"We were good together, and you know it."

The minute the words came out, she regretted them.

"You don't have to remind me, angel," he said, taking a step closer, his gaze colliding with hers.

She swallowed, steeling herself against the onslaught of memories. "I was talking about our business relationship."

"I wasn't." He moved closer, his breath warm against her cheek.

"Nash, I—"

His lips crushed down on hers. She opened her mouth, welcoming him inside, reveling in the feel of his tongue. It was take-no-prisoners contact, as much a battle of wills as an expression of emotion.

The power of his touch almost more than she could bear...

DARK
DECEPTIONS

DEE DAVIS

FOREVER

NEW YORK   BOSTON

This book is a work of fiction. Names, characters, places, and incidents are the product of the author's imagination or are used fictitiously. Any resemblance to actual events, locales, or persons, living or dead, is coincidental.

Copyright © 2010 by Dee Davis Oberwetter
Excerpt from *Dangerous Desires* copyright © 2010 by Dee Davis Oberwetter. All rights reserved. Except as permitted under the U.S. Copyright Act of 1976, no part of this publication may be reproduced, distributed, or transmitted in any form or by any means, or stored in a database or retrieval system, without the prior written permission of the publisher.

Book design by Giorgetta Bell McRee
Cover design by Claire Brown

Forever
Hachette Book Group
237 Park Avenue
New York, NY 10017
Visit our website at www.HachetteBookGroup.com.

Forever is an imprint of Grand Central Publishing.
The Forever name and logo is a trademark of Hachette Book Group, Inc.

Printed in the United States of America

First Printing: April 2010

10 9 8 7 6 5 4 3 2 1

To Kim, Amy, and Alex.
Couldn't have done it without you.

Scientia Potéstas Est...Knowledge Is Power.

PROLOGUE

Hotel Montague—Paris

So do you think we're ever going to feel like a normal couple?" Annie asked as they stumbled back into their hotel room, Nash's hands cupping her breasts, his breath hot against her cheek.

"Trust me, angel, normal is overrated." He pushed her back against the wall, his thumbs rubbing heated circles through the soft silk of her halter top. "And anyway, I kind of like what we've got."

"Right," she sighed, shivering as he kissed her neck. "Sex on the run."

"Well, it's not like we have a lot of free time." His mouth slanted over hers, his tongue sending fire lacing through her belly. It was always like this. Combustible. Their desire heightened by the possibility that each time could be the last.

"Maybe we should adjourn to the bedroom?" She nodded toward the doorway of the suite, and then gasped as he pushed her skirt up around her thighs.

"What's wrong with right here? Right now?" He teased her with his fingers, the friction of satin against skin threatening instant explosion. She lifted her hips, but he pulled back, his slow smile taunting her. "Unless of course you've changed your mind?"

"Not on your life." She reached up to unbutton his shirt, her fingers tracing the scars that laced his chest. Twisted mementos of their life together. "Tell me what you want," she whispered, her breathing labored.

"You, Annie. All I ever want is you."

"So take me," she taunted, anticipation coiling inside her, hot and heavy. Sometimes she thought maybe she wanted something more. Something that resembled normalcy—commitment. But not now. Not in this moment. Right now all she wanted was Nash.

For a moment their passion stretched taut between them; and then, trembling with the sheer power of the feelings he evoked, she arched her back, welcoming his hands and mouth as he crushed her against him. This was what she craved. What she wanted. As long as she had Nash, she could endure anything.

Anything.

"The bed...I can't...please." She gasped the words as they stumbled backward, the need so intense now she thought she might die of it.

His dark eyes reflecting her passion, Nash swung her up into his arms and in two strides they were through the door and on the bed, the cool cotton sheets a counterpoint to the heat that pulsed between them.

Annie pressed against him, her eyes riveted for a moment on the mirror across from the bed and the image of their interlocked bodies moving in tandem. Two shattered souls desperately seeking release. She sighed, and then froze as something else in the mirror moved.

A shadow detached itself from the wall, and Annie dug her nails into Nash's back, instinct and training over-riding passion in an instant. Nash's muscles tightened in response, and moving with a precision gained from years of working together, they sprang apart, a bullet smashing into the headboard between them. Annie rolled to the floor, reaching for the gun she kept strapped to her thigh. In her ardent haste she hadn't had time to remove her weapon.

But Nash had. He'd thrown his on the table as he'd carried her to bed.

Damn it all to hell.

From her vantage point beside the bed, she couldn't see Nash or their assailant. Which meant she needed to move. Popping up to fire a round in the direction of the shadow, she rolled out from the bed, diving for cover behind a chair as a bullet shattered a lamp just above her head.

Nash was cornered between the bed and the wall, the bed giving protection, at least for the moment, but the gunman had the advantage. He stood between them and the door, with a large wardrobe to his left blocking her from taking a clear shot.

"Well, isn't this a pickle," their assailant said, his accent a smooth blend of American and French. She should have known. Adrian Benoit. They'd only just been in his apartment. Looked like he was returning the favor.

"Seems we've got ourselves a Mexican standoff," he drawled.

"Except that none of us are Mexican," Nash quipped. She could see him now reflected in the mirror. And when he smiled, she realized he could see her as well. Which meant he had a plan.

"Doesn't matter," Benoit continued. "I've clearly got the advantage."

"So what, you want us to come out with our hands up?" Nash queried, nodding almost imperceptibly toward his gun lying on the table about five feet in front of her.

"It would certainly make things easier. But what I really want are the files you stole from my computer."

"And then you'll let us go? Right. And I've got some swampland…" Nash's laugh was harsh as he tipped his head slightly, signaling for her to stand ready. Annie nodded, already shifting her position.

"Well now, there wouldn't be any fun in letting you live, would there?" Benoit responded, anger clouding his voice.

Annie drew a breath, rolled out from behind the chair, fired once, and then dove for the table, her hand closing around the butt of Nash's gun. "Two o'clock," she yelled, as she chunked the weapon overhand toward Nash, still shooting in Benoit's direction in an attempt to provide some modicum of cover. Her ploy worked, Benoit turning to return fire as Nash emerged from behind the bed in a flying leap, intercepting the gun as it tumbled through the air.

Two seconds later and it was over. Benoit lay dead in a pool of his own blood.

"Are you all right?" Nash asked, pushing to his feet.

"I'm fine," she said as they met halfway, Nash's arms closing around her.

"You sure?" He ran his hands down her now trembling body, double-checking to ascertain if she'd told him the truth.

"Really. He didn't hurt me. You were the one without the gun."

"Evened the odds." He shrugged, his voice buoyed by adrenaline, his smile edged with a ruthlessness that had kept him alive more times than she cared to remember. "So where were we?"

"I think that ship has sailed," she said, her gaze falling on the body.

"I suppose you're right," Nash said, brushing a strand of hair from her face. "We've got to get out of here before someone starts asking questions. Benoit was using a silencer. But we weren't."

"I'll start wiping things down." She pulled away and reached for a pair of gloves, falling effortlessly into a pattern they'd perfected over countless operations.

"So what was it you said earlier?" Nash called from across the room where he was packing their gear, his tone teasing, the fact that they'd just survived death—again—already an afterthought. "Something about wondering if we'd ever be a normal couple?"

Despite the gravity of the situation, Annie smiled. She loved this man. With every ounce of her being. And the cold hard truth was that she wouldn't change a single thing about their life. "I think," she said, reaching down to retrieve Benoit's gun, "that I just answered my own question."

CHAPTER 1

Island off the coast of Southeast Asia—eight years later

"Get the boats under cover," Nash Brennon said, keeping his voice low as he dragged one of the dinghies behind a pile of moss-covered rocks. "We should have about five minutes until the perimeter guard make their way back here. Everyone know their assignment?"

It was a rhetorical question. Although sometimes personnel varied, for the most part A-Tac members had been working together for years, and they'd certainly had operations far more difficult than this one. Only difference here was that their commander, Avery Solomon, wasn't present. The big man was in Washington. Some top brass bullshit. Which meant Nash was in charge.

It wasn't that he hadn't the experience. Trained in covert operations, he was an admitted adrenaline junkie. He'd started his career as an operative in Europe—with Annie. But then after a particularly difficult mission she'd deserted him. Disappeared. Almost as if she'd never existed.

He pushed the memories away. He'd moved on. To A-Tac. The CIA's most elite black ops unit. Hell of a step up from European operative. He didn't need Annie. He didn't need anyone. And right now he had a mission, and he couldn't afford a fuckup.

"Can everyone hear me?" Emmett Walsh asked, his voice crackling as Nash's earpiece sprang to life.

"Yeah, like a freakin' bullhorn," Drake Flynn said with a wince. The com system was new. Emmett's design. And even though the man was a genius when it came to playing connect the operatives, that didn't mean there wouldn't be hiccups. "Can you turn the damn thing down?"

"The controls are right here," Tyler said, tapping her ear with a grin as she looked up from a backpack full of explosives. Tyler was Nash's second in command for the mission. An army-trained demolitions expert, she had yet to meet a building she couldn't destroy. And she'd saved their asses on more than one occasion, disarming incendiary devices most people would never even know existed.

"I'm patching Jason through now," Emmett said. Jason Lawton, along with Hannah Marshall, served as long-distance eyes and ears for the team. Tonight that meant keeping watch over the operation from Sunderland in New York, which, at the moment, seemed a hell of a long way away. But at least, thanks to a couple of strategically placed satellites, they had the benefit of Jason and Hannah's constant vigilance.

"You've got two more minutes," Jason intoned, as usual cutting right to the chase. "I'm showing two hostiles—both armed and ready to rumble."

"Always good to have big brother watching." Nash laughed, signaling the team to move out. "We're heading east. Target ETA ten minutes."

The operation was simple in conception. Destroy a communications array and its accompanying computer systems. The property of an Asian terrorist group known as the Red Sword, the array was used to coordinate organizational efforts within the region as well as operations abroad. Taking it out would severely cripple if not completely destroy enemy operations.

Unfortunately, the island's heavy jungle undergrowth impeded movement, rendering the straight line between points A and B anything but. The moisture-laden air was heavy and oppressive, making every breath an effort. The team had fanned out, Nash on point, Drake keeping back, making sure they weren't being followed. Even with Jason and Hannah watching over them, Nash didn't like taking chances. And there was no one he'd rather have at his back than Drake Flynn.

A specialist in CIA extractions, Drake had been with the team just over a year. Rumor had it that before A-Tac he'd been with one of the CIA's D units. Operations even more off the books than A-Tac. Not that the man ever talked about any of it. Hell, Drake didn't talk seriously about much of anything. But he got the job done, and at the end of the day, that's all that really mattered.

Something rustled in the bushes next to him, and Nash signaled the others as he spun, gun ready. But it was only a bird, eyes glowing red in the moonlight. Focusing again on the barely discernible trail, he moved forward, careful to keep Tyler flanking him on the left. She nodded toward an opening in the trees, and together they moved forward,

Emmett following a pace or so behind on the right, with Drake still bringing up the rear.

The jungle opened out on cleared space below them. Tall grass mixed in with stands of bamboo and a few straggling trees led up to a concrete wall enclosing four buildings. Off to the left, separated from the rest of the compound by about fifty yards, sat the array. It was small—just three dishes—but Nash had learned long ago that small packages could be just as lethal as larger ones, and the members of Red Sword weren't prone to wasting time with empty platitudes. They were far more interested in terrorizing innocents under the guise of some perverted cosmic justice.

Only not for much longer.

"What have we got?" Nash whispered as he dropped to his stomach, using infrared glasses to scan the area below. "Any surprises?"

"Everything looks pretty much as we expected," Drake's voice echoed in his ear. "You can see the surveillance camera mounted above the wall near the entrance. And if our intel holds true there should be additional units every fifty feet or so."

"With a blind corner to the southwest in the back, thanks to an uprooted jackfruit tree," Emmett added.

"What about the array?" Nash frowned as he studied the compound. He'd seen satellite photos, and rendered maps, but there was nothing to beat firsthand observation.

"Three sixteen-foot dishes on machined counterbalanced mounts," Tyler said, her goggles trained on the array. "Should be easy enough to destroy. I've just got to get close enough to rig the explosives."

"Don't worry, Nash and I will get you in," Drake assured. "Piece of cake."

"Maybe not so much so," Jason said, his tone grim. "I'm showing at least eight hostiles inside the compound."

"Son of a bitch. There were only supposed to be two."

"Sorry," Hannah Marshall said, her voice cracking in transmission as she took the com-link from Jason. "Looks like some kind of an impromptu meeting. I've got three boats moored off the pier. No way we could have predicted this."

"So what do we do now?" Jason asked, patching through another com-link. "Abort?"

"Depends on where this little meeting is taking place," Nash said, sorting through the alternatives. "Can you verify location?"

"Yeah. Hang on," Jason said, his voice moving away as he shuffled through something on the other end. "I've got five in the building farthest north. And two more in the guardhouse at the entrance."

"And the eighth?" Drake barked.

"Give me a minute. He's moving." Silence stretched, tension building. "Looks like he's heading back to the north building."

"Can you confirm the location of the communications computers?"

"Little building closest to the array," Hannah said, her voice coming in on a whisper. "The one without windows."

"I see it." Nash nodded, even though she was thousands of miles away. "So if our hostiles will just stay put we ought to be able to get in and out without notice."

"And if they don't—well, that will only make it more of a challenge."

"This isn't a game, Drake." Emmett's tone bordered on harsh.

"Hell if it isn't." There was laughter in his friend's voice, and despite himself, Nash smiled. Nothing wrong with kicking a little Red Sword ass.

"All right then, we're agreed. We're going in."

"We'll watch your back," Jason said.

"I don't know..." Hannah started, only to be cut off by Tyler.

"No guts, no glory."

"It's not up for discussion," Nash said, his tone brooking no argument. "We're going in. But first we wait for the perimeter guard to pass. If I'm marking it right, they should be showing up about now." As if to underscore his words a jeep with two armed men turned the corner onto the rutted road that ran in front of the compound. It continued as the guards drove in front of the wall, slowing momentarily at the gate and then proceeding south. At the corner, the vehicle turned into the jungle, presumably heading back toward the beach and the outer edge of the island.

"I'd say you've got about twenty minutes," Jason confirmed.

"Should be more than enough time," Drake said, swinging his utility pack over his shoulder as he rose to his feet.

"Assuming we don't run into a welcome party," Emmett muttered as he double-checked his gear. "Nothing like discovering a nest of hostiles on site at the last fucking minute."

"I heard that," Hannah said.

"Sorry." Emmett clearly wasn't, but the apology seemed to placate Hannah.

"Let's move out," Nash said, signaling the others, falling in line with Tyler as they made their way down the hill.

"I hate to agree with Emmett, but it does seem like Hannah might have given us a heads-up a little sooner."

"Maybe the satellite wasn't in position. I don't know. You know as well as I do that intel is an inexact science." Nash shrugged. "Point is that we know now. And with a little luck we'll avoid an encounter altogether."

"And if we happen to run into them?" Tyler asked.

"We've faced worse."

"True enough," she sighed. "It just seems like lately something always goes wrong."

"Comes with the territory. Anyway, we'll be fine. You'll see." Nash shifted his weapon to the other side and moved ahead, the four of them falling into their former positions.

They managed to make their way down the incline without incident, emerging from the grass at the far southeast corner of the enclosure. Two minutes later and they'd arrived at the fallen tree, the resulting gap in the vegetation opening the canopy to the star-studded sky.

"The camera is definitely missing," Drake said, pulling a climber's rope from his pack. "Way to go, Hannah; you called it right."

"Hey, I aim to please." Even long distance you could hear the smile in her voice.

"Anything on the other side we should know about?" Nash asked.

"Looks clear from here," Jason responded. "But you'd better go quickly; I've got one of the front gate guards on the move. About a hundred yards out. Heading your direction."

"Okay, people. Let's move," Nash called, as Drake tossed the rope, and the grappling hook dug into the top of the wall with a soft thunk. With a jaunty grin, Drake was up and over, Tyler following on his heels.

"You next, Emmett," Nash said, turning slowly to survey the area, making sure they didn't have additional company.

Emmett vaulted over the wall, and after waiting a beat, Nash turned and followed suit, straddling the barrier to remove the rope and hook before jumping lightly to the muddy ground of the compound.

"Where's the guard?" he barked into his earpiece.

"Moving the other way." Despite the distance, Jason clearly sounded relieved. "For the moment you're good to go."

"Should we split up?" Tyler asked. "It might be more time-efficient."

"Normally, I'd agree with you," Nash said, "but considering the number of hostiles present I think we're better off sticking together."

Tyler nodded.

"I suggest we get a move on," Drake urged, already heading in the direction of the tiny communications building.

The heat closed around them, the still air oppressive, drops of rain spattering the ground as they walked. Nash positioned his silenced Sig Sauer, finger on the trigger. Better to be ready. The shrouded building loomed out of the mist, and they stopped in the shadow of a large acacia tree.

"Drake, you and Tyler stand guard while Emmett and I deal with the computers. How much time will you need once we hit the array?"

"Seven minutes tops." Tyler shrugged.

"All right, we'll be out in three."

The building was dark and surprisingly cool. A narrow hallway ran from the door to the far end, flanking a large room full of computers that was even colder than the hall.

"The computers can't function in this humidity, so they've got to control the temperature," Emmett explained, as he opened a small bag at his waist.

Banks of computers lined the room on both sides, LED lights blinking off and on, giving the room a hazy green glow. Emmett pulled out a pen drive the size of a lighter, and after a brief search opened a drawer with a keyboard and inserted the drive in the CPU above it.

The computer's gauges lit up, moving up and down as the machine downloaded the information on the drive. Designed to immobilize not only the computers present but anything networked to the system, the virus Jason had created was geared to reach beyond the compound itself into the very heart of Red Sword's technical infrastructure.

"How's the security?" Jason's voice crackled into the earpiece.

"Can't tell yet," Emmett replied. "So far they haven't even detected the fact that we're in the system. You getting anything?" The plan was for Jason to remotely detonate the virus seconds before Tyler blew the array, keeping outside interference to a minimum. However, there was always the chance that Emmett's download would trigger some kind of inner systemic security.

"Everything seems fine," Jason replied.

"Five more seconds," Emmett whispered to no one in particular.

Nash held his breath, waiting for the all-clear. In truth, he'd rather face a horde of Uzi-toting hostiles than a simple bank of enemy computers. There were just so many variables, and nothing he could do to control them. Technology had its moments, but push come to shove, he could live without it. Hell, he never even remembered to turn on his cell phone, a shortcoming Tyler never failed to remind him of.

As if giving voice to his concern, the room was filled with an ominous beeping sound—some kind of alarm. "What the hell?"

"I don't know," Emmett said, typing furiously as the screen above him scrolled through various commands. "Jason, you got anything?"

"You tripped some kind of security," Jason answered. "Maybe the firewall."

"Well, that much I knew. But it's not responding to the codes you gave me. Anything you can do from your end?"

"Hang on."

Not exactly words to instill faith. Nash pulled his gun and turned to face the door. "You guys getting this?" he asked, speaking into his headpiece.

"It's all quiet out here," Drake responded. "At least so far. Nothing's moving."

"Keep your eyes open." The beeping increased in intensity, lights flashing now along the bank Emmett was working on. "Jason. We could really use some help here."

"I'm trying." The sound of frantic typing filled both

the room and Nash's earpiece as both men worked to stop the alarm. Nash tightened his hand on the Sig, almost wishing for an intruder—anything to break the tension.

Then suddenly the alarm stopped.

"Got it," Emmett said, retrieving the hard drive before pushing the drawer with the keyboard closed. "Jason, you should have control."

"Hannah?" Jason asked.

"We're in," she confirmed. "Now you guys get the hell out of there."

"With pleasure." Still leading with the gun, Nash made his way out of the computer room, down the hallway, and out the front door. Drake and Tyler were standing back to back watching the pathways for signs they'd been discovered.

"Looks like I'm up," Tyler said as they ducked low, making their way across the open ground between the compound and the array.

The rain was coming down in earnest now, providing a gray cloak that helped to obscure their progress. Still, Nash kept himself on hyper-alert. The alarm in the computer room had to have alerted someone. Which meant that sooner or later they were bound to have company.

They reached the array in seconds, Tyler already pulling the prerigged plastique from her backpack. She knelt at the base of the first dish and, using duct tape, carefully secured the explosive in place.

"Do we have to connect the three of them?" Drake asked, his attention fixed on the compound behind them.

"No." Tyler shook her head as she moved to the second dish. "They're wireless. I've got a detonator."

"And if something happens to you?"

"Nothing is going to happen to me," she said. "But worst case, Jason can trigger the charges remotely."

Nash nodded. "How much more time?" Things were still quiet, but he had the distinct feeling the other shoe was about to drop.

"Just a couple of seconds. I need to arm them." Using a tiny screwdriver, Tyler made an adjustment on the first device, the small red pinprick of light on its face turning green. "One down. Any action out there?"

Clearly Tyler was having the same thoughts about impending intervention. She moved to the second device and in less than a minute had it armed as well. But the third mechanism proved to be stubborn, the red light refusing to change to green.

Tyler let out a curse, just as a shot rang out.

"Company," Drake called, returning fire. Emmett followed suit, the two of them moving between the gate to the array and Tyler, who was still struggling with the third unit.

"Just leave it," Nash said. "Better to get the hell out of here. We can blow the two you do have set."

"It's okay," Tyler said. As the reticent light turned green. "I've got it. Let's go."

The four of them raced for the far wall behind the array, the shots moving closer but the gunmen still not in sight. Skidding to a halt, Drake threw the grappling hook again and was up and over almost before it was embedded in the wall. Tyler and Emmett followed suit while Nash kept the shooters at bay with return fire. Then after a last volley, he pulled himself over the wall, hitting the ground on a roll.

Springing to his feet, he followed his friends as they

sprinted for the cover of the jungle, quietly trying to raise someone on his com piece. No one answered, and he wasn't certain if the problem was his alone or if somehow the entire system was down.

But there was no time to figure it out. Bullets exploded in the mud at his feet, and he dropped to a crouch, still moving, veering back and forth to keep his path unpredictable. Ahead, he saw Emmett fall, but Drake was quick to pull him back to his feet, the two of them moving in tandem. Tyler was just off to the right, almost to the cover of the trees.

All she needed was time to detonate.

Swerving back toward the road and the gunmen, Nash rolled to the ground again and came up firing, satisfied to see a burst of blood as one of the gunmen hit the dirt. Two more shots and another man was dead.

Two down.

Knowing that he was still too close to the blast zone, he pulled to his feet just as the jeep rounded the corner, machine guns blazing. Reaching into his flak jacket, he produced a grenade and, without slowing, lobbed it over his shoulder. Seconds passed, but not enough time for the jeep to react, and the resulting explosion flipped the vehicle into a ditch.

Hitting the top of the ravine and the line of trees, he ran into the jungle, scanning the area for signs of Tyler.

"Here," came her whisper, from the shelter of a clump of bamboo. "I'm here."

"Did you lose com or is it just me?" Nash asked, dropping to his knees beside her.

"Whole system is down, which means no remote detonation. It's got to be me."

"How's Emmett?" The shooting had subsided for a moment, but there was no doubt that it would resume as soon as the dust from the grenade had cleared.

"He's fine. Bullet to the groin. I don't think it's life-threatening, but there was a lot of blood, which meant he was no good to us here, so I sent him ahead with Drake to the rendezvous point. I figured better to get them out of harm's way. Easier for me to concentrate on blowing this pop stand."

"Literally." Nash shot her a brief smile. "What about the computer virus?"

"With loss of com we can't be sure that Jason can launch it. Emmett is going to try to do it manually as soon as they're out of range of the gunfire."

"Good. At least we've got that much taken care of. So are we far enough away from the blast zone to detonate?"

"Yeah, we're good. I just need to verify the signal." The machine-gun fire resumed, this time much closer. Clearly the perimeter guards had survived the grenade.

"I'll see if I can buy you some time." Without waiting for an answer, he jammed a new cartridge into the Sig, and keeping low, moved in the opposite direction from Tyler. Once he'd managed to put some distance between the two of them, careful to keep himself between the encroaching terrorists and her position, he twisted to a standing position and lobbed another grenade.

His last one.

For a moment everything moved in slo-mo, the shooters first freezing as they recognized the impending disaster and then running and diving for cover as the grenade exploded, sending chunks of mud raining down into the night.

Firing over the top of a fallen log, Nash kept the pressure on, all the while waiting for Tyler's signal. There were six shooters now. And despite the momentary obstacle created by the grenade, they had resumed their press forward.

One of the men stepped out from the protection of the vegetation to get a better angle on Tyler's position, but fortunately, Nash was faster. Three down, five remaining, and two more unaccounted for. A quick flash of light from above him indicated that Tyler was ready, so, still firing, he moved back again into the cover of the jungle, making his way over to her position.

"You ready?" she mouthed, holding up the transmitter.

"Go," he bellowed, shooting as a man broke through the vegetation, his body breaking bamboo as he fell.

Tyler pressed a button, already moving deeper into the woods, but nothing happened.

"Shit," she said, pressing again. This time, however, the motion was rewarded as a maelstrom of thunder and light split the night, embers and debris raining down into the jungle.

For a moment everything was quiet, and then all hell broke loose, shots volleying off the trees.

"Run," Nash yelled. And the two of them sprinted through the jungle, the shots growing fainter as the distance grew. As they neared the rendezvous point they slowed, and Tyler pulled her gun.

"It's awfully quiet," she said.

"Too quiet, if you ask me."

Together they inched forward until they had a clear view of the beach. Drake and Emmett were huddled next to one of the dinghies, two Red Sword thugs holding them at gunpoint. Emmett's pant leg was stained with blood and Drake had a bloody nose, which meant he hadn't gone down easily, but it was clear that for the moment at least the terrorists had the upper hand.

Of course they hadn't counted on Nash and Tyler.

With a mutual nod, they separated, shifting so that they each had a clear shot. And then on a silent count of three, they fired. Nash's man was dead before it even dawned on him that he'd been hit. Tyler's had enough time to get off a shot, but it went wild, and he, too, went down as Nash and Tyler broke free of the undergrowth and sprinted into the clearing.

"About damn time," Drake said with a grin.

"You get the virus launched?" Tyler asked.

"Do we look totally incompetent?" Drake quipped. "Of course we got it off. Truth is we had everything under control."

"Yeah, right," Nash returned as they pulled the boats into the water and helped Emmett on board. "I don't know what I was thinking."

"We should have let them shoot you," Tyler said, pulling the cord to start the outboard motor.

Still grinning, Drake did the same with the other dinghy, and the two boats headed for the safety of open water, the jungle glowing silently behind them, backlit by the eerie fire of the burning array.

CHAPTER 2

Creede, Colorado

Annie Gallagher stood at the window watching the fairy fall of snow, each flake glistening as it fell through the swath of gold cast by the lamplight. Tomorrow she'd have to shovel, but tonight she was content to simply enjoy the magic.

She thought about waking Adam, but resisted the urge. It was late and he had school. Still, the idea of building a snowman appealed. Behind her the clock struck twelve and she laughed. Definitely too late for Adam to be up. Even with the temptation of a midnight snowstorm.

She turned her back on the snow, shivering as she walked through the drafty hallway into the warmth of the firelit parlor. The old Victorian was a rare find in these parts, especially way up here on the mountain. It had been pretty run-down when she'd first found it, but Annie had recognized its beauty despite the disrepair, and she'd never been afraid of a little work.

The quiet of the San Juans had been just what the

doctor ordered. And now she and Adam had made a life here, far away from the world she'd inhabited for most of her adult life. The shadowy world of espionage. Sometimes she missed it. But she'd never regretted her decision. Isolation was the best thing for Adam.

And for her.

The little town of Creede was the perfect place for escape. High in the mountains, occupied mainly by others who wanted a quiet life away from the real world. No one asked questions. Folks here weren't interested in who you'd been, just who you were now. And that suited Annie just fine.

She picked up a poker and shifted the logs on the fire, the flames crackling as they danced along spines of spruce and aspen. Above the firebox, on the mantel, was the only thing that remained from her old life—well, almost the only thing—an intricately carved wooden box. She'd found it in a market in Krakow. The day Adam had been conceived.

Of course she hadn't known that then. Or just how much her life was going to change.

She looked down at the objet d'art cupped in her hands. It was a puzzle box. The kind that only opened for someone who knew its secrets. At the time she'd just thought it beautiful and interesting, but as the years passed, she'd come to realize that it symbolized her life. She was the box, the secrets of her past locked deep inside alongside parts of her she no longer wished to acknowledge.

With fingers long practiced, she manipulated the crevices and curves, and with a small squeak of protest, the box sprang open, revealing its treasure.

The faded petals of a rose.

Cliché, really. But she smiled, her mind drifting back to the market square and the sweet smell of roses. No one had ever given her flowers before. And in that moment—everything had been perfect.

But nothing was forever.

She closed the box and put it back on the mantel, ashamed suddenly of her vulnerability. It was only a memory. Turning her back on the mantel, she sat in the wing chair, snuggling into the warmth of its cushions as the snow fell and the fire snapped and hissed.

Life was in the present. Here in the mountains. With Adam.

And on that note...

She stood up and began gathering the myriad toys scattered throughout the room. A Tonka truck, a Leapfrog cartridge, a Lego pirate, a Happy Meal racecar, and a stuffed turtle named Timmy. Crossing the room, she tossed the toys into a plastic basket, and satisfied that she'd tidied a bit, started for the kitchen and a hot cup of tea.

Before she'd taken two steps, she stopped, instinct sending a warning as the hairs on her arms rose ominously. She waited, hardly daring to breathe, trying to figure out what it was that bothered her.

And then she heard it—a low screeching noise as if a window were opening or something were being dragged across the floor. She froze, concentrating on identifying the location of the noise, her heart hammering to a stop as something moved again.

Upstairs.

With Adam.

Mind scrambling, she quickly went through the possibilities. Most likely an animal. The worst of which would be a bear. Thanks to the summer drought, food was in short supply. But bears were more interested in the kitchen than an upstairs bedroom. Burglary was possible, but uncommon here in the mountains, which meant if the intruder was human, it was most likely a vagrant looking for a warm bed for the night. Unless, somehow, her cover had been blown.

She discarded the notion as quickly as it had occurred. It had been too long and she'd been too careful. Probably just the wind. But better safe than sorry. She grabbed the poker and headed toward the stairs. She'd have preferred her Beretta, but it was upstairs in a lockbox. Too far from Adam. There simply wasn't enough time.

Moving silently on bare feet, she crept up the stairs, straining for further indication of where the danger lay. If only she could get to Adam's room, they could crawl out the window. The gable would give them a way down to the roof of the porch and from there to the ground—and safety.

The landing at the top of the stairs was shrouded in darkness. It provided cover, but made it difficult to see. At the end of the hall, the glow from Adam's night-light spilled out into the corridor, the soft light almost comforting in its normalcy. She started to move, pulling up short as a shrill moan echoed through the house, the sound emanating from the spare room.

Adrenaline flooded through her and she lifted the poker as she stepped from the landing into the hallway, ready for a fight.

Nothing moved.

Waiting another moment, just to be certain, she inched forward, back to the wall, sucking in a breath as she swung into the spare room. A breeze lifted the curtain as snow spilled through a broken window. Jammed into the hole, a twisted tree limb moved back and forth, screeching against the jagged glass. Annie sighed, relief washing through her, her warrior instincts dissipating as quickly as they'd come.

She'd meant to cut back the tree. Remove that branch. But there'd always been something else to do and she'd kept putting it off. Now she'd be replacing a window as well.

First thing tomorrow.

Grabbing a towel, she stuffed it into the hole between the glass and the branch. Then, after bending to retrieve the poker, she headed back into the hall to check on Adam. The hall was warmer than the spare room, but she shivered anyway. The aftermath of her scare.

Adam's room was chaotic as always. No matter how easy she made it to put away toys or how often she managed to do it herself, there was still always a mess, her son fond of throwing things every which way.

His bed was shadowed, his covers piled high. As usual, he'd burrowed his way to the very bottom of the bed. As a toddler he'd always managed to turn himself round about. Head under the blankets, tiny little toes pressed against the pillow. Nothing had changed.

She smiled, lifting the covers, and then choked on a scream as she realized there was no Adam. Only a pile of abandoned stuffed animals, their friendly faces adding horror to her rising panic. The wind outside whistled, drapes flying high as she whirled to face an open window.

Heart shriveling, she called Adam's name, her mind conjuring images of him hurt and frightened.

Outside, in the softly falling snow, she could see

fading tire tracks on the drive. Someone had been here. Someone had taken her little boy.

"Adam," she screamed again, but the wind whipped her words away, taunting her terror. "Adam…"

But she was too late.

Adam was gone.

"So in the final days of April, General Hooker leads the Army of the Potomac upstream to slip around Lee's left flank." Nash drew a hooked arrow on the board to illustrate the point, just as the beeper on his belt vibrated twice. "Lee responds aggressively and during the first week of May wins what may have been his greatest victory." The beeper vibrated again, this time repeating its message twice, but Nash ignored it, looking instead at his students. "Who can tell me what happens next?"

Several hands shot up, while others thumbed through their text.

"Hillary?"

The girl smiled, shifting provocatively in her seat. "The Confederates march into Pennsylvania."

"Right," Nash said, nodding encouragingly, his beeper practically dancing against his hip. "Then what?"

"General Meade kicks his ass," Reggie Fenderman said, accompanied by general laughter.

"I don't know that I'd have chosen those exact words, but you're right. The Army of the Potomac did indeed defeat Lee at Gettysburg in July 1863. Which, as we know, changed the course of the war. And tomorrow, we'll find out why. For today, time's up." He nodded at the students, reaching down to shut off the insistent electronic device. Damn technology.

Three giggling coeds waited at the foot of the dais. "Professor Brennon? We have a couple of questions."

He groaned inwardly. It wasn't that he didn't welcome inquiring minds, but these three were more about chatting up the prof. "Ladies, you know I'd love nothing better than to stay here and discuss the war with you, but I'm afraid I'm late for a meeting."

Emmett appeared in the doorway, assessing the situation with a mocking grin. When Nash had started teaching American history eight years ago, enrollment had jumped 25 percent—most of them female, much to the amusement of his colleagues.

"They're getting younger every year." Emmett grinned.

"Don't remind me." Nash closed his briefcase and shrugged into his jacket. "I got a pair of panties in the mail last week. Jesus, you'd think they'd be more interested in guys their own age."

"Hey, you're our resident rock star," Jason said, joining them as they walked down the hallway, stopping in the doorway of another classroom.

Nash was currently chairman of the history department, and his dissertation on the role of espionage during the Cold War was considered, by some, the preeminent document on understanding various intelligence strategies used by both the United States and the U.S.S.R.

"Tomorrow, your essays on Lenin are due," Hannah was saying from a lectern at the front of the room. Her dark hair was cut short, strands spiking in every direction. "And starting next week, we'll begin our discussion on Trotsky and the effect he had on the communist movement in Russia, so I'll expect you all to have read the text. And, Martin, that means you."

Ignoring the resulting laughter, she quickly strode to the back of the room. "I swear to God, next year I'm going to petition to teach Western civ. It's got to be a hell of a lot easier than trying to get this lot to understand the differences between communism, fascism, and democracy. So what's with the summons?"

"No idea," Emmett said, still limping a bit from his injury in Southeast Asia. "Text just said to head downstairs."

"I'm betting it's Avery," Nash said as they walked out of Fischer Hall into the bright May sunshine.

Sunderland College was located in central New York not far from the Connecticut border. Surrounded by rolling hills, stately farms, and vast nature preserves, the ivy-clad institution, founded in 1823, was a liberal arts college of the highest reputation. Nationally ranked among small colleges, Sunderland drew some of the greatest minds in the country. And serious students flocked to the tree-lined, bucolic campus to learn from the very best. There was even a joke that the reason the trees had lights in them was so that the squirrels could study at night. Which Nash had to admit had a certain ring of truth.

"Great," Emmett sighed. "Just when I was getting through to them about the subtle nuances of inflation, Avery calls. Every time my TA takes over, the upper-level classes regress at least a month."

"You should choose your TA more carefully next time," Jason said, waving at Tyler, who had emerged from the humanities building.

Teaching assistants were a way of life at Sunderland, particularly for those professors who were a part of the Aaron Thomas Academic Center. Created fifteen years ago by the CIA in response to the increased threat of terrorism, the nationally renowned think tank was home to a dozen or so of the best minds in the country, Ph.D.s who also handled some of the nation's most dangerous counterintelligence operations.

There were eight permanent members of the American Tactical Intelligence Command (A-Tac), all tenured professors with expertise in both academia and espionage. And from time to time, as missions demanded, they were joined by other experts in their field, the think tank acting as cover for their association and affiliated operations.

Since A-Tac professors were often called away to "advise" on top national issues, their teaching assistants were given the chance for more hands-on classroom experience than their colleagues at other universities. All of which meant that competition for graduate positions was extreme. And the winners, like their mentors, were usually the best of the best.

"I had no choice." Emmett shrugged. "The kid's a senator's son. Strings pulled and all that. Probably has visions of running the Fed one day."

"Well, he's lucky to have you," Hannah said. "I mean it's not every day you get to work with a Draper fellow." The coveted prize was given annually to the country's most noted economist. Emmett had actually won twice.

"I'm not sure he sees it that way." Emmett grinned. "But thanks."

"So anyone know what's going on?" Tyler asked as she joined them.

"Not a thing." Emmett shook his head. "But Nash thinks it's Avery."

"Well, that's a given. No one else summons us in the middle of class."

"It wasn't the middle," Jason said. "And we go when called. It's part of the job."

"Actually, just at the moment," Tyler sighed, "I think I might prefer Avery to Chaucer. Or at least the endless complaints about Middle English."

Nash smiled, knowing that her protestations were cursory. The truth was that Tyler was as passionate about her teaching as she was about ordnance.

They'd crossed the campus in short order, making their way up the steps of the Aaron Thomas Academic Center. Crossing into a narrow side hallway, the group stopped in front of an elevator marked "professors only," and Nash inserted a key. The doors slid silently open as the assembled company stepped inside.

"This always makes me feel like Maxwell Smart," Emmett said, inserting another key and pressing a button hidden behind an Otis elevator sign.

"I know what you mean," Hannah said as the elevator started to move downward. "Although, for me, it's more Bruce Wayne. I always half expect Alfred to be waiting at the bottom with my utility belt."

"It is sort of like the bat cave," Tyler agreed, "but considering the money the suits in Washington have spent on it, I kind of think they'd resent the analogy."

"Depends if you're talking the campy television show or the movie," Emmett said as the elevator stopped and the doors slid open.

"They all sucked," Jason protested. "The original comic is the only way to go."

"Batman, I'm assuming?" Lara Prescott said as they stepped into the austerely appointed reception area. The room served more as a buffer than as a real welcoming area. From time to time, students had tried to gain entrance to the coveted elevator.

Thanks to CIA fail-safes, the very few successful attempts had all ended in an upper-floor lounge and general disappointment. But just in case there was ever a breach to this level, the reception area was designed as a decoy and, without proper identification, the precursor to a not-so-pleasant meeting with Avery—who also happened to be the dean of the college—and a one-way ticket out of Sunderland altogether.

"Are we that obvious?" Tyler asked, pressing her hand against what looked like a professorial bust, but was really a biotechnical scanner.

"Not you." Lara shook her head, slapping her hand against the statue of the center's namesake, Aaron Thomas. A prominent early American scholar from New York, Thomas had been quite the rabble-rouser. Famous for his treatise *Scíentia Potéstas Est—Knowledge Is Power*—Thomas also served as a spy for General Washington, making his role in A-Tac all that much more apropos.

"Jason. You have to admit he does have a rather well-documented obsession with all things Batman."

"And you love it," Jason said, dropping a kiss on the top of her head. With an impressive Ph.D./M.D. combo, Lara chaired Sunderland's chemistry department and served as A-Tac's expert in biochemical weaponry, as well as the unit's medical officer. She and Jason had been living together for the past year. Although such relationships were frowned upon by their bosses at Langley, the team nevertheless turned a blind eye to their relationship.

Life was short and it was best to take what you could

while you had the chance. Nash knew that firsthand. And even though in his case it hadn't ended well, he still didn't regret the fact that for a little while at least, he'd been lucky enough to find someone who'd accepted him for what he was.

But nothing was forever.

"So anyone seen Drake?" Hannah was asking as they walked through the now-open panel in the rear reception wall.

"He had an off period," Tyler said. "So my guess is he's already down here."

As if to verify the fact, Drake appeared in the doorway to the war room. "Nice of you to join us," he said with his customary grin.

"So have you got any idea what this is all about?" Jason asked.

"Why don't you ask the big guy himself." Drake moved aside to reveal Avery Solomon standing at the head of the conference table. The man dwarfed even Nash. An ex-marine with service in both the CIA and the Pentagon, the fact that Avery had worked with three different admin-istrations said a lot about his loyalty to country and his ability to sway even the most strident of critics.

His appointment as commander of A-Tac eight years ago had coincided with Nash's arrival in the unit, the two of them hitting it off instantly. They'd worked countless operations together, and now, along with Tyler, were the senior members of the team.

"So what's up?" Nash asked with a frown. "You've got your serious face on and that's never a good thing."

"If everyone will have a seat, we'll get started," Avery said, his tone no-nonsense. The rest of the team took their places, the jovial mood from the elevator replaced with somber anticipation. "I just got word that we've received a credible threat against a high-ranking official."

"That's not exactly something new," Drake said. "We get hundreds of threats on a weekly basis."

"Yes, but as I said," Avery continued, shooting him a censorious look, "this one is credible. More than credible, actually. It's verified. According to Langley's intel, a splinter group of Al Qaeda is planning an assassination."

"Which group?" Hannah asked.

"Ashad."

"Out of Pakistan. Didn't we have a run-in with them a few years back?" Tyler asked. "The massacre in Peshawar." Seventeen innocents had been slaughtered when a bomb exploded in the central marketplace. Despite serious A-Tac efforts, the culprits were still at large.

"Yup," Avery said. "That's the one. But they've gotten more ambitious. This time they're targeting the United States. A top-level government official. We haven't been able to confirm the target, but we've narrowed it down to three."

"The president?" Jason asked, tapping away on his computer, already trying to secure new information.

"No. Secretary of State Wright seems most probable, but it could also be Evan Packard."

"Head of the Senate Homeland Security and Government Affairs Committee," Nash inserted, considering the possibility. "His stance on terrorism hasn't exactly made him the darling of Islamic extremists."

"Well, Richard Wright is, if anything, more militant than Packard," Hannah said, like Jason, already working on her laptop. "So who's the third candidate?"

"Blake Dominico."

"The U.S. ambassador to the U.N.?" Drake asked, clearly surprised.

"There was considerable objection to his being appointed, if I remember correctly," Jason said, looking up from his computer. "If he had his way most of the Middle East would become U.N.-occupied territory."

"So we've got three good candidates," Nash said, still frowning. "But why us? I mean, Homeland Security has entire divisions to handle this kind of threat."

"Because we've got credible intel identifying the contract shooter as former CIA."

"One of ours?" Tyler asked, her tone terse.

"Not A-Tac, no. But just being ex-CIA puts the operation in our backyard."

"And we've been tapped for the mission," Drake said.

"Got it in one." Avery's smile lacked humor. "And, as you can imagine, time is of the essence."

"And we've got no idea who exactly it is they've hired?" Emmett asked.

If possible, Avery's expression grew even more fierce. "Langley's best guess is that it's Annie Gallagher."

"Is this some kind of a joke?" Nash asked, his stomach clenching into a writhing knot of battling emotions.

"I wish it was," Avery said, shaking his head. "But we've got credible intel. And I'm afraid it all points to Annie."

There was silence as Nash swallowed, trying to think. To make sense of the nonsensical. But it just didn't compute. Even after everything that had gone down between them, he'd never have pegged Annie for a traitor.

"Son of a bitch."

CHAPTER 3

There's got to be a mistake," Nash said, his mind still reeling. "There's no way Annie would sign on for that kind of thing."

"People change." Avery shrugged.

"Someone want to tell me who the hell Annie Gallagher is?" Drake asked, his dark gaze falling on Nash.

He tried to find words, but couldn't, his brain still trying to make sense of the idea that Annie was playing for the other team.

"She was Nash's partner before he came to A-Tac. A trained assassin. One of the best, if rumors are to be believed," Tyler said, coming to his rescue. She and Avery were the only ones who knew just how much Annie's defection had cost him. "Nash and Annie worked special ops. Mainly in the former Eastern Bloc. Some of the Company's most dangerous missions."

"So what happened?" Hannah asked.

"She jumped ship in the middle of a mission," Nash

said, fighting against his anger and the memories. "Fucking disappeared. And I damn near died because of it."

"Maybe something happened to her," Emmett offered. "I mean, our line of work doesn't exactly lead to winning popularity contests."

"That's what I thought at first," Nash said, his tone laced with bitterness. "And believe me when I say that I explored every possibility. But everything I managed to discover only underscored the idea that her disappearance was planned. Annie was always good at details."

"Sometimes there are good reasons to jump ship," Drake said, eyes narrowed, "but that doesn't excuse her leaving you to die. What the hell happened?"

"Long story." Nash shook his head. "But the short version is that we got cornered in a building in Lebanon. Saida. My last mission before leaving to join A-Tac. Anyway, Annie and I got separated and I got pinned down in the firefight. There was an explosion and half my shoulder got ripped off. I was trapped, but she never came back. Just left me there to die."

"But you made it out okay," Tyler said, her eyes dark with anger.

"Yeah, I did. No thanks to Annie."

"She betrayed your trust," Emmett said.

"Which shouldn't be all that surprising. Hell, it's part and parcel of the gig." Drake grimaced. "They train us to doubt everything we see and hear. Trust nothing and no one."

"Except your partner. If you can't trust him or her, you might as well pack it in." Lara frowned, shooting a look in Jason's direction.

"Maybe I just picked the wrong person," Nash sighed,

shaking his head to clear his thoughts. Whatever the hell kind of relationship he'd had with Annie, it had imploded in Lebanon. Along with any loyalty he might owe her. "So, Avery, what have you got that makes you think it's her?"

"Intel picked up three separate references to Titian while picking through the chatter," Avery said. "Two of them directly referencing what we believe to be plans for the assassination."

"Titian as in the painter?" Jason asked, typing furiously on his laptop.

"Indirectly." Avery nodded. "Annie has red hair. Titian was her code name."

"Bit of a blinding glimpse of the obvious." Drake frowned.

"Sometimes the best way to hide is in plain sight." Emmett shrugged.

"Yeah, but in this case it doesn't make sense. Annie's disappearance was without sanction. That means that she's persona non grata as far as the CIA is concerned. So surfacing now using an old CIA code name would set off all kinds of alarm bells." Nash shook his head, frustration cresting. "I think it's far more likely that someone's playing us. Trying to make us believe it's Annie, when, in fact, it's not."

"The possibility occurred to me, too," Avery said, his expression, as usual, masking any emotion. "But there's more." He picked up a remote and pressed a button, the screen behind him filling with the photograph of a man entering a small hotel. "This picture was taken yesterday afternoon in D.C. The man is Emanuel Rivon, a Bolivian national with known terrorist ties. He operates a coffee conglomerate and uses it to cover travel in and out of questionable countries. Including Pakistan."

"Has he been specifically linked to Ashad?" Lara asked.

"Not specifically, no." Avery shook his head. "But intel can establish that he does business with people who do have ties to the group."

"Guilt by association," Drake said to no one in particular.

"Sometimes it's all we've got. But in this case we can verify that Rivon met recently with two suspected Ashad sympathizers. Both Pakistani and both alleged to have strong ties with radical Islam. This photo was taken about sixteen hours after that meeting."

"I assume you have something connecting Rivon to Annie?" Lara asked.

Avery nodded, hitting the remote again. The screen filled with another photograph, same hotel, but this time the camera had captured the image of a woman. Nash struggled to breathe, long-sequestered emotions threatening to overwhelm him. Despite the passing years, Annie looked just the same. The fall of her hair, the slant of her eyes, even the small scar that bisected her left eyebrow—a souvenir from a particularly incendiary operation—nothing had changed.

"This photo was taken fifteen minutes after Rivon entered the building. If we hadn't been watching him, we'd probably never have seen this."

"It could be coincidence," Nash started, trailing off as he realized just how delusional he sounded. Annie was clearly a part of something big. And the fact that she'd fucked him over eight years ago only gave credence to the idea.

"In our business there's no such thing," Drake said, his expression hard, as he stared at the photograph.

"Is there anything more?" Tyler asked.

"More chatter. This time a veiled reference to a meeting between Titian and El Halcón."

"The Falcon," Emmett repeated. "Rivon's code name?"

"Exactly." Avery nodded, his expression harsh.

"And if you play connect the dots," Drake said, "you end up with Rivon hiring Annie to do Ashad's dirty work."

"Makes sense." Hannah shrugged. "With security what it is, it's a hell of a lot easier to hire someone already in country. Especially if said person is a professional assassin."

The label hung in the air, no one willing to look at Nash.

"So you think Annie's turned mercenary?" Nash said, his jaw clenching as he fought his anger. It was a reasonable assumption, but that didn't make it any easier to swallow.

"She wouldn't be the first." Jason shrugged.

"I don't know," he said, frowning as he tried to sort through the facts. "Don't you think it's a little suspect that she's showing her hand after all these years? Usually when people fall off the grid, they go out of their way to stay that way. Meeting with a known terrorist in the middle of D.C. is like waving a red flag."

"Or maybe she's just lost her edge," Lara said. "It's been a long time."

"You don't know Annie." Nash shook his head, anger mixing with frustration.

"But you do," Avery replied, his tone brooking no argument. "Which is exactly why the boys in Virginia dropped this in our backyard. They want you to spearhead the effort to bring Annie Gallagher down."

Annie paced in front of the hotel window, the traffic below indicating that it was rush hour in Baltimore. Time had lost all meaning, her every waking moment occupied with thoughts of finding her son. It had been almost thirty-seven hours since Adam had disappeared.

Less than two days. But it felt like years. The kidnappers had made their instructions clear. A phone call that had sent her across the country to D.C. and a meeting with a man named Emanuel Rivon.

It was dangerous coming out into the open after so many years, but she hadn't had a choice. The kidnappers had made it clear that there would be no negotiation. And that they were watching. Any attempt to contact the authorities, particularly the CIA, would result in Adam's death.

Not that she was tempted to go that route. She wasn't foolish enough to believe anyone from her old life would step in to help her now. For all practical purposes, black ops agents operated off the radar. And once they'd ceased to be useful, they ceased to exist, all ties with the past severed irrevocably. In return for her safety and her freedom, she'd agreed to a cover story that painted her a deserter.

It was for the greater good. At least that's what she'd been told. But now, standing here waiting for Rivon's call, she wondered if she hadn't made a bargain with the devil. In trying to save her son, she'd opened the door to a far more hideous danger.

So far they hadn't allowed her to speak with Adam. The only proof she had that he was still alive was a grainy photograph Rivon had given her. She picked up the picture for something like the thousandth time, studying every angle, looking for something—anything—that would give her some idea where they were holding him.

But the generic room gave nothing away.

She clenched her fists and stared at the PDA on the nightstand, willing it to ring or signal an incoming text message. Rivon had given her the phone at their meeting. Untraceable, it was no doubt rigged to track her movements as well. Although she hated the idea, she couldn't ditch it. It was her only link with Adam's kidnappers. Rivon had said they'd call her when everything was finalized.

He'd also promised a video call from Adam.

But so far...nothing.

She blew out a breath and leaned her forehead against the cold glass of the window. Life below her went on without so much as a pause. It was as if the universe were completely unaware of the nightmare she'd been thrown into.

Rivon hadn't exactly been a font of information. He hadn't even told her who it was he was working for. But clearly it was someone who knew who she was. Who she'd been. Someone who knew that taking Adam was the only way to pull her back into the game.

She fought against a sob, knowing that this was no time for emotion. She had to keep a clear head. Figure out where they were holding her son and find a way to get him out. And failing that, she'd have to follow through with their demands.

It meant crossing a line, but the choice was an easy one. Adam was her son. And if necessary she'd sacrifice her life for him. Or someone else's. Rivon had made that much perfectly clear.

She sighed, a shiver working its way up her spine.

It wasn't as if she'd never killed anyone. But in the past, she'd always believed she was working on the side of right. Fighting against corruption and evil. Making the world a safer place for children like Adam.

Maybe it had all been bullshit. Maybe there was no right or wrong. At least not in any absolute kind of way. The world was a dangerous place. And her involvement with the darker side of espionage was the only reason she was standing in a seedy hotel room praying for word from her son. All she knew for certain was that she'd do whatever it took to make sure that Adam was freed. Securing his release was the only thing that mattered.

She still had no idea who the target would be. Someone of great importance, Rivon had said. A major player. A roadblock in the continuing battle to bring America to its knees.

She sank down on the end of the bed, desperation threatening all rational thought. Nothing had changed. It was the same war. Different opponents maybe. But still the same fight. And her son was caught in the middle of it.

Beside her the phone rang, and heart pounding, she snatched it off the bed, fumbling with the buttons in her rush to answer.

"Hello?" She held her breath, waiting. "Adam, is that you?"

"No, Ms. Gallagher. I'm afraid it's not your son."

"Rivon." The word came out more a curse than a name. "I want to speak to Adam."

"In good time. But there are a few things we need to discuss first."

She wondered if it was possible to hate anyone as much as she did this man. "So speak."

"It's almost time for you to make your move. And so I've been instructed to reveal the target."

"Aren't you worried that I'll tell someone?"

"Not particularly," he said, his tone smug. "You're more than aware of what would happen if you were to try to bring in outside help."

She sighed, knowing there was little point in arguing. Better to play along and keep alert. She needed to talk to Adam. "So who is it you want me to take out?"

"Spoken like a consummate professional." He laughed. "The target is an official with the U.N. Blake Dominico."

"The U.S. ambassador?" She tried but couldn't keep the dismay out of her voice. Not only was the man a patriot, he was probably, thanks to his often extreme views on eradicating the country's enemies, one of the most protected men in the country. "You're asking the impossible."

"That's why we have you. Your reputation precedes you."

"I haven't been a part of that world in years. And even then I wasn't operating on my own. I don't have the resources to pull something like this off by myself."

"I think you're underestimating your abilities, Ms. Gallagher. And besides, you've got more resources than you realize. Which is why I want you to go to New York

and survey the situation. Then when you've come up with
a plan, we'll see that you get whatever it is you need to
make it happen."

"I'm not sure you have access to the kinds of resources
that might be necessary. Blueprints, surveillance equipment, entrance codes, not to mention weaponry. Since
9/11, access to U.N. diplomats has become increasingly
difficult. Particularly at the Secretariat."

"Yes, but Dominico doesn't spend every waking hour
at the General Assembly. You'll find a way, Ms. Gallagher. After all, we have Adam. And it would be a shame
for his life to end so soon. Wouldn't you agree?"

Blind rage threatened to overtake all rational thought,
but she clenched the phone until the plastic cut into her
fingers, the sharp bite of pain pulling her back from the
edge. "I won't do anything more until I see my son. I need
to know that he's okay." She paused, sucking in a breath
of air, as her mind considered the unthinkable. "That he's
still alive."

"You're not really in any position to be making demands,"
Rivon said. "But as it happens, we're prepared for you to
speak with your son as soon as we've finished here."

"So what else do I need to know? You've made your
objective crystal clear."

"I'll be texting a file with information and final
instructions within the hour," he said, ignoring her open
hostility.

"What about transportation? It'll be difficult to stay
under the radar if I have to use my credit cards."

"All of that has been arranged. You'll receive everything you need."

"And if I don't? How can I contact you?" It was worth

a try. A phone number would be the quickest route to tracking him down.

"You can't. At least not by any direct method. But again, arrangements have been made, and as I just said, you'll be apprised of the details very soon."

"Whatever," she said, her impatience growing by the second. "Let me talk to Adam."

"As you wish." The line went dead. And for a moment she panicked, fearing Rivon's promise had been nothing more than empty words, but two minutes later the phone signaled an incoming video. And holding her breath, Annie waited for the call to connect.

"Mommy?" Adam's face swam into view, blurred as much by her tears as by the quality of transmission.

"I'm here, baby. I'm right here." She leaned closer to the picture, as if in doing so she could somehow physically connect with her child. "Are you all right?"

"I think so." He nodded, his little face looking older than it should. "At first I was really scared. But there's a nice man here. He has a Wii. And we've been playing Super Smash Brothers. It's really cool." He paused, his chin quivering. "But I want to come home."

"I know, sweetie. And I'm doing everything I can to make that happen."

He nodded again. "Come soon, Mommy. Please."

Tears ran down her cheeks in earnest, her heart threatening to shatter. "I will, Adam. I promise. And in the meantime, you be brave."

"Like Daddy?"

"Like your daddy." She nodded, wondering for the millionth time why she'd made the man seem so much larger than life.

"He was really brave, right?"

"Yes," she said, frustration and anger blending with agony. "And so are you. Just hang in there, baby. I love you."

"I love you, too." He nodded.

"Everything's going to be okay. I swear it is. We'll be home before you know it."

"Can we have hot dogs?"

Annie felt a bubble of laughter but before she could say anything the screen went blank. Adam was gone.

"Hello?" she said, her voice cracking with emotion. "Adam?"

"He's no longer on the line," a disembodied voice said.

"When can I talk to him again?" she asked, desperation mixing with dread.

"When you've accomplished your objectives. I need for your focus to be complete."

"You have to know that I can't do anything well, knowing my son is in danger."

"Don't be ridiculous. You're a professional, Ms. Gallagher," the tinny voice said.

"That was a hell of a long time ago."

"Just get the job done." The connection went dead and Annie stood staring down at the phone. For one second, she considered forsaking common sense and calling in help. She and Nash might be estranged, but he'd never let her hang in the wind. Especially if he grasped the true significance of the situation. Even as she had the thought, she rejected it. She'd reached out to him once before, and he'd turned her down flat.

And besides, even if for some reason he did agree to

help, she still didn't trust the CIA. At least not with her son. His death would be viewed as nothing more than collateral damage, the primary objective being to take out the threat, no matter the cost.

No. She couldn't risk asking for help. Nash was a Company man to the core. He'd proven that in no uncertain terms eight years ago. Which meant she was in this alone. And she'd find a way to save her son. Even if it meant killing an innocent man.

CHAPTER 4

This is crazy," Tyler said, lowering her field glasses. "We don't even know that Blake Dominico's our man."

"That's why Avery assigned secondary teams to watch over Wright and Packard. But Hannah believes Dominico's the most likely target. And she's not wrong that often." Nash shrugged, dropping the aerial photograph he'd been studying back onto the table. Something about it felt off to him, but staring at it didn't seem to be helping.

They'd been in Manhattan following Dominico for just over twenty-four hours. And in that time they'd agreed that the man's most vulnerable access point was his apartment. Situated on the southeast corner of a building fronting the East River, it was lined with windows and a wraparound terrace. The setup was perfect, with a variety of places for a seasoned shooter to find concealment.

Attempts to convince Dominico to move somewhere

safer for the duration of the threat had been met with his signature arrogance and a blunt refusal, the fortitude that had helped make him a first-class negotiator also making him a blind fool.

So they'd secured the building immediately across the way. A man on the roof was tasked with protecting egress and Dominico's men were taking care of additional security in the ambassador's building. That meant fewer options for the killer, but it was impossible to eliminate everything. Which left Tyler and Nash stuck doing surveillance from a conveniently empty studio apartment directly across from Dominico's.

Nash sighed. There was nothing worse than trying to protect an idiot. Especially a politically connected one.

"There's no way we can cover every angle." Tyler frowned, echoing his thoughts. "Where do you think she's most likely to set up?"

"The most obvious," Nash said, joining his friend at the window. "Because we're the most likely to dismiss it. Annie is fond of hit and run. She's in and out before anyone has time to realize what's happened."

"Sound strategy."

"Except this whole thing feels off to me. Annie's been out of the game over eight years. Why get back in now?"

"Money." Tyler shrugged, lifting the glasses again as she scanned the skyline, looking for anything out of the ordinary. "You've got to admit it's a great motivator."

He turned away from the window, not bothering to answer. Whatever her motivation, if Annie really was planning to kill Dominico, she'd crossed a line he couldn't even contemplate. Nash was as ruthless as anyone in the game, but he was also clear about which side he was fighting for. And as far as he was concerned, there were no shades of gray—only stark black and white.

"So tell me honestly," Tyler asked, swinging away from the window, her expression reflecting her concern. "How are you handling all this?"

If it had been anyone else asking he'd have given a flip response, something that firmly closed the door. But he and Tyler went way back. If nothing else, he owed her honesty. "I've been better."

"Look, I know this is rough. Nobody would blame you for sitting this one out."

"Avery made it pretty clear the suits want me involved."

"So be an armchair quarterback."

"Not exactly my style," he said, allowing himself the sliver of a smile.

"I figured you'd say that. But I'm afraid there's one more fly in the ointment." She paused, her expression rueful. "Avery called while you were checking on the roof-top surveillance."

"And I take it you weren't pleased with what he had to say?" Nash leaned back, waiting for the other shoe to drop.

"It's not really me he was worried about. Apparently the powers that be have asked Tom Walker to be part of our operation."

"But he's Homeland Security. Why the hell would they want him in on this?"

"It's not a matter of wanting him. It's more about playing nice with the other boys. Homeland Security has access to the same intel that we do, and they don't much like the idea of our handling something that normally would land in their backyard. So after some wrangling it was agreed that someone from HLS would sit in on our operation."

"Tom. But why him, specifically?"

"Oh, come on. I think that's pretty obvious. You and Annie worked with him for what, ten years?"

"Nine." He frowned.

Tom Walker, acting as a CIA division head, had coordinated most of Nash and Annie's Eastern European operations. He'd been their handler, the man primarily responsible for getting them into and out of trouble. The latter more times than Nash cared to count.

Tom had also been the one who'd secured Nash's shot at A-Tac, his influence key in convincing higher-ups that Nash was the man for the job. And it'd been Tom who'd pulled his ass out of the fire after things had gone south on the last mission in Saida—literally. Tom had rescued him when Annie had left Nash high and dry. And Tom had been there to help put the pieces back together.

But shortly after Nash had joined A-Tac, Tom had left the CIA for a suit job in Homeland Security. It was a huge promotion for Tom, a coup of sorts. In part because of the rescue in Lebanon. Nash had been happy for him, but after a couple of congratulatory phone calls, the two of them had more or less drifted apart, their friendship a casualty of political turf wars between two agencies whose objectives collided more often than not.

"I've got no problem with Tom," Nash said, shaking his head, "but I thought we were supposed to handle this. The CIA taking care of its own."

"You know there are always layers in these kinds of

operations. Accountability. And you know as well as I do that Homeland Security can get pretty pushy when they believe someone is treading on their territory."

"So they wrangled their way onto the team."

"Well, this isn't the first time we've had to play nice." She shrugged. "And who knows, maybe the two of you sharing history will make it easier."

"Or maybe it'll just make an already difficult situation worse."

"Way to look on the bright side." She smiled. "Anyway, Avery says it's just a temporary inconvenience."

"Avery doesn't know Tom Walker."

"What do you mean by that?" She frowned.

"Nothing ominous. Just that Tom's a by-the-book kind of guy. Real results-oriented. That's how he's risen so far so fast."

"You think he'll go hard on Annie." Tyler frowned, cutting right to the heart of the matter.

"I don't know. Hell, if she's really hired herself out to the highest bidder maybe she deserves what she gets."

"You don't believe that."

"Yeah, actually I do. But I'm done discussing it."

"All right," Tyler said, holding her hands up in surrender. "We'll stop with the heart-to-heart. I just wanted you to know that I'm here if you need me."

He appreciated the thought, but was uncomfortable with the sentiment. He'd paid once before for allowing himself to get too close to his partner, and he wasn't about to do it again. "So what have we got?" he asked, moving back to the window.

"Nothing at the moment. Everything is pretty quiet. So far Dominico's managed to stay off the balcony and away from the windows. Which means for the moment, at least, he's safe. There's no way anyone unauthorized is getting into the building. And I'm not seeing any identifiable threats out there." She nodded at the terraced buildings across the way. "Of course I'm just one pair of eyes."

Tyler hated surveillance. She preferred the heated exchange of a firefight to the incessant waiting that was an integral part of this kind of operation. Annie had been just the opposite. Comfortable with her own company, Annie had the ability to outwait and therefore outmaneuver even the most elusive of targets. It had made her a valuable asset to any team. And a woman impossible to read when it came to relationships.

She'd held things close to the vest. Too close, if he'd had any say at all. But he hadn't, and that was, at the end of the day, the whole point. He blew out a breath and angrily pushed his memories firmly back into the past where they belonged.

"I'll check the video feed," he said as he walked over to a monitor bank sitting against the far wall. The top row of screens showed Dominico's apartment from every conceivable angle. Dominico himself was currently sitting at the dining room table reading the paper, the scene looking deceptively ordinary. On the next monitor over, his housekeeper was chopping vegetables in the kitchen, while some kind of soup boiled away on the stove.

"Anything?" Tyler queried.

"Nothing worth reporting." Nash shook his head as he turned his attention to the bottom row of monitors, their affiliated cameras homed in on the buildings across the way, highlighting possible areas of access. "Pretty dead on our side, too. The only action's in the park. And that's been limited to a dog walker or the occasional jogger."

Dominico's building sat at the end of the street, parallel to the FDR and the river. The park sat about three levels below the street, connected to it by two flights of steep stone steps. A cement walkway extended from the first flight of stairs across the highway to connect with the river walk on the opposite side.

"They're too far down to be a danger," Tyler said, coming up to look over his shoulder. "And the angle is wrong to shoot from the highway, even if Dominico was standing on the railing waving his arms for attention."

"I wouldn't put it past him. But I agree that the FDR isn't an option. The park is all wrong, too. Like you said, it's too far down. Which leaves us with a big fat zero."

"So what did the guy on the roof have to say?"

Andre was an NYC man. He seemed competent, but Nash had never liked working with unknowns. "Nothing. Just that everything seemed normal."

"Beats the alternative."

"I don't know," he said, watching a jogger below on the walkway using the railing to stretch and warm up. "I don't like the quiet."

"The optimal time to make a move?" Tyler frowned. "You think Annie knows we're here?"

"I doubt it. She's working without backup, which puts her at a distinct disadvantage. She'll have done her homework, though. Which means she's more than aware of Dominico's security detail. And she'll factor in the possibility that others are watching. Hell, it's standard protocol."

"But she won't be expecting you."

"Not sure how that matters. But no, she won't."

Tyler shifted to face him, her brows drawing together in concern. "You sure you're up to this? I mean, if things go south..." She let the words trail off, her meaning more than clear.

"You're asking if I can take Annie out."

"I wouldn't blame you for saying no."

His jaw tightened as he contemplated the unthinkable. "If the situation presents itself, I'll do what has to be done. Satisfied?"

"I wasn't trying to—"

"I know," he said, shaking his head. "And you had every right to ask. Anyway, push comes to shove, you'll be there, too. So I'd say we've got it covered."

"And if we're lucky we won't have to deal with it at all," she said, turning back to the window. "Why don't you check in with Hannah? Maybe she's seen something we haven't."

Hannah was watching the feed from Sunderland. Analyzing all activity. Using various technological applications to enhance the information the cameras provided.

"Hannah?" Nash said, as he sat down at the table and slipped his headset on. "You there?"

"Copy that," she responded, her voice tinny as it carried over the wires. "Not seeing anything interesting from this end. What about you?"

"Nothing suspicious."

"Much to your dismay." There was a hint of laughter in Hannah's voice.

"Hey, I've never pretended to be a sit-on-my-ass kind of guy."

"You and Drake both."

"He complaining, too?"

"Not complaining. Just lamenting the lack of action." Drake and Emmett were stuck in Maine watching over Senator Packard. "Packard's pretty much sequestered himself at his family's compound. It's on an island and security is pretty impregnable. So if he's the target, we're probably not going to see any action there."

"At least one of the three's taking the threat seriously. What's happening in Annapolis?" Jason and Lara were there, eyes on Richard Wright as he addressed a group of top military brass.

"Overkill. Whatever Wright's private security hasn't got covered, the Pentagon does. Although Jason's not complaining." This time Hannah's laugh was audible.

"Downtime with Lara."

"Exactly. Anyway, I don't think either team has anything to worry about."

"You're still thinking it's Dominico?"

"Everything I've seen points in that direction. He's the most outspoken of the group when it comes to Islamic extremists."

"Which means that thanks to the man's stubborn streak he's made himself the perfect target for a group like Ashad." As if to underscore the remark, Dominico stepped out onto his balcony, five cameras adjusting automatically to follow the movement.

"You guys see that?" Tyler called over her shoulder.

"Yeah, we got him," Nash said, frowning at the monitor. "Where the hell are his bodyguards?"

"In the hallway," Hannah said. "Monitor five."

Nash's gaze moved to a grainy image of two men in black flanking the door in the hallway outside Dominico's apartment. "Fat lot of good they're going to do him there."

"Nothing else is moving," Tyler said, studying the row of buildings opposite them. "Still, I don't like the odds of his being out there on his own."

Nash scanned the monitors, and then, still wearing his headset, walked over to the windows. "Hannah, can you radio Dominico's security?" Dominico stood near the railing, his eyes on the park below him. Nothing seemed out of the ordinary, but Nash couldn't shake the feeling that Annie was out there somewhere and the clock was ticking.

"Got them," Hannah's voice crackled over the headset. "They should be pulling him out now."

Moving back to the monitor, Nash watched as the guards appeared and, after a brief argument, hauled Dominico back into the relative safety of his apartment. "Well, that takes care of that."

Blowing out a breath, he studied the various camera shots for a moment and then the corresponding points in the buildings across the way. None of the angles seemed right to him, somehow. Too much of a risk, both for access and for making an escape. This was a high-rent neighborhood, which meant building security was at a maximum.

He picked up the aerial shot again, studying the photo, trying again to figure out what it was that bugged him about it. The park consisted of an L-shaped strip of land situated at the bottom of a cliff. On top of the cliff sat the grounds of the building he was in now, a sixteen-foot stone wall insuring residents' privacy and effectively keeping intruders out. Dominico's building also had grounds, but they were protected by fencing and a sheer rock face cutting down to the highway itself.

He frowned and then looked up at the monitor showing the park. The walkway over the highway was directly below the camera, only a part of it visible. He typed coordinates into the connected laptop and the camera's angle shifted, the entire walkway now visible. The west side, nearest the buildings, sat well below street level, but as it moved toward the river, the path rose almost imperceptibly until, near the end, it was actually almost level with Dominico's balcony.

The jogger he'd noticed earlier was still there. Still stretching, but farther down, closer to the river. He maneuvered the computer, moving the camera lens closer. The woman's face was obscured by a Yankees cap, but as she twisted, a strand of hair caught the light, gleaming russet in the sun.

"Shit," Nash said, a sense of urgency knotting his gut, as he jumped from his seat, already heading for the door. "She's been out there all along. On the walkway. Right under our fucking noses."

He took the stairs two at a time, Tyler hot on his heels barking orders to Andre on the roof and to Dominico's security guards.

"Tell them not to do anything to give their positions away. She'll bolt if she thinks we're onto her. And no shooting. I want to take her alive." For any number of reasons, none of which he was about to analyze now.

They swung into the hallway on the bottom floor heading for the back way out and the garden. A small gate in the side wall gave access to what had once been a stairway, removed years ago for safety. The resulting overgrowth hid Nash and Tyler from view as they stepped out onto the rock ledge that surrounded the wall. The walkway was only a few feet away.

"Wait here," he said, signaling Tyler to stay put. "Keep me covered, and if I get into trouble, take her out."

Tyler nodded, gun already in hand.

Without giving himself time for further thought, Nash leaped across the gap, landing silently on the cement walkway, staying out of view behind the overgrowth of rhododendrons.

Annie had shifted again, moving closer to him. He could see the outline of her face under the cap, her profile as familiar to him as his own. She was still feigning stretching, her attention locked on the building across from her.

Thanks to the incline and a bend in the walkway, his approach would be almost invisible. Sucking in a breath, he drew his gun and moved forward, closing the distance between them. Annie's attention was still on Dominico's apartment, and as the man appeared in the window, she shifted, straightening her arm as she lined up the shot, but Nash was faster, leveling his gun at the back of her head.

"Give it up, Annie," he said, his voice cracking on her name. "Please. Don't make me shoot you."

CHAPTER 5

"Give us some time alone," Nash said, his jaw tightening with the request.

"Are you sure that's a good idea?" the blonde asked, her green eyes speculative as she looked from Annie to Nash.

"Tyler, just do it." There was a note of command in Nash's voice that Annie remembered well.

"Fine." Tyler shrugged. "I need to call Avery, anyway. I'll do it from the parlor." She walked toward the door, stopping first to lay a hand on Nash's shoulder, the gesture comforting and intimate.

Annie fought against a rush of emotion, forcing herself to focus. Nash was nothing to her anymore. An obstacle to finding Adam. The thought of her baby out there somewhere with God knew who was beyond frightening. She clenched her teeth, trying to maintain control. There had to be a way out. She just needed to find it.

She had no idea where exactly they were. Lower

Manhattan somewhere. A brownstone from the looks of it. Probably a safe house of some kind. From here, they'd no doubt take her to a secured facility. Somewhere where she'd have little chance of escaping. Which meant that she had to capitalize on the moment. Find a way out now before reinforcements arrived.

Rivon had been clear. No outside help.

She wasn't carrying the phone, and she'd been careful to cover her tracks. So there was a chance that they didn't know about her capture, but that didn't rule out the possibility of being followed. And if Rivon knew—then Adam could already be dead.

Her heart pounded in her chest, tears welling, and she struggled to calm herself. There was nothing to be gained by letting her fear take control. She'd been in worse situations and managed to escape. She could do this.

Releasing a long breath, she turned to face Nash. "So where are we?" she asked, her frown more of a prop than anything else. A mask to hide her tumultuous feelings. The longer she was here, the more risk to Adam. She had to find a way out.

"A safe house," Nash said, his tone curt, his attention on a sheaf of papers in his hand. He'd hardly made eye contact since he'd trapped her on the bridge, leaving most of the physical contact to the blonde. Which was just as well. She wasn't sure she could handle him touching her. Not after all this time.

"And the blonde?" she asked, playing for time as she tried to case the room. "Is she your partner?"

"Tyler's part of A-Tac. Expert in munitions," Nash said, his dark eyes giving away nothing. "And she's a friend."

"I see." She nodded, her gaze darting around the room, looking for some means of escape. "And this Avery?"

"He's my boss. Heads up the team. He'll be escorting you to Langley. Along with Tom Walker."

"Tom?" she frowned, fighting off another rush of memory. Tom had been her friend once. An ally when her life had turned to shit. He'd helped her escape. Helped her go underground. He was the only one who had known the whole truth. But he'd moved on to bigger and brighter things, cutting her off in the process. Just like everyone in her life—he'd walked away.

But now apparently he was back, and more of a threat than she wanted to acknowledge.

"He's Homeland Security," she said, scrambling to figure Tom's angle in all of this. Tom always had an angle. "Some big muckety-muck, right?"

"Nice to know you keep up."

"I don't. Not really." She shook her head. "But it was headline news. Kind of hard to miss. So if this is a CIA matter, why Homeland Security?"

"Treason tends to bring out the big guns, Annie. Homeland Security has priority. But since you were ex-CIA," he said, emphasis on *ex*, "we drew the short straw when it came to running you to ground."

"But you and Tom…" she trailed off, knowing there really weren't words.

"Had the dubious honor of knowing you," he finished for her, the words not meant as a compliment. "That's why we were called in."

"I see."

Silence stretched between them, a ticking clock on the mantel sounding abnormally loud. She tried to focus on the room. Find access for escape. But concentration seemed out of the question. Maybe she'd been away from the game too long. Or maybe it was her proximity to Nash. Either way she was having difficulty staying on task.

Adam, her mind whispered. *Nothing matters but Adam.*

She nodded, pushing away everything else. Nothing was more important than her son. It was as simple as that. Once they'd transferred her to Langley, she'd be out of the game for good. Of no use to Adam. And even if she told them the truth, it wouldn't change the fact that she'd been caught gunning for Dominico. Tom was a stickler for the rules, and Nash's boss was an unknown quantity. They'd ship her off to Washington. And once Rivon figured it out—she struggled to breathe as the image of her son filled her brain. He was so little.

She had to find a way out.

"So," she said, pushing to her feet, testing her boundaries, "until this Avery arrives, I'm a prisoner here?"

After arriving at the brownstone, they'd made no further effort to restrain her. Nash had said it was a safe house. Which meant one of two things. Either an off-the-books place out of sight of prying eyes. Or a stronghold meant to keep people out—or in. She was betting on the latter. But at least from what she could see, it felt more like the former. A safe place agents could go to recuperate. Find center again.

There had been a place in Vienna. An escape she and Nash had used...

But those days were gone.

"I'm not giving you a chance to get out of here, if that's what you're thinking," he said.

"But I'm free to stretch my legs?"

He watched as she moved toward the window but made no effort to stop her. The street below looked like any other Manhattan street. Garbage bags littering the sidewalk, spindly trees stretching upward trying to find their way out of the grime-laden air. Just for a moment she closed her eyes, thinking of home—of Colorado.

But Dominico wasn't in Creede. And neither was Adam.

She turned to face Nash, leaning back against the sill, feeling surreptitiously with her fingers to see if the window could be opened.

"It's no use," he said, circling closer. "The windows all have motion sensors."

"Nobody in. Nobody out." She moved away from the window, accepting the futility of trying to use it as a mode of escape. But that didn't mean she'd given up. Not by a long shot.

"You know the drill." He shrugged, then lifted his eyes, his gaze colliding with hers, his anger an almost tangible thing. "What the hell were you doing out there, Annie?"

Electricity arced between them as their eyes dueled. Once upon a time, she'd believed she'd known this man better than she'd known herself, but that was ancient history. The truth was she didn't know him at all. Which meant she couldn't afford to drop her guard. It would be too easy to fall into old patterns. To trust a man that she knew damn well couldn't be trusted, at least not when it came to the things that really mattered. She pulled in a cleansing breath, steeling herself. "I was doing what I had to do."

"Killing the ambassador." His tone was dismissive, his disdain apparent.

"Sometimes we have to choose the lesser of two evils."

"That's not an answer."

"It's all I've got." She shrugged, her repertoire seemingly reduced to the simplest of gestures.

"Well, you're going to have to do better than that," he said, exasperation coloring his tone. "If not with me then with Avery and Tom."

"I've got nothing to say to any of you."

"It's not like you can make it go away, Annie. You had your sights on Dominico. I saw you. And even if I were inclined to look the other way, Tyler saw it, too. As well as four different security cameras."

"I haven't denied anything," she said, searching the room for other ways out. The door wasn't locked, but Nash's partner was out there. Given the right circumstances, Annie might be able to take the woman, but first she'd have to make it past Nash. Not impossible odds, but she'd need to find the right moment. Preferably before reinforcements arrived. She blew out a breath and forced herself to focus on what Nash was saying.

"You're in a hell of a lot of trouble, Annie. There's no getting around it. And the only thing you can do to help yourself is to tell us what you know. Help us catch the bastards behind this."

And kill her son in the process.

She shook her head, sequestering her emotions. "How do you know I wasn't working on my own?"

"Because we know you met with Emanuel Rivon several days ago," Nash said, his eyes narrowing. "And that he's been meeting with known associates of Ashad."

"You've certainly done your homework," she said, stalling while she tried to gauge the distance between the window and the door.

"Maybe you've forgotten," he said, moving closer, his eyes narrowed, "but I'm really good at what I do."

"How could I possibly have forgotten?" The tension in the room ratcheted up another level. "You put your job before everything else."

"At least I know how to follow through on what I start."

They were standing inches apart, their anger tying them together in a way their love affair clearly never had. And in that moment, Annie knew this was her best chance. Probably her only one. Without giving herself the time to analyze further, she clasped her hands and swung upward, her fists connecting with Nash's chin. He staggered backward as she followed through with a knee to the groin, his gasp of pain indicating she'd hit target.

Taking advantage of his momentary disorientation, she sprinted for the door, wrenching it open and stepping onto the brownstone's landing. Stairs extended in both directions, but Tyler's voice carrying from below meant that "up" was the better option. Praying that there'd be some kind of access to the roof, she headed for the third floor.

Below her, his anger erupting in expletives, Nash burst through the door and started after her. With only seconds separating them, she increased her pace, her attention focused on the landing above her.

Then, without warning, the stairs curved abruptly and in her haste, she stumbled, grabbing for the railing. Her last-minute handhold kept her from falling, but the mistake cost her valuable time. Nash quickly closed the distance between them, his fingers tightening on her wrist as he yanked her to a stop.

Reacting on instinct, she whipped around, shoving hard against his chest, then wrenched away, fleeing up the remaining steps, fighting against the urge to turn and make sure that he was okay.

Whatever he might have once been to her, he was her enemy now. A major obstacle to freeing Adam.

She hit the top of the staircase and moved quickly onto the landing, searching for some way to exit. There were rooms opening off to her right and left, but there was no time to explore. She might have slowed Nash, but she certainly hadn't stopped him. Fighting against panic, she searched the hallway, relieved when she spotted a ladder and the outline of a trap door at the far end.

Sprinting now, she raced forward, praying that the ladder led to the roof and not the brownstone's attic or some forgotten crawl space, but knowing that either way, she had to make it work. Taking the rungs two at a time, she reached the top just as she heard Nash hit the landing.

"Annie," he called, his tone deceptively calm. "You're wasting your time. There's no way out."

"There's always a way out," she called back as she pushed the trap door wide. "You taught me that." In seconds, she was up and through the opening.

But instead of blue sky, she was greeted with dusty gray walls. Which meant she was still trapped.

Damn it all to hell.

With a sigh of frustration, she slammed the trap door back into place, shoving a rotting old crate over it in an effort to keep Nash out. It wouldn't hold for long, but it might buy her enough time to figure a way out.

The room was small, the walls lined with insulation. A small window at the far end was the only source of light. She searched the ceiling for signs of another opening out onto the roof, but there was nothing visible. Cursing her luck, she ran for the window as Nash slammed into the trap door from below, the crate listing drunkenly in response.

It wouldn't be long before he managed to break through her makeshift barrier.

The window was cracked and grimy. A quick search of the sash and sill yielded no sign of security. She tried to yank it open, but age and weather had lodged it firmly into place. Behind her the crate slid forward as the wood and metal trap door slammed into the floor.

Wrapping the bottom of her T-shirt around her hand, Annie punched out the glass, relieved to see a rickety ladder extending upward from a grated metal walkway just outside the window. Slipping through the opening, she pulled herself out onto the ledge, heart pounding as she listened for the sound of Nash's footsteps as he crossed the floor of the attic.

Instead silence reigned. It could be a trick, but she wasn't about to wait to find out. Better to keep moving. Without bothering to test stability, she scrambled up the ladder, relieved when it held her weight.

At the top, two curved iron railings provided final access over the wall that bordered the roof. Grasping each side, she pulled herself up and over the ledge, landing in a crouch.

"What took you so long?" Nash asked, his smile cold as she pushed upright, already moving in retreat. Behind him, an open doorway signaled a second entrance to the rooftop. She must have missed it in her cursory examination of the hallway and attic. "I told you it was pointless to try to run."

"You always did underestimate me," she snapped as she reached behind her for the railing. Pushing off with her feet, she flipped backward, her intent to regain the ladder she'd just left. But Nash was faster, grabbing her by the waist and pulling her back onto the roof, the effort sending them both sprawling.

Gravel dug into her back, and she swore as she tried to push her way free. "Let go of me."

"Not on your life," he whispered, his grip tightening. "This isn't a game, Annie. And even if it were, you'll remember I'm not big on losing."

"I remember a lot of things," she said, twisting left, slamming her knee up into his gut. He grunted in pain, and she pulled herself free, scrambling to her knees, only to have him tackle her again.

They rolled across the rooftop, each trying to gain the upper hand. They'd sparred like this hundreds of times over the years. Each with their share of wins. But this time the stakes were much higher. This time her son's life was at risk.

She pushed off, trying for leverage, but only managed to lose her grip, Nash flipping them so that he straddled her. His face was flushed, his breathing coming in gasps. "When did I become the enemy, Annie?"

"When you let me go," she whispered, the words coming of their own accord.

He frowned, the pain in his eyes a reflection of the ache in her heart. With gentle fingers he pushed the hair from her face, and she turned away, not willing to explore the emotions coursing through her. There was too much time between them. Too much hurt.

"You all right?" Tyler asked, appearing in the rooftop doorway, her gun serving only to increase the tension between them.

"I'm fine. Everything's under control," Nash said, his grip tightening.

Tyler surveyed the situation and nodded. "Avery's downstairs. With Walker. I figured you'd just as soon him not find you up here—like this."

"You figured right." Nash pushed to his feet, then reached down to pull Annie up. "We're coming," he said, his fingers locking around her arm.

Tyler nodded, moving back to give them access to the stairwell, her gun still trained on Annie. Nash held his ground, his dark gaze giving away nothing. Annie shivered, but refused to look away. "What the hell happened to you?" he asked, a tiny muscle in his jaw the only sign of emotion. "We used to be on the same side."

"Yeah, well, things change," she said, unable to keep the sarcasm from her voice.

"I don't buy it. There's something else going on. I can see it in your eyes. Come on, Annie, you used to tell me everything."

"That was a hell of a long time ago," she whispered, her thoughts tumbling over each other. After all these years, he was here. With her. And in so many ways, it felt the same. And yet it couldn't be. If for no other reason than the lies that lay between them.

Hers.

His.

They were unavoidable. And she'd be a fool to believe him now.

"Annie, whatever it is—you can tell me." His eyebrow raised in question, the gesture so familiar she wanted to cry.

She swallowed, her heart pounding so loud that she was certain he could hear it. Maybe she was a fool. Or maybe she was just desperate. Either way she was certain there would be a price to pay. But beggars couldn't be choosers. She'd blown her chance at escape. Which meant that Adam's only chance now was for her to come clean.

At least in part.

"I didn't agree to kill Dominico for money. Or for political reasons." She swallowed, praying she was doing the right thing. "I did it because they have my son."

CHAPTER **6**

So you're telling us that Ashad has your son." Avery frowned from his perch on the arm of a chair. "And that's why you agreed to take out Dominico."

"I don't know who has him," Annie said, the line of her shoulders defiant. "Rivon refused to say. And he's been my main contact."

Nash watched the proceedings with caged emotion. There were so many questions he wanted answered, none of them having anything at all to do with Ashad. He should have asked her on the stairs. Made her spell out the truth. But Tyler had intervened, insisting that any further conversation occur downstairs.

With Avery and Tom.

She'd been right, of course, but that hadn't stopped Nash from wanting to shake the truth out of Annie anyway.

"So why didn't you bring this to us in the first place?" Tom asked.

"You already know the answer to that," she said, her jaw tightening as she watched him warily. "Under the circumstances, I wasn't exactly discharged with honor. I wasn't burned, but I'm definitely persona non grata. I had no reason to believe after all this time that anyone would lift a finger to help me. Besides, I was warned against bringing in outside help."

"So you decided to handle it yourself," Nash said, his anger making his words sharper than he'd intended.

"I didn't have a choice. My son comes first."

"There's always a choice, Annie." But she'd never really seen that. Never trusting anyone. Always believing she was better off on her own.

"Yes, but you had to know that Ashad was a top priority." Avery frowned, pulling the conversation away from emotional land mines.

"I already told you that I didn't know it was Ashad. And if I had, it would have been even more reason not to bring in outside help, because I knew that any involvement on a national scale would mean emphasis on taking out the people behind the kidnapping, not on rescuing my son."

"How old is he?" Nash asked, surprised at himself for interjecting the question.

She shifted so that her eyes met his, her jaw tightening at the implication of the question. "He just turned six."

Disappointment mixed with relief, the latter edging out the former by only the smallest bit. Annie had a child.

And it wasn't his.

"What about the father?" From his peripheral vision, Nash could see Tom frown. These weren't the questions he should be asking, but he couldn't seem to stop himself.

"Not in the picture." Annie's words were terse, her anger evident as she looked first at Tom and then back at him.

"You didn't think he had the right to know?" Again the words came of their own volition, the subtext hanging heavily between them.

Annie's laugh was bitter. "I don't think that's really any of your business. You lost all say in my life a long time ago."

"I'm not questioning your decisions, Annie. I'm asking if the father is around."

"No. He isn't."

"So there's no chance that he's a part of this?" Nash asked, scrambling to pull the conversation onto more stable ground.

"Absolutely none." She narrowed her eyes, anger making her cheeks flush. "He's dead."

"I'm sorry," he murmured automatically.

"Don't be," she snapped. "Turns out he wasn't the man I thought he was."

"I see." Silence stretched between them, the others in the room seeming, for the moment, to have disappeared.

"I think," Tom said, clearing his throat to break through the building tension, "that we've gotten a bit off track. What's past is past. There's no need to rehash it here." He paused, his eyes dropping to Annie, and Nash frowned as something passed between the two of them.

He started to object, but Tyler cut him off. "The key here is for us to figure out who's behind this and stop them."

"The *key* is to find my son," Annie snapped, her lips compressed with anger.

"That's not your call," Tom said. "You pulled yourself out of the equation when you decided to act on your own."

"The hell I did." She rose to her feet, every muscle in her body ready for a fight.

"Again, we've gotten off point." Avery's voice was deceptively calm, but Nash recognized the tone. "Our task was to neutralize Ms. Gallagher and trace the plot to its source. I see no reason we can't make rescuing the boy part of finding the culprits."

"As long as he doesn't get in the way," Annie said, clenching her fists.

"I have never knowingly put a child in harm's way, Ms. Gallagher." Avery's eyes narrowed as he studied Annie. "And I don't intend to start now."

"I wish I could believe that."

"Well, for the moment, we're all you've got," he said. "And I'd submit that it's in your best interest to suspend hostilities. The only way any of our objectives are going to be accomplished is if you give us whatever you've got on the people behind your son's kidnapping."

Annie held Avery's gaze for a moment, still defiant, and then with a sigh sank back into her chair. "What do you want to know?"

"Everything," Tom said, pulling up a chair to sit in front of her. "No detail is too small."

From his seat on the radiator cover, Nash listened as she told them about discovering her son missing, and the first phone call from Rivon. Her pain was evident, her fear for her son coloring every word. Despite all that Annie'd done, she didn't deserve this. And even if she did, the boy certainly didn't.

Nash quashed the conflicting emotions battling inside

him, forcing himself to concentrate on the conversation instead.

"The initial call came from Rivon?" Tom was asking.

"I think so, yes." Annie nodded. "Although he didn't identify himself at the time."

"And the call came right on the heels of your discovery that your son was missing?" Tyler was transcribing the conversation on a laptop, presumably linked in to Hannah at Sunderland.

"Yes. It was maybe fifteen or twenty minutes later. I'm not sure exactly. I was pretty frantic."

"And you never considered calling for outside help?" Nash asked, shifting so that he could better see her face.

"Of course, I thought of it. But as I said before, I wasn't certain who I could trust." Her words zinged across the room, taking on a life of their own. "And once they called, all I could think of was getting to Adam."

"And there was no mention of Ashad?" Avery asked.

"No. They made no effort to identify themselves." She shook her head. "You mentioned Ashad earlier. Are you certain they're behind this?"

"We have credible intel that links them to Rivon," Tyler said, looking up from the computer. "And there's chatter connecting you to them as well."

"Well, I didn't even know it was Rivon until I got to D.C. And he's never mentioned anyone specifically. Just the ever-present 'they.' Frankly I'm surprised I'd be on their radar. Not only has it been eight years, but most of my career was spent in Eastern Europe."

"You know as well as I do that these groups have cells everywhere," Avery said. "Besides, reputation carries a lot of weight."

"But it was all such a long time ago. Why would they think I was any good anymore? I mean surely there are people out there better than I am."

"Quite possibly," Tom said, "but if they were aware of your abilities, they were also aware of your circumstances. Which means they'd recognize the fact that you were uniquely vulnerable."

"Because of Adam."

"That and the fact that you'd separated yourself from any kind of support."

"I suppose that makes sense, but it still feels off to me somehow."

"Actually, I've felt the same way from the beginning," Nash said, surprised to find himself voicing his support.

"Have you had dealings with Rivon before?" Avery asked.

"No," she said. "And believe me, I've racked my brain trying to be certain. But I can't remember ever having heard of the man before we met. Of course after the fact, I did a little research. But even that only supported the idea that I'd never dealt with him. He works primarily in Central and South America. With some admittedly dubious ties to the Middle East and, of course, his corporate work here in the States. But his rise in power has been mostly within the last five or six years. Which means there was little opportunity for our paths to cross."

"What about in Colorado?" Tyler asked. Annie had admitted that she and Adam lived on the eastern slope of the Rockies. Some long-forgotten mining town on the Rio Grande. "Could your paths have crossed there?"

"I don't see how." She shook her head. "We kept pretty much to ourselves and I was really careful. I worked as a guide. Climbing. So I was mostly working with folks on a one-time basis. And the people I did have regular contact with didn't know anything about my life before. Look, I'd never seen Rivon until I met with him in D.C. I'm sure of it."

"Okay, so we'll assume for the moment that Rivon is just the go-between." Tom stood up to pace restlessly in front of the fireplace. "That means the idea to use Annie had to have come from Ashad."

"And it really isn't that great a stretch to assume that they'd have heard about Annie's work for the Company and her defection after Lebanon," Nash said.

"If it is Ashad," Avery said, his expression inscrutable. "I tend to side with Ms. Gallagher on this one. Something seems off."

"Under the circumstances, I think you should call me Annie," she said.

"So tell me more about the phone call."

"There isn't much. It didn't last more than a few minutes. They said that they had Adam, and that they had proof. But that I'd have to come to D.C. to see it."

"Could you tell where the call originated from?" Tyler asked.

"I tried to track it. But my resources were limited. And to make matters more difficult, best I could tell, the phone was on a relay of some sort."

"Which means that even with the best technical help you couldn't have traced it." Nash watched as she pushed her hair out of her face, the gesture familiar.

"So you left for D.C.?"

"Yes. Immediately. I drove to Colorado Springs and got the first flight out. I was in D.C. by ten-thirty the next morning. I made my way to the hotel he'd indicated.

When I arrived, there was a message. A time and place for the meeting."

"And the proof of life?"

"That makes it sound so cold," she said with a shiver. "But yes, he gave it to me when I met with him. It was a photograph of Adam, with a newspaper. Pretty standard stuff."

"Do you have the picture?"

"Not on me," she said. "It's in my hotel room with the phone."

"Phone?" Tom frowned, coming to a halt in front of her chair.

"Yeah. Rivon gave me a phone when we met. Told me it was to be our primary means of communication. I figured it had a tracking device and I didn't want it with me while I was scoping out Dominico's apartment."

"To kill him," Tom said, his eyes flashing with disgust.

"Obviously, I was hoping it wouldn't come to that," Annie replied. "But as I said before, nothing is more important than my son."

"Did they tell you where to stay?" Avery asked.

"Initially, but I moved almost immediately after checking in. And then again last night. So far at least they haven't made an effort to stop me. Which is why I figured the phone probably gave away my position."

"So Rivon asked you to kill Dominico when you were in D.C.?" Tom asked.

"Yes. But not in the original meeting. He made it clear at that time that the people he worked for wanted me to take someone out, but he wouldn't say who it was. And I refused to go along with any of it without first talking to Adam. The photograph was already old."

"And I'm assuming he agreed," Nash said, "considering the fact that I interrupted your plans for Dominico."

"I told you, I wasn't going to shoot him. At least not then. I was just trying to ascertain my options."

"Annie, that's bullshit and you know it. I was there, remember?" Nash shook his head, still not comfortable with the idea that Annie could so easily have killed an innocent. Even to save her child.

"You're always so quick to believe the worst." She shook her head, her mouth drawn tight. "Everything black and white. God, to think that I—"

"It doesn't matter now," Tom said. "The point is, you're here. And for the moment at least, that means Dominico is safe."

"But they still have Adam," Annie said, her voice breaking on her son's name. "And if I don't contact them soon, they'll think I've double-crossed them and gone for help. Which means my son's life will be worth nothing."

"When did they tell you that Dominico was the target?" Avery asked.

"Just before a video call with Adam."

"So you have talked to him."

"Yes." Tears filled her eyes, and she angrily brushed them away. "They seemed to be treating him okay. He'd said he'd been playing video games."

"With Rivon?" Tyler asked, looking up from the computer.

"No. At least I don't think so. I talked with Rivon first— in a separate call. He told me the target was Dominico. Then a few minutes after he hung up, the phone rang again and this time it was Adam. If he'd been there, there wouldn't have been a need to terminate the first call. And after I talked to Adam, there was another voice—electronically altered so that I couldn't identify it. But I had the distinct feeling I was talking to whoever is really behind all of this."

"And there was nothing that gave you any clue to his identity?" Tom frowned, dropping down into the chair next to Avery.

"I can't even really be certain it was a man." Annie shook her head. "As I said, the voice had been altered. It sounded like one of those really bad computer programs. Definitely seemed male, but that could have just been a trick. I did try to record the call. The phone they gave me is pretty high-tech."

"Smart move," Nash said.

"Just because I've been out of the game, doesn't mean I've lost my edge," Annie snapped, sounding just this side of losing it. Which wasn't really all that surprising when one considered that her son was trapped out there somewhere while she was stuck in the brownstone rehashing the past couple of days with them. "Although in the end it didn't work. I got nothing but static."

"We still need the phone," Tyler said. "Hannah might be able to use the phone to triangulate a location."

"Hannah?" Annie repeated.

"She handles our intel," Avery explained. "We'll need the picture, too. There's a chance she could pull something from that, as well. Has she contacted Jason?"

"Yeah." Tyler nodded. "Per your instructions, he and Drake are on their way here now. Emmett and Lara are heading back to Sunderland."

"Good," Avery said, with a satisfied shake of his head. "If anyone can find something on the phone it'll be Hannah and Jason."

"Jason's IT," Nash said, in answer to Annie's obvious confusion. "He's really good," Nash assured her. "The best actually. If there's something there, he and Hannah will find it."

"And in the meantime?" she queried.

"You'll be transferred to Washington for further questioning," Tom said. "Despite the mitigating circumstances of your son's kidnapping, you still attempted to take out a U.S. dignitary. Which means you're in serious trouble. Worst case you could be tried for treason."

"Don't you understand? I can't go anywhere," she protested, rising to her feet. "If they don't hear from me at the appointed time, Adam is dead. They made it perfectly clear what would happen if I contacted anyone. Please, you can't send me away. I've got to stay and see this through. It's Adam's only chance." Tears spilled down her cheeks as she clenched her fists, her body taut with anxiety. "Please."

"If we can get Rivon," Tom said, his attention on Avery, "we'll get him to flip. And from there, we'll have a chance to dismantle the entire operation."

"Maybe," Avery said. "But she's right; if she disappears, the principals are going to go underground fast. And the kid becomes a liability."

"Oh, God," Annie whispered, her voice cracking.

"Look, Tom," Nash interjected, her pain cutting him in a way he hadn't expected, "if we use Annie, we'll have an almost guaranteed shot at getting to the real culprits. And at the end of the day, isn't a sure thing better than a long shot? Especially when the payoff is the same? The truth is that Rivon has reason to fear Ashad as much if not more than he fears the CIA. Which means that getting him to turn may not be as easy as you think. And you're assuming that you'll be able to find him. Annie's right; if he doesn't hear from her, he'll probably disappear completely. And then the whole thing falls apart."

"Including the plot against Dominico." Tom's tone remained stubborn.

"Not necessarily." Nash frowned. "And even if you're right, do you really want Adam's blood on your hands?"

"He's just a child," Annie added, her voice pleading.

"Well, we certainly can't let you just waltz out of here."

"I don't think anyone is suggesting that, Tom," Avery said, as usual the voice of reason. "But I do think that Nash has a point. We're far more likely to make inroads with Rivon and the others if they think Annie is still a player. What time are you supposed to make contact?"

She sucked in a ragged breath and glanced down at her watch, flinching as she read the dial. "Just over an hour."

"Can't she just call from a secondary phone?" Tyler asked.

"No." Annie shook her head, her eyes still on the watch. "That won't work. I'm not calling them. They're calling me. On the phone Rivon gave me. If I'm not there..." she trailed off, pain flashing in her eyes.

"You'll be there," Avery said.

Annie nodded gratefully, sinking back onto the chair.

"So you're agreeing that we still need Annie?" Nash asked.

"Yes. I think it's the best option." He paused, his gaze meeting Annie's. "For everyone."

"Maybe, but I'd argue that this is a job for Homeland Security, not A-Tac," Tom said. "Annie is our problem." There was a proprietary tone in Tom's voice that set Nash on edge. Tom had always been Annie's champion. And yet now it seemed he was determined to bring her down. Or maybe this was about marking territory. Tom's versus Avery's.

"Not so," Avery said, his tone firm. "Annie is ex-CIA, and this operation was given to A-Tac. You're here representing Homeland Security because my bosses made a deal with yours, but that doesn't change the fact that I'm in charge. And I say we use Annie to find her son and take out Ashad."

"Well, she can't be allowed to go out there on her own," Tom insisted. "She's perfectly capable of disappearing the moment we lower our guard."

"I'm not a fool, Tom," Annie said.

"No, but you're desperate. And you know as well as I do that desperation doesn't make for good decisions."

"Annie's not going to run." Avery lifted a hand to stop Tom's protest. "She's not going to run because we're going to be with her every step of the way."

"But you can't do that," Annie protested. "They'll be watching the hotel. If I'm seen with anyone, it'll blow the whole thing sky-high. My son's life hangs on my following their rules."

"Then we'll just have to make certain that Nash stays out of sight." Avery stood up, a sure sign that the discussion was over.

"Me?" Nash said, surprised at the choice.

"Yes, you," Avery said, his gaze knowing. "The two of you worked together for years. So who better to keep watch? You know Annie better than anyone."

Which of course was exactly the problem.

CHAPTER 7

This is as far as we can go together." It was the first time Annie had spoken to Nash directly since they'd left the brownstone other than "yes" and "no" and the occasional "this way."

They were a block from her hotel in the West Village. A nondescript two-star affair, used primarily for temporary corporate housing, it wasn't exactly the Waldorf; but it was serviceable and, more important, the kind of place where no one particularly noticed anyone else's comings and goings.

Avery had secured Nash a room on the same floor as hers. Its proximity would allow for Nash to monitor goings-on without drawing undue attention. She was still concerned about the possibility that if someone had her under surveillance Nash might be recognized, but it wasn't as if he hadn't done this kind of thing before. And with his baseball cap and jacket he blended in seamlessly with other New Yorkers.

"You're sure this is going to work?" she asked nervously. "Adam's life depends on it."

"Annie," he said, laying a hand on her arm, the contact sending a shiver racing down her spine. "It'll be fine."

"You don't know that."

"We'll get him. I swear." They stood for a moment, the past and present merging. "Here," he said, reaching into his pocket to produce her handgun. "You might need this."

She took it from him, slipping it into her own pocket. "You're trusting me with a gun."

"I'm trusting you with a lot of things." His words resonated in places that had nothing whatsoever to do with her brain, but she chose to ignore the fact.

All that mattered was Adam. It would be so easy to run...

"You're not going to run," he said, reading her mind. "That would force Tom's hand. He'd come after you with everything he's got. He wouldn't have a choice. Adam be damned. You know it. I know it. And Tom knows it. So there's no room for trying to play it solo."

"I suppose you're right." She sighed, nodding to emphasize the point, although, in truth, the gesture was more about convincing herself than convincing Nash.

"Nice to hear you say so," Nash said with a twisted smile. "Okay, so give me five minutes' head start and then you can follow."

"All right." She nodded, glancing down at her watch. "Go already. They're calling in less than twenty minutes."

Nash nodded, gave her arm a squeeze, and then loped off down the street, keeping his head down as he made his way toward the hotel.

Annie closed her eyes, still fighting the desire to run. For so long now, she'd trusted no one, depending only on herself and her own ingenuity. But it was that very independence that had put Adam at risk. Nash was right—her best hope now lay in cooperating with A-Tac, no matter what her instincts were telling her.

Forcing herself to keep her pace neutral, she made her way down Bleecker. The entrance to the hotel was sandwiched between a bodega and a Verizon store, the revolving door adding to the place's anonymity.

She stopped at the desk to request an extra key, then walked through the lobby toward the elevator. The small room was almost empty, a woman in a blue sweatshirt on a cell phone and a man with a baseball cap standing in the corner casually perusing a copy of the *Post*.

Nash.

As the elevator doors slid open, he moved forward, entering the elevator on her heels. Sweatshirt was right behind him, still on her cell, the three of them filling the small space. Shifting to make room, Annie stepped sideways to stand right in front of Nash. Making a point of staring up at the numbers over the door, Annie casually slipped her arm behind her, passing the keycard to her room off to Nash.

Two floors later, the elevator opened, and the two of them got off, Annie walking slightly ahead of Nash. Even after all this time she was still acutely aware of his presence.

She shook her head and stopped in front of her door, sliding the keycard through the lock. The red light flashed for a moment and then blessedly turned green. She opened the door and stepped into the room, Nash's shadow brushing across her as he walked by.

Forcing herself to focus, she walked through the tiny foyer and into the bedroom. The first thing she noticed was that her suitcase had been moved from its corner of the floor to the bed. It lay open, her belongings scattered across the sheets.

The second thing she noticed was that the balcony door was open. Drawing her gun, she moved carefully across the room toward the open French door, its gauzy curtain shifting in the breeze. Her hotel room was on the sixth floor, which meant that access was limited. But the facts seemed to belie the logic.

As she approached the terrace doorway, she leveled her gun, grasping her wrist with her left hand to steady the shot. Sucking in a deep breath, she swung into the opening, just as something hard hit her from behind.

The weight propelled her forward into the window flanking the door, the impact shattering the glass and sending her gun skittering across the cement to the far edge of the balcony where it lay wedged against the wrought-iron railing.

She pushed to her knees, instinctively reaching for the gun, but her assailant had other ideas, yanking her backward as a fist connected with her cheek. Pain exploded, and she fought against a sharp wave of nausea. Tightening the muscles in her legs, she pushed off against the floor and, using her attacker as a fulcrum, she managed to flip over him, gaining her feet.

Without giving him time to react, she kicked upward, connecting with the man's jaw, and then spun to kick again, this time hitting him squarely in the solar plexus. He staggered back a pace or so but kept his balance using the railing, producing a knife in his left hand.

He was dressed in black jeans and a black hoodie, a baseball cap jammed backward onto his head. His eyes were narrowed and his stance combative. He lunged at her, the blade slicing through her upper arm, the metallic stench of blood filling the air.

With a howl of protest, she kicked again, but he deflected the blow with one massive arm, slashing out with the knife in the other hand. Diving to avoid the blade, she hit the floor, rolling toward the corner of the balcony and the gun. As her hand closed on cold steel the man smiled, lifting the knife, his arm arcing downward in a deathblow.

Annie tried to lift the gun, but her arm refused to work, the sticky flow of blood coating her fingers. Using her feet, she pushed back against the concrete floor, trying to roll away from the inevitable, but the railing barred escape, and reacting on pure adrenaline, she lifted her good arm in defense.

"Adam," her brain screamed. *Adam.*

For one moment, sunlight glittered against the metallic blade, and then the man's eyes widened as the curtains in the doorway billowed outward. Cursing, her assailant spun away and then vaulted over the railing, the knife clanking against cement as it landed on the floor.

Annie scrambled to her feet and grabbed her gun, training it on the French door. "Don't move," she hissed.

"It's just me." Nash emerged from behind the drapery, gun in hand.

"Son of a bitch," she whispered, turning back to lean over the railing, searching the roof below for signs of the intruder.

"You see him?" Nash asked, coming to stand beside her.

"No. He's gone," she sighed, frustration mixing with equal parts relief. "Thanks to you."

"Hey," he said, raising his hands. "I was just saving your ass."

"I had things under control," she said, her labored breathing making a lie of the statement. "But I suppose you evened the odds a bit." She nodded at the knife as she leaned back against the balcony.

"You're hurt." He frowned, reaching out to check her arm.

"It's just a graze." She shook him off, knowing that if he touched her she'd lose it. "I'm fine."

"Why don't you let me be the judge of that," he said, helping her back into the hotel room.

"No. We need to follow the man with the knife," she said, already moving toward the balcony. "He could lead us to Adam."

"Annie," he stopped her, his hand on her arm. "He's long gone by now."

"I suppose you're right." She clenched her fist and then winced in pain. "I just feel so helpless." She moved into the bathroom and grabbed a towel. After wetting it, she returned to the bedroom. "Everything..." she started as Nash stepped back into the bedroom from the balcony, but he shook his head, lifting a finger to his lips as he quickly searched the room for signs that they were being monitored.

"Looks clear to me," he said, finally.

"I searched yesterday and came to the same conclusion. Although maybe the intruder was trying to change that. None of this makes any sense at all."

"Did you recognize him?" he asked, as he closed the door and drew the drapes.

"No. I've never seen him before." Annie shook her head as she tried to picture the man's face. "It was hard to make out his features. He was wearing a hoodie. One thing's for certain though: whoever he was, he wasn't here to talk."

"So the big question is whether he's tied in to Adam's kidnapping." It was the first time he'd used her son's name, and the emotional rush was almost more painful than the gouge on her arm.

"Oh, God," she said on a shuddering breath, "if he saw you—then they'll..." Words failed as panic washed through her, and she fumbled with the wet towel, cursing when she pressed too hard.

"Here," Nash said, taking the towel, "let me."

She shook her head, pulling away, her hands shaking as she gulped in calming breaths, trying not to let her imagination go on overdrive.

"Annie, you're not alone here." His voice was full of emotion. Frustration, anger, and something else—concern. It had been so long since anyone had cared.

"I can't." She shook her head. "Nash, I just can't. We've covered this ground before. And we both know where it ends."

"Just let me see your arm. Bandage it." His voice was soft now, coaxing. "I was always better at triage than you were."

She nodded, offering her arm, shivering as the heat of his fingers seeped through her. So many memories.

"Annie, I..." he stopped, his dark eyes meeting hers.

She leaned closer, his pull magnetic. It would be so easy to let herself go. To lean on him. To fall back into the patterns of the past. But he'd hurt her so badly. And nothing had really changed. She shook her head, pulling back, breaking the moment. "We need to focus on Adam," she said, her words cutting through the building tension. "My son is out there and he needs me."

"Right," he said, his mouth tightening as he quickly cleaned and bound the wound, using the bottom of one of her T-shirts for a bandage. "It's not as bad as it looks," he said, tying off the soft cotton. "Can you move your arm?"

She tested the limb, bending it at the elbow and then moving it gingerly to the right and left. The motion hurt, but the arm seemed to be working again. "It's fine. Thanks."

"No problem. It's not like I haven't done it before."

"You're right; you were always better at field dressing than I was." She closed her eyes, fighting against the memories engulfing her. Other moments like this one— standing in the chaos after facing an all-but-inevitable death. It was all horribly familiar, but this time the stakes were higher than ever. This time Adam's life was in jeopardy. "So what made you check on me? Surely you couldn't hear us?"

"No." He ducked his head, then moved off the bed.

"Then what?"

He shrugged, his expression wry. "I thought maybe you were going to make a run for it."

"I'll admit I was thinking about it," she acknowledged. "But the intruder didn't give me the chance." A bubble of laughter rose in her throat as she recognized the incredible irony of Nash's action. His lack of trust had probably saved her life. "So what about you?" she said, steeling herself against her fear. "Did you get a look at him?"

"Nothing definitive. I was trying to save you, not memorize his features, but I think maybe he was Asian."

"That narrows it down." She stood up, then sat down again, restless energy heightening her frustration.

"Let's check the room," he said. "Maybe the guy dropped something in the scuffle. Where did he attack you?"

"Door to the balcony." She nodded toward the opening. "I think he was hiding in the curtains."

Nash walked over to the doorway, searching the floor and the area outside. "We might be able to get a print off the knife if we're lucky." He pushed back the curtains to check the floor. "Hang on," he said, as he bent to retrieve something from the floor. A slow smile spread across his face. "Look what we have here." He brandished a card of some kind, careful to grip only the edges. "Gym membership. Looks like the man is into fitness."

"Does it have a name or address?" she asked. "Something that might lead us to Adam?"

"Not directly." Nash shook his head. "But the gym's in Brooklyn, and the card's issued to one Leland Evan Bruebaker."

"Doesn't sound much like a terrorist." She frowned, sorting through her belongings until she found a bottle of ibuprofen. Swallowing three, she tipped back her head, clearing her thoughts. "You think maybe the attack was incidental? That he was just robbing the place?"

"It's possible." He shrugged.

"But if he is involved in all this..." she said, staring down at her bloodstained hands.

"Then we'll figure out how to deal with it." He shook his head. "Did he attack you or the other way around?"

Again she pushed her fear away. She wasn't going to help her son by falling apart. "He jumped me when I went to check the balcony. The door was open and my stuff was all over the bed."

"But he wasn't in plain sight."

"No." She shook her head, picturing the scenario. "Definitely hiding."

"All of which supports the idea that it was a break-in."

"Except that the room door wasn't open."

"It isn't that difficult to secure a keycard. Especially in a place like this. All kinds of people have master keys."

"So why didn't he just run? I mean, I was headed for the balcony; he could have made it to the door."

"If he saw your gun, he'd have known better. Or maybe he was hopped up on something. Either way I think his attempt to take you out only supports the idea he's not involved with Adam's kidnapping. I mean, there's no reason for them to want you dead. At least not yet."

"What if they know about you?" she said, her panic rushing back, threatening to swamp her. "About A-Tac. They told me they'd kill him if I talked to anyone. Oh, God, what have I done?"

"Let's not jump to conclusions," he said, dropping down on the bed beside her. "There's no reason to believe that they know you were taken. We took precautions. And so did you. Besides, if they did know, there are a hell of a lot easier ways to take you out than sending someone to attack you in your hotel room."

"Maybe they wanted it to look like a robbery?" she asked, her breath coming in gasps. "Maybe Adam's already dead."

"Annie, stop it," he said, gripping her hands. "You know as well as I do that the only way we can help Adam is to keep it together. He needs his mother."

She nodded, releasing a breath and squaring her shoulders.

"That's my girl," he said, reaching into his pocket for his cell phone.

"What are you doing?" She reached out to stop him, alarm bells ringing in her head.

"I'm calling Avery. We need someone to sanitize the scene."

"It's my mess," she said, defiantly, her momentary panic passing. "I'll clean it up."

"There's no point in you calling attention to yourself. Besides, we need to check for evidence. Maybe there's something here besides the gym card and the knife. And they're professionals, Annie. They know what to do."

"I'm a professional, too. Or did you forget that?" She sounded petulant and she knew it, but then Nash did have a tendency to bring out the worst in her.

"Of course I didn't forget." He frowned. "But you have to admit you're out of practice."

Considering Bruebaker had almost killed her, she didn't have much ground for argument, so she decided to ignore the comment. "Okay, but what if someone is watching?"

"I think we just established that they're not. You've changed hotels several times already and, if I know you, taken all kinds of other evasive measures. But if it makes you feel better, we'll clear out and then I'll call."

"What will make me feel better is to hear from Rivon. I need to know that Adam is still alive."

"It's the same as with you, Annie. Until Dominico is dead, they have no reason to hurt Adam. He's their only bargaining chip."

"I'm sure you're right, but that doesn't stop me from worrying." Turning her back to hide the tears filling her eyes, she made a play of straightening her things.

"Look, I know this is hard for you."

"You have no idea. It's been Adam and me on our own for so long. I thought I could protect him. I thought that I was enough. That as long as we stayed under the radar, nothing would happen. No one from the past could find me."

"I can't imagine what it was like for you." He frowned, studying her. "On your own with a kid. It must have been hell."

"Adam is my child. I would do anything for him. Anything. He's changed everything. All my priorities now center on him. Simple as that. Unlike you, I've never had trouble stepping up." The last bit came of its own accord and she immediately wished the words back.

"What the hell is that supposed to mean?"

"Nothing. I'm sorry. I was just sounding off." The last thing she needed was to alienate her only ally. "I guess I was thinking of us. Of the fact that we couldn't make it work."

"No need to apologize," he said, his mouth folded into a grimace. "You're right. I don't do relationships."

"So there's no wife hidden away somewhere?" Again with the wild words. "I'm sorry. My mouth seems to be working overtime. Your private life is none of my business."

"Doesn't matter," he said, shaking his head. "You already know the answer anyway. There's no one. My lifestyle isn't exactly conducive to white picket fences."

"Espionage will do that to you." She tried to keep her voice light but it cracked anyway.

"Maybe"—he shrugged—"or maybe it's just me. But *you* made it work, with Adam—and his father."

"With Adam, yes. But not with his father. I seem to have made a practice of putting my faith in the wrong men."

"That's sounds pretty cynical."

"You know my history." She shrugged. Her father had walked out on her when she was just a kid. Left her to fend for herself after her mother's death. She'd survived. But she'd never forgotten his betrayal. It had taken years for her to work up the courage to trust Nash—to take a chance on the two of them. And then he'd thrown it back in her face, rejecting her just like her father. "If I'm cynical, it's with good reason."

"I'm sorry." His voice was soft, and she felt the weight of his body as he sat down next to her on the bed, his hand warm against her shoulder. It would be so easy to melt into his arms. To let him hold her close. But it was only an illusion, and Annie had learned long ago the cost of believing in something that wasn't real.

"Don't," she said, shaking her head, pulling back. "I'm hanging on by a thread here. And I'm not sure I can take it if you're nice to me."

He nodded, his expression grim as he released her. "So where's the phone?"

She whirled around, reality slamming back into place, as she plowed through the things scattered across the bed, heart pounding. "It's not here. Oh, God, what if he took it?"

"Just stay calm. We haven't even had a look yet."

"You're right. I'm jumping to conclusions. I'm just not thinking clearly," she said, angry with herself for letting fear get the upper hand. "Help me search the room."

She checked her duffel and under the bed, then carefully went through the drawers of the bedside table. All to no avail.

"Nothing in the television cabinet," Nash reported, heading for the bureau to check the drawers. "Where did you leave it?"

"Over there on the table by the landline."

She walked to the cubicle serving as a closet, but except for her leather jacket, the space was empty. That left the bathroom. She walked inside, scanning the countertop, her stomach sinking when there was no sign of the missing phone.

"Where the hell is it?" she muttered, anger warring with dismay.

As if on cue, the staccato *brring* of the phone filled the hotel room, Nash and Annie both scrambling to locate the source of the sound. By the fourth ring, they'd found it, on the floor behind a chair where it must have fallen when Bruebaker was rifling through her things.

Annie scooped it up, only to stand staring as it vibrated against her hand.

"Answer it," Nash said. "Just pretend nothing's happened. And if you can, try to arrange a meeting. That way if we can't get anything from the phone, we'll have another firsthand shot to get information."

She nodded and swallowed, then clicked the button to answer the call. "Gallagher."

"Where the hell have you been?" Rivon's angry voice filled her ear.

"Actually, you're late. You were supposed to call"—
she glanced down at her watch—"seven minutes ago."

"I called half an hour ago and nobody answered."

"I went out for something to eat," she said, sounding much calmer than she felt. "I didn't take the phone
with me."

"Well, I suggest, in the future, you keep it with you."

"When can I talk to my son?" she asked, her heart
pounding.

"After you've given us something to verify that you're
cooperating."

"Other than handing you Dominico's body, I'm not
sure how you expect me to do that. I did spend the morning casing his apartment. I think it's our best chance
at access. But it's going to be more difficult than I
expected."

"In what way?"

"The man's got security out the wazoo. My best
chance is a long-distance shot, and for that I'll need spe-
cialized equipment."

"So get it."

"It's not something you can just pick up on the street,
and as you are well aware, I haven't got those kinds of
contacts anymore."

"And you think I do?"

"I think if you don't, you'll know someone who
does."

"So what is it exactly that you want?"

"I can't explain it over the phone. The modifications
are tricky. I'll have to show you specifically what it is I
want. I'll draw up schematics."

"And if I refuse?"

"Then all bets are off. I can't just waltz in and take the man out. It doesn't work like that. It takes planning. Which brings me to another point," she said, frowning over at Nash, as she frantically tried to think of something else to convince Rivon they had to meet. "I'm going to need blueprints of the building across the way, as well as a floor plan for Dominico's apartment. The one you gave me isn't to scale, and I need everything to be precise if this is going to work."

Nash nodded, circling his hand to urge her on.

"I'm not sure we'll have access to blueprints," Rivon said.

"If you want this to happen, you'll find a way." She hoped she sounded more confident than she actually felt. She was bargaining with Adam's life. "And I'll need to talk to Adam again."

"I'm not in a position to make that kind of promise. But if I can make it happen, it won't be until after we finalize plans. As I said, we need proof of cooperation."

"So when do you want to meet?"

"I need to clear everything with my bosses. But I know they're anxious to conclude our business."

Annie nodded, shooting a thumbs-up at Nash. "Well, move as quickly as you can. The window of opportunity isn't going to last forever. People are always watching and listening, and if they figure out Dominico is a target, you can bet your ass they'll pull him from public access."

"So you'll just have to work a little harder. I'll be in touch."

"Make it soon." She clicked to disconnect, and then sank down on the bed, all signs of bravado evaporating. "Oh, God, Nash, what have I done?"

"You've set the wheels in motion to rescue Adam. All we need is to figure out where they're holding him. And Rivon is our best bet."

"You can't take him." She lifted her head. "They'll kill Adam if anything happens to that bastard."

"Only as a last resort. As I said before, Jason is a whiz with all things electronic. So first order of business is to show him the phone. It may be possible to trace the call back to wherever they're holding Adam. And if that doesn't work, he'll figure out a way to use the meeting with Rivon to tag him."

"And then we follow him to Adam."

"At least it gives us options."

She nodded, not certain at all that she'd made the right decision, to work with Nash and his friends, but oddly relieved nevertheless to have him here—on her side.

At least for now.

CHAPTER 8

T he phone's clean," Jason said, looking up from the
    body of Annie's disassembled phone. "There's noth-
ing here connecting back to the source. But on the plus
side, there isn't a tracking device either. So if they're
watching you, it isn't through the phone."

"But there's no way to use the phone to give us
Adam's location?" Nash asked from his perch on a chair
in the corner.

The three of them were in the latest of Annie's hotel
rooms, this one a little smaller than the last, but not quite
as seedy. Annie had wanted to meet Jason here instead
of at the brownstone. She wasn't all that keen on dealing
with Tom. And although Nash had no problem with the
guy, there was no avoiding the fact that as far as A-Tac
was concerned, his old handler was an outsider working
his own agenda. So meeting here had suited him as well.

"No," Jason said. "My guess is they're scrambling
or relaying their locations. We might be able to pull

something off it if we run the next call through our computers. But it's far from a sure thing."

"And there's always the chance they'll figure out we're trying to get in, right?" Annie asked, eyes narrowed as she considered the possibilities.

"Exactly." Jason nodded, working to reassemble the phone. "Which makes it an option of last resort, in my opinion."

"So we've got nothing." She offered a tight smile, then stood up and walked over to the window out of Jason's earshot.

"We're going to get him back, Annie," Nash said, coming to stand behind her, his hands on her shoulders. He knew the words were an empty promise, but he couldn't seem to stop himself. In truth, Annie's pain felt a hell of a lot more personal than it should have. And the idea that she could lose her son—well, it just wasn't an acceptable option. At least not as long as he had any say in the matter.

She nodded, still staring out the window. "He's just so innocent. You know? And none of this is his fault. It's mine. I'm the one with the past. A mother should protect her son, not throw him in the middle of danger."

"You couldn't have known any of this would happen."

"Yes. But I knew there was a risk."

"Annie," he said, turning her to face him, "thinking like that isn't doing anyone any good."

She looked up at him, tears brimming in her eyes. "But it was my job to keep him safe."

"Well, right now he's counting on you to find him. So you've got to stay focused. Concentrate on us bringing him home. Okay?"

"Yeah," she sighed, lifting her chin. "You're right. I'm sorry, I don't know what came over me."

"You'll be fine," he said. "If for no other reason than because you have to be. Adam is counting on you."

He grimaced, flashing back to the days after she'd left. The weeks in the hospital, waiting for her to come back. To explain why she'd walked out when he'd needed her most. She was his partner. He'd trusted her. But she'd betrayed him. At the time, he'd thought he would never forgive her. But in this moment, watching her pain, he suddenly wasn't as sure.

Maybe...

Anger surged, and he jerked away, ignoring the flash of hurt in her eyes. There was nothing to be gained in letting his imagination run away with him. It was over. And he'd survived. Lesson learned.

It was better to stay detached. To keep his head clear.

"Here you go," Jason was saying as he handed Annie the restored cell. "I've got it all together again. No one will be the wiser."

"I hope you're right," she said, her expression guarded.

"Believe me, we're not going to do anything to jeopardize the mission," Nash said.

"It isn't the mission I'm worried about."

Behind them, someone rapped on the door. Instantly all three of them swung to face it, guns drawn.

Annie held a finger to her lips, shaking her head for silence as she moved toward the door, Nash flanking her to the right, Jason to the left. "Who is it?"

"Drake Flynn." The voice was deep and resonant.

Annie turned to Nash, eyebrows raised in question.

"It's okay. He's with us," Nash confirmed as he

lowered his gun and opened the door. "So what have you got?"

"Everything's sanitized. Hotel will never know any-thing happened," Drake said, striding across the room as Jason and Annie lowered their weapons. "You're letting her carry?"

"Seemed prudent at the time." Nash shrugged. "People do seem to be trying to kill her."

Annie shot him a look and then turned her attention back to Drake. "I take it you looked for the guy."

"Yeah. No sign of him. Nothing much on the roof either."

"But everything's all sorted?"

"Yeah," Drake snarled with a frown. "Like I said, it's sanitized. Look, it's not like we don't know what we're doing. Although you sure as hell didn't make it an easy job with all the action on the balcony."

"I'm sorry I didn't have time to negotiate terms of attack." She glared up at him, her shoulders rigid. "I was kind of busy trying to stay alive."

"Kinda mouthy for a suspected assassin," Drake said with a nod. "Did she have this much attitude when she was with you?"

"More." Nash laughed. "Much, much more."

"Like hell," she responded, swinging around to face him. "If anything I was the one who kept things grounded."

"Right. Like now." He glanced pointedly down at her clenched fists. "Completely calm and in control."

She opened her mouth to argue, but then clearly thought better of the idea, turning to Drake instead. "We haven't been formally introduced." She stuck out her hand. "Annie Gallagher. Although you already know that."

"Drake Flynn," he said, shaking her hand. "Nash's right-hand man."

"Tough gig."

"Don't I know it." Drake shrugged and then sobered. "Looks like your missing man was into impersonations or the card wasn't his."

"What do you mean?" Nash asked, dropping back into the chair in the corner. Jason had already settled in at the desk and his computer. Annie'd moved across the room to lean against the window sill, leaving Drake to sit on the end of the bed.

"Seems that Leland Bruebaker died a year ago," he said. "In Queens. Hit by a street sweeper while walking his dog."

"So our guy wasn't Bruebaker," Jason sighed.

"Not unless he's discovered the secret to everlasting life."

"So what does that mean? Are we back to thinking the intruder was working for Rivon?" Annie asked.

"Not necessarily." Drake shook his head. "It's possible the card wasn't our guy's at all."

"So you're saying a dead guy leaves his gym card in my hotel room and some other yahoo just happens to be breaking in as well?" Her voice cracked, her fear making her sound harsh.

"Well, when you put it like that." Nash shrugged, purposely keeping his tone neutral.

"So what the hell was he doing there?" she asked.

"Waiting for you, if I had to call it." Drake frowned.

"Or maybe he was just casing the joint," Nash suggested.

"Why would he do that?" Annie shook her head. "I've

been jumping through their hoops from the very beginning. There's not much use in checking me out."

"So maybe we're looking at a third player," Nash mused. "Someone separate from Rivon and whoever's pulling his strings."

"I'm with Drake," Jason said. "I'm betting the guy was after Annie. Any chance they know we've joined the mix?"

"Anything's possible." Drake shrugged.

"Well, pray that they don't know," Annie said, expression defiant. "Adam's life depends on it. Anyway, Nash and I have been over it. You guys took precautions. And I'm pretty damn certain I covered my tracks. I haven't gone totally soft. And Rivon seemed perfectly normal when he called. I can't imagine he'd have agreed to a meeting if they had any doubts."

"There's truth in that," Jason conceded. "Maybe it was Rivon's guy and he was just supposed to rough you up. Convince you that they were in control."

"Doesn't make sense," Annie said. "As I said, I've been playing by their rules."

"I still think we can't discount the possibility of a third party," Drake said. "We know Rivon's not running the show. So maybe someone is keeping tabs on the situation. Only Rivon wouldn't know about it."

"So basically, we don't have any idea what the hell he was doing in my room," Annie said.

"Do we have any leads on the man's real identity?" Nash asked, still watching Annie. She was keeping tight rein on her emotions, but he could see the tension in her face, the fear in her eyes.

"Not yet," Drake said. "We managed to lift a couple

of partials from the knife. Hannah's running fingerprints now. If we get lucky, he'll turn up in one of our databases. But until then your guess is as good as mine."

"Well, whoever the guy is," Nash said, "if he's involved in this, he'll be reporting back. And that means there's a risk that he saw me and put two and two together."

"I don't know," Annie said. "Everything happened really fast. And you were behind the curtain most of the time. I doubt he got a good look at you."

"At the very least, though," Jason said, "he'll know you're not alone."

"Shit." Annie sank down on the bed.

"It could have been housekeeping, for all he knew," Drake said, shaking his head. "Anyway, whether he saw Nash or not, our hands are tied. Until Annie meets with Rivon, or until Hannah has a breakthrough, there's nothing much we can do."

"What about the photograph of Adam?" Annie asked. And Nash immediately flashed on the little boy in the picture. He had Annie's eyes. And he looked like a fighter. Just like his mom. "Did Hannah find anything that might help?"

"Nothing," Drake said. "Except that it's definitely residential. But that could be an apartment. A house. Hell, it could be a decorated room in a warehouse. There's just no way to know. Have you set a time for the meeting yet?"

"No." She shook her head. "Rivon hasn't called. But he said he had to talk to his bosses."

"Any chance he'd have tried to call while the phone was down?" Nash asked.

"None," Jason responded. "I rigged it so that if a call came through, Annie could answer through the computer."

"Too damn high-tech for me." Nash shrugged.

"Clearly some things never change," Annie said with the arch of an eyebrow.

"Hey, it's not like I can't deal with it when I have to. I just prefer doing things the old-fashioned way."

"Especially if it involves shooting someone," Drake goaded.

"Too bad I didn't have the chance."

"Well, somebody did some damage. Tyler found blood on the roof."

"That'd be me," Annie said, looking pleased with herself, not that he blamed her. Given the chance he'd have blown the guy's head off—right after he forced the man to spill Adam's location. "I got in a couple of good punches. Definitely enough to draw blood."

"We sent the sample to Lara to see if it was viable for DNA."

"And?"

"Haven't heard anything yet. But between the DNA and the fingerprints, we'll figure out who this bastard is."

"So where is Tyler?" Nash asked.

"Downstairs. Making certain we weren't followed. She'll come up after she's sure it's all clear."

"You guys think of everything." Annie tried to smile, but missed the mark, the skin around her eyes lined with worry.

"Once Rivon calls," Jason said, "we'll be ready. I've worked up the schematic you requested. For the sniper rifle." He produced a small folder and held it out for Annie. "I based it on the description you gave me on the phone."

She pushed away from the window to take the file. Opening it, she studied it for a moment, and then smiled—the first real one Nash had seen. "This is amazing work. Right down to the notations. Rivon will think I drew it myself."

"That was the plan," Nash said. "But it's a hell of a lot more than just a drawing."

"What do you mean?" she asked, frowning down at the schematic.

"It's also a tracking device," Jason said, unable to contain his excitement. "It's actually embedded in the portfolio."

"I've never heard of such a thing," she said, lifting the schematic to the light.

"That's because I'm the first to develop it. In fact, this will be its first time in the field."

"You're putting my son's life on the back of technology that hasn't even been tested?" Her jaw tightened as she surveyed the three of them.

"Oh, it has been tested," Jason assured her. "Vigorously. Just not in an actual operation. But we've simulated them and believe me when I say that the device is virtually undetectable."

"And it's got an impressive range," Drake added. "More than ten miles."

"You've worked with it, then." Her frown deepened as she continued to examine the hand-drawn blueprint. "Nash?"

"I haven't had the chance to test it." He shook his head. "But Drake is our expert at extraction. So if he's signed off on it, I'm good to go."

"Hey, I invented it," Jason protested. "Which means I believe in it. Shouldn't that count for something?"

"Of course." Annie nodded. "It's just that there's so much riding on our being able to track Rivon. I mean, it makes sense that he'll take it to whoever he's working for. But there's nothing to assure that that will get us to Adam."

"Well, we know he was there when you talked to Adam," Drake said. "And Adam said the guy had been playing games with him. So it's reasonable to believe they're together."

"It's our best shot," Nash added.

"I promise, Annie," Jason said. "The device works."

"All right then. All I've got to do is get it to Rivon."

The phone vibrated against the metal of the radiator cover. The sound stopped all conversation as everyone turned to stare at the undulating cell.

Annie nodded for quiet and then answered the phone. "Gallagher." Mouthing *Rivon*, she waved them to the far corner as she moved into the bathroom, well out of range of their voices.

"Jason?" Nash nodded toward Annie.

"I'm on it." Jason hit a key and adjusted his earphone. "I've got her. It's definitely Rivon." He turned back to his computer, focusing on the call.

"So do you really trust her?" Drake asked, keeping his voice just above a whisper, his gaze probing.

"There's no easy answer to that question," Nash said. "Eight years ago, I trusted her with my life. And then she betrayed me in the worst possible way. Throwing everything I thought I knew about her in question."

"I'm not asking about the past. I'm asking about now. She did, after all, try to take out Dominico."

"Well, she had a pretty damn strong motivation. You know as well as I do that if someone you loved was in danger and the only way to save them was to cross the line, you'd be over it so fast it'd make your head spin."

"Maybe. But then again, maybe I wouldn't get myself into that position in the first place. We carry a hell of a lot of baggage in this business. Most of it armed and dangerous."

"Sometimes there isn't a choice. It's not like Annie knowingly put her son in danger. How was she to know someone wanting to use her past was waiting in the wings?"

"She wasn't. But for my money, she should have known it was a possibility."

"And what? Terminated her pregnancy? Abandoned her son? That seems a little harsh."

"Nash, I'm not trying to debate the pros and cons of people like us having serious relationships. I'm just trying to figure out if we can trust Annie."

"Look, the truth of it is that I'm the last person to make that call. I've got too much history. But if I had a kid and someone took him, I can tell you without doubt that I'd do anything to get him back. Which means that as long as we're an asset, she has no reason to do anything counter to our mission."

"And if she finds out our primary mission isn't to rescue Adam?"

"She already knows that. She may have been out of the game a long time, but believe me she's more than aware of how it's played."

"If we're lucky," Drake said, shrugging, "maybe we'll figure out a way to achieve both goals. Save the kid and take out his kidnappers. I say we take things one step at a time. We get the schematic to Rivon, let him lead us to Adam, and then we'll use the information to figure out our next move."

"And besides, even if we can't trust Annie, I've got things covered," Jason said, pulling the receiver out of his ear. "She'll be wired to the gills."

"How so?" Annie said, stepping back into the room.

"You'll be wearing these." Jason held out his hand, revealing two intricately carved earrings, silver drops sporting pearls at the ends. "They're a one-way transmitter. As long as you're wearing them, we'll be able to hear everything that you and Rivon say. And I'll be able to relay it all back to Sunderland so that Hannah can record and analyze it."

"I see," she said, her eyes narrowing in thought. "Covering your asses in case I make a break for it?"

"Never hurts to err on the side of caution." Nash shrugged.

"True enough," she said, her words hanging almost tangibly between them.

"So what did Rivon have to say?" Drake asked, cutting through the tension.

"I thought Jason was monitoring the call?"

"He was," Nash admitted. "But Drake and I weren't listening in."

"I'm sorry. I didn't mean to snap. This is just so damn hard. I feel like I'm being yanked all over the place. First by Rivon. Then by all of you. I just want to get Adam back."

"That's what we want, too," Jason assured her.

"And all of this," Drake said, waving at the earrings and the schematic, "is just the easiest way to make that happen. So tell us what Rivon had to say."

"He's agreed to a meeting," she replied. "And he wants to do it tonight."

CHAPTER 9

Carl Schurz Park lay enveloped in the dark shadows of a moonless night, the shoreline of Queens eerily illuminated across the churning waters of the East River. Annie walked slowly, her gait casual, but inside her heart was pounding. So much was riding on this exchange.

The park, bustling with locals in the daytime, was deserted now. In the distance, parked along a side road, Annie could just make out the bulky shape of the utility van where Drake and Jason were waiting to monitor her meeting with Rivon. A part of her wanted to toss the earrings in the nearest trash can. If nothing else, just to prove that she was in charge.

But the cold hard truth was that she'd lost all semblance of control the moment Nash had leveled his gun at the back of her head. He was out there now. Waiting, watching. His presence should have made her feel more secure. But it didn't. Not one little bit.

A gust of wind blew off the water, whipping through

trees, leaves rattling in protest. Annie shivered, thinking of Adam. Somewhere out there her little boy was waiting. And she'd be damned if she'd let anyone get in the way of bringing him home.

Located in the Eighties on the Upper East Side, the dimly lit park was hilly and narrow, with pathways that rendered it almost mazelike, complete with dead ends, blind corners, and hidden grottoes. Rivon had chosen a circular courtyard honoring Peter Pan as a meeting place, the draw, no doubt, the statue's tree-shrouded isolation at the park's northeastern end.

As if to intensify the mood, tendrils of mist curled along the edges of the path, shifting and turning as she moved. Moisture-laden trees, amplified by the fog, loomed larger than life, their crooked branches reaching up into the night.

"If you're listening, this isn't exactly my idea of a good time," she whispered, immediately feeling stupid. Next time, she was insisting on a two-way radio, regardless of the risk.

With a sigh, she glanced down at her watch, the illuminated dial showing that it was almost eleven. Speeding her pace, she made her way through the park, passing basketball courts and swing sets, leaving behind pavement for the rock-studded woods that covered the north end of the park.

At the top of a rise, she stopped and watched as a barge made its way up the river, green lights winking through the mist. Turning back to the park, she walked slowly down the stairs that led to Peter in his grotto, the shadows deepening as she descended, her senses on high alert.

Here in the dark, it was almost possible to imagine

that she was actually in Neverland. She was more than familiar with Peter's story. She'd read the book to Adam. And of course, they'd watched the movie. Even collected all the Disney characters. Adam loved Peter, Wendy, and the Lost Boys. He'd even liked Smee. But he'd been so afraid of Captain Hook, he'd moved the little plastic figurine to the back of his bookshelf, Hook's nose firmly pressed into the corner. Annie'd laughed at the time, but here in the dark, she wasn't so sure that Adam hadn't had the right idea.

At the bottom of the stairs, the courtyard yawned black, the bronze statue rising up above the mist like one of Peter's mermaids on her rock in the sea. Shaking her head to break the fantasy, Annie let her eyes adjust to the gloom, then searched the circular clearing for signs of Rivon. At first glance, the grotto seemed empty, bordering bushes and trees stark against the sharp outcrop of stone that surrounded the clearing. Benches lined the circle, Peter serenely holding court in the center.

Then a shadow on the far side separated itself from the wall. Rivon. Annie's fingers closed around the gun in her pocket, the cold metal comforting. There was only one way in or out of the clearing, and using instinct honed by years of training, Annie moved cautiously around the circle, careful to keep from turning her back. Rivon watched her move, his features obscured by the gloom.

"You're certainly taking your time," he said, as she came to a stop in front of him, her hand still on the gun in her pocket.

"I always err on the side of caution." She nodded at the entrance, now off to her right. "Anyone with you?"

"No. Although I'd have preferred to come with an

army. Never have liked this city. No matter how much they pretend to clean it up, it still always seems dangerous." His gaze darted nervously around the courtyard.

There was irony in his statement, but she didn't have the luxury of examining the fact. "How is my son?" she asked, trying to hold her voice steady. No sense in alerting this goon to her fear.

"He's fine."

"Is he eating? Has he been sleeping? He doesn't function well when he hasn't had enough sleep." The words came tumbling out as she watched Rivon, praying for some kind of news.

"I told you, he's fine," Rivon said, his hooded gaze darting around the clearing. "But he won't be if you don't hold up your end of the bargain."

"Right," she said, steeling herself, digging deep, calling on the woman she'd once been. "Did you bring the plans I asked for?" She'd already decided it was best to make that seem the more important concern.

"Yeah. Right here." He offered a manila envelope. "The floor plan is old. But there haven't been any major renovations." She nodded, pretending to care. In actuality, she already had the plans. Updated. In point of fact, Dominico was actually quite fond of redoing his apartment.

"And the blueprints of the buildings across the way?" She shifted slightly, constantly checking the pathway and bushes for signs of company.

"They're in there, too. All but one. But I'll have it for you the next time we meet. When I bring you the gun. Do you have the plans?"

"Yes." She held out Jason's portfolio. "We should go over a few things."

"Fancy presentation," he noted, opening the folder.

"I like to be thorough."

He nodded, producing a penlight to study the drawings.

Annie held her breath. She was fairly certain Rivon didn't have the technical know-how to spot the embedded device, but the knowledge didn't make her any less nervous. One mistake on her part and her son was dead.

"The key changes are to the scope." She pointed to a diagram lower on the page, moving in closer to make sure that her earrings were picking up the conversation. "You can see what's needed here and here. A long-distance telescopic, preferably with laser sight—thirty to forty power. And a free-floating barrel with a threaded muzzle. In addition, I'll need the cheek piece customized. The specs are here." Again she pointed to a diagram on the schematic. "And finally, I need the whole thing to break down in seconds and some kind of backpack to fit the pieces. So that it's easy to carry in and out without being noticed."

"Not asking for much, are you?" Rivon said, his tone sarcastic.

"If you want me to take out Dominico, this is what I'll need to get the job done."

"And if we can't find one?"

"You can have it built. There are military versions that can serve as a starting place for the modifications. Both American and Russian made. And there are any number of gunsmiths capable of making the necessary changes. But you'll need to be careful. This kind of weapon sets off all kinds of alarms if the transaction goes public."

He frowned down at the document in his hand. "I don't think it'll be a problem."

"How long do you think it will take?"

"A couple of days. Maybe longer. I'm not an expert on sniper rifles. I'll get back to you with an ETA."

"And what about my son?"

"I told you he's fine. Quite the little gamer."

She shifted nervously, fingering her gun, the desire to take Rivon out overwhelming. But there was nothing gained in his death.

At least not yet.

"You promised me something to show that he's still okay."

Rivon reached in his upper coat pocket and produced a cell phone. After clicking several keys on the keypad, he handed it to her, the screen filling with the image of her son. He was sitting at a game console, clearly enthralled with the characters on screen. A half-eaten sandwich lay at his elbow. The camera panned slowly and then moved in for a close-up. Adam looked tired, but healthy, his hair clean and his clothes new. She fought off a sob as she traced the line of his jaw, her fingers remembering the silky softness of his hair. "How do I know this is recent?" she asked.

"The newspaper," Rivon said, pointing to a white square on the table beside Adam. As if on cue the camera zoomed in on the cover. "See, it has today's date."

She squinted down at the tiny screen, the lines of the newspaper coming into focus, confirming that it was in fact today's *Post*. Two seconds later, the screen went blank. "I want to see it again."

Rivon frowned, his annoyance apparent, but he shrugged and leaned over to restart the video sequence.

Annie studied the visual, trying to find something in

the shots that might yield location, but her eyes kept locking on her son. The video ended, and her heart wrenched as if Adam had been taken away from her all over again. "I want to talk to him."

"Not a problem. Just kill Dominico and you can talk all you want." Rivon snatched the phone from her hand.

She clenched her fist to keep from snatching the cell from his hand. Better to play along. Keep him believing she was playing the game by his rules.

"So we're good," she said instead.

"I think I have what I need." He patted the portfolio. "I'll call if there are any questions."

Behind them, near the entrance, the bushes rattled ominously, a spray of gravel skittering across the path. They both swiveled, Rivon producing a gun.

"What the hell was that?"

"The wind," Annie said, squinting into the shadows to be sure.

"Sounded like more than that to me." He took a pace forward, still holding his weapon. Annie followed behind, moving cautiously, her fingers closing again on the gun in her pocket. Not certain who she'd shoot if it came to it, Rivon or an intruder.

The bushes rattled again as something fell from the steps above them.

"Who's there?" Rivon called, his voice swallowed by the mist.

Annie leaned down and picked up a piece of cement, a chip off the balustrade above them. "I'm telling you it's just the wind," she said, tossing the chunk of debris.

Rivon stared upward for a minute or so and then lowered his gun. "Yeah, well, I'm sure you'll understand if I don't take your word for it. Anyway, we're through here. I'll go first. We don't want anyone seeing us together."

"Might be better if you put the gun away as well."

Rivon scowled at her, but slid the gun into his waistband. "I'll be in touch as soon as we've got the weapon."

"You do that," she said, holding her ground as Rivon walked away, instinct screaming that he was her only link to Adam. That she shouldn't let him walk away. Better to take him down. Try to trade his life for Adam's. But intellectually she knew it wouldn't work. The people holding Adam didn't give a rat's ass about Rivon's life. He was nothing more than a means to an end. An expendable one at that.

Better to let him go. Let A-Tac do their thing.

She glanced down at her watch, waiting an agonizing five minutes before bidding Peter Pan and his grotto adieu. She walked up the steps, careful to keep a close watch for any sign that she was being monitored. If things had gone as planned, she should be on her own, Nash and Drake already on their way to finding Adam.

At the top of the stairs, the air grew colder, the wind wilder as it raced between the undulating branches of the canopy of trees. Quickening her pace, she retraced her steps past the basketball court and playground.

In the distance, she could see that the van was gone. The street empty. Beyond that the East River flowed. Backward now as the tide reversed itself. She crossed in front of an equipment building, its walls momentarily blocking what little illumination the park's lighting provided. She stopped to give her eyes a chance to adjust to the gloom, and as she did so she heard the telltale sound of a footstep behind her.

Drawing her gun, she pressed her back to the wall, listening for something to help her identify the direction of the intruder. Silence hung heavily as she held her ground. If someone was indeed behind her, he had to round the corner of the building before he'd be able to see her. Which meant that she had a two- or three-second advantage.

Holding her breath, she inched forward, leading with the barrel of her gun. Then froze on her side of the corner, waiting—listening.

Again she heard the soft sound of leather on concrete, this time no more than a few feet away. Adrenaline rushed through her as the shadowy shape of a man rounded the corner, his own gun glistening in the misty half-light. Resisting the urge to fire, she pressed back against the wall, deep into the shadows, until he was almost even with her. Then, moving with a speed acquired through years of training, she kicked up and out, sending the man sprawling onto the concrete pathway.

"Don't move," she said, leveling her gun at the back of his head.

"Put the fucking gun down," came the beleaguered answer. "It's just me."

"Son of a bitch," she whispered, anger only adding to the adrenaline rush. "What the hell did you think you were doing? I could have killed you."

Before she had time to say anything more, Nash grabbed her behind the knees, pulling her down and flipping her over, her gun sliding across the pavement as his weight pinned her to the ground. "I think maybe you're overestimating your abilities."

"You know as well as I do that you'd be dead right now if I hadn't recognized your voice. You just got lucky."

"Think whatever you want." He shrugged, pushing to his feet. "But I think the facts speak for themselves. After all, I was the one who ended up on top."

"Bastard," she taunted, ignoring his extended hand as she rolled to her feet.

"Hey. I just call it like I see it."

She glared at him, then bent to retrieve her gun. "What are you doing here anyway? Aren't you supposed to be following Rivon?"

"Drake's on it. Avery tasked me with watching you."

"Afraid I'd run?"

"You admitted yourself you were thinking about it." He frowned. "You always seemed to prefer acting on your own."

"That's bullshit, and you know it. We were good together." The minute the words came out, she regretted them, her words morphing into something bigger than she'd intended.

"You don't have to remind me, angel," he said, taking a step closer, his gaze colliding with hers. "I was there, remember?"

She swallowed, steeling herself against the onslaught of memories, emotion threatening her composure. "I was talking about our business relationship."

"I wasn't." He moved closer still, his breath warm against her cheek.

"Nash, I—"

He swallowed her words, his lips crushing down on hers. Sensory memory kicked in and she opened her mouth, welcoming him inside, reveling in the feel of his tongue, entering, possessing. It was take-no-prisoners contact, as much a battle of wills as an expression of emotion.

He brushed her lips with his and then tugged softly at her lower lip. She tensed, thinking to push him away, but her body rebelled at the thought, and of their own volition, her lips opened to his kiss.

She pressed closer, feeling the heat of his hands against her back. His mouth moved, tracing the soft skin along the inside of her neck, kissing the pulse at the base of her throat. Shivers racked through her, and her mind raced with memories—their bodies pressed together, skin to skin, hot and sticky.

Sliding her hands inside the warm leather of his jacket, her palms flat against his hard muscled chest, she closed her eyes, allowing sensation to wash over her in hypnotic waves of heat, igniting her, filling her, the power of his touch almost more than she could bear.

His mouth closed over hers again, the heat inside her building to a fever pitch. When his thumb rasped across her nipple, she moaned, the sound swallowed by his kiss. Then he lowered his head and took her breast into his mouth, his tongue rasping through the thin cotton of her shirt. Her nipple hardened and throbbed and she moaned, her voice trembling with passion.

He suckled harder, rolling the nipple between his teeth, his other hand pulling her closer, the flame inside her building in intensity until she wasn't certain she could survive it, wasn't sure anything could be as wonderful as the feel of his mouth on her breast. So many memories. But this wasn't a dream, he was here...now...

Somewhere, beyond the magic of his touch, she heard the wail of the wind, the sound bringing reality crashing in.

Adam.

How could she have forgotten her child?

She shoved back, anger replacing any semblance of passion. "We can't do this."

"Annie." He reached for her, his face awash with the same confusion she was feeling.

"No." She shook her head, holding up a hand to ward him off. "This was a mistake."

"I see." There was an edge to his voice, but she was too agitated to analyze it.

"Oh, come on. You know as well as I do that whatever we had died a long time ago. The only reason we're together at all is because of the mess I'm in. And the only thing that matters now is finding my son."

"My bad," he said, stepping back, the distance stretching between them. "Clearly I was out of line."

Annie winced at the chill in his voice. "Nash..."

"Let it go." He shook his head, his expression hardening. "You're right. There's nothing between us anymore. You made your choices and I made mine. There's no going back."

She should have been pleased. He was agreeing with her after all. And yet, instead, his words cut deep, hurting more than she could possibly have imagined. Especially after all this time.

But then again, maybe the saying was wrong—maybe time didn't heal a goddamned thing.

CHAPTER **10**

I still think she should be under the protection of Homeland Security," Tom said, arms crossed as he paced in front of the fireplace. "This should have been our case in the first place. But now that she's done her part, I figure the sooner we get her to Washington the better."

"I can understand your misgivings," Avery acknowledged, "but so far she's followed our instructions to the letter."

"More or less," Nash mumbled, still trying to deal with the aftermath of his hormones or pheromones or whatever the hell they were called. He and Annie had made it back to the brownstone without further incident, but that didn't mean things were settled between them. It was as if all the shadows of the past had raised their ugly heads the minute he'd kissed her.

What the hell had he been thinking?

At least for the moment, he had a reprieve. Tyler was debriefing Annie in the next room while everyone else waited in the parlor for the final word from Drake.

"Are you saying she tried something at the park?" Tom frowned as Nash pulled his attention back to the conversation at hand.

"No." He shook his head. "Of course not. Nothing happened. I was just sounding off."

"I'm not sure I believe you," Tom said.

"Well, I don't give a flying fuck what you think," Nash snapped. It was clear that the man didn't trust Annie. Which under the circumstances probably wasn't that far off base. Hell, he had his own set of conflicting emotions to deal with. But something in Tom's tone pissed Nash off.

"Maybe I was wrong to bring you into this." Avery frowned.

"No." He shook his head. "I'm the best person for the job. It's just harder than I thought it would be. Can we just leave it at that?"

"Yeah," Tom said with a nod. "Your feelings are understandable. Hell, I've got issues, too. We all worked together a long time, and it's hard to think of Annie as one of the bad guys. But that doesn't negate the fact that she tried to assassinate a U.S. dignitary." Nash opened his mouth to argue, but Tom raised his hand. "I realize there were mitigating circumstances, but that doesn't change the reality of what she tried to do."

"Look, I understand where you're coming from, Tom, but you know as well as I do that there's no such thing as black and white in this business," Avery observed. "Only shades of gray. She might have chosen the wrong way to deal with the situation, but it's an understandable decision nevertheless."

"I suppose," Tom replied, clearly unconvinced.

"Anyway, the bottom line here is that until we see

how Drake fares, I think we're better off having Annie go through the motions of following Ashad's instructions."

"You're in charge." Tom shrugged, dropping down into the wing chair across from Avery. "But I want my objection to go on record."

"Duly noted." Avery nodded, turning his attention to Jason, who was monitoring a computer satellite hookup. "What's the word from Drake?"

"Rivon's still on the move," Jason said. "Drake's about a mile behind him. They're just outside the city now. Heading north on Highway 9."

"Our luck, he's headed for his mother's." Tom stood up again, nervous energy getting the better of him.

"So what's the plan?" Nash asked.

"As soon as Drake's ascertained that he's not on a wild-goose chase," Avery said, "he'll give us coordinates and you'll join him in the field. He won't make a move until you're in place."

Nash walked over to the window and looked outside. The city was still awake. Even at this hour, there were people on the streets and lights in the windows. Life—24/7. He dropped the curtain back into place.

"So do we have any more information on Bruebaker? Or whatever the hell his real name is?" he asked. "I know Hannah's been working on it."

"Nothing yet." Avery shook his head. "Fingerprints aren't in the system."

"We're running everything a second time," Jason said. "As well as waiting for Langley to confirm our findings."

Nash frowned. "Anything on the DNA?"

"The sample was good. But unfortunately that doesn't speed the process of using it for identification purposes,"

Jason said. "Besides, if this guy's working with Ashad, then I'm figuring he won't be in any of our databases anyway."

"What about your team, Tom?" Avery asked. "They come up with anything?"

"It's too soon to say. Hannah sent the prints and copies of Lara's preliminary report on the DNA, but like you said, it all takes time."

"Well, in the meantime," Jason said, "Hannah's still working on finding something. Hell, she's got sources even Langley doesn't know about." Nash smiled. Hannah's intuition alone was worth anything Langley and Homeland Security could throw at the problem.

"What about Annie?" Nash asked. "I mean, once Drake reports in."

"She stays here in New York."

"The hell I do," Annie said, walking into the room, followed by an apologetic-looking Tyler.

"She wouldn't stay put."

"Not surprising," Nash observed, the tension in the room ratcheting up at least five degrees as Annie faced off with Avery.

"I'm not staying here. I'm going with Nash to meet Drake."

"Annie, that's not a wise idea and you know it."

"I don't have to be involved in the operation itself. I'll just stay in the background. But I need to be there. He's my son."

"Exactly why you need to stay in New York," Avery said. "You know that emotions are only a handicap in the field."

"I'm more than capable of keeping my emotions

in check. It's not like I haven't been dealing with this already. And so far I've managed just fine."

"Look," Avery said, holding up his hands, his voice placating, "there's a good chance that Rivon will try to contact you after he drops off the plans. You need to be available in case we need to take action from this end."

"If your team is as good as you say they are, Rivon won't have the chance to call me. And besides, I can take the damn phone with me." She glanced over at Jason, looking for support.

He shrugged. "It'll be okay. I can rig it so that if they ping it, it'll register a false location."

"And you can monitor me. Nash and Drake will be there. So it's not like I won't have babysitters."

"They're going to be a little busy," Tom said. "And for the record, I think this is highly irregular."

"Well, it's not your call," Avery said, his eyes narrowing as he studied Annie. "How do I know you won't take matters into your own hands?"

"Because if I were going to do that, I already would have. If I wanted to rid myself of you and your people, I could have done so any number of times. But I didn't. I'm here. And I'm playing by your rules. But I won't sit by idly while my son's life is in danger. I'm going with Nash."

"Actually, I think she's right," Tyler said.

Annie swung around to look at Tyler, her surprise almost comical.

"What's your thinking?" Avery asked.

"No matter where she is, her head is going to be out there with Adam. And she's correct in thinking Rivon isn't likely to call. And if he does, she'll have the phone. But more important, if she's on site, she'll be able to provide intel. Things about Adam that might facilitate his rescue. Or even Rivon, for that matter. I'm not advocating that she take part in the operation. Just that it seems feasible, practical even, that she be allowed on site."

"You're not for one minute considering this?" Tom asked, clearly appalled. "What if the worst happens? What if the boy is collateral damage? What's to keep her from taking matters into her own hands?"

"Nash?" Avery queried, ignoring Tom. "What do you think?"

"She knows the risks," Nash said, nodding his support. There was no question in his mind that if someone he loved were in danger, he'd want to be there.

"I'm not going to endanger the operation," Annie said, her eyes shooting daggers at Tom. "It's the only chance my son has. All I'm asking is that you let me be there. I promise I'll stay in the background."

"Well, I vote no," Tom said. "Not that any of you are going to listen to me."

"You realize that our primary objective is to stop Ashad?" Avery asked.

"I do." She nodded.

"And you'll do exactly as you're told. Stay in the background. Out of sight. And out of the line of fire."

"Unless I'm needed."

Nash couldn't help but admire Annie's strength as she stood up to his boss. Avery wasn't the type to give in to civilian requests. And no matter how much experience she'd had, she was still technically an outsider. But she'd stated her case well, and Tyler had provided solid support.

"All right. You're in. But only as an observer," he said, his tone brooking no argument.

"Hang on," Jason said, interrupting the moment. "Drake's online." He gestured them over to the computer, and the five of them stared down at the satellite photo on the screen, a flashing blip showing Drake's location. Jason hit a couple more keys and a small window at the bottom of the monitor opened to show video feed directly from Drake. "He's live."

"Drake, can you hear me?" Avery asked.

"Loud and clear."

"I assume Rivon's reached his destination?" Avery queried.

"Exactly. I've sent Jason the coordinates." Jason tapped the blinking light on the satellite photo in response. "I'm currently about half a mile back. Didn't want to take a chance on them monitoring our conversation. But they're holed up in a house about two miles off Thompson Road between Graystone and Hastings-on-Hudson."

"How isolated?" Nash asked.

"Completely. It's fenced off, with a gravel road that leads down to the house itself. It's surrounded by thick overgrowth on three sides with a lake pretty much lapping at the foundation at the back. Can you see it?"

"Yeah, Jason's got it onscreen," Avery confirmed as he shifted the view and zoomed in on the rooftop of the house Drake was describing.

"Have you seen Adam?" Annie asked, her face tight with worry. "Is he all right?"

"No. I haven't been able to make visual confirmation. Couldn't get close enough. Figured it was better to wait for backup. But if I was going to kidnap someone, this is exactly the kind of place I'd bring him to."

"What about personnel?" Avery asked.

"Unconfirmed. Once we're ready to move, maybe I can get some help from satellite and infrared."

"Shouldn't be a problem," Jason said.

"Great," Drake said, "so all I have to do is wait here until the posse arrives."

"That'd be me," Nash said, picking up a backpack containing assorted gear and com equipment.

"Glad to hear it. Although I'm a little surprised. Figured Avery'd have you babysitting."

"I don't need babysitting," Annie said, her words clipped.

"Actually, she's coming along for the ride." Nash tossed the bag to Annie, and she caught it one-handed, swinging it over her shoulder, their teamwork coming automatically, as if they'd never been apart.

"And Avery agreed to that?" Drake's surprise carried over the line.

"I did." Avery broke in. "But only as an observer."

"Good luck with that," he said. "Listen, company's coming. It's probably not related, but I'd better go dark. You guys need to get a move on. And Nash, bring some firepower. Assuming we're really dealing with Ashad, I've got a feeling these boys mean business. Over and out." There was a moment's silence and then static as the video screen went blank.

"Guess it's time to get a move on," Nash said, already moving toward the door.

"Annie," Avery called as she started after Nash, "see to it that you don't make me regret my decision."

CHAPTER 11

Ready to rumble?" Nash asked as he dropped to the ground beside Drake.

The two of them were hidden in a copse of trees on a small rise just above a dilapidated house. It was flanked on the left by a weathered outbuilding and on the right by what looked to be a farmyard dumping ground. A rusting tractor, an abandoned pickup, and myriad barnyard implements lay half-buried in overgrown weeds and grass as the first pale fingers of dawn appeared on the horizon.

"Thought maybe you weren't coming," Drake said with a grin.

"Hey, you know I never miss a party."

"Where's Annie?"

"Back with the SUV. Avery's orders. But thanks to Emmett's magic, she's linked in by com. Annie, can you hear us?"

"Yeah, I'm here. And I feel totally useless."

"I don't know," Drake said, "I always feel better knowing someone's got my back."

"I thought that was my job," Nash protested. "Anyway, Annie, you promised Avery you'd stay in the background. That was the deal."

"I know," she sighed. "But I don't have to like it."

"So consider yourself the backup backup," Drake said.

"So what's happening?" Annie asked. "Any action from below?"

"Not since Rivon went in." Drake shook his head. "That's his car on the left. The blue sedan."

"And the others?" Nash motioned to the two SUVs parked near the shed.

"No clear idea about owners. But I've seen at least two men besides Rivon. They were checking the perimeter."

"I'm assuming they're carrying?"

"Both with LMGs. M-249s if I had to call it," Drake said, offering Nash his field glasses.

"So they're playing for keeps." He scanned the area slowly, mentally noting possible locations for cover. "What about inside?" he asked, returning the glasses.

"I haven't been down there yet. Figured it was best to wait on you."

"Not up to facing machine guns on your own?" Nash quipped.

"Yeah, right," Drake grunted, then sobered as a shadow passed in front of the house's front window. "Looks like maybe we're about to get another gander at the ground patrol."

The front door opened, and a man moved onto the porch, machine gun draped over his left shoulder.

"Annie, you getting this?"

"Yeah, I can the see the man from here."

"Doesn't seem to be worried about anything," Nash said. "Guess he doesn't know he's got company. Jason, you there?"

"Roger that," Jason's voice crackled into his ear.

"You got a body count for us?"

"Not yet," he said. "I'm still waiting for the satellite to move into position. There's no hurrying three tons of extraterrestrial titanium."

"How much longer?"

"Maybe two minutes," Hannah chimed in. "Hang on. The satellite's downloading the image now. Looks like two clusters of heat. One in the front and one in the back left corner. I'm zooming in."

They waited, Drake still watching the house through his field glasses. The rising sun washed the compound in pale morning light, the shadows from the trees and rocky hills effectively camouflaging the perimeter topography.

Below them, the guy on the porch performed a cursory visual search of the area, his gaze passing, uninterested, over the copse of trees where they lay hidden. "I've got one hostile in sight," Drake reported. "Armed, but no threat at present."

"So how many others are there?" Nash asked. Static crackled in his ear. "Hannah, you there?"

"I'm here," she said. "Jason?"

"Present and accounted for," he acknowledged. "Probably just a hiccup in the communications hookup. Everything seems to be fine now."

"So what have you got?" Nash asked again.

"Looks like you've got three warm bodies in the front

of the house. Not counting your man on the porch. And two in the back."

"Anyone else? In the back, outside, maybe?"

"Nothing I can see," Jason said. "Hannah, you got anything different?"

"Nope. Annie, can you see anything more from your vantage point?"

"I've got nothing new."

"Well, it looks like you guys have your work cut out for you," Hannah said. "Assuming one of the thermal images is Adam, that leaves five hostiles. Four of whom are probably loaded for bear."

"Whatever the hell that means," Drake mumbled.

"Carrying enough ammunition to kill a bear," Hannah answered, ever the literalist.

"Well, idiomatic lesson aside, we know that at least two of them are toting M-249s. I can see one. And Drake IDed the other. And we know that Rivon was carrying in the park. Annie, it was a Beretta, right?"

"Yes. And as far as I know that's all he was carrying."

"So that's three confirmed with weapons. And the odds are good the others are armed as well," Jason said.

"We've fought worse odds."

"Yeah, and the last time Emmett wound up with a bullet in his groin." Jason's tone was light, but there was a note of concern as well. "Maybe you should wait for backup."

"Nah," Drake said, watching as the guy on the porch flicked his cigarette butt into the bushes and went back into the house. "We're better off with the original plan. Surgical strike. In and out. Grab the kid before they even know we're here. If we encounter trouble, we'll fall back. But we need to at least establish that the boy is here."

"Nash?" Hannah queried. "What do you think?"

"I'm with Drake. Better to go in now," Nash said, sobering at the thought of Annie's child down there all on his own. "Annie?"

"I haven't got an official vote, but you know what I want. Adam. Now."

"Okay then," Drake said, "it's a go. Jason, we're counting on you and Hannah to be an extra set of eyes."

"Globally speaking," Hannah said. "Anyway, whatever the capacity, we're here."

"I'm thinking our best bet is to head for the back of the house. You still seeing two people back there?"

"Affirmative," Jason said. "They're pretty much still in their original position."

"And the guys in front?"

"Still there. Two stationed near the windows," Hannah replied. "Annie, can you see them?"

"Shadows maybe?" she answered. "But not positive confirmation."

"They're there," Hannah said. "Possibly on sentry duty. And the other two are still inside center. Most likely out of visual range."

"All right then." Drake nodded. "On my mark, we go."

"Good luck," Annie whispered as Drake signaled Nash to move out.

The two of them started to make their way down to the compound, using rocks and trees for cover. At the bottom of the rise, they moved into the junkyard to the right of the house, careful to keep positioned so that each was watching the other's back. Nash squatted behind the back axle of an old flatbed Ford, flecks of rusty turquoise clinging tenaciously to what was left of the frame.

Ahead of him, from the shelter of what looked like a plow, Drake motioned toward the back of the house and the edge of a window just visible behind a clump of overgrown rhododendron.

Nash nodded and then followed as Drake began to make his way to the east side of the house. From somewhere in the distance, a dog barked. Nash froze, waiting to see what, if any, reaction there would be from inside.

The compound remained quiet.

"Everything okay?" Annie whispered.

"We're fine," Nash said. "It was nothing."

"Just a dog," Drake confirmed as he moved into place behind a large oak tree about three feet from the rhododendron. Motioning Nash forward, he crouched low, ready to provide covering fire if necessary.

But again nothing moved, the bucolic scene belying the true nature of the situation at hand. "Not sure I see the appeal of a rural life," Nash said as he dropped down beside Drake.

"Rest and relaxation?" Hannah quipped, but her words were cut off by another burst of static.

"Hannah?" Nash said as the noise retreated into silence. "Jason? Annie? Can you guys hear me?"

"We're here but we're picking up some kind of interference," Hannah said, her words backed up by strong static. "Could be someone's picking up our signal. Better we sign off. You know the drill."

"Roger that," Drake said, already reaching up to switch off his headset.

"Maybe it's just because we dropped below the line of the trees." Nash waved toward the spot they'd just vacated. "It's possible the hills are interfering with transmission."

"Either way it looks like we're on our own."

"Wasn't much they could do anyway." Nash shrugged. "If we switch to the local channel we ought to at least be able to talk to each other without risk of anyone uninvited listening in." He reached up to twist the tiny dial on the com-link's base. "Can you hear me?"

"Yeah, you're coming through fine." Drake nodded.

"Annie?" Nash asked. "You there?" Static filled his ear. "She doesn't know to switch channels."

Nash nodded. "At least I can signal her that we're okay." He reached into his pocket and produced a pen-light. Pointing it toward the hilltop where Annie was concealed, he flashed twice. "Hopefully she'll see it."

"If not she probably can see us. Which means she knows we're still good to go."

"Roger that," Drake responded, shifting so that he could better survey the surrounding area. "Guess we're good to go. I'll hold position here while you check the window to try and hopefully verify Annie's son's position."

"Sounds like a plan, but we'd better move fast. Without our guardian angels we have no way of knowing if those clowns are in motion."

Nash moved across the open area, slipping underneath the cascading branches of the rhododendron. The area beneath was dank and dark, but it provided the kind of cover that meant he couldn't easily be detected.

Working his way to the edge of the house, he pushed between overcrowded branches, following the foundation line until he was directly beneath the window. "I'm here," he whispered into the com-link. "Getting ready to check the window."

"Copy that," Drake replied. "Everything's still quiet on this end."

Nash twisted until he was between branches and then slowly inched his way up to the base of the window. Then after a silent count of three, he moved the rest of the way, his eyes just above the edge of the window sill.

He squinted as he tried to focus through the grime that coated the glass. He was looking into the kitchen. A dilapidated-looking refrigerator sat in the corner next to an old free-standing gas range. Below him, Nash could just make out the edge of a sink filled with dirty dishes, the remains of a peanut butter sandwich giving credence to the possibility that Adam was indeed inside.

Directly across from the window an open door revealed tantalizingly little of what he supposed was the dining room. The corner of a chair or maybe a table of some kind, and the faded floral print of what appeared to be some kind of drapery. No sign of hostiles, and no sign of Adam.

"The kitchen's empty," he whispered as he shifted so that he could better see the right side of the room, "but I've got a closed door leading to a back room." Instinct prickled, and he frowned. "I'm going to try to move around the corner. See if there's another window."

"Hold position," Drake answered, his voice crackling over the com. "I've got a hostile coming off the porch. Same guy as earlier."

Nash dropped down, shifting to try to see through the thick curtain of rhododendron, but the tangled branches blocked everything from view. Frustrated, he leaned back, fingering his gun, waiting for word from Drake. At least there was some comfort in the fact that if he couldn't see out, no one else would be able to see in. For the time being, at least, his position was secure.

"All right," Drake said finally. "He's gone. Bastard only wanted to take a leak."

"I'll bet that was a tempting target."

"No shit." Drake's soft laughter filled the com. "Anyway, you're clear to move."

"Okay, I'm heading around back."

Nash crawled forward again, still using the bushes for cover. After about ten or twelve feet, the rhododendron gave way to some kind of holly, the thorny leaves making progress more difficult, even as the dark leaves provided shelter from prying eyes. Swallowing a curse, he made his way around the corner, and in another two feet, reached a second window.

This one was less protected than the first, the holly bush growing thinner as it disappeared into the overgrowth between the back of the house and what appeared to be the lake Drake had mentioned earlier.

Daring exposure, Nash pushed upward until his line of sight cleared the window ledge. The room was darker than the kitchen, the trees behind him casting shadows along the walls and floor. A small bed in the corner showed signs of recent use. Tangled sheets wadded up in a ball against the wall. Across from the bed, a dilapidated table held a surprisingly new-looking game system with a large monitor. The screen showed what looked to be a video game of some kind. Heart quickening, Nash scanned the room again, looking for other signs that the boy might be there, but the room yielded no further clues.

"Damn it," he whispered to no one in particular, and then froze as the pile of sheets on the bed moved.

First a hand emerged, and then two feet. And finally a head.

Adam.

There was no question that it was Adam. He recognized him from the picture. But even without it, he'd have known it was Annie's child. He had her hair, her freckles, and the same determined look in his eyes. Nash lifted a hand to signal his presence, but before he had the chance, the door slammed open, a dark-haired man appearing in the opening, weapon in hand. Ducking out of sight, Nash cursed himself for not moving faster. Something was definitely wrong.

"Drake?" he whispered, his back pressed against rotting wood. "Are you there?" Static cracked in his ear, followed by a clicking noise and then silence. He opened his mouth to repeat the question, but stopped short, instinct keeping him quiet.

Drawing his gun, he headed back toward the corner of the house, staying low, still using the bushes for cover. He slowed as he reached the rhododendron, pushing the leaves back so that he could see. From this vantage point, he couldn't verify Drake's position beneath the towering oak. But he was relieved to find the side yard quiet. No sign of intruders or danger of any kind.

But there was no sign of Drake either.

Staying within the protection of the rhododendron, Nash carefully made his way back toward the oak tree. And then, only after waiting a full five minutes in silence, did he dare to step from the bush's sheltering confines.

One minute he was moving toward the safety of the

oak tree, and the next something struck him hard on the back of the head. White-hot light exploded in his brain as he stumbled to his knees, trying to hang on to consciousness. Using sheer power of will, he grabbed his gun and pivoted, his effort rewarded with the shadowy outline of his attacker.

He lifted his hand and fired. But there was only a quiet click as the gun jammed. Nash tried to push to his feet, but his attacker was faster, knocking the Sig away, his own weapon pointed directly at Nash's head.

CHAPTER 12

Annie gripped the field glasses, her heart beating double time. The man holding Nash and Drake at gunpoint was gesturing toward the house, which meant that for the moment at least they were safe. Still, with the communications blackout, she wasn't about to take a chance. The handgun Nash had given her was of little value, unless she could fly. She needed something more powerful. And she needed it now.

Running over to the Land Rover, she yanked open the back and felt along the front seam of the carpet covering the floor for the notched indentation that opened the weapons cabinet.

Standard issue even in her day.

She selected a rifle and fitted the scope, feeling a hell of a lot more secure, in her element. She'd already checked out the farm, if you could call it that. Looking like something out of a Thomas Cole painting, the graying old house set against the yellow-pink of the sunrise had looked almost peaceful. The Hudson River School at its very best. But this wasn't a painting. Hell, it wasn't even a real farm. At least not anymore.

Now it was nothing more than a prison. A place to hold her son. And it had taken every ounce of self-restraint Annie possessed to keep from running down the hill to try to free Adam. But now all bets were off. Nash was in trouble.

Grabbing some extra ammo, she stuffed it into a small backpack, adding a couple of grenades and a Sig Sauer for good measure. Better to be overprepared. She closed the hatch and moved back toward the farmhouse. Although it was daylight, clouds had moved in to cover the sun, the overcast day giving her an unexpected advantage when it came to stealth.

At the top of a small rise, she dropped to the ground, using the rifle's scope to reevaluate the situation. The group had moved about fifteen feet, Drake and Nash both with their hands in the air. It wouldn't be long before the man called for reinforcements or forced them out of sight. Either way, she didn't have much time.

She lowered the scope and sat back on her heels, considering her options. The first thing to do was remove the immediate threat—the man with the machine gun. She could take him out from here. But the shot was long, even by her standards. She'd move closer and then take the bastard out.

Gauging the distance between their position and the rise, she decided on a point halfway down the slope, a large pine tree huddled against an outcropping of rock providing the perfect place to conceal herself. The only trick was to make the distance between here and there in one piece, but considering the kidnappers probably weren't expecting reinforcements, she figured the odds were on her side.

Moving at almost a crawl, she skittered down the hill, stopping once behind a boulder, relieved to see that her movement had gone unnoticed. Another ten yards or so and she was sheltered by the pine. Reattaching the rifle's scope and silencer, she knelt, taking aim, as the man waved his machine gun again in the direction of the house. The three of them moved forward, stepping into the shadow of a stand of trees, Drake blocking the angle of her shot.

"Move, damn it," she whispered, heart thudding as she waited.

As if he'd heard her, Drake bent down, and Annie closed an eye as she gently squeezed the trigger, the motion at once intimate and deadly, everything coming back to her with one fluid motion. She was a trained killer and nothing— not her life in Creede, not her absence from the Company, not even her love for her son—could change that fact.

Using the scope, she ascertained that the man was indeed down. Nash and Drake had already pulled his body deeper into the shadows. She struggled for breath, the past and present coming together in nightmarish fashion. Angrily, she pushed away her rioting emotions. There was no time for introspection. Her son's life and quite possibly Nash and Drake's depended on her ability to keep a cool head.

Keeping the rifle at the ready, she swung the pack back onto her shoulder and cautiously worked her way around the perimeter of the farmyard to the copse of trees where she'd last seen Nash and Drake.

Whistling softly, she prayed Nash would remember their old signal. It had been eight years, after all. She didn't relish the idea of coming up on them blind, but she didn't have much choice. Fortunately, the breeze carried his answering call.

Keeping low, careful to keep watch on the house, she moved into the shelter of the trees. "Nash?" she called softly.

"Over here," came the reply.

Nash was crouched over the body, Drake next to him keeping watch, the dead man's machine gun trained on the house.

"Nice shot," Drake said as she dropped down beside them. Everything was still almost eerily quiet.

"I'm a little rusty," she said, shrugging, "but once a shooter always a shooter, I guess. Any sign of company?"

"Nothing so far," Nash said as he finished searching the body. "The man wasn't carrying a radio. So that's a break in our favor."

Drake winced as he shifted his position, gingerly rubbing the back of his head.

"You okay?" she asked.

"Yeah, the guy just clubbed me upside the head. But it's nothing."

"So what the hell happened?" Annie asked. "I assumed that even though Jason and Hannah bugged out, the two of you were still in communication."

"We were," Drake said. "But the guy caught me unaware. Knocked me cold from behind."

"And then went after Nash." She nodded, turning back to Nash, who was camouflaging the body with rocks and leaves. "I saw that much. But I thought you had him."

"Gun jammed," he replied, his mouth tightening with anger. "I hope to hell you've got another one in the bag?"

"I do," she said, reaching in to toss him the gun. "Also

some extra ammo and some grenades. I kinda hate going into a situation unprepared."

"Grenades could be useful," Drake said. "And at least for the moment we seem to have the upper hand. We're still alone."

"Yeah, but sooner or later someone's bound to come looking for our friend over there."

"Which means we need to move fast," Drake said, the machine gun still trained on the farmhouse.

"What about Adam?" Annie asked, her heart in her throat.

"He's here," Nash said. "I saw him."

"And?" she asked, fear shimmering in her voice.

"There wasn't time to see much, but he's definitely alive."

"Thank God," she whispered, her heart slipping back into place again. "What about the others? Do you think the man from the phone call is here?"

"No way to tell. There was a man with Adam, but there was nothing to signify who he was."

"And we don't have time to sit here and debate. Once they figure out they're a man short, we'll have lost advantage," Drake said. "We need to make our move now."

"I'm ready," Annie said, and nodded, sliding a clip into her gun. "So what are we facing?"

"According to Jason's intel, we've got five hostiles including Rivon," Nash said.

"So that means we're down to four," Annie said. "Jason placed two up front. Which I'm assuming includes the guy I took out. And two midhouse."

"Which is probably Rivon and maybe the guy in charge," Nash added.

"And then there's one in back with your son," Drake concluded. She noticed he didn't call Adam by name. That was protocol. It made it less personal when working on a retrieval, but the thought made her gut churn.

"So what's the plan?" she asked, remembering that Nash had said that Drake was an expert in extractions.

"I'm thinking a two-pronged attack," Drake replied. "I'll create some kind of diversion. Something that will pull Rivon and company to the front of the house or, even better, outside. Then once we've managed to grab their attention, you guys can sneak in the back and grab the kid. From what I could see, there were two rooms at the front of the house. A living room on the west side and a bedroom on the east. The living room opens onto a dining room."

"Which leads to the kitchen," Nash said, sketching a crude diagram of the house with his finger in the dirt. "Adam is in a room on the back. Here." Nash pointed to the northeastern corner of the house.

"And according to the plans Jason showed us, there should be a door near the opposite corner."

"So all we've got to do," Annie said, studying the diagram, "is get in the back door and through here to Adam." She drew a line to indicate what seemed to be the shortest route.

"While Rivon and his cronies are outside chasing after me." Drake nodded.

"It's still risky," Nash said with a frown. "Maybe it would be better if I handled the retrieval on my own. After all, Avery told Annie to stay in the background."

"If I'd stayed in the background, you'd both be dead."

"Point well taken," Drake said. "Besides, we need all

the personnel we can get. If everything goes well, I'll be able to take out the four remaining hostiles. And your job will be easy. But if I fail, or if someone stays behind with the kid, you could run into trouble. And an extra gun could be just the ticket." He waited a moment for dissension, and when there was none, nodded. "All right, so we're agreed. I'll attack the front while you and Annie hit from the back and free the kid."

"Adam," Annie said through gritted teeth. "His name is Adam."

"Right." Drake nodded.

"Annie," Nash said, his fingers closing around hers. "It's going to be all right."

"I know." She nodded, forcing herself to sequester her fear. She could fall apart later, after Adam was safe. "It's just that he's my son."

"Are you sure you're going to be okay?" Nash asked, his eyes dark with worry.

"Yeah," she said, her gaze meeting his. "I have to be. For Adam. Besides, it's not like I haven't done this before." She blew out a breath and squared her shoulders. "So what do you say we get this show on the road?"

"Sounds like a plan," Drake said. "Give me a couple of minutes' lead time to get into place. Then assuming everything's still quiet, you guys head for the back door and hold your position until you hear the fireworks."

"Fireworks?" Annie asked, stealing a surreptitious look in Nash's direction.

"Call it creative grenade work." Drake shrugged, holding up the backpack.

"Just take the bastards out," Nash said, holstering his gun.

"Not a problem." Drake gave them a jaunty salute, then shouldered the bag and picked up the rifle and machine gun. "Here's to good hunting. And with a little luck, I'll see you both on the flipside."

"With Adam," Annie whispered.

And then he was gone, disappearing into the undergrowth that bordered the edge of the property.

"Annie," Nash said, his brows drawn together in a fierce frown, "I want you to know that I'm going to get him out. And nothing is going to stop me."

"Thank you," she whispered, reaching up to stroke his cheek, the gesture automatic. "I know he's not the main objective. But he's just a little boy."

"Your little boy."

The words hung between them and he leaned forward, his eyes still locked with hers, their breathing intertwined. She swallowed, frozen, pinned by his gaze, and for a moment she thought he was going to kiss her. But instead, he turned, moving to the edge of the trees, his eyes on the house, a muscle in his jaw working overtime.

There was a time when she'd have known just what he was thinking.

But not anymore.

They'd both moved on. Or at least he had. She was still tied to the past, every single day with her son a reminder of what she and Nash had once been to each other.

"It's time," Nash said, his voice breaking into her thoughts. "You ready?"

Now there was the sixty-four-thousand-dollar question.

CHAPTER **13**

Let's do it," she said, her hand tightening on her gun as they stepped cautiously out of the shed, circling back to back as they searched for enemies, the familiar choreography coming naturally. The farmyard was quiet, the cars still parked in the drive, the dead man still safely hidden in his pile of leaves.

Moving as quietly as possible, Nash and Annie continued to flank each other as they made their way to the back of the house. There was no sign of Drake. But that was to be expected. If everything was going as planned, he was on the opposite side of the building setting up his pyrotechnic display.

As they neared the corner, the sound of a screen door opening broke through the stillness. Annie froze, back to the wall, finger on the trigger of her gun. But Nash shook his head, lifting a finger to his lips. She strained into the silence, then heard the familiar clanking of a garbage can lid, followed by the repeated screech of the door opening and closing.

"Close call," she whispered. "Didn't figure Rivon for the environmentally conscious type."

Keeping her back to the wall, Annie slid forward until she could just see around the edge of the building. The small area that constituted the yard was empty, two trash cans leaning against the remains of a fence, the trees on the lake's edge spreading upward to block the sky.

"It's all clear," she said, sliding back into place next to Nash. "So what do you want to do?"

"Wait for Drake's signal and then storm the castle."

"Nature of the beast," she said.

"Some things never change." His smile was almost lost in the shadows of the overgrowth.

She fingered her gun, wondering how in the hell she'd managed to wind up right back where she'd started. Maybe there was no such thing as second chances. The sins of the mother revisited on the child. She shuddered, thinking of Adam. He needed her. Now more than ever. And she'd be damned if she was going to let some specter from her past take him away from her.

Suddenly the crack of an explosion shattered the still air, the reverberations joined by a second, even louder blast. For a moment, the sky above the house turned orange and then black as plumes of smoke and fire shot up into the air.

"That's our cue," Nash said, already on the move.

Annie followed him around the corner, crouching low as they made their way through the undergrowth to the back door. There was shouting from the front of the house as well as gunfire. Hopefully, Drake had the upper hand. But either way, the diversion seemed to be working.

The two of them held their position on either side of

the door for a full minute and then on Nash's count, they yanked it open and stepped inside the house, guns at the ready. They were standing in what had probably been a pantry or mud room. The floorboards were buckled and the wallpaper peeling. Dusty crates and boxes were stacked against the left wall near a doorway, a rudimentary bathroom directly across from it on the right.

Pointing toward the door, Nash started forward, Annie keeping watch from behind. Moving in tandem, they worked their way across the floor, Annie holding position as Nash pivoted into the adjoining room, leading with the Sig.

"Clear," he whispered as she followed him into an empty bedroom, her body still on high alert. "This is where I saw him."

The rumpled bed, a half-empty juice glass, and the laptop on the table were all familiar. Annie recognized the room from the photos and the video feed. But there was no sign of Adam now. Stifling her rising fear, Annie moved into the kitchen, Nash following behind her. Like the rest of the house, the room was dilapidated, the appliances covered in dust. Dirty dishes in the sink were the only real sign of life.

But the deadly quiet coming from both inside and outside the house left Annie with a sick feeling rising in her gut.

There were two additional doors leading out of the kitchen, one directly in front of them and another to the right, next to the refrigerator, opening onto what appeared to be a dining room. Nash signaled her to hold position as he moved to the wall flanking the dining room doorway. On a count of three, he swung into the room, the Sig catching the light as he moved.

"Take another step and I'll kill the boy."

From her angle, she couldn't see Rivon, but she recognized his voice, fear chasing down her spine as the meaning of his words sank home.

"I'm assuming that's your man outside," Rivon said. "The one responsible for the explosions. I told Lloyd things were too quiet."

Annie took a step forward and then froze. Rivon had no idea she was present, which meant that for the moment at least they had an advantage.

"One of your men gave us a little trouble, but we managed to take him out," Nash said.

"I take it he's dead."

"As a doornail. Which I suspect is the fate of the rest of your colleagues."

A volley of shooting rang out in protestation, and Rivon smiled. "I think you might be just a little bit ahead of yourself. Besides, as long as I have the boy, I win."

Annie fought against a surge of rage and backed slowly away from the doorway, moving instead toward the closed door leading to the front of the house. A bedroom, if she remembered right. Leading to the living room. Which in turn connected with the dining room. If Nash could keep Rivon from shifting position, she just might be able to sneak up on him from the back. It would be tricky with Adam there, but not impossible.

The room, like the rest of the house, was in tatters. A broken bed frame listed toward the front wall, its torn and tufted mattress long ago surrendering to local vermin. Keeping the wall to her back, Annie slid forward until she reached the door to the living room. From her new vantage point, she could see Rivon. And Adam.

Rivon had her son in a stranglehold, his gun pressed against Adam's temple. She drew in a breath, calculating angles. And then sighed, frustration cresting. Even if she could manage the shot, Rivon might still manage to shoot Adam, his reflexes following through even if his brain was already dying.

"Throw me your gun," Rivon said, tightening his hold on Adam.

"What guarantee do I have that you won't shoot the boy the minute I do?" Nash asked, moving slightly to the right, his gun still pointing at Rivon. She could almost see him now. Just a few more inches.

"You have my word," Rivon said with a shrug.

"Which we all know isn't worth a damn." Nash shifted a little more to the right, his movement almost imperceptible, but now she could see him full on. She smiled as their gazes met. Feigning throwing her gun, she nodded toward the far corner. Away from Adam.

Again almost imperceptibly, Nash tilted his head toward Adam, with a slight nod.

And just like that the plan was set.

This was a game they'd played a million times before.

She nodded, her grip on the Beretta tightening as she anticipated the next move.

"Look, I don't know who the hell you are," Rivon bellowed, "but I do know you're after the kid. So if you don't want his blood on your hands, throw me the god-damned gun."

"Fine." Nash shrugged. "You win." He tossed the Sig Sauer to his right, just beyond the other man's reach.

Everything else happened at once. Rivon instinctively

moved toward the careening gun, releasing his hold on Adam. Nash dove across the room, pulling her son to the floor. And Annie fired, her bullet hitting Rivon dead center. He dropped to his knees as his gun fell from lifeless fingers.

Annie stood for a moment, frozen to the spot. Afraid to look in Nash's direction. Afraid of what she might see.

"Mommy?" Adam's voice broke through her fear, and after handing Nash the gun, she swept her son into her arms.

"I'm here, baby. Right here." She stroked his hair, looking over his head as Nash checked the body and retrieved the Sig.

"Is he dead?" Adam asked, his voice quavering.

"Yes, baby," she answered truthfully, tears filling her eyes. "He can't hurt you anymore."

"I knew you'd come," Adam said, his chin trembling. "You were just like Zelda in my Wind Waker game." He shot a shy look in Nash's direction. "And he's like Link."

"You play too much Nintendo," she chided automatically, her mind still dealing with the ramifications of what could have happened. "Anything from Drake?"

"Nothing yet," Nash said from his position by the front window, "but I can see at least two down from here. Which is a good sign."

"Third guy's trussed up like a turkey. Figured he might be of use," Drake said from the kitchen doorway, the machine gun still draped over his shoulder. "I came in the back way, in case you needed help. But it looks like you've got it all under control."

"Wow," Adam whispered, eyes wide at the sight of Drake's fatigues. "You brought the army."

"Something like that." Annie smiled, smoothing his hair.

"Anyone else here? Like maybe someone in charge?" Drake asked.

"Nope. Just Rivon." Nash shook his head.

"What's with the beeping?" Drake frowned, his gaze sweeping the room.

"I don't know," she said, "I didn't hear it before. Nash?"

"It's coming from over there. Could be Rivon or maybe the table." Drake moved toward the dining room table as Nash dropped down beside Rivon, and Annie shifted to shield Adam's view.

"Son of a bitch," Drake said from beneath the table.

"What? What is it?" Annie asked, her heart rate ratcheting upward again.

"A bomb."

"Looks like Rivon had the detonator," Nash said, holding up a small box with a pulsing green light. "He must have pressed it when you took him out. Or maybe he triggered it when he fell."

Drake pushed to his feet. "Either way, we've got to get out of here. Now."

Adrenaline surging, Annie jumped up, pulling Adam with her. "Come on, baby, we've got to go," she said, swinging him up into her arms, already beginning to run. But their combined weight was more than the old floor could bear. She felt it give even as the crack of splintering wood echoed through the house, her left leg driving straight downward, Adam tumbling from her arms.

Annie tried to push herself upward, the incessant beeping reminding her just how little time they had left, but her body refused to budge, her left leg jammed through the floor, dangling below her with nothing to push off of.

"Get Adam out of here," she yelled, still struggling for a foothold.

"Mommy," Adam shrieked as Drake scooped him into his arms and ran for the door.

"Hang on, Annie," Nash said as he slipped his hands underneath her arms. "I think this is going to hurt."

"Beats the hell out of being blown to bits," she said through gritted teeth as he yanked her upward, the splintered wood scraping at her skin.

"Just like old times," he said.

Without further conversation, he swung her up and over his shoulder, carrying her fireman style as he made for the front door, the syncopated beep accompanying them step for step. Slamming through the screened front door, they hit the porch and were about halfway down the stairs when the house blew.

"Move it, Brennon," she yelled as she watched the fireball shooting through the house, the heat preceding it making the paint on the porch blister.

Nash made it another fifteen feet or so before the surge of the blast caught up with them, throwing them both into a stand of rhododendron another ten feet from the house. Ash and debris rained down as he rolled to cover her body with his, the arching branches of the bush providing additional protection.

"Are we still alive?" she groaned after the worst of it had passed.

"I think so," he said, rolling off her. "But to tell you the truth, it's kind of hard to tell. How's the leg?"

"Not broken. But it hurts like hell." She pushed to a sitting position. "You?"

"Everything seems to be working."

"Can you see Adam or Drake?" She tried but couldn't keep the worry from her voice.

"Not from here." He shook his head. "But I know they're okay. Drake got them out well before the blast."

She nodded, knowing intellectually that he was right, but terrified nevertheless.

"Annie. Nash. Can you hear me?" Drake's voice filtered through the dense vegetation.

"We're here," they called in tandem.

"Is Adam all right?" Annie asked as Drake helped Nash to his feet.

"He's fine. I think he's more worried about you than anything else. That was some leap the two of you took."

"We had a little help," Nash said, reaching down to lift her up. "For the first time in my life I think I really understand the concept of the booster rocket."

"So where is he?" she asked, leaning against Nash for support.

"Don't worry. He's with Tyler and Emmett."

"Famous last words," Nash quipped as they slowly limped forward. "But I guess that means reinforcements arrived."

"Yeah. A little late if you ask me," Drake said, tipping his head toward the group huddled in front of a couple of SUVs. "If for no other reason than they missed all the fun."

"I can think of better ways to spend an afternoon,"

Annie said, searching the assembled group for signs of her son.

"Mom," Adam cried, breaking into a dead run at the sight of her.

"Careful," Nash said, catching his shoulders as he tried to throw himself at his mother. "You've got to be gentle. She's got some battle wounds."

"From flying," Adam said, his voice quavering. "I saw you both."

"Hey, it's okay," Annie said, reaching for her son. "I'm all right. And besides, you know I'd never turn down a hug from you."

Over her shoulder, she mouthed the words *thank you* as Adam nestled his head against her waist. There really weren't words to express her gratitude toward Nash— toward all of A-Tac. They'd given her back her son.

The nightmare was over.

She released Adam, the two of them turning to head for the cars at the end of the drive. But as she lifted her foot to move forward, an alarm sounded in her head, her body sensing what she could neither see nor hear.

"Get down," Nash yelled, already diving forward, his big body sending them crashing to the ground. Behind her, Annie heard the bullet splintering wood as it embedded itself in a tree directly behind where they'd been standing, the ricochet echoing through the suddenly quiet farmyard.

Drake and the others, instantly on alert, moved in the direction of the sniper, guns drawn. But the woods stayed silent.

"You okay?" Annie asked, searching her son's face for signs that he'd been injured.

"I think so." He nodded, his voice a whisper, his eyes as round as saucers. "Is the bad man out there?" He shot a look at the woods, his mouth trembling.

"It's all right," Nash said, his mouth tight with anger, as he searched the tree line for signs of danger. "No one is going to hurt you."

As if to mock his words, Rivon's phone vibrated against Annie's thigh. In all the excitement, she'd forgotten it was in her pocket. Careful not to alarm Adam, she pulled the cell free, flipping it open as her gaze met Nash's.

He nodded, and she forced herself to talk. "Gallagher."

"Consider that a warning," the disembodied voice said, the sound sending a shiver of dread racing down her spine. "I can get to you any place—any time. So enjoy this moment with your son because, I promise you, unless you complete your end of our bargain, it isn't going to last."

She opened her mouth to argue, to tell him exactly where he could put his threats, but her effort was wasted—the line had gone dead.

The cold wind howled as it moved through the wreckage of the farmhouse, the wailing monotone underscoring the fact that she'd been wrong. The nightmare wasn't over—it had only just begun.

CHAPTER **14**

"All right, people," Avery said, his voice carrying over the chatter in the room, "settle down."

Nash pulled up a chair, straddling it, as the rest of the team found seats in the war room. Avery had called everyone back to Sunderland for debriefing, dispatching a forensics team to secure the scene. Annie, much to her frustration, had been sent to medical along with Adam, with Lara assigned to check them both out and keep watch. Annie hadn't been thrilled at being left out of the briefing, but Avery hadn't been interested in her arguments.

In light of everything that had happened, Nash was conflicted about Avery's decision to keep Annie out of the loop. To some extent, at least, she deserved to be in on their findings. But that didn't negate the fact that she remained a wild card, and that the only thing stopping her from taking matters into her own hands was being sequestered here at Sunderland.

Avery was just doing his job.

"So someone want to tell me what went wrong out there?" Avery asked, his tone probing.

"A hell of a lot went right," Drake protested. "We rescued the kid."

"True." Avery nodded, his expression resolute. "But you and Nash almost got killed, and the farmhouse was blown to smithereens. Not to mention the sniper and the phone call. So humor me and let's start at the first sign of trouble. Why did we lose satellite communication?"

"It wasn't my system," Emmett said. "I ran every conceivable diagnostics program and everything checked out."

"You said the same thing about the communications failure in Southeast Asia," Nash reminded him.

"Yeah, well this is different. In Southeast Asia, the whole system went down. This time it was interference. And there's no way we were the source."

"I can vouch for that," Hannah said. "The interference was definitely external. Which means that either they tapped into our communications and jammed us, or there was some kind of satellite snafu."

"Any way to know for sure?" Avery asked.

"Not at this point." Emmett shook his head. "There are feedback reports filed on all our satellites, but the data isn't available in real time. Anyway, considering there was no way to verify the source, Hannah and Jason followed the proper protocol. They went dark at the first evidence of trouble."

"If the kidnappers were jamming us, it wasn't from the farmhouse," Nash said. "I didn't see any kind of satellite linkup. Did they find anything on the bodies?"

"A couple of short-range two-way radios and a cell phone," Emmett said. "I've got people pulling information off them now. But nothing that could account for the interference."

"Well, I'm not sure it's relevant now other than as part of the postmortem," Avery observed. "But I want all the systems double-checked again. Never hurts to be overly cautious."

Emmett nodded, making a notation in his BlackBerry.

"Which brings us to the weapons malfunction." Avery looked down at the paper he held in his hand. "Nash, you said that the firing mechanism jammed."

"Yeah, although it shouldn't have. I've turned it over to ballistics. They should be able to identify the source of the problem. But I can tell you one thing for certain, it wasn't me. I always make it a point to clean my guns after I use them. And I always check everything before going into a mission."

"Anyone else have an opportunity to handle it?"

"No one..." he trailed off, an ugly thought filling his head.

"What?"

"It's nothing," he said, regretting he'd said anything out loud. "Really. Just that the gun was in the bag with the other gear for the operation. And I gave it to Annie."

"But Annie had more reason than anyone to want us to succeed," Drake said. "Doesn't make sense that she'd try to sabotage things."

"And besides," Nash said, his brain still turning over the idea, "Annie saved our asses. Hell, guns jam all the time. It was probably just an accident."

"We'll wait to see what ballistics has to say." Avery

nodded. "And in the meantime, everybody be extra-careful about checking weapons. Tyler, where are we with the bomb?"

"Still a ways to go. But we'll know more once my team sifts through the rubble." She hit a button and the screen was filled with a shot of the explosion, the scattered debris underscoring the reality of how close they'd come to getting blown to bits. "We know that the epicenter of the explosion was the dining room."

"Which is perfect placement for taking out the whole house," Drake said.

"And everything else in the vicinity." Tyler switched to a second photograph. "This is the device Nash found on Rivon. It's definitely the trigger. A remote one at that. Which seems to support the supposition that Rivon triggered it by accident. Or maybe after Annie shot him. He'd have known it was over. And taking out the compound is a hell of an endgame."

"I'd agree with that," Hannah mused, studying the photograph. "Rivon doesn't really strike me as the type to sacrifice himself unless there were no alternatives."

"Well, it definitely fits the MO of a religious zealot," Drake said, "but I agree, not Rivon. He was definitely more about self-preservation than self-sacrifice."

"I don't think the idea was to blow himself up." Avery frowned. "I think it was more about destroying evidence once the operation had played through."

"You don't think they were planning to release Adam." Jason leaned back in his chair, his expression grim.

"Doesn't follow with the facts." Avery shook his head. "There appeared to be no attempt to hide their identities. And if he'd seen them all, then he could identify them."

"Which means they had to take him out." Drake's eyes narrowed as he considered the idea. "My guess is that after Annie took out Dominico—"

"Assuming she'd have actually gone through with it," Nash interrupted, anger flashing.

"Don't kid yourself, Nash. I've seen her in action. If she thought her kid's life depended on it—she'd have done it." Drake shrugged, apologetically. "Anyway, the point is, I think they were planning to take out Annie, the kid, and any evidence, all in one fell swoop."

"We just got in the way. And then when Annie shot him, Rivon triggered the bomb."

"But what was he doing with it in the first place? I mean, where was the guy in charge?" Emmett asked. "The one who called Annie?"

"Maybe he was on his way. Or maybe there was going to be some kind of remote contact," Hannah said. "There's really no way to know for sure."

"So what else do we have?" Avery asked, bringing everyone's attention back to Tyler.

"As I said, there isn't much. It's still early. But on first pass, I did find three frags from the bomb. I'll need to run tests to make definitive conclusions, but there are a few things I can be fairly certain of, one being that the bomb wasn't of Arabic design. Particularly not something I'd have expected from Ashad. They're fond of duct tape and homemade pipe bombs. This was far more sophisticated."

"But you said you only had fragments," Hannah said. "How can you tell so much from so little?"

Tyler smiled, clearly in her element. "It's amazing how much you can discern if you know what you're looking for. One of the pieces we found was the corner of a circuit board. Probably part of the electrical detonator on the bomb itself. It's far more advanced than the kind of thing Ashad usually uses. Plus at least two of the components were American made."

"So maybe they used locals," Avery said.

"Anything's possible." She shrugged. "But if I had to call it, I'd say Ashad wasn't behind the bomb."

"What about the prisoner?" Avery asked. "He said anything?"

"I interrogated him," Drake said. "But he isn't exactly a font of information."

"Maybe we need to turn things up a notch," Emmett suggested.

"Not the problem." Drake shook his head. "He's just not part of the inner circle. Says Rivon hired them to watch over the kid. Didn't know about the kidnapping or that there was a bomb. Scared the shit out of him when the thing blew. Anyway, his name is Eduardo Montez. Basically just a thug for hire. He's worked for Rivon before."

"Fingerprints verify his ID," Hannah confirmed. "He's got jacket as long as my arm. Armed robbery, assault, and trafficking stolen goods. But nothing political."

"What about the dead men?"

"Same thing. Lowlifes with a record for penny-ante stuff. Nothing that would flag them as working with terrorists. And certainly nothing international."

"Hired guns?" Jason queried.

"Maybe." Hannah shrugged. "But if I were smart enough to get to Annie to take out a key government official, it seems to me that I'd be able to pull in higher-level people for the operation. Mercenaries at the very least. Like Drake said, these guys were just thugs."

"So how is that different from most terrorists?" Emmett asked.

"It's not. I mean, you're right, most terrorists are thugs," Hannah admitted. "But usually there are commonalities. Ideology if nothing else. And at least with the dead guys we've got nothing connecting them to each other. They're from different parts of the country. They've all got varied backgrounds. And none of them has ever done anything that could remotely be considered extremist behavior."

"I'm assuming they're all Americans?" Avery asked.

"Yes." Hannah nodded. "As I said, with long records. But nothing that makes me think there's a link to Ashad. Or to Rivon, for that matter."

"And we've got nothing on the shooter?"

"No." Tyler shook her head. "Of course we'll go over it again. But whoever it was, they knew what they were doing. We worked off trajectory and covered the immediate area where the sniper would have been but there was nothing."

"How the hell did he get past you, anyway?" Avery's expression was thunderous.

"There wasn't time to cordon off the area. The explosion happened just as we got there, and our attention was on making sure that Nash and Drake came out of it alive. Not to mention Annie and her son."

"We've got people canvassing the area now. Maybe someone nearby saw something," Emmett said. "The area's pretty deserted, but there's a trailer park about a half mile away. And another farmhouse about a mile to the east."

"So what about the kidnapper's threat?" Avery said. "Anything there that might give us a clue to who this guy is?"

"Nada," Jason said, shaking his head. "Annie gave me the transcript. Which you all have a copy of. There was no time to do a trace, and nothing in his words to give us anything to go on except that he obviously still expects Annie to do something. His exact words were 'complete your end of our bargain.'"

"Which could be kill Dominico."

"Or maybe there's something more," Avery said. "Something Annie hasn't told us."

"Well, one thing is for certain, he wants her to stay scared," Nash mused. He'd seen how freaked she'd been. Hell, he couldn't say that he blamed her. Not when the guy had just taken a potshot at her kid.

"So what about Dominico?" Jason asked. "Do we consider the threat to him ongoing?"

"I don't think we can ignore it," Avery said. "But clearly as long as Annie is with us, she's not going to be taking out Dominico."

"She's got her son back." Nash frowned. "So she's got no reason to take him out at all."

"Agreed. Which makes this whole thing feel off. I mean, obviously the kidnapper knows that we're involved. He had a witness on site. Which means he also knows that Annie's got protection. Speaking of which, I've upped security on campus just to be on the safe side."

"What about if she's shipped off to Washington?" The jury was still out as to whether Annie would be charged with anything. Tom, working as usual off his own agenda, was still advocating her being prosecuted.

He'd flown to D.C. to make his case with his bosses and with the higher-ups at Langley. But nothing had been decided.

"Then it'll be Langley's headache. However, for now, we're the babysitters."

"And Dominico?"

"I've contacted his security and they've convinced him to hole up for the next week or so. He has a country house about an hour from here. Emmett, I want you to head that way and make sure everything is locked down. Just to be on the safe side."

"Will do." Emmett nodded.

"In the meantime," Avery said, "I've got a call in to Langley. I still think Annie and Adam should fall under the CIA's jurisdiction. She's ex-CIA and she saved your asses. If nothing else that makes it worth arguing her case."

"I can't disagree with your logic," Hannah said. "But we've also got to tread carefully. I mean, we don't really know anything about her." She waved Nash silent. "I know that she was your partner. And that she saved you and Drake. But she also left you to die in Lebanon. And we don't know anything about what happened to her between now and then. And for all we know there's something more playing out here. Something beyond her son and Dominico. I'm just saying we should be cautious."

"Hannah's right," Drake said, his somber gaze moving to Nash. "There's nothing more dangerous than letting emotions rule the day."

"There's nothing left between Annie and me." It wasn't completely true, but Nash was smart enough to recognize the wisdom in Drake's words. "So what do you want to do about Adam?" he asked, in a transparent effort to change the subject.

"I'm not sure what you mean," Avery said.

"I'm just wondering if maybe he knows more than he realizes? Something that might help us figure out who's behind all of this."

"Anything's possible," Jason began, "but hell, he's just a kid. If we have to depend on his coming up with viable information I'd say we're screwed."

"Still," Avery said, "Nash is right. It's worth talking to him."

"I can do it," Nash volunteered, the words coming out before he had the chance to stop them. He didn't exactly have a lot of experience with kids. And talking with Adam meant talking to Annie. Which was probably the exact opposite of what he ought to be doing.

"I think it's worth a try," Avery said, clearly unaware of Nash's inner turmoil. "And in the meantime, we all need to try to put the pieces together. Figure out who the real culprit is. Somebody set this thing in motion. And I think we're all agreed that it wasn't Ashad."

"I concur with that." Jason nodded. "None of this follows their pattern. Usually, if they want someone taken out, they just do it. Damn the consequences. This had a much more orchestrated feel."

"Nine-eleven was highly orchestrated," Hannah said.

"And highly public." Nash frowned. "When these kinds of organizations take action, they want credit. So why go to a middleman?"

"Access in the United States?" Jason suggested. "With tighter regulations surrounding getting in and out of the country it's a hell of a lot harder to just walk in and blow someone away."

"I think the real question," Drake said, "is why go to all the effort to pin the plot on someone else?"

"To keep it from being linked to the real puppet master," Jason mused. "But that changes the motivation. Passing a murder off on someone else, even a high-profile one, indicates a very clear head, and someone who doesn't want to get caught."

"So our mystery man wants Dominico dead, but decides to let Ashad take the fall," Hannah said. "Hence the planted intel."

"It wouldn't be the first time," Drake observed.

"Except that I'm usually pretty good at sorting through the chaff." Hannah shook her head, her frustration evident. "So if this was planted it had to be done by someone who knows what they're doing."

"So basically, we're saying that the intel about Annie and Ashad was a cover. But for what?" Jason frowned.

"For *whom* is actually the better question," Drake said.

"Which," Nash said, trying to sort through his thoughts, "puts us right back at square one."

"So what?" Jason asked, putting words to everyone's frustration.

CHAPTER **15**

How are you doing?" Nash asked as he strode into the suite that served as A-Tac's medical facility.

"How do you think I'm doing?" Annie spat back, gingerly edging off the table where Lara had just finished stitching her up. "Some crazy guy is threatening my son and taking potshots at us. And I'm stuck here in hospital hell." She waved at the room, its stark features and antiseptic smell underscoring her words.

"I meant your leg," he said with a frown, his expression not giving anything away.

"It's fine." She winced as she tried a step or two. "Or at least it will be. Couple of stitches and some abrasions. No permanent damage. Nothing to stop me from running the bastard to ground who did this to us."

"I think maybe, for the time being," he said, his scowl deepening as he helped her over to a chair, "you need to leave the heavy lifting to us."

"Nash, it's my son in jeopardy. I'm not going to just sit on the sidelines and hope it all turns out okay."

"You may not have a choice," he said, crossing his arms over his chest and leaning back against the table. "How's Adam?"

"He's asleep in the next room. Lara says it's the best thing for him. I just wish I could wipe the fear out of his eyes. He's too young to have seen the things he's seen."

"But he's safe now. And children are resilient."

"Lara said that, too, but he saw his mother kill a man," Annie said. "That's not something you can just white-wash away."

"You saved his life. That's the way he's going to look at it. I'm not going to pretend that there aren't going to be repercussions. But the main thing is that you rescued him. He's safe now."

"The hell he is. The man who did this is still out there. Waiting for the opportunity to strike again," she said, fists clenched. "To hurt me—to hurt Adam. The question is who?" She sucked in a breath and released it, the soothing motion allowing her to think. "It's got to be someone from my past. At the very least someone who knew I had the skills to take out a target."

"What if it's something more personal?" Nash asked, his face thoughtful as he considered the idea. "Someone who has a grudge or wants revenge."

"There's a long list, but no one in particular comes to mind. I mean, I'm sure there are people out there with long memories, but I've been out of the game a long time now."

"So maybe someone found you," he said. "Is there anything you haven't told me?"

"Like what?" She frowned, angry that he still didn't trust her.

"Well, according to your transcript of the phone call the kidnapper said something about completing your end of the bargain."

"I just assumed that meant Dominico."

"Except that you're under our protection and you've got your son. Both of which would seem to negate any possibility you'd off the ambassador."

"I wasn't going to kill him," she said. "At least not if it could be avoided."

"Your intent is irrelevant. The point here is that the kidnapper lost his leverage when we rescued Adam. And even with his continued proximity at the farmhouse, it doesn't make sense that he'd think you could be lured into assassinating a public official without his holding something over your head."

"And so you think he's talking about something else. Something I'm not sharing with you and your friends." She choked out a bitter laugh, pushing up off the chair to move farther away from him. "Why is it you always think the worst of me? First, that I'd kill Dominico simply for monetary gain. And then that I'm in league somehow with Adam's kidnapper." Tears pricked the back of her eyes, and she wiped them angrily away. "Are you insane?"

"I'm just covering all the bases," he said, his placating tone ratcheting up her anger. "You know how this works."

"I don't know anything," she bit out, "except that you continue to doubt me. For God's sake, Nash, we were partners once. Lovers. We shared everything. Surely that has to mean something?"

"Of course it does." His jaw tightened, his eyes dark. "But that was a lifetime ago, Annie. People change. Life goes on. You found someone else. Made a new life for yourself."

"And you?" she asked, her gaze colliding with his.

"I got exactly what I wanted. I'm happy here. I've got friends, but no entanglements. The one thing I learned from my mistakes was that working black ops isn't conducive to that kind of happily ever after."

"And you're good with that?" She sucked in a breath, still fighting tears, her heart breaking all over again.

"I am. I told you as much in Vienna. The night I told you I was transferring to A-Tac."

"The night you left me." She remembered that night. Remembered the anger. The betrayal. There'd been so much she wanted to tell him. But she'd never gotten the chance. Instead, he'd blindsided her.

"I didn't leave you," he said, his eyes narrowed in anger. "That one's totally on you, baby."

"You told me I had no right to be upset. That what we had wasn't real. That it was only a by-product of living in constant danger."

"I was angry. But you know there was truth in what I said."

"I don't know anything except that you decided unilaterally that you were leaving."

"It was my choice to make. My life. And it was a hell of an opportunity. A-Tac is the best of the best. And I'd have been a fool to turn them down."

"So I was just collateral damage?"

"I don't know," he ground out. "You didn't give me the chance to figure it out."

"That's the point. It wasn't for *you* to figure out. It was something we should have done together. Only you forgot there was an us."

"Or maybe it was just never meant to be," he said, the muscle in his jaw working overtime now. "Truth is, I'm not that kind of guy. I thought you understood that."

"Well, if I didn't, I certainly do now."

"Look"—he raised a hand, stepping back—"this isn't getting us anywhere. It's ancient history. We need to let it go."

"It's not that easy." She turned away, trying to push back the pain, old wounds seeming new again.

"I know," he said, his voice gentle as his hands settled on her shoulders.

"What happened?" she whispered as she turned to face him, her eyes searching his. "What happened to us?"

"I don't know." He reached out to cup her face, the feel of her skin against his palm waking sensory memory, hunger and need blending together with the familiar urgency of raw desire. It had always been like this between them. Chemistry overriding everything else. Right or wrong, it was undeniable. And impossible to resist.

He leaned forward, tracing the line of her bottom lip with a finger.

"Mommy?"

Annie jumped back, her heart stutter-stepping as she turned to her son. "Hi, baby, are you okay?"

He nodded, his little head tousled, his eyes still heavy with sleep. "I was afraid the bad guys might come back."

"No one's going to hurt you, sweetie. Momma's here." She pulled him close, his heart beating next to hers.

"Hey, buddy," Nash said, coming over to squat beside

them. "There's no need to be afraid. You've got all kinds of people watching over you."

"Even the army guy?" Adam pulled out of her arms, curiosity overcoming shyness.

"Yeah." Nash smiled. "Even him. So there's nothing for you to worry about. Okay?"

He nodded, his expression serious again. "And my mom? Are you going to watch out for her, too?"

"I'm not sure your mother needs anyone to watch out for her," he said, his eyes meeting Annie's. "I mean, after all, she's got you."

Annie's heart swelled as she watched Adam lift his shoulders and nod solemnly.

"I've got another favor to ask," Nash said. "I'd like to talk to you a little about what happened. At the farmhouse. That is if it's okay with your mom."

They both looked up at her, their expressions almost exactly alike. She nodded, fighting against her rioting emotions, centering her attention on her son. "If it's okay with you, it's okay with me."

Nash stood up and Adam walked over to sit on the chair, his feet dangling, his legs swinging a good six inches off the floor.

"So can you tell me about what happened? The night the bad men took you away?"

Adam shot Annie a nervous look, and she smiled and nodded as she leaned back against the examination table. "Well, at first I thought it was a dream," he said, chewing the side of his lip. "A really bad one. There were men and they were wearing snow boots—inside. And one of them smelled funny." He wrinkled his nose. "Like the food you ate at that restaurant in Alamosa."

"The Thai place?" Annie prompted.

"Yeah." If possible his nose scrunched even more. "Like that."

"It was a fish curry," Annie explained.

"That sounds pretty awful." Nash nodded. "I don't like fish much either."

"I like fish," Adam said. "Just not that stuff."

"So how many of them were there?" Nash asked, moving them back on topic. "In your room, I mean."

"Two. They carried me out the window. I remember it was really cold."

Annie's stomach clenched as she thought about how terrified he must have been. "It's okay, sweetie, it's all over now."

"Did you try to call for your mom?" Nash asked.

"I couldn't." He shook his head. "They used tape. The shiny kind."

"Duct tape. I bet that hurt." Nash nodded sympathetically. "So what happened next?"

"They put me in the backseat of a car. I was really scared." He swallowed, remembering.

"But you were brave, too, I bet," Nash said.

"Like my dad." He smiled, memories forgotten. "Mommy said he was a hero. He saved lots of people and kept our country safe. But then he got killed fighting bad guys."

"Your mom told me a little about him." Nash glanced her way, but Annie made a play of studying her hands. "Did you know him?"

"Nope." Adam shook his head, his feet still swinging. "He died when I was just a baby. I've never even seen a picture of him."

"But I bet you have something of his."

"Yeah, I got his watch." Adam grinned, then frowned. "But it's back home in Creede. Momma, when are we going to go home?"

"I don't know, baby," Annie said, her throat tightening. "There are still some things I've got to work out. So for the time being we're going to stay here. Okay?"

Adam nodded, his lower lip trembling.

"So tell me about the watch," Nash said, pulling Adam's thoughts back to the positive. Annie could have kissed him.

Adam's eyes brightened. "I keep it by my bed. It's supercool. It tells time in three different places at once."

"I had one like that, too." Nash frowned at the memory.

"You all right?" Adam asked as Annie tried to read Nash's expression. She'd given him the watch. A birthday present. "Your face looks funny."

"I'm fine." He smiled, with a shake of his head. "Just remembering something."

"Something bad?" Adam cocked his head to one side, his little face scrunched up in sympathy. "Mom says you can't let them get the best of you. Bad memories, I mean."

"She said that?" He lifted his head, this time their gazes connecting. Annie swallowed and shrugged.

"Yeah." He nodded, solemnly. "She has real bad night—"

"I don't think Nash cares about my dreams, sweetie."

"So what happened next?" Nash asked, his mouth tightening as he turned his attention back to Adam. "After they put you in the car?"

"They drove away. I couldn't see much cuz I was on the floor. And then they put me on a plane. A real fancy one with really big seats. The two men were there, too. We flew a really long time," he said, looking down at his hands, still chewing on his lip, "and I fell asleep."

"That's okay, sweetheart," Annie said, her stomach still churning as she considered all that he'd been through. "It was probably the best thing you could have done."

"Your mom's right. Better to save your strength. That's exactly what I'd have done."

Adam's mouth curled into a weak smile.

"So then what?"

"We landed. But it wasn't like any airport I'd ever seen. The landing place was dirt. And there weren't any buildings."

"And then they took you to the farmhouse?"

"Yeah." He nodded, frowning as he tried to remember the details. "I was in the back of the car again. But this time they let me sit up."

Annie clenched her fists, her gaze meeting Nash's. There'd been no need for secrecy. They'd never meant for Adam to walk away.

"And it was the same two guys?"

"No. Different ones. They didn't talk much. And then when I got there, two new guys were waiting. One of 'em was the guy Mom shot."

"You know she had to shoot him, right?"

Adam nodded. "Or he'd have taken me away again."

"So who was the other guy?"

"The man with the Wii."

"I beg your pardon?" Nash frowned, his confusion obvious.

"It's a gaming system. Supercool," he explained, looking exasperated.

Annie bit back a smile. "It's the latest thing."

"I see. And this man, was he there when we came to get you?"

Adam shook his head. "No. He'd already gone. I only saw him twice. Once when I first got there. I was really scared, but he was kind of nice."

"And the other time you saw him?"

"He brought a camera. You know, the digital kind that makes movies. He fixed it so I could talk to my mom. He even talked to her on the phone. Then he gave the other men some orders and said if I was really good and did what he said, he'd take me home. But he left. And he didn't come back." Tears welled up in his eyes.

Annie pushed off the table, intent on comforting her son, but Nash was faster, reaching out for his hand. "But then we came, right? Your mom and me. And everything was okay."

Adam nodded. "You even made the house blow up."

"Well, actually that wasn't us, sweetie," Annie said.

"But it was pretty exciting, wasn't it?" Nash asked as Annie shot him an incredulous frown, and Adam grinned. "So you think you can tell me what this guy looked like?"

Adam screwed up his face as he thought about the question. "He had dark hair," he said. "As dark as yours, only it was smooth. And there was a streak of gray."

Nash nodded. "Was he tall like me?"

"Nope. But not short either. And his face was kinda pinched up, like he was mad all the time. You know, with a tight mouth and squinty eyes."

"If I can round up some pictures, do you think you

could look at them for me?" Nash asked. "Maybe you'll recognize someone."

"You think you can do that?" Annie asked, reaching out to smooth his hair, needing to feel his skin, to assure herself that for the moment at least, he was all right.

"Sure," Adam said, shaking off her touch, Nash hiding his smile behind his hand. "And I could maybe draw a picture of him, too. They always do that on TV."

"Hey," Lara said, appearing in the doorway, "look who's up! How are you feeling?"

"Hungry," Adam said.

"I think I can do something about that. I know where Jason keeps his cookies. And I'll bet he wouldn't mind if you had some. If that's okay with your mom?"

Annie nodded, her throat tightening at Lara's kindness. "Go on," she said. "Go with Lara. I'll be right here when you finish."

"Thanks for your help," Nash said as Adam followed Lara out the door. "He's a good kid."

"I know. I'm pretty proud of him," she said, moving back to stand by the table. "You don't really think a drawing is going to help, do you?"

"Not unless Adam's an art prodigy." He shook his head.

"Unfortunately not." She smiled, surprised at how at ease she felt. "He's not much past finger paints and crayons. You were really good with him."

"He made it easy." Nash shrugged.

"You haven't said anything about Tom," she said, pulling up to sit on the examination table, her leg throbbing.

"Now there's a non sequitur." He frowned, dropping down into the chair.

"Not really. I mean, if he has his way I'll be shipped off to Washington to face charges, and Adam..." She swallowed a sob, the thought of losing her son more than she could bear.

"That's not going to happen, Annie."

"You don't know that. You know as well as I do that Tom can be pretty determined about things once he's made up his mind. So is he here?"

"No." He shook his head, his expression guarded. "He's in D.C."

"Doing what? Trying to convince the powers that be to transfer authority for my case to Homeland Security?"

"Avery's not going to let that happen. He's got a call in to Langley. The situation is far from cut-and-dried. And if nothing else, there's the fact that you're ex-CIA."

"*Ex* being the operative word," she sighed. "Who'd have thought we'd have wound up on different sides of the fence?"

"It's not as bad as all that," he said, his words meant to be comforting, but Annie knew he didn't believe them any more than she did. Whatever they'd shared was gone. Or maybe Nash was right and it had never existed at all.

One thing was for certain, though. It'd be a hell of a lot easier if she could just accept the fact that it was over and move on. But the heart was a stubborn thing. And love, it seemed, had no statute of limitations.

CHAPTER 16

Annie closed the bedroom door. It had taken three stories, and a lot of reassurance, but Adam had finally fallen asleep. She walked down the hall, stopping at the top of the stairs, glancing out the window at the perfectly manicured neighborhood. A block and a half off campus, the cul-de-sac felt more like a back lot than reality, especially when one considered that the occupants of the half circle of houses were all members of A-Tac.

Dubbed "Professor Cove" by students, the mixture of Cape Cods, Colonials, and Saltboxes recalled an earlier time. A more gentle America. The irony was not lost on Annie. She'd dreamed of living in a neighborhood like this, of having a shot at normalcy.

But this was only a facade. Play pretend. CIA meets Ozzie and Harriet.

She and Adam had a real life. In Colorado. And if she was lucky, they'd find their way back or at least have a shot at building something new. But in the meantime, she was stuck here. Avery hadn't left her with a choice. He'd managed to keep Tom and Homeland Security at bay for at least a little while longer, but that didn't mean she was totally off the hook, just a stay of execution. And for the duration, she and Adam had been assigned quarters in Nash's house, which meant she had to play nice.

Easier said than done.

Sucking in a breath, she headed down the stairs and into the kitchen. Lightning flashed on the horizon, the wind whistling through the open French doors. The air was heavy with the smell of roses, and Annie frowned at the sensory memory, her mind jumping to the black lacquer box nestled in her gear upstairs.

She'd grabbed three things when she'd left Colorado: Adam's favorite stuffed bear, her Beretta, and the puzzle box. An odd trio, yet somehow indicative of her life. She shook her head, dismissing her troubled thoughts.

"Is Adam asleep?" Nash asked, appearing in the doorway, his dark gaze shuttered.

"Yes. But I'm not sure for how long. This has all been really hard on him." She frowned, wishing for the millionth time that she could have somehow prevented the kidnapping.

"You couldn't have known," Nash said, reading her thoughts.

"Maybe not. But that doesn't change the fact that my son has been through hell—because of me."

"And some bastard with an ax to grind." Nash held out a glass, the wine glowing crimson in the soft half light. "I thought maybe you could use a drink. I know I could."

She took the glass with a nod, settling into an Adirondack chair facing the garden. Lightning flashed like a strobe, momentarily filling the small garden with color, green grass against the red and white of a rose-covered gazebo. The pink of a lily contrasted against the dark green leaves of a rhododendron.

"I don't suppose you've heard anything new?" she asked, closing her eyes as she sipped her wine.

"Nothing of substance. Drake is still working on the prisoner. And Hannah's trying to sort through intel. But basically we're just waiting."

"I've never been any good at that."

"Like hell." His smile was fierce, and her heart quickened. "You've made an art form out of stillness. Hunting—waiting."

"That was before." She shook her head. "But not anymore. Not when my son's life is hanging in the balance."

"He's safe here."

"Is he?" She turned to look at Nash, her gaze probing. "I thought he was safe in Creede, too. And I was wrong."

"Avery's doubled security. That has to count for something."

"Yes, but Avery is also charged with finding the person behind this. And if that means using me or my son..." she trailed off, dropping her gaze to the glass in her hands.

"Every effort will be made to keep Adam safe."

"I know how the game is played, Nash. And besides, this guy has already gotten to us twice. Once in your protection. I'm not sure that anywhere is truly safe."

"You know, sometimes you just have to have a little faith."

"In what?" Annie's laugh was bitter. "The CIA? The

system? I've seen firsthand how that works. As long as you play the game, they're on your side, but the minute things go wrong—they turn their backs and you're on your own. I've been there, Nash. More than once." She stood up and walked to the edge of the patio, the storm clouds billowing dark and threatening as the wind whipped through the garden.

"Annie…" He came to stand behind her, his breath stirring the back of her hair.

"No." She shook her head, resisting the urge to lean back into his strength. "You're talking bullshit. Faith is just a foolish person's way of staving off the dark."

Behind her, his phone rang, and she turned as he pulled it from his pocket and flipped it open.

"Brennon." There was a moment's silence as he listened to the person on the other end of the line. "I'm sorry, Annie," he said, his expression shuttering. "I've got to take this."

Just as well, she thought as he walked into the kitchen, closing the door behind him. They'd been treading on dangerous ground. She released a breath, turning back to the garden. It stretched the length of the backyard, separated from the woods beyond the back of the house by a wooden fence. Beyond the roses and peonies she could see pine trees and sumac whipping in the wind. White oaks, leaves trembling with the onslaught of the coming rain, standing sentry as the sky filled with nature's fury.

For as long as she could remember, Annie had loved storms. Once when she was little, she'd snuck out in the middle of the night, thunder thrumming in the air, the dark clouds silhouetted with crooked streaks of lightning. The wind had whipped through her hair, and she'd felt supercharged, as if she were capable of flying high into the clouds.

She'd have stayed until the maelstrom descended, but then her mother, realizing she was missing, had pulled her back into the house. At the time she'd been angry, certain her mother lived to ruin her life. But now, as a mother herself, Annie realized the danger she'd been in, and that her mother's anger had been the result of fear for her child.

She smiled, remembering her mother. If she closed her eyes, she could still smell her perfume—*L'air du temps*.

Or maybe it was just the roses.

Her mother had been the one bright spot in her life. Laughing, loving. Always there for her. Until the cancer took her away, emaciating her body, eroding her mind. And then Annie's father had shown up, taking everything but his daughter, his rejection still haunting her after all this time.

"I'm sorry," he'd said, his voice cold and distant, *"but there's no room in my life for a kid. I told your mother that over and over again. And now that she's gone—well, you'll just have to find your own way, won't you? Men like me aren't made for family and kids. Your momma never understood that."*

He'd turned then and walked away, leaving her sitting on the porch of an empty house, never once looking back. In the space of a heartbeat, Annie had been forced to face the fact that she was truly on her own. She'd been nine years old, and her first great life lesson had been driven home. Count on no one but yourself. Ever.

The sky splintered with light, the air crackling with

electricity. Walking out into the garden, she lifted her chin, letting the storm carry her away from pain and rejection of the past, from the nightmare that threatened her present.

The thunder echoed through the garden, the roses shimmering in the wind. She raised her head to the sky, the cold breeze washing across her face. She couldn't change the past, but she could protect her child.

The wind whipped through her hair, the first drops of rain falling like a fine mist against her skin. She breathed deeply, the cool air filling her lungs, filling her soul. Clearing her head. There was no going back. No matter how many times she considered the possibility, the answer was always the same.

The risk was too great. She could never allow Adam to be hurt the way she had been. It was her job to protect him. And that's exactly what she'd continue to do. Nothing had changed. Nash had made that more than clear. Still, her heart was having trouble accepting the fact. There were so many wonderful memories. But none of them negated the fact that he'd made his feelings clear—no relationships. Like her father, he wasn't that kind of man.

Annie shivered as the wind wailed through the fence boards. Staying here, close to Nash, was a mistake. She needed to go. To walk away. To take Adam and simply disappear again. To hell with the danger. She'd manage. She always did. All she had to do was pack her things and walk out the door.

But instead, here she sat, in Nash's rose garden, watching the lightning slice through the sky. Maybe she was a coward. Or maybe she just didn't want to say good-bye—*again.*

"Annie?" His voice reached out through the darkness, caressing her. "I see you still like storms."

"You were right," she said, still struggling to keep her demons at bay. "Some things never change."

"Are you okay?" His brow knotted in a way she remembered so well. She'd known every nuance in those days. Every quirk of the eyebrow and tilt of the lips.

"No," she whispered, shaking her head. "No, I'm not." She hated the idea of admitting weakness. But somehow, here in the face of the storm, she couldn't find the strength to lie.

"Oh, Annie," he said, coming to sit beside her, the soft lilt of his voice almost as good as a kiss. "I wish I had the power to make it all go away."

"You know," she sighed, "there was a time when I actually believed that you could, but I was a fool. And you'd think that by now I'd have gotten over it—*over you*."

"Some connections are hard to sever."

"And harder to forget." Lightning flashed as the thunder rolled, the rain so close it teased them.

He lifted a hand, his fingers cupping her face. "You look just the same."

"You're blind." She laughed, the feel of his palm against her skin bordering on heaven.

Time stretched between them, the past and the present blending together until she couldn't tell the difference anymore. The only thing that existed was the two of them and the storm.

The wind lashed through the garden, the trees and bushes bending in protest, but Annie only lifted her face.

With a groan, Nash took possession of her lips, and

she sighed, the taste of him more heady than the finest of wines. She'd forgotten how much she loved the feel of his body against hers. How much she reveled in the strength of his fingers twining in her hair.

She opened her mouth, their tongues dueling, the choreography so familiar she ached with the contact. He deepened the kiss, and she accepted him. Familiar and yet foreign.

"Annie," he whispered, and she pressed against him, desperately needing to feel him hard against her.

His lips stroked hers, feeding the fire burning deep inside her. Some part of her, the part that still made sense, called for her to stop. But God help her, she didn't want to. There would be time for regret. But not now. Not here.

Lightning split the sky, the crescendoing thunder chasing behind it. The fury of the storm fed their fire. His hands cupped her breasts as he kissed her, his thumbs circling, desire mixing with pleasure until she could hardly breathe.

"Annie," he whispered again. "Are you sure?"

"Yes," she answered, her voice hoarse with desire. "I've missed you so damn much." It was far more than she'd ever meant to admit. But in this moment, with him touching her, there was no turning back. He reached to pull her into his arms, to take her inside, but she shook her head. "I want it here. Now. In the rain."

"What about your leg?" He frowned. "You're hurt."

"I told you before, I'm fine." She tipped her head back, the wind lashing through her hair. "Better than fine, actually."

His teeth were white against the night as he laughed. "In the storm, then."

And, as if cued, the rain fell, lashing against them with a violence only nature could emanate.

He smiled and pulled her close, his lips making hot tracks against her neck. She pushed against him, wanting to feel closer—to feel a part of him, if only for a moment.

His mouth moved lower, tracing the line between her neck and breast. She arched upward, needing more, and he obliged, sucking her nipple, the resulting heat almost her undoing.

There was something to be said for solitude, but for the life of her, with Nash touching her in the exact way that he was, she'd forgotten why. She arched back, offering herself, and he slid his hand beneath the soft cotton of her sweatpants, his fingers hot as they moved against her skin. While gently biting her nipple, he slid a finger inside her, the friction setting off shivers of pleasure. She fought for breath, even as she pressed closer.

Wanting more. *Wanting him.*

It had been so long.

He lifted his head, his smile rakish as his fingers began to move faster and faster until she thought she'd die of sheer joy.

"Tell me what you want," he said as he bent, his kisses blending with the rain as he stroked her neck with his tongue. His finger moving in and out. Each succeeding stroke—deeper. Stronger.

"Tell me, Annie."

"You," she whispered, her voice snatched away by the wind. "I want you, Nash. Only you."

The thunder drowned out her moans as the rain and his mouth and his fingers played her like a finely tuned instrument, pulling the string tighter and tighter, higher and higher, until she felt herself falling, pleasure careening through her in shuddering waves.

"Please," she rasped. "Please. I want more. I want you inside me."

Again the thunder rocked through the garden, the sound taking on almost physical proportions. With a crooked smile, Nash lifted her into his arms, cradling her close, kissing her forehead, her cheeks—her lips. His touch infinitely gentle, as if she were his most precious possession. As she shuddered against him, he caressed her, pressing her close with murmured words, nonsensical nothings that held more meaning than any sonnet could ever possess.

Then, eyes burning with passion, he carried her to the gazebo, laying her on a cushioned chaise as the rain fell like a silvery curtain all around them, the cool air scented with roses and geraniums.

She sat up, straddling the lounger, and smiled up at him, running her hands along the curve of her breasts, letting her fingers trail across the swollen flesh at the juncture of her thighs. And then she reached for the hem of her T-shirt, sliding it slowly upward, undulating to the rhythm of the rain. With a slow smile, she pulled it over her head, her hair swinging free as she tossed the shirt aside.

His intake of breath was audible as he watched her hungrily. And she rose to her feet, pushing her sweats over her hips, twisting so that they fell to her feet. Then, after stepping out of them, she waited as he closed the distance between them and reached out to skim his palms along the bare skin of her breasts, his teasing touch promising so much more.

With a strangled gasp, she reached for his shirt, popping buttons in her haste to free him from his clothes and feel his skin next to hers. He shrugged out of his shirt, and with fumbling hands, she helped him remove his pants. And finally—finally, there was nothing between them but the moist night air.

They moved together almost as one, the fierce longing in her heart reflected in his eyes. His mouth possessed hers as she closed her fingers around the hard heat of his penis, the velvety skin moving with her hand. Up and down. Up and down. Desire pierced through her, her own need building again, the fire inside her licking at her as she fought to contain it. To keep her focus on pleasuring *him*.

Pulling him closer, she traced the line of his teeth with her tongue, then thrust it deep inside his mouth, the motion a prelude—a mirror image of things to come. Then, with a wicked grin, she pushed him back onto the chaise, kneeling beside him as he rolled toward her, offering himself.

Lightning split through the sky, illuminating the rugged planes of his body, and she reached out to trace the jagged line of a scar. So many memories. With a soft sigh, she took him in her mouth, tongue circling, the salty smell and taste of him intimately familiar. Circling the base of his erection with her hand, she moved her fingers in time with her mouth in syncopated rhythm. Moving slowly at first and then faster and faster, feeling him harden beneath her touch, his pulse blending with hers as she sucked him.

Then suddenly she felt him tense, his hands tightening

on her shoulders as he pushed her back, lifting her to her feet.

"I want to be inside you," he growled, his eyes dark with passion.

"Patience," she said, enjoying her moment of power. Turning her back, she straddled him, taking him in one downward thrust, the feel of his throbbing penis sliding inside her almost too wonderful to bear.

Arms braced on the chaise, she gyrated slowly, reveling in the feel of him moving inside her. Then, with a murmured oath, Nash grabbed her hips and pushed her downward, the pressure exquisite as he took control. For a moment, they balanced on the edge of the cliff. Then, in perfect tandem, they began to move in earnest, her hips pushing downward as he arched up to meet the motion, their slick heat combining, friction sending tendrils of pleasure curling through her body, the sensation ratcheting up, stroke by stroke, as she tightened around him.

This was what she remembered. What she dreamed about. Not just the pleasure, but the belonging. The joining. No longer two souls, but one.

His right hand teased her nipples, while his left moved downward, stroking her, matching the harried rhythm of their thrusting. And then his fingers slid lower, his thumb slipping inside, stroking the tiny heart of her desire.

Gasping with pleasure, she bucked against him, the movement driving him deeper inside, and she tightened her muscles, wanting to hold him—stroke him—to give him as much as he was giving her.

"You ready?" he whispered, the touch of his breath against her ear almost as sensual as his sinewy movements inside her.

"Yes," she sighed, pressing downward, wanting only to pull him deeper still. "Please, Nash. Oh, please."

His arms circled around her, anchoring her to him as he thrust upward, impaling her with his strength, their bodies fusing together as they moved faster and faster, their movements frenzied as they followed a sequence older than time.

Lightning flashed and the thunder roared, and the night shattered into shards of blinding white heat. Nash's fingers closed around hers as he shifted for one last powerful thrust. She screamed his name as he drove deeper, taking her over the edge.

Her vision exploded into fire. White on white. Everything going blank as sensation overrode all rational thought. There was only the two of them, together. Nothing else mattered.

At least for now.

Annie rolled over, reaching for Nash in the dark. After the storm had subsided—in more ways than one—they'd moved inside to his bedroom and made love again, this time more slowly and sensuously. New memories. Annie smiled, then sobered, as her hand met an empty pillow.

No Nash.

Frowning, she glanced at the clock, surprised to see that it was still relatively early. Just past midnight. Climbing out of the bed, she slipped into one of Nash's shirts and headed out into the hallway toward Adam's room.

He'd managed to kick off his covers, and true to form had flipped around in the bed so that his feet were on his pillow. Annie gently slid the pillow from under his toes and placed it under his head. He sighed once, then

nuggled against the blanket as she covered him once
gain. There was a normalcy to the action that brought
ears to her eyes. Her little boy.

And Nash's.

Annie swallowed, her stomach churning as the words
ormed in her mind. Maybe she'd been wrong. Maybe he
vould have wanted to know.

Just because her father had rejected her didn't necessar-
y mean Nash would reject Adam. Although he'd made it
retty clear—both then and now—what he thought about
ommitments and family. Still, the reality of a son was a
ar cry from an abstract discussion about relationships.

She ran a hand through her hair, looking down at
Adam as he slept.

She'd die before she'd let him be hurt. But maybe…

She shook her head. Nash had made no bones about
vhat he'd wanted. About his life. And none of it had
ncluded her. Or Adam.

What if she told him the truth now and he rejected her
on? The thought made her heart ache. It had all seemed
o simple in Colorado. But now, here, standing in Nash's
ome, still warm from his bed, she wondered if maybe
t could have been different. If she and Nash could have
ound a way to make it all work.

If wishes were horses, then beggars would ride.

Annie sighed, pushing away her tumbling thoughts.
oo much had happened too quickly. She needed time
o think. Time to make the right decisions. Adam's hap-
iness was in her hands, and she wasn't going to let him
own. The most important thing right now was to keep
im safe. Everything else would just have to wait.

She squared her shoulders and walked back into the

hallway, heading downstairs to find Nash. Halfway down
she stopped, the sound of voices surprising her. Instinc
tively, she crouched low into the shadows of the stairwell
straining to hear the conversation.

"I'm sorry to get you out of bed," Avery was saying
The two of them were standing in the foyer, but Annie
could only see Nash's back. "But I figured you'd want to
know that someone deliberately messed with your gun
She sleeping?"

Nash nodded, his head bent as he studied something in
his hand. "Any fingerprints on the thing?"

"Yours...and Annie's."

"So you think I was right? That she sabotaged the
gun?"

Annie's stomach clenched, anger warring with
disbelief.

"I don't know what to think. But you said it yourself
she had access to the gun. And the necessary knowledge
to fuck with it. The question is why?"

"I don't know." Nash shook his head. "None of this
really makes sense. Unless maybe she wanted to save the
day. Make herself look good so that we'd trust her? What
if this whole thing is a ruse of some kind? A way to get
inside A-Tac?"

"Seems like there'd be easier ways to gain access. But
maybe you're onto something."

"Well, whatever's going on, I don't like the idea that
Annie played us," Nash said, his voice harsh. "Hell, played
me. But the truth is that it wouldn't be the first time."

"Any chance she's aware of your suspicions?" Avery
asked.

"No way." He shook his head, his tone almost glib

Annie fought a wave of nausea. How could she have been so stupid?

"Good," Avery said. "I'd hate to think we'd exposed ourselves any more than necessary."

"So what do we do next?"

"Nothing. At least for now. We need more proof than just the gun. Along with a workable theory for motivation. And besides, Tom will be here sometime tomorrow. He's taking her back to D.C. Which, it turns out, may not be such a bad thing."

"And the kid?" Nash asked. "What happens to him?"

"Not our problem. You just keep an eye on Annie. I don't want anything else to go wrong."

"Right." Nash nodded, his face still hidden in shadow. "Keep her happy. I know the drill."

Annie gripped the banister with shaking fingers. He'd done it again. Pulled her in. Made her believe. But it was nothing more than a trick. A way to gain her trust. To trap her into saying or doing something she'd regret.

Holding her breath, she waited until Nash and Avery stepped out onto the front porch, then hurried back up the stairs. Instinct demanded that she grab Adam and run, but she'd played this game before, and that meant waiting until the time was right to make her move.

She slipped back into the bedroom, dropping the shirt and climbing back into the bed just as she heard his footsteps on the stairs. Closing her eyes, she feigned sleep, willing her body to relax as he rounded the bed and pulled off his clothes to slide in beside her.

She fought a gag as he pulled her close, his arm around her waist, his leg thrown over her hip. Nothing was gained by losing it now.

"Annie?" he whispered.

She forced her breathing to slow. Inhale. Exhale. Inhale. Exhale.

All she had to do was wait.

Sunshine streamed through the window and Nash pulled the pillow over his head, trying unsuccessfully to block out the light. For a moment, irritation won the day, and then he remembered the reason he was so tired.

The storm.

The chaise.

Annie.

With a smile, he rolled over, reaching for her, surprised when his hands met only the cotton of the sheets. He sat up, alarm replacing the remembered heat of the night. Avery's words came crashing back.

The gun. Annie's fingerprints. And the possibility that she'd purposely jammed his gun. It didn't make sense. But he'd meant what he said. She'd screwed him before. He wasn't about to let one night of mind-blowing sex make him forget that fact.

But she'd been asleep when he'd come back to bed. Looking so damn desirable—it had taken every bit of his willpower not to wake her. Even now, just the thought of her writhing beneath him had his body reacting, hardening. Cursing, he pulled on a pair of sweats and headed for the bathroom, checking the shower, and then down the hall to her bedroom.

Nothing. No sign that she'd been there at all.

He sucked in a breath, his suspicions warring with the memory of the evening's untethered heat. The intensity had been amazing. Better than before even, if that were possible.

He shook his head with impatience, wanting nothing more than to find her and take her back to his bed.

He rounded the corner and stopped, the morning light spilling from Adam's doorway. *Of course.* He smiled, striding forward, certain that he'd find her with Adam. Her son came before everything else. She'd even insisted on checking on him when they'd come in from the garden, the moonlight playing against her skin as she smoothed the hair from her son's eyes. She'd never looked more beautiful.

He stepped into the room, and his smile faded.

The room was empty.

As were the kitchen, the living room, and the dining room. He double-checked the bedrooms, and then, taking the stairs two at a time, he headed for the garden, hoping to see the two of them playing ball or laughing in the sun.

But the backyard was as empty as the house. He clenched a fist, his jaw tightening with anger, as he fought against the obvious. She'd played him. Again.

He checked the front garden, the garage, and even the attic, although by then he'd already accepted the truth.

Annie and Adam were gone.

CHAPTER 17

thought you were going to watch her?" Avery said, his features harsh, his expression formidable.

"I was. Hell, she was right next to me most of the night." Nash ran a hand through his hair, pacing in front of the white board in the war room. He still couldn't believe she was gone. That he'd been stupid enough to believe things had changed between them. "I honestly didn't think she'd run."

"Even after our conversation last night?"

Nash shot a glance at Drake, who was straddling a chair on the far side of the table.

"It's all right. He knows. So does Tyler." Avery nodded. "I haven't told the rest of the team about the gun yet. I wanted to be sure we had hard proof that it was Annie."

"Seems to me her running pretty much seals the deal," Drake said with a shrug.

"Any way she could have overheard you and Avery talking?" Tyler asked.

"Shit. I didn't even think about that." He stopped for a moment, turning the idea over in his head. "But no. She was asleep when I came back to bed." He'd admitted his remarkable lack of self-control. It hadn't been his first choice, but if they were going to figure out where she'd gone, they needed all the facts. Even if they painted him an idiot. "If she'd heard me, she'd already have bolted."

"What about surveillance?" Drake frowned. "Surely security caught something?"

"I had Hannah pull the tapes the minute Nash called," Avery confirmed, a slide filling the screen. "This is from just beyond Nash's backyard." The camera panned once across the woods and then rotated slowly to cover the back of the fence. And then suddenly the screen filled with static.

"She disabled the camera," Tyler said to no one in particular.

"Went through a broken board in the fence. Not a bad plan actually. That field leads straight to the highway."

"But we've got people stationed out there," Tyler said. "How did she get through?"

"Security got a call for backup on the east side of campus around five o'clock."

"Was there a disturbance?" Nash asked, anger burning in his gut, adrenaline making his nerves feel like they were all firing at once.

Avery shook his head, his expression grim. "No. Turns out the call was bogus. And it traced back to a campus phone."

"So no way to tie it to Annie," Tyler said. "But I'm betting it was her."

"She's pretty damn resourceful," Nash growled. Hell, she'd seduced him right into believing she'd changed.

"So what else have we got?" Drake said, pushing away from his chair. Obviously he was as anxious as Nash to get on with the hunt.

Avery nodded. "A car was reported stolen about a quarter mile from the far side of the woods. Owner came out early this morning to head to work. Car was gone. I've got people looking, but so far no sightings. It's a black Honda CRG. 2005. New York license, ADL-4681."

"But we don't know for sure that it was Annie who stole it," Tyler said, writing down the number. "And even if she did, the first thing she'd do is ditch it when she had some distance and find something new."

"Yeah, but she's traveling with the kid," Nash said. "That's got to slow things down."

"Or make her more desperate," Drake observed. "I mean, the truth is Annie has a hell of a lot of experience with running, not to mention staying off the radar. And the cold hard facts are that we have no idea where she's going or what she might have planned."

"The way I see it," Avery said, "there are two scenarios. The first is that something spooked her. Maybe she did overhear our conversation, or maybe she was always planning to run, but if that's her motivation, then she's going to want to move quickly and get as far away from here as she can."

"And the second alternative?"

Avery sighed. "We could be right about her being involved in this whole scheme somehow. Either trying to fulfill some bargain she made with the kidnapper— Dominico's assassination or something she's kept from us—or worse, maybe she's in league with whoever has been pulling the strings and this whole thing is a lot uglier than we anticipated."

"Either way, sitting here talking isn't going to do us any good," Nash said, sliding a clip into his gun. "We need to get out there now."

"I agree." Avery nodded. "Drake, I want you to follow up on the Civic. See if you can run it to ground. Hannah will handle things from here. She's already been working with our security and local law enforcement. And, Tyler, I want you to work on other transportation options, any other stolen vehicles, airports, buses. Hell, anything that comes to mind. Jason will provide backup."

"What about me?" Nash asked, hands fisted as he waited for orders, Drake and Tyler already heading for the door.

"I want you at Dominico's country house. With Emmett. It's possible the ambassador is still a target."

"But I—" Nash started, but Avery shook his head, brushing the words aside, his expression brooking no argument.

"I need you on point with Dominico."

"Fine, I'll go," Nash said. "But, Jesus, Avery, she's got Adam with her. There's no fucking way she's going to kill someone else in front of her son."

Annie jerked aside the curtains of the Sweet Rest Motel room, peering out at the almost-empty parking lot. She knew that stopping was a risk. Nash and his friends would be looking for her by now. She needed to keep moving. But Adam had been hungry. And tired. And confused.

So she'd stopped, the mother in her overriding the

operative. After wolfing down three White Castle burgers, Adam had fallen asleep, and she hadn't wanted to wake him. So instead she watched out the window, wondering how the hell she'd wound up here. Running.

She hated the idea. Had hated it the first time, too. But as in Saida, she'd been given no other option. For a brief moment, she'd been fooled into believing that Nash truly cared, that there was still a chance for them and for Adam. But after overhearing his conversation with Avery, she'd realized it had all been a fantasy.

Despite all his grand talk about having faith, he'd been playing her, believing all the time that she was in league with her kidnapper, certain that she was in some way betraying him and his precious A-Tac. It was an insane assumption, but then he had always been quick to believe the worst.

And even if somehow she'd managed to get past his betrayal, there was still the matter of Tom, another supposed ally turned enemy. It was clear that all Tom cared about was his career. And bringing in the woman who turned traitor and tried to kill an ambassador was headline-making stuff. She had no doubt that he'd use her situation to promote himself.

It's what he'd always done.

He'd used her before, but at least then it had been mutual. He'd needed a way out of a situation gone bad, and she'd needed to disappear—to reinvent herself and build a life for the baby she carried.

She'd trusted Avery and Nash. Thought that they'd had her back. CIA taking care of CIA. But they'd made it more than clear last night that that wasn't the case. Tom was on his way to take her back to Washington. And neither Nash nor Avery was going to lift a finger to stop him.

She'd be charged with attempted murder at best. Treason at worst. And either way, she had no doubt that they'd take Adam from her. Her little boy would be on his own. Just as she'd been all those years ago.

She closed her eyes, memories sliding past, pain raking through her. She'd managed to survive. But she wasn't about to let the system get her son.

"Mommy?" Adam's voice broke through her tumbling thoughts. "Are we going home now?"

"No, sweetie," she said, coming to sit beside him on the bed. "We can't go back there anymore. It isn't safe. But I promise you we're going to make a new home. And it'll be even better than before."

"What about the bad men?" Adam asked, his eyes darting toward the window. "Won't they find us?"

"No." Annie shook her head, praying it was the truth. "I won't let them."

"Can't we make our new home with Nash?" her son asked, his eyes wide with confusion and innocence. "I thought he was your friend."

"I thought so, too. But sometimes grown-ups make mistakes. Just like kids."

"But he saved me."

"Yes, he did. And I'll always be grateful. But it's more complicated than that."

Adam nodded solemnly, reaching over to squeeze her hand.

"Anyway," she said, struggling for a lighter tone, "it's always been just you and me, right? We're a team."

"But I promised to help Nash find the man with the Wii."

"I know, baby, but sometimes things happen and we have to break our promises. I'm sure he'll understand."

Adam frowned, but didn't argue. He trusted her. It was there in his eyes. Her heart tightened. This was all too much for a little boy. And for the millionth time, she questioned the wisdom of running.

Behind her, the phone rang. And she whirled around, pulse pounding. It wasn't the landline. It was the phone Rivon had given her. With shaking fingers, she picked it up, turning her back so that Adam couldn't see her fear.

"Gallagher," she whispered, working to keep her voice calm.

"Running was a stupid idea," the disembodied voice said. "But all the better for me." Annie reached for her gun, moving between Adam and the window. "I hope your son had a nice nap," the voice continued, "because, now, it's time for you to pay."

"Glad you're here," Emmett said as they walked through the overly ornate foyer of Dominico's country house. "The ambassador's not the easiest man to deal with. I can use the backup."

"How many in his security detail?"

"There's six altogether. Three working the perimeter and three in the house. They seem like good men, but with Dominico's tendency to roam we could use ten more—easy."

"Where is he now?" Nash asked, taking the com unit Emmett offered.

"In the orangery." He shook his head with a grin. "Whatever the hell that is."

"This place is huge." Nash followed as Emmett cut through what looked to be a ballroom of some kind. It was big enough to hold a basketball court. Upholstered velvet chairs stood like sentries against garishly floral walls.

"Makes our job so much more fun," Emmett said. "Nothing like a game of finding Dominico. Anything new on Annie?"

"Yeah, maybe a lead. I just got off the phone with Drake, and they found the stolen Honda in a Wal-Mart parking lot. They're interviewing employees now. If we're lucky, maybe someone saw her. Noticed where she went. What kind of vehicle she's in now. But it's a hell of a long shot. A needle in a fucking haystack."

"It just takes one mistake." Emmett rounded the corner into a long mirrored hallway.

"Like mine." The words were meant more for himself than for Emmett, but his friend answered anyway.

"We've all been there. They teach us to be cynical, to stay unattached, but sometimes even the best of us get drawn in. Hell, I believed her, too."

"Yeah, well, you didn't sleep with her."

"I might of if I'd had the chance." Emmett smiled, then sobered as he glanced down at the GPS on his watch. "Shit."

"What?"

"Dominico's on the move," Emmett barked into the microphone on his com-link, still staring down at the moving blip on his watch face. "Who's supposed to be on him?"

"Me," came the static-filled reply. "Said he was going to the can. I figured he was safe in there, but he's gone."

"Goddamn it." Emmett blew out a breath, picking up the pace as he moved through the room. "Which john?"

"The one near the kitchen."

"How could you possibly have lost him?" Emmett asked, pulling his gun now as they walked into the kitchen, the security man standing near the open door of what was clearly a bathroom.

"He asked me for a magazine," the man said sheepishly. "When I got back, he was gone."

"Anyone out there got him?" Emmett barked again into the microphone.

Nash pulled out his gun, motioning toward a glass door open just a crack.

Emmett nodded, signaled the security man, and the three of them, guns drawn, moved across the kitchen. Emmett waited a beat, then pulled the door open, swinging through, his Smith & Wesson at the ready. Nash followed, the security man on his heels.

"You see him?" Emmett asked, his voice just above a whisper.

Nash scanned the enormous tree-filled yard and was just about to shake his head when someone stepped out from behind a large elm tree. The man was dressed in a yellow golf sweater and green plaid pants. "That him?"

"Yeah," Emmett said, lowering his gun as Dominico gave them a casual wave. "Asshole." They started across the lawn as the ambassador began to make his way toward them. There was maybe ten yards separating them when something flashed in the woods behind Dominico.

"Get down," Nash yelled, but the warning came too

late. A shot rang out, and the ambassador fell to his knees. "Son of a bitch."

Emmett and Nash moved in tandem, Emmett dropping down beside Dominico. "No pulse. He's dead."

Nash nodded, his eyes still on the stand of trees where he'd seen the flash. The bushes moved slightly, and he saw a shadow detach from the undergrowth. "Someone's out there. I'm too far away for a shot. I'm going after them."

Nash ran across the grass, using the shrubbery and trees for cover, vaulting over the hurricane fence that bordered the property. Unlike the manicured lawn, the woods were full of undergrowth, slowing his progress as he fought against entangled tree branches. There was no sign of the shooter.

"Emmett, I've lost him. Maybe your security guys can intercept him. I'm going to head for the place where I thought I saw someone."

"Roger, that," Emmett said. "I'm right behind you."

Nash reached the stand of birch, surprised to find that the killer had left his gun. Then again, maybe it was easier to move through the trees without the encumbrance of an assault rifle. He leaned down, careful not to touch it, and felt a shock as he recognized the modified specs.

Floating barrel, 40x telescopic with laser sight. This was Annie's gun. The one on the schematic she'd given to Rivon.

His blood ran cold as he turned slowly around the clearing, looking for something else—something to negate the image of Annie. Here. Killing Dominico.

Something glistened in the dappled light of the trees. He moved forward, his gut churning.

"What is it?" Emmett asked, coming to a stop behind him.

"There," Nash said, anger mixing with a rush of pain so great he had to fight just to breathe, "caught in that branch. It's a clump of hair. Red hair."

"Adam?" Annie said, her eyes on the parking lot outside the window. Nothing moved. "Honey, I need you to move into the bathroom."

"Is the bad man out there?" His little voice trembled as he moved to follow her instructions.

"I don't think so. I think he was just trying to scare us. But I don't want to take any chances," she said, still watching for any sign of danger. "So we're going to go out the back way. Just like we practiced."

She'd picked the room because, unlike some of the others, it had a window in the back. She'd parked the pickup back there, too, figuring that if anything happened, it was logical to assume the attack would come from the front.

"I'm going to boost you up, and I want you to crawl through the window. Then duck down behind the truck, okay?"

"I can do it." Adam nodded as she lifted him upward. He scrambled through the open window and dropped safely to the ground below, moving quickly to crouch behind the beat-up Ford she'd liberated from the Wal-Mart.

Annie followed Adam through the window and crouched beside him, checking for signs that someone had seen them. Like the front, everything was quiet. But something felt off, the hair on her arms prickling as she tried to figure out what it was.

"Mommy," Adam said, fear filling his voice as he tugged on her jacket. "I know that man. He was in the car. After the airplane." Annie's heart stopped as she turned to see a man in a black T-shirt standing by the ice machine, his attention focused on the front of the motel.

She was too far away to take him out. And she wasn't about to leave Adam to get closer. Better to just get the hell out of Dodge and pray that he didn't turn around. "Okay," she whispered, reaching up for the truck's door handle. "I'm going to open the door, and when I do, I want you to get inside and lie on the floor. And I want you to stay down, no matter what happens. Promise me."

"I will." He nodded.

She pulled the handle, and the door opened with a soft groan of protest. The guy at the ice machine didn't move. Either he hadn't heard the noise, or he'd written it off as nonthreatening. She motioned to Adam, and he climbed up into the cab of the truck, crouching on the floor under the dashboard.

With what she hoped was a comforting smile, she followed him in, keeping low as she slid across the bench seat and turned the key. The truck wheezed for a moment, and then the engine caught, the noise seeming deafening.

The man in the breezeway turned, his face darkening as he recognized her. Shouting out something to someone behind him, he raised his gun, shooting as Annie gunned the old Ford. The truck lurched forward as the bullet slammed into the passenger-side door.

"Adam, you okay?" She risked a look at her son, then clenched her teeth, yanking the wheel, the old truck's tires spinning as she pulled it into a one-eighty. In the rearview mirror, she saw the guy shoot again, but they'd moved out of range. Gunning the engine, the Ford shot forward, past the motel office and onto the highway, gravel spewing.

Behind her, she could see a blue sedan pulling out of a parking lot, slowing only slightly as the man from the ice machine wrenched the door open and jumped inside. Then it sped up again, intent on pursuit.

She pressed the pedal to the floor, praying the old engine would hold out. The truck fishtailed as she cut around a pothole, the sedan closing the distance between them fast. Reaching into her pocket, she grabbed the cell phone and dialed.

"Come on, Nash," she screamed into the phone, trying to keep an eye on the road, on Adam, and on the car behind her. "Pick up." The sedan moved closer as the machine kicked in. "Damn it, Nash. Where are you?" The electronic voice told her to wait for the beep, and she momentarily considered hanging up.

But sometimes a person had to choose between the rock and the hard place. And right now, she and Adam needed help. She had a gun and plenty of ammo. But with her son in the car, she couldn't afford a shoot-out. The best option was to outrun them, but the heat indicator on the Ford was climbing, and she didn't have a lot of faith.

Faith.

She laughed, the sound bitter against her throat.

Finally, the beep sounded, and she stumbled over her words. "Nash, it's Annie. Adam and I are in real trouble. They found us somehow. Adam recognized one of them. Anyway, they're on my tail. Two of them. And I could use some help. I'm on Route 82 heading south. Back to Sunderland." She stopped, drawing a breath. "Nash,

I know you're angry. But we can deal with all of that later. The only thing that matters now is Adam. Help us. Please."

She clicked to terminate the call and threw the phone on the seat. The car behind them was gaining—the Ford's hot light flashing red now.

"Mommy?" Adam asked, his eyes wide, his voice quavering as the truck shuddered in protest. "Are we going to be okay?"

"We're going to be fine," she answered, forcing what she hoped was a reassuring smile. "I can deal with this, I promise." She pulled her gun from her pocket, balancing it on her knee, keeping her attention focused on the road ahead and the rearview mirror.

"And if you can't?" he asked, chewing on his bottom lip.

"I will. I just called Nash for backup."

"He's your plan B," Adam said with a weak grin. "Like the window in the motel bathroom."

"Exactly." She smiled down at her son. "We're going to be fine, Adam. You'll see."

As if to counter the thought, the blue sedan slipped up beside her, the driver slamming his front bumper into the side of the pickup. The truck lurched to the right, the front wheel sliding off the road onto the rocky shoulder.

Annie jerked the wheel to the left, using the weight and force of the Ford against the sedan. The sedan's front quarter panel crumpled with the impact, the car falling behind them again.

Pressing her foot to the pedal again, the old truck shot forward just as a shot rang out from the car behind. The bullet crashed through the back windshield, shattering the glass.

"Stay down," Annie yelled as she pushed the pickup to its limit, the floorboards rattling in protest as they started across a bridge.

Another shot whistled past her. This time the bullet shattered the front windshield, the spidery cracks making it impossible to see. In front of her, she heard the frantic sound of a car horn and swerved instinctively to avoid impact. The truck skidded off the pavement, slamming through the guardrail, flipping over as it landed with a frightening crunch at the bottom of a ravine.

Annie fought against a scream, knowing that they only had minutes before they had company. "Adam. Baby? Where are you?"

"Out here," came the answer, his voice reedy, but strong. "I think I flew through the window."

"Are you okay?"

"Yeah, I think so. My knee's bleeding."

"Stay put, honey. I'm coming." Using her feet, she knocked out the rest of the windshield behind her and, after pocketing her gun, climbed out onto the pickup bed. Adam was crouching beneath a tree.

"I think they're coming." He pointed up the steep embankment, at two figures working their way down.

"I see them." She nodded, trying to decide if it was better to run or to make a stand. She reached inside the pickup window and grabbed the bag with her ammo. Maybe a bit of both. The truck blocked them from being seen from above, which meant that the men had no idea they were still alive. "Can you move okay?"

"Yeah." He nodded, hopping to his feet to prove the point.

"Stay down, baby." He dropped back to his knees as

she crawled over to his position. "What I want you to do is head over there behind those rocks." She pointed to a couple of moss-covered boulders a few yards away. "They'll give you some protection."

"What about you?"

"I'm going to stay here and try and stop them." She reached for her son's hands. "I know I'm asking a lot. But you're the bravest guy I know. All you have to do is stay behind the rocks and wait for me to come and get you. Okay?"

He nodded, glancing upward at the two men still working their way down to the wreckage.

"They won't be able to see you. I swear it."

He nodded again. "I love you, Mom."

"I love you, too." She gave him a quick hug and sent him scrambling for the boulders, turning back to concentrate on the threat from above. She only had a handgun. But she had the advantage of surprise and expertise.

She held her breath, waiting. There'd only be one chance. Once they hit level ground she'd lose sight of them. Which meant she had to wait until they rounded the truck to take her shots. They'd see her the minute she popped up to fire.

After glancing behind her to make sure Adam was safely out of sight, Annie held her breath as the men disappeared into the undergrowth. She could hear them moving, which meant they probably thought she was dead. All the better to blow their asses away.

She lifted the gun, bracing her hand on the back of the pickup bed. One Mississippi...two Mississippi.

The man from the ice machine appeared in her sights. She squeezed the trigger. One bastard down. The second man ducked back behind the truck. And Annie edged forward slightly, trying to improve her angle, but the heel of her boot caught on a branch or debris, sending her flying into the dirt.

"Don't move," the second man said, rounding the far side of the car. She started to roll back, to shoot the guy, but before she had the chance her son came flying out from behind the rocks.

"Leave my mother alone." He stopped directly in front of her, blocking her line of fire.

The man's face darkened and he lifted his gun.

Annie dove for Adam, screaming his name as the gun's report filled the air.

The quiet that followed was deafening. Still covering her son, Annie lifted her gun, searching for the shooter. But the man was down.

Drake Flynn knelt beside him, his expression stony as he checked to be certain the shooter was dead.

"Thank God," Annie said, checking Adam for signs of injury. Relief made her giddy. "I thought... I thought we were dead. Did Nash send you?"

"In a manner of speaking," Drake said, his face still giving nothing away. "I found someone who saw you take the pickup. And then Nash called to tell me what you'd done."

"What I'd done?" she asked, suddenly wary.

"Yeah, pretty neat trick. Anyway, Nash is the one who figured out where you'd be. But I drew the lucky straw because I was closer. I'm afraid I'm going to need that gun." He motioned toward the Beretta she still had clutched in her hand.

Adam turned to look at her, confusion filling his face.

"Fine," she said, handing over the gun, not willing to do anything more to put Adam at risk. "But I still have no idea what you're talking about."

"Annie, we know what you did," Drake said, motioning for her to stand. "Nash was there."

"What the hell are you talking about?" she asked, her brain scrambling to make sense of his words.

"I'm talking about killing Blake Dominico. Just over an hour ago, you blew the ambassador away. And we have the evidence to prove it."

CHAPTER **18**

What the hell is going on here?" Annie said, shaking off the guard as he escorted her into the war room. She was holding it together, but just barely. Drake hadn't said more than three words on the drive back to Sunderland, his accusation hanging heavy between them.

She'd sat in back with Adam, holding her son, feeling as if she'd lost her mind. Everything had seemed so clear last night. Disappear. Make a new life for herself and for Adam. And then everything had gone to hell. First the kidnapper's call. And then the car chase and then Drake and now Dominico—dead.

None of it made any sense. And the only thing her mind could focus on was the fact that Adam had seen her kill another man. What kind of mother did that make her? She'd fought so long to protect him, and yet it was because of her that he'd been thrown into danger.

He was with Lara now. Safe, for the moment. And she

was here, in the war room, facing an inquisition. Annie glared at the assembled company. Tyler and Drake sat to her immediate left, Drake with his chair tipped back, one foot propped against the table, his hooded eyes unreadable. Jason was in his customary spot in front of a computer keyboard. Avery sat just to her right, his expression, as always, unreadable. A man she'd never met, probably the elusive Emmett, sat at the far end of the room. Only Lara and Hannah were missing—and Nash.

She'd seen him only once since her arrival back at Sunderland, the look of disgust in his eyes stirring up an uncomfortable mixture of anger and despair. No one was saying anything, and all of them were avoiding eye contact.

Behind her the door opened, and Nash walked in, his expression stony as he moved to take a seat next to Emmett. She tried to make eye contact, but he made a play instead of looking at a stack of papers he held in his hand.

Swallowing her fear, she called on years of training and conditioning, some of it in the CIA, some of it growing up on the streets. All of it in preparation for ambushes just like this.

"I repeat. What the hell is going on?"

"I think you're in a much better position to answer that," Avery said, crossing his arms over his massive chest.

"Drake accused me of killing Dominico," she said, her brain still scrambling to figure out where this was headed. Nowhere good, that much she was sure of. "He said there was proof." First rule of interrogation: Turn it back on the questioner. Play for time and information. It was amazing how easily she'd fallen back into their world.

"Emmett and Nash found a long-range rifle at the scene," Avery said.

"And because I'm a sharpshooter that means it's me?" At least she'd correctly identified the stranger. Score one for the condemned.

"It had the same modifications as the one you designed for the schematic." This from Drake. Nash was still pretending fascination with the pages on the table.

"The modifications are hardly unique." She frowned. "And even if they were, it still wouldn't be enough to make even a circumstantial case."

"There were fingerprints." Nash lifted his gaze, his eyes filled with accusation as he handed her the report with the identified prints. "They were found on the gun. And there's a hair sample as well." He tossed a photograph on the table. A tree branch with a clump of red hair.

"We're doing DNA analysis as we speak," Jason said, heading off her next question.

"But I wasn't there." She tossed the report back onto the table. "Drake, you saw me. I was fighting for my life—and Adam's. You killed one of them yourself."

"You were definitely fighting off someone," he admitted. "No question about that. But that doesn't change the timeline." He leaned forward, his eyes narrowed, as he recited what he believed to be the facts. "We know that you left Sunderland around five this morning. We've got the disabled security camera to prove it. Then we have the car you stole from the farm just down the highway. Turns out Mr. Johnson's had some trouble with vandals and he had a security camera. You missed it. And we've got you hotwiring the car at five-forty-five."

"Then," Jason continued, this time flashing a photo up on the console screen, "you drove about sixty miles to the Wal-Mart parking lot. Where at approximately seven o'clock, you left Mr. Johnson's car and about forty minutes later, stole a pickup truck."

"You managed to avoid the security camera in Wal-Mart," Tyler said, "but one of the employees recognized Adam. And the guy who rounds up the baskets remembers seeing a woman matching your description driving off in the green Ford Drake found you and Adam hiding behind."

"From there, you apparently drove to Dominico's country house. It's about an hour and a half from the Wal-Mart. You cased the house, waited for Dominico to make a wrong move—and took him out."

"The only reason we got the evidence we did," Nash said, his mouth set in anger, "is that I saw the gun flash. Because I was in pursuit, you didn't have a chance to sanitize. Either that or you wanted to get caught."

"I wasn't there," she said.

"Once you'd managed to get off the property," Drake continued, ignoring her denial, "you made your way back to Route 82 and headed south—toward the interstate. That's how we figured out where you'd be. Best location based on time elapsed from the shooting. I was close by so I got the order to intercept."

"You've got it all figured out," she said, leaning forward, hands on the table.

"The facts fit."

"Especially when you add in Nash's suspicions about my sabotaging his weapon. Right?" She narrowed her eyes, glaring at Nash. "You actually believe I'd have put you in harm's way?"

"You've done it before."

"Jesus, you're a piece of work." She pulled her gaze away from Nash. "All of you. First you say you'll help me. But you bungle that and I have to save the day. Then you promise to help me deal with the fallout, and turn around and sell me out to Homeland Security because you decide I'm in league with Adam's kidnapper. And on top of that"—she leaned closer, her eyes only for Nash—"you actually believed that I'd willingly kill a man in cold blood in front of my own son."

She clutched the edge of the table, her body going cold, her legs suddenly weak. How could she have thought that he was on her side?

God, she was a fool.

"Let me make myself very clear," she said, sequestering her emotion and turning back to Avery. "I did not shoot Blake Dominico."

"But you're not denying that you ran away." It wasn't a question.

"No. I overheard you and Nash talking last night. And I wasn't going to stick around and wait for Tom Walker to throw the book at me. I had my son to think of. Besides, you made it very clear what you thought of me." She shot a look at Nash, who was back to staring at the papers on the table. "I realized that I was wrong to believe that you'd help me, and that the only one I could truly depend on was me. I had to do what I thought was best for my son. But Dominico wasn't part of the plan."

"So what happened?" Tyler asked, her expression grim, but at least not condemning.

"Pretty much like you said. Except that when we left Wal-Mart, Adam was tired. And hungry. So we drove through a White Castle, and checked into a no-tell motel. Sweet Rest or something like that. Adam ate and then slept—a couple of hours maybe. I tried to figure out what my best options were. I even considered coming back."

Nash's head shot up, and for the first time she felt as if he was really seeing her.

"But before I could make a decision, the phone rang. The one Rivon gave me." She filled them in on the rest of what had happened. The threat, the guy with the gun, the car chase, the crash, and her attempt to fight her way out. "And then Drake arrived and you know the rest."

"Can you substantiate any of this?" Avery asked.

"Adam will back up everything I said. He was there."

"He's only six," Tyler said, her words gentle.

"Fine," she said, scrambling to think of hard proof. "I used a fake name at the motel, but the clerk should remember me and the name will be on the register. And I called Nash. That's why I thought you were there." She looked over at Drake. "I thought Nash had sent you."

"There were no incoming calls," Nash said, throwing his cell phone out on the table. "Check it yourself. I've had it with me all day."

"That's impossible," she said, shaking her head. "I left a message."

Tyler picked up the phone. " Maybe it wasn't on." She pressed the button and the phone whirred to life, then beeped loudly.

Annie sucked in a breath, her gaze colliding with Nash's. "Go ahead. Check your voice mail."

He grabbed the phone, still glowering, punched in a

code, and then listened as the phone spat back the message. "It's just like she said. She called." He handed the phone to Avery, his hand brushing hers in the process. Annie shivered and stepped back, needing the distance, unsure how to process the flash of remorse in his eyes.

"Maybe she's just using the phone call as a decoy," Emmett said. "It doesn't change the timeline or the evidence we found at Dominico's. And we all know that Nash has issues when it comes to Annie."

"I'd never let anything interfere with an operation and you know it," Nash said, pushing to his feet.

"Calm down," Avery said, nodding for Nash to sit back down. "Emmett is just presenting options. And he's right, the phone call isn't enough to negate the evidence found at the scene. We need to verify the motel records."

"Already on it," Jason said.

"But even that doesn't clear her completely." Tyler shook her head. "I mean, she could have gotten the call and been scared enough to follow through and kill Dominico."

"But I didn't," Annie protested, feeling like a broken record. "And besides, what about the people chasing me? How does that fit the scenario of my cooperating?"

"I don't know." Tyler shrugged.

"They were going to try to kill you before," Drake offered. "Maybe they were just tying up loose ends after the fact."

"So they followed me all the way there. Waited until I'd done the deed, consoled my son, and driven away before chasing after me in an attempt to take me out? Seems like it'd be easier to plant another bomb, on the truck maybe."

"I'll admit none of it fits together easily," Avery said. "But, Annie, it's going to be hard to ignore the facts."

"Especially now," Jason said, his expression hardening. "Lara just sent me the preliminary DNA report. Looks like the hair Nash found is a match with Annie's."

"Evidence can be planted," she argued, feeling like she was fighting one of the immortal monsters in Adam's games. "We've all done it ourselves when the situation called for it."

"She does have a point." Jason shrugged. "It could be done. But if Annie's telling the truth, and someone tried to frame her for Dominico's murder, what's the motive?"

"Million-dollar question," Avery said, pondering the idea.

"And a hell of a good one," Hannah agreed, bursting into the room, her breathing ragged, her spiky hair even more disarrayed than usual. "Sorry to be late, but I have good news. At least I hope it's good. I was going over the transcript of Adam's debrief." She dropped down into the chair next to Annie. "And I noticed he said that the guy with the Wii had been at the farmhouse."

"Wii?" Jason asked.

"Adam plays a lot of video games," Nash said.

"Too many," Annie admitted. "Anyway, we think the man with the Wii is the one who's been calling me."

"So you say." Nash glared.

"I'm telling the truth." Their gazes caught and held—and Annie's breath stuck in her throat.

"I want to believe that." The words were whispered, almost as if he'd spoken against his will, but for the first time since she'd landed back at Sunderland, Annie felt a small stirring of hope.

"I hate to interrupt," Hannah said, clearing her throat, breaking through the ratcheting tension, "but as I said, I've got good news. For everyone."

"And..." Avery prompted, his frown more for show than any sign of true anger.

"*And*—I figured that if Adam had seen the guy in charge, then our prisoner was lying. Montez would have had to see him, too. So with a little persuasion I managed to get him to give me a description. Used Jason's new computer program. Anyway, the guy was amazingly gifted when it comes to remembering features. So I let the computer do its work and then printed out the picture and showed it to Adam. He confirmed that it looks like Wii Man. So what about you, Annie? Do you recognize him?" Hannah held out the computer-generated photo.

"Oh, my God," Annie said, her legs going all wobbly again.

"What?" Nash asked, moving to her side, automatically reaching out to support her. "What is it?"

"Look." She nodded at the photograph in her hand.

"Son of a bitch," Nash said. "Kim Sun."

"Who the hell is Kim Sun?" Avery demanded. "And what's he got to do with the two of you?"

"He was Korean ambassador to the United States eight years ago," Nash said. "It was because of him we were in Lebanon. We were there to rescue his son."

"Actually," Annie corrected, the world tilting again, "we were there so that I could kill his son."

CHAPTER **19**

A nnie's words hung suspended in the room, and she immediately wished them back. Even after all this time, the operation was classified. She'd held on to the truth for so damn long. And now in one unguarded moment, she'd broken her silence.

"All right, people," Avery said, waving Annie to a seat at the table. "Let's clear the room. I think this is something I need to sort out with Annie and Nash. In the meantime, I want confirmation of Annie's story. And IDs on the two men you took out on Route 82. In addition, I want everything you can dig up on Kim Sun. Until we find him, this thing isn't over."

"So, what, you're saying we're just going to forget the evidence we found at Dominico's?" Emmett protested, clearly not happy with this turn of events.

"Emmett," Avery said, the name as good as an order.

"Fine," he said, following Tyler to the door, Hannah and Jason on their heels. "But I'll be in the lab with Lara if you need anything. Dominico was killed on my watch. Which makes it personal."

"Hang in there," Drake whispered as he passed Annie and Nash. Annie knew his words were meant for Nash, but she took comfort just the same. She'd forgotten how nice it was to be part of a team.

Shaking her head, she rose to her feet, unable to avoid the anger in Nash's eyes. She wasn't part of anything anymore, and she'd do well to remember that fact. There was an uncomfortable silence as the two of them took seats on opposite sides of the conference table, Avery splitting the difference and sitting in the middle.

"All right," he said. "The room's clear. Does someone want to tell me what the hell is going on here?"

"Don't look at me," Nash said, lifting his hands. "I have no fucking clue. Until about five minutes ago, I thought we were sent to Lebanon on a rescue mission. But apparently there was more to it than that. I just wasn't in on it. An omission, I might add, that almost cost me my life."

"It wasn't my idea not to tell you. Tom insisted. And I—"

"Decided for the first time in your life to follow orders?" The sneer in his voice was backed by a flash of hurt she couldn't ignore. They'd always been honest with each other. Until the night they'd fought over his transfer to A-Tac. After that things had changed, something shifting, their relationship forever altered.

She'd meant to tell him everything that night. The truth about the mission, the truth about the baby. But instead he'd dropped his bombshell, insisting that there was no room in their lives for permanent relationships.

No room for family of any kind. And she'd known then that there was no chance he'd welcome her pregnancy.

So she'd walked away, determined to finish the operation and find a way to make a life for her and her baby. Tom had understood. He'd offered his help. All he'd asked in return was her silence. And until now, she'd honored their agreement.

"Why don't we stop with the accusations and start at the beginning." Avery frowned.

"I've already said too much," Annie said. "The computer rendition of Kim caught me off guard."

"Look," Avery started, his expression turning stern, "if Kim Sun is indeed behind all of this, we need to be sure that he's stopped. And the only way I can help with that is if I have the full facts about what really happened in Lebanon."

"But it's classified. Highest levels."

"I've got clearance." His steady gaze brooked no argument. And besides, Annie was tired of running.

"You'll cover me with the big brass?" she asked, realizing immediately just how ludicrous the question was. She was already suspected of killing Dominico. Revealing a classified operation was just a drop in the bucket by comparison.

"I promise." He nodded, solemnly.

"And Nash?" Despite the fact that he'd believed the worst of her, she still didn't want to hurt him any more than necessary. His career was his life, and she didn't want to do anything else to damage his standing with the Company.

"I don't need your help," he snapped, her heart wrenching at his tone. "You've already done more than enough."

"Stop." Avery raised a hand. "Sniping at each other isn't going to help. The charges against Annie are serious. Emmett wasn't exaggerating. The evidence against her is damning. And if you expect A-Tac to help, you've got to shoot straight with me." He leaned forward, his expression fierce. "Both of you."

"Fine." Nash sat back in his chair, his face purposefully blank, but Annie knew he was still angry over her perceived betrayal. That and the fact that he obviously believed she'd killed Dominico.

Her own anger surfaced again and she fought for control. Avery was right, the only way things were going to get better was if she leveled with him. If Kim Sun was behind Adam's kidnapping, then he was behind Dominico's execution as well. And the only way she was going to clear her name and keep Adam safe was to find Kim. And to do that, she needed A-Tac.

"It started out like a regular operation. Tom came to us and said we had been assigned an extraction in Lebanon."

"I thought you worked Eastern Europe."

"We did," Nash acknowledged. "We wondered at the time why we'd been called in. But Tom just said the operatives in the division were stretched too thin and that we'd drawn the short straw."

"It's not like we hadn't had other assignments out of our area. Sometimes our expertise was needed. Sometimes, like Nash said, they just wanted to get something done and the only way to do it was to call in other folks."

"So your initial objective was to rescue Kim's son."

"That's what we were told," Nash said. "At least that's

what I was told. Anyway, Jin really wasn't a kid. He was nineteen, I think. Reputedly, he'd been on a trip through the ancient world, studying architecture. While in Lebanon he disappeared. Kim was concerned and used his diplomatic influence to get the United States involved, and the problem landed in our laps. The CIA did some digging and found out Jin had been kidnapped by a group of insurgents."

"Our job was to get him out. So we prepped for the extraction," Annie interjected, picking up the story. "And once we got the green light, everything was set. Until Tom received additional orders. According to last-minute intel, the kidnapping was a fake. Jin was actually working with his 'kidnappers.' He'd secretly converted to Islam and was actually in Lebanon for training."

"So why specifically did they want you to take him out?"

"Conceivably to remove the threat of blackmail against Kim Sun," Annie said. "Because of his position he had access to potentially sensitive information about U.S. policies. And his son's alleged association with the insurgency in Lebanon meant that there was a legitimate fear that Jin would try to use his father to access sensitive information. Intel that could at the very least embarrass the country and at worst aid in planning a terrorist attack. So Langley wanted to use the opportunity to eliminate the threat without creating an international incident."

"And you got nominated for the job," Avery said.

Annie nodded. "And because the situation was so volatile politically, they wanted to keep as few people as possible in the loop. Which is the only reason Tom didn't tell Nash about the change in plans."

"I can understand Tom's reasons," Nash said. "It's yours I don't get. We were partners."

"Past tense. You'd just told me you were leaving—remember? And that you didn't have room in your life for me. So when Tom asked me to keep it quiet, I respected his request. What did you expect me to do?"

"Watch my back maybe? I thought we meant more to each other than that. Obviously I was mistaken."

"You're the one that threw what we had away," she said, heart pounding as the memories threatened to overwhelm her. "Don't lay that on me. And as to having your back, you wouldn't be sitting here if it weren't for me. You have no idea what I risked to go back in there and get you. So don't you dare play the guilt card on me."

"Saved my life." He laughed, the sound harsh and bitter. "That's a good one. *You* left me there to die. Payback for choosing A-Tac over you, I guess. Anyway, the point is when I needed you—you were gone. Tom's the one who pulled my ass out of the fire."

"Tom never left the fucking helicopter."

"Look," Avery said, his voice cutting through the building tension. "I realize that this is hard. That there are things going on here that go way beyond reliving an old operation. But accusing each other isn't going to get us any closer to finding the truth. So if you can sheath the verbal swords, maybe you can walk me through what happened without the emotional subtext."

"That's not as easy as it sounds," Annie said.

"I know." Avery's eyes were kind. "But Tom's going to be here any minute and I guarantee you he's not going to listen to any of your protestations."

"So why are you?" Annie asked, stomach roiling.

"Because this whole thing stinks. It has from the beginning. I just haven't been able to figure out why. And now for the first time maybe we're getting somewhere. But I can't know that for certain until I understand the extent of Kim Sun's connection to all of this. So do you think you can tell me what happened without tearing each other apart?"

Annie nodded, shifting to avoid looking at Nash. "We went in undercover, posing as aid workers. Once we were near Saida and the building where they were allegedly holding Jin, we holed up and waited until nightfall."

They'd hardly spoken at all. Each of them lost in their own thoughts. So many angry words had already been exchanged, there seemed little point in rehashing the inevitable. Instead they'd focused on the mission. Or at least what Nash had believed was the mission.

"Once it was dark, it was simply a matter of infiltrating the warehouse," Nash continued. "We had two other operatives with us. One handling communications, the other fluent in Lebanese. My Arabic is passing but not up to regional dialect. We hadn't worked with either before, but they were good men."

"Were?" Avery prompted.

"They're dead." The words hung in the air, radiating between Annie and Nash.

"You think it's my fault," Annie said.

"I'm not saying anything, except that they shouldn't have died."

"Well, it wasn't because of me or my part in the mission." She blew out a breath and pushed back her hair, trying to do as Avery'd asked and keep the emotion out of it. "We made it inside the warehouse without incident.

Took out two of their guards, before either of them had a chance to radio for help. In fact, in hindsight, maybe we should have known something was off. It was just too easy."

"According to intel, Jin was being kept in a room on the top floor of the building," Nash said. "We secured the stairwell, and had made it about three flights when Jake, the communications guy, got a garbled message from base. We couldn't make out any of the details, but it was clear that something was wrong. Somehow the kidnappers had learned we were coming and set up an ambush."

"We thought about aborting, but we were so close to our objective it seemed ridiculous to bail."

"We'd been in tougher spots and come out in one piece." Nash nodded. "Anyway, we were all of one accord. Find the kid and get the hell out of there."

"So we came out on the top floor and started making our way toward the room intel had designated. But before we were halfway down the hall, all hell broke loose."

"They were coming at us from everywhere," Nash interrupted. "They'd definitely been expecting us. It was full-out war. Everything was chaos. All I could think of was trying to get the team out alive. But when I tried to signal for retreat, Annie had disappeared."

"Mission always comes first. And I knew I had to complete mine. So I made it to the room where they were supposed to be holding Jin. It was empty, but as I turned to go, a man rushed me, firing all out. I hit the ground, rolling to try to avoid the bullets, and shot on instinct. The fighting outside in the hallway was gaining momentum, but the room was suddenly silent. I realized I'd managed to take out my attacker. And when I turned him over, I saw that it was Jin."

"Well done. While the rest of us were getting the shit kicked out of us, you managed to accomplish your objective," Nash said, bitterness coloring his voice.

"I tried to come back into the hall," she snapped, reliving the fear she'd felt in that moment, "but the fighting was too heavy. So I climbed out a window and managed to maneuver my way down. Once I was out of range, I started to call for backup, but before I could make contact with anyone, the building exploded. There was fire and smoke everywhere. Debris raining down. The damn thing was like a beacon inviting all comers, all chance of secrecy blown with the building. So I radioed Tom and told him what was going down, and then I went back in." She met Nash's gaze, her own steady. "To get you."

He opened his mouth to argue, but then closed it again, waiting.

"At first I couldn't see anything. But I could hear. There was still gunfire. Which meant someone was still alive. So I made my way back to the stairwell. The smoke was so heavy I could hardly breathe. Parts of the stairway were completely gone, and I had to literally claw my way up.

"But I kept going. The only thought in my mind was that you were trapped up there somewhere. I made the third-floor landing and realized there was no way to go any farther. The entire staircase had collapsed in the blast.

"So I made my way into the hallway. Everything was on fire, masonry crumbling around my head. There was no one on the floor, at least no one alive. So I moved forward, remembering finally that there was a workman's passage in the west wall. A crawl space between floors.

"Above me, the shooting slowed and then stopped. I knew I had to move quickly. So I made my way into the work space and up the ladder leading to the fourth floor. By the time I accessed the hallway, there was fire everywhere. I found Drew—the interpreter—first. He was already dead. Bullet wound to the head.

"Jake was next. He was still alive. Barely. Shrapnel had torn off his right arm. He was bleeding to death, and before I could do anything, he was gone. I'd taken too long."

Annie paused, gulping for air, but when Avery started to speak she shook her head. "I need to finish this." She dragged her hand through her hair, the memories coming fast now. "I was certain, then, that Nash was dead. I don't think I've ever felt as alone as I did in that moment. There were other casualties. Enemy combatants. And I have to tell you I rejoiced in their deaths.

"And then there was a noise, coming from the far end of the corridor. I pushed my way past debris, praying that I hadn't imagined it, that somehow, Nash had managed to survive. And then he was there. Battered and broken, but alive." She smiled despite herself, her eyes filling with tears as she looked at Nash. "I tried to explain what had happened but you were bleeding badly and totally beyond comprehending. And the fires were getting more intense. I knew I couldn't carry you. And I sure as hell wasn't going to leave you.

"So I dragged you to a window and shot off a flare. I knew it was the equivalent of a Hail Mary pass. But it was our only chance. And miracle of miracles, a helicopter appeared out of the smoke. Tom riding to the rescue. Clearly, that's the part you remember.

"But I was there, Nash. I held Jake as he died, and I pulled you out of the rubble. I didn't leave you. I wouldn't do that. Not ever."

"Then why didn't you come to the hospital?" he asked, his voice rough with emotion. "Why did you just disappear?"

"I did come. Once. But you were pretty out of it."

"And after that?"

"Tom said it would be best if I didn't come again. That to protect the operation I had to disappear. So I left."

"Hell of a story," Avery said, his eyes narrowed in concentration as he considered her words.

"Exactly the word I would have chosen," Nash said, anger and confusion coloring his voice. *"Story."*

"So you don't believe her?" Avery asked.

Annie held her breath, waiting. Feeling as if somehow everything that mattered depended on his answer.

"I don't know," he said, avoiding eye contact. "Some of the details fit with what Tom told me. Others don't."

"What about your own memories?" Avery frowned. "How does Annie's story match up to that?"

"I don't have any memories," he sighed, his frustration evident. "At least not cognizant ones. The doctors said it was normal to forget, my brain protecting me. I remember everything up to our arrival in Saida, but after that I've got a big gaping hole. There are fragments, but most of them don't make a hell of a lot of sense. I'm afraid all I really have to go on is what Tom told me. And, at the end of the day, he wasn't actually there."

"I'm telling the truth," Annie said, her own frustration

cresting. There was so much riding on their believing her. "It happened just the way I described it."

"Then why would Tom let me believe you deserted me?" Their gazes collided and she willed hers steady, her stomach tightening with anxiety.

"I don't know," she snapped. "Maybe for the same reason he didn't tell you about the real objective of the mission. Maybe he didn't trust you anymore. After all, you were the one deserting the ship."

"Oh, for God's sake, Annie. I wasn't deserting anything. I was just seizing an opportunity. A good one, I might add. And besides, Tom supported the move. He even helped me secure the transfer. So I hardly think trust was the issue."

"Then I guess it was just need to know." She shrugged, the gesture an attempt to hide the fear and doubt crashing through her. "Maybe he lied to protect me. To keep me safe." It was a comforting thought, but she knew in her heart the facts weren't there to support it.

"And maybe you're the one who's lying," Nash said, his voice taunting.

"You don't believe that." She leaned forward, her hands clenching the edge of the table, feeling as if everything important depended on his answer.

"No," he said, shaking his head. "I guess I don't. But that doesn't change anything."

"You're wrong," she whispered. "It changes everything."

Silence stretched between them, and for a moment, everything else disappeared. Avery, the war room. All of their problems. For just one second out of time, there was nothing but the two of them and the emotions that bound them together.

Then Avery cleared his throat, and the fragile connection broke, placing them back on opposite sides again. "So what happened after the rescue?"

Annie leaned back in her chair again, forcing herself to breathe. To clear her mind of everything but the situation at hand. "Nash was evacuated to a military facility in Germany. And the CIA went all out to create a cover story for the incident—an American construction company helping to advise a Lebanese conglomerate. Something went wrong and the building exploded. A horrible accident with limited casualties. Fortunately for everyone, the fire destroyed most of the evidence."

"What about Kim Sun?" Avery asked.

"He was told his son perished in the fire. I don't know the particulars. I wasn't there."

"Where were you?"

"After the airlift, I went back to Vienna—" Annie paused, looking down at her hands. "There was a safe house there. My cover was blown, so I waited there for word on Nash, and for orders from Tom."

"How exactly was your cover compromised?" Avery asked.

"Someone who saw me in Saida and connected me with the explosion? I never really knew for certain. Once Tom got the ball rolling, things moved pretty quickly. I went to visit Nash, and from there I was sent back to the States."

"Did the CIA handle your relocation?"

"I assume so, although I never had contact with anyone beyond Tom and a few people he said he trusted."

"Did you stay in touch with him?" Nash asked.

"No. Only a couple of times in the beginning. I needed

his help with a few things. But after that, he made it pretty clear that I wasn't to call him anymore. I shouldn't have been surprised. I mean, they tell us from the beginning that we're expendable. That for all practical purposes we don't even exist. I knew if things ever went really wrong I'd be on my own. But I guess I never expected to be completely cut off."

"So you had no contact with anyone from your old life?" Avery asked.

She swallowed tears as she fought against memories. "There was no one to contact."

"And Adam's father?" Nash queried, his words cutting through her doubts. "Did he know the truth?"

"I told you, he wasn't in the picture." She wrestled for control and won. "Just a mistake I made. Although that isn't really accurate, I suppose, considering Adam is the greatest gift I've ever had. Look, I know you're trying to figure out if I inadvertently gave myself away. And I can't tell you that it's impossible. But I did everything I could to keep my past buried. I had to, for my son."

"Still," Avery said, "if Kim knew you killed his son, he'd have had the motivation to find you."

"And make me pay," Annie said, shivering as she remembered Kim's words. "That's what he said on the phone—in the motel room. He wanted to make me pay."

"By kidnapping and killing your son."

"So you believe me?" Hope flooded through her even as she forced herself to remain wary.

"There's no denying he kidnapped Adam. We've got witnesses who can identify him," Avery allowed. "And when you couple that with the events of eight years ago, it all falls into place."

"And Dominico?" she asked, keeping her expression guarded as she watched Avery. "Do you still think I killed him?"

"I'm not sure it matters what I think once Homeland Security gets hold of the evidence. But, no, I don't think you did it."

"So you'll help me?"

"If I can," Avery said. "But you have to do things my way. Is that understood?"

Annie nodded, her gaze darting between the two of them.

"And the two of you have to find a temporary truce. I can't have you working at odds with each other. There's too much riding on this."

"Fine," she said, her agreement a necessary evil. She knew she couldn't trust them. Nash, most of all. Last night, he'd made her feel as if anything were possible. And then he'd callously ripped it all away, his doubt negating the love she'd thought she'd seen in his eyes, a love she'd thought long dead.

Hope was a dangerous thing.

Especially in the hands of a fool.

CHAPTER **20**

One of the things Nash loved most about Sunderland was the campus. Set among towering trees, the ivy-covered brick buildings, some dating back to the 1800s, were surrounded by stone walls and cobblestone walkways. The quiet hush of the grassy lawns lent an air of academic solitude even when the grounds were flooded with students. And now, on a Saturday, with only a few students out and about, it was positively peaceful.

Or it would have been if only he didn't have so much on his mind.

For eight long years, he'd believed Annie had betrayed him. Left him to die in Saida. And now, in the space of only a couple of hours, everything he'd believed had been turned on its end.

He headed up the steps to the Aaron Thomas Center. Usually he prided himself on staying removed from operations, on keeping his personal feelings locked away. But this was different. This was Annie.

And yet, he'd doubted her. From the beginning, he'd believed she had crossed over to the other side. And with Dominico's death, the evidence of her guilt had seemed irrefutable. But if he truly cared about her, surely he'd have never allowed himself to be swayed.

It was all so damn complicated.

And it was far from over. Avery was right. There were other forces at work here. People who didn't give a damn about Annie's past. About Kim or his son or the things she'd done for love of country. All they were going to see was a scapegoat. And the evidence mounting against her.

Which was why it was crucial that Avery win Tom over when he arrived. That he convince the powers that be to let A-Tac work with Annie to take down the real culprit—Kim Sun.

Nash blew out a breath and nodded at a couple of passing coeds as he stepped into the faculty elevator. The girls giggled and whispered as they passed. Nash suddenly felt old. And tired.

It was all so twisted. Or maybe that was the problem. Maybe twisted was the norm, part and parcel of who they all really were, damaged individuals who chose danger and adrenaline in an effort to avoid anything at all resembling real life.

He stepped off the elevator and slapped his hand against Aaron Thomas and walked through the open door. To the left, in one of the computer rooms, he could see Adam, feet swinging off the floor as he concentrated on something on the screen.

"Hey, dude, whatcha up to?" he asked, stepping past the security guard to look over Adam's shoulder at the fight on the screen. "Pretty bad-ass dragon."

"I know, but he isn't that hard to defeat." Adam hit a key and then another and the dragon bellowed fire and then disappeared. "See?"

"You're really good," Nash said.

"Nah." Adam shook his head. "It's an easy game. I've beat it a couple of times. There's a sequel out, Wings of the Dragon II, but Mom won't buy it for me. She thinks I play too much."

"Moms can be like that." Nash shrugged.

"Did your mom let you play computer games?" The boy tilted his head to one side, considering the idea of Nash as a gamer.

Nash laughed. "She did, but our games weren't nearly as good as yours. I started with something called Space Quest. The graphics sucked but the game was pretty fun. There was this one part where if you let a monster kiss you, then later on, a monster jumps out of your stomach."

"Cool," Adam said. "Like *Alien*."

"Yeah, only not as scary. I'm surprised you've seen it."

"I wasn't supposed to. Mom watched it on Halloween. She likes scary movies. And I snuck to the top of the stairs and watched from there." He stopped, clearly regretting the admission. "You won't tell her, will you?"

"No way." Nash held out a fisted hand. "Swear." They bumped knuckles and Adam grinned, the first true smile Nash had seen from the boy. He looked so damn much like his mother.

"You want to try?" Adam said, hopping up from the chair. "I can coach you."

Nash nodded, sliding in front of the computer screen.

"Okay," Adam continued, leaning close. "The arrow

buttons move you right and left. And the space bar makes you jump. The up button is your sword. All you got to do is remember that dragons have really mushy bellies."

The dragon roared, and Nash started swiping the air with his sword, jumping to miss the dragon's bursts of fire.

"Careful," Adam warned as Nash moved too close to the dragon's claws.

Nash swung again, hitting the dragon on the chin. The beast howled and the green life bar above his head dropped down to halfway. Adrenaline surged as Nash focused in on the fight, parrying to the left, then faking the dragon to move right.

"Go," Adam cheered. "You're almost there. Now."

Nash thrust upward, pressing the appropriate computer key for everything it was worth. "Come on, buddy, die already." He moved to the side, then thrust again, this time cutting into the beast's leathery hide.

"Just a little more to the left," Adam counseled.

Nash lunged right, then struck left, his sword slicing through the soft belly of the beast. The dragon roared, then burst into flames and disappeared.

"See," Adam said. "I told you it was easy."

"No way I could have done it without your help," Nash said, feeling his beeper vibrate against his thigh. He reached into his pocket and checked the message.

"You gotta go?" Adam asked, looking disappointed.

"Afraid so. I've got to go to a meeting, but I'd like to play again later if you're up for it."

"And in the meantime," Jason said, appearing in the doorway, "you can play with me."

"Cool," Adam said, hopping on one foot with excitement. "Jason's really good."

"Which I guess puts me in my place." Nash laughed, surprised at how at ease he felt—and how much he hated to break the mood. "But I learn pretty quickly."

"You did great," the boy added supportively. "Honest, you did."

"Thanks." Nash smiled. "But now I'm afraid I've got to go to work."

The kid's expression sobered. "To help my mom."

"Yeah. And to keep you safe."

Adam nodded solemnly, his eyes looking way too old. "You gotta kill the dragon."

"Exactly," Nash said. "But first we've got to find him."

"So what have we got?" Nash asked as he walked into the war room, dropping down into a chair next to Drake. Annie was sitting across the table. Their gazes met briefly, but she turned away. Hannah, who was sitting at the head of the table next to Emmett, raised an eyebrow, and Nash shrugged. No one said working with Annie was going to be easy.

Tyler sat at the other end of the table, next to Lara. The only ones missing in action were Avery, who was working on arrangements for their meeting with Tom, and Jason, who, having drawn the lucky straw, was still playing computer games with Adam.

"I was just telling everyone that I'd managed to ID the two bodies Annie and Drake took out. And it looks like the stakes are getting higher. These men are both players. Antoine Marcel is a French mercenary.

International connections. No political agenda. Just follows the money."

"And the other one?" Drake asked.

"Yuri Atomov. Russian dissident with ties to radical communist splinter groups. No known relationship with Ashad. And nothing to connect him to Kim or Rivon. But he's definitely got a history of providing muscle when the price is right. So my guess is that they were both just hired guns."

"What about the scene?" Nash asked Tyler. "You guys find anything?"

"Nothing concrete. The car was clean. And there was nothing on the bodies except a couple of cell phones."

"Both throwaways," Emmett said.

"So nothing at all to help clear my name." Annie's tone was bitter and she still kept her gaze averted from his.

"I wouldn't say that." Drake shrugged. "I did find corroboration that you were at the Sweet Rest. The name on the register was just as you said it would be and the manager identified your picture."

"I told you I was telling the truth," Annie said, her chin lifting as her eyes met Nash's.

"It wasn't enough, Annie," Lara said. "Nothing the manager said changes the timeline. You could easily have checked in and then driven on to Dominico's."

"What about the room?" she asked. "There should have been prints. Something to prove we were there? The White Castle trash?"

"The room had been wiped clean." Emmett shook his head. "Professionally, if I had to call it. So either you did it, or someone wanted it to look that way. Jason and I went over the phone Rivon gave you again, and there was still nothing. Which leaves us, I'm afraid, with a hell of a lot of questions."

"You've all been briefed, I take it, on what happened in Lebanon?" Nash asked.

"Yes." Hannah nodded. "And I've been working up some information on Kim Sun."

"So what did you find?" Annie's hands clenched and unclenched, her nails biting into her skin as she struggled against her demons.

"The guy pretty much disappeared after his son was killed," Hannah said, flashing a picture up on the overhead screen. "The notoriety surrounding Jin's death and the resulting investigation pretty much doomed his career. He resigned his post, but there's evidence he was actually forced out of the diplomatic corps."

"For a time," Drake said, taking up the story, "he worked as a consultant. But there are at least some indications that his dealings began to move toward the political fringes."

"We can't substantiate this, of course." Hannah shrugged. "But there have been indications that Kim has become a key player in the effort for Korean reunification."

"But he's South Korean," Annie said with a confused frown. "I thought they were happy with their freedom."

"Most of them are," Nash agreed. "But there are those who feel the country was better off united. And communist."

"Like the pro-Soviet movement in Russia," Tyler added.

"Exactly." Hannah nodded. "Part of it is nationalistic pride, and part of it is the belief that the communist path is the right way. Anyway, bottom line is that we believe Kim Sun is involved in clandestine operations to work toward reunification of Korea under communist rule. Actions that certainly wouldn't endear him to the United States. And worse, Kim's political proclivities have led to involvement with other, more violent fringe groups, primarily Asian. Although there is some reason to believe that he's also had contact with several Arabic extremist groups as well."

"All of which makes him a dangerous man with even more dangerous friends," Annie acknowledged, "but I don't see how it relates to his vendetta against me."

"It doesn't." Emmett shook his head. "At least not directly. But it does mean that Kim is tied in to a pretty evolved underground network, which will make it all that much easier for him to stay under the radar."

"Meaning it could be impossible to find him," Annie said.

"No. I'm not saying that. I'm just saying that our work is going to be cut out for us."

"When was the last time he was seen in the United States?" Lara asked.

"Five years ago," Hannah said, punching up another photograph, this one more recent. "He attended an international peace conference. After that, nothing shows up in current immigration or airport security records. So if he's here, he's under an assumed name."

"The guy's like a ghost," Emmett confirmed. "The CIA's got a file on him, but most of it pertains to the incident in Saida, most of that limited to the official story."

"That there was an industrial accident." Annie nodded.

"Exactly," Emmett said. "And according to the official record, Jin was touring the area when the explosion occurred, his death ancillary. There were no charges filed, although there was an official protest by the Korean government on Kim's behalf."

"But after doing their own investigation, they ended up satisfied with the official explanation." Hannah crossed her arms and frowned. "Kim, however, was never convinced. He was certain there was more to the story."

"And apparently there was," Nash acknowledged, surprised that the idea no longer made him feel betrayed.

"How the hell do you think he found out that Annie was involved?" Drake asked. "I mean, our government went to great lengths to cover up what really happened. And not to blow our own horn, we're pretty good at that kind of thing. Not to mention that Annie was totally out of the picture with her defection."

"It wasn't a defection," she protested. "I was supposed to go underground to protect the sanctity of the mission."

"No way to question the plebes if they've left the building," Emmet said to no one in particular.

"It doesn't matter how deep they buried it." Tyler shrugged. "If someone is patient and tenacious, anything is possible. There had to be people that knew what really went down. Tom for one. But there would have been others as well. Maybe someone spilled the beans."

"For the right amount of money." Drake's contempt was blatant.

"Hey," Lara said, "there are all kinds of reasons to release information. Some of them actually understandable. Although I'll admit, nine times out of ten it's about greed."

"It's also possible that maybe Annie just slipped up," Tyler said, shooting Annie an apologetic look.

"No way," she said, shaking her head. "Not with Adam to think about. If anything, I was overly cautious. Well, whatever the source, I think we can all agree that Kim knows the truth. It's the only thing that ties it all together."

"But why now?" Emmett mused. "I mean, the operation is old news. And Jin's been dead for a hell of a long time."

"There's no statute of limitations on a father's love," Tyler said.

"Or on his need for revenge." Drake's take, as usual, was the more cynical, but Nash had to agree.

"So somehow Kim finds out the truth about what really happened in Saida, and then with a little digging he figures out that Annie was the guilty party."

"But how the hell did he find me?"

"There's no way to know," Emmett said. "If he had someone on the inside, maybe they had access to whatever Tom kept from the original mission. The truth is there are countless ways he could have found you."

"Anyway, once he did, it was just a matter of planning and executing his revenge," Drake said. "First he kidnaps your son, using Adam to maneuver you into killing an American dignitary. But why? What'd he have against Dominico?"

"I don't think it was ever about Dominico," Nash said. "Except maybe as a bonus round. Dominico wasn't exactly pro-Korea, especially the movement for reunification. But I think the real goal here was to punish Annie."

"To make her pay for what she'd done to Jin," Lara prompted.

"That and what she'd done to Kim Sun himself. I mean, for all practical purposes she ruined his life. And I expect he wanted to ruin hers as well."

"First by killing her son," Tyler said. "An eye for an eye."

"So why not just kill me, too?" Annie asked, her voice cracking as she struggled with the enormity of Kim's threat and the reasons behind it.

"Dying would be too easy," Drake said. "Killing Dominico would mean you'd be charged with treason or murder, take your pick. Couple that with the loss of your son. Can you think of a better way to ruin someone's life?"

"Annie's in particular," Nash mused, avoiding Annie's gaze. She'd always prided herself on helping to rid the world of dangerous men, people determined to take out all vestiges of civilization and democracy.

"And so when things went wrong," Emmett mused, "and we rescued Adam—"

"—he moved on to plan B," Drake concluded. "Kill Dominico himself and frame Annie. Same ending, just a different way of getting there."

"But then why go after me at the motel?" she asked.

"Maybe the goal was to get you out of there, so they could sanitize. That would explain the phone call. Or maybe it was just a reaction to your running," Lara said.

"Without Kim to answer our questions definitively we're not going to have anything but conjecture." Emmett shook his head. "The more important thing is to consider the fact that if there was a plan B, then that means Kim had to have already planned for the possibility of failure with his initial scenario."

"You're talking about the fingerprint and hair sample." Tyler frowned.

"Yes." Emmett nodded. "It's easy enough to transfer a print from one surface to another if you know what you're doing. All Kim had to do was have one of his flunkies secure Annie's print and while he was at it, grab a hair sample."

"Rivon could have managed it," Lara suggested. "He met with her several times. Or maybe Kim's people pulled the samples when they took the kid. Annie's hair and prints had to be all over the room."

"Or maybe it was the man in the hotel room," Annie said, her brows drawn together as she considered the idea. "It would certainly explain his presence."

"Makes more sense than anything else we've considered," Nash agreed. "I don't suppose you have anything new on his identity?"

"No." Lara shook her head. "Langley verified that the fingerprints we lifted weren't in any of our files. And the DNA hasn't popped yet either."

"But maybe we have a new angle," Hannah said, already typing furiously on her laptop. "Annie, you told me the guy was Asian, right?"

"Yeah." She nodded. "But I can't be sure. I didn't get that good a look at him."

"What about you, Nash?" Drake asked.

"I didn't see him except for a brief moment, and that was through the haze of the hotel curtains. He was definitely Asian but he wasn't old enough to be Kim, if that's what you're getting at."

"No." Hannah shook her head. "I wouldn't expect Kim to do his own dirty work. But usually when people plan an operation as big as this one, they have someone they trust. Someone at the top who is privy to all the planning and is part of the implementation."

"But we haven't seen any evidence of that at all," Emmett said. "None of the accomplices we've turned up so far have a Korean connection. Hell, not even an Asian one."

"Understood," Hannah said, still typing. "But the people we've uncovered so far have just been lackeys. Paid help, so to speak. Even the big guns were the kind of folks that couldn't easily be tied to Kim. But nobody operates in a vacuum. And the intruder at Annie's hotel room has never fit what we knew of the plan."

"So you're saying that he's the inside guy?" Nash frowned, turning the idea over in his mind. "Someone Kim knows and trusts?"

"Exactly." Hannah nodded. "The lower-level operation was for Annie's benefit. So that she'd believe that she had to kill Dominico. By having unknowns on the payroll, Kim had insurance that if things went badly, Annie wouldn't have anything to implicate him. Just Rivon and the planted information about Ashad."

"But Kim was at the farmhouse," Annie said, shaking her head. "Which meant Rivon and the others saw him."

"And they were all supposed to die," Tyler reminded them. "That bomb was meant to take out the whole lot— except Rivon."

"Well, it definitely wasn't Rivon in my hotel room," Annie said.

"It was someone Asian," Hannah reiterated, still typing.

"So maybe we need to be checking the fingerprints against Asian databases," Drake suggested.

"Korean in particular." Lara nodded. "Although I have to say that even if it is a Korean, Kim could have been working with anyone. And figuring out who isn't going to be easy."

"Yes, but maybe we were looking in the wrong places," Nash said. "And if we can tie the intruder to Kim, it'll go a long way toward proving Annie was framed."

"Needle in a haystack," Emmett muttered.

"Can't you check DNA for that kind of thing?" Drake asked. "Alleles or something?"

"Come again?" Nash asked.

"Alleles are part of a pair of genes. They're used to identify particular characteristics. Race, among other things," Lara explained. "But I'm not sure that identifying the intruder's nationality is going to definitively tie Kim to the intruder."

"It might. If the man is related," Hannah said with a triumphant smile as she flashed a new photograph on the overhead screen. The man looked like a younger version of Kim. "It seems there were two brothers. Jin and Chin-Mae." She waved at the screen. "Meet Chin-Mae."

"So why are we just now hearing this?" Tyler asked.

"Because Chin-Mae was just a kid when his brother died. And because his father's always kept him off the radar. I stumbled across a reference when I was searching for info on Kim. But I hadn't put two and two together until you mentioned the age of the assailant in the hotel room. Anyway, I know it's a long shot. But the CIA has a DNA sample on Kim. Which means we should be able to compare it to the DNA we found on the hotel balcony. Right?" Hannah asked.

"It's possible." Lara nodded. "Assuming I can obtain the full records. It's just a simple paternity test."

"And if we can prove that it was Chin-Mae in my room," Annie said, hope mirrored on her face, "then we'll be a whole lot closer to proving the connection to Kim."

"Which would be a good thing," Avery responded, striding into the room. "Sorry to have to break up the meeting, but I need Annie and Nash to come with me. Tom Walker's here. And I'm afraid he's gunning for Annie."

CHAPTER **21**

don't care what the fuck you think you know," Tom said, his expression guarded. "I've got the authority to take Annie back to D.C. for prosecution. And that's exactly what I intend to do."

Avery had sequestered the four of them in a conference room deep in the bowels of headquarters, away from prying eyes, although Annie figured the room was probably wired for sound. Her head was still reeling from all the developments of the day, her primary concern still Adam's safety. But not only had Avery doubled security, he'd had someone from A-Tac with the boy all day.

So at least for the moment, she felt like she could concentrate on the present. On fighting for her life—possibly quite literally—as they tried to present the case that Annie'd been framed. Needless to say, Annie still felt as if she were caught in a dangerous tug-of-war. And worst of all, she was having trouble concentrating with Nash in the room.

She knew he had doubts. And until those doubts were

assuaged, she knew that he wouldn't be able to trust her completely. Professionally, she needed that trust. Needed him to believe in her innocence and the necessity of finding and taking out Kim Sun once and for all. And on a personal level—well, she wasn't certain she was ready to deal with all of that. He'd hurt her as much as she'd hurt him. Maybe there was no recovering from that.

The thought was more painful than she could have imagined.

"Until I verify the truth about what happened in Saida," Avery was saying, his expression thunderous, "and until we hear from our respective commanders, you're not going anywhere. I don't like being played."

"No one has been playing you, Avery." Tom shook his head. "Saida is just old news in light of today's assassination."

"But we have proof that Kim Sun was involved," Nash argued.

"You have theories. *I* have proof." Tom waved the file with the fingerprint and DNA evidence.

"And I have the ear of the president," Avery said, pulling all attention firmly back to his corner of the table. "Which means that I expect you to tell me the truth. Were there counterorders for the mission to Saida?"

"You know as well as I do that I can't confirm or disconfirm anything without proper clearance." Tom crossed his arms over his chest, his face guarded. "Annie shouldn't have shared classified information. It's a breach of protocol."

"There is no protocol on an eight-year-old mission," Annie snapped, her patience wearing thin. She'd never been much on playing the political game, and despite the fact that she'd once considered Tom her friend, the day's revelations had left her doubting the validity of her memories.

His motives, seen from her new vantage point, seemed suddenly suspect. Especially considering the fact that Homeland Security and the CIA weren't particularly good at playing nice with each other, turf wars regularly erupting as their missions intersected and overlapped.

Annie might not be ready to completely commit to trusting A-Tac, but in a firefight she'd take Avery and Nash over Tom every time.

"Even if there was protocol," Avery said, his voice deceptively soft, "Annie's no longer bound by it. And considering the enormity of the situation at hand, I think the time for full disclosure is at hand."

"I haven't got the authority," Tom insisted.

"What am I missing here?" Avery asked, shaking his head. "You said it yourself—the operation's old news, which makes it a dead issue as far as internal agencies are concerned. All I'm looking for is confirmation that Annie's version of events is true."

"What about the evidence against Annie?" Tom asked, deftly turning the argument away from the past. "Are you just going to pretend it doesn't exist?"

"It's not like that kind of thing can't be faked," Annie ground out. "Besides, if nothing else, there's my word that I didn't do it. That used to mean something. What happened to you? You've turned into the kind of blustering bureaucrat we used to make fun of."

"I care about our country's security. And I care about bringing Dominico's killer to justice."

"Well, you're barking up the wrong tree. I didn't kill the man."

"So you say." Tom shook his head, clearly not buying the idea.

"There are definitely signs that she's being played, Tom," Nash said. "The timeline is there for her to have been at Dominico's, but the rest of the facts don't line up."

Tom's eyebrows shot up. "Surely you of all people aren't buying into this?"

"I don't know what to think." He shook his head, his eyes narrowing as he watched Tom. "But I also don't understand why you're out to get Annie. She's right, you know her. Know us. And yet, you're not interested in helping her at all."

"I'm interested in justice."

"You're interested in you," Nash said. "That's always the way it's been. I just didn't realize how much."

"You always had a weakness when it came to Annie." Tom shrugged. "But I'm not as easily fooled. And I just can't ignore the fact that we've got evidence that places her at the scene. And nothing you've told me here is strong enough to refute those facts."

"It's enough to cast reasonable doubt," Avery said. "And last I checked that's all that's needed. We know that Kim Sun was behind Adam's kidnapping. And if the child is to be believed, Kim is behind the phone calls as well. And once we establish for certain that the man in Annie's hotel room was Kim's son, we'll have incontrovertible evidence that the two of them are part of this."

"Maybe. But that only gives testament to Annie's motivation. If Kim is still threatening her son, it follows that she'd finish what she started. And there's the fact that she ran away from here. Why would she do that when this is probably the safest place she could be?"

"Because she overheard us talking about your coming to get her," Nash admitted, his words sending Annie's stomach reeling. Listening to Tom, even she was starting to believe she was guilty.

"Seems to me that just supports her guilt. I mean, why would an innocent person run?"

"I was fighting for my life—and Adam's." Annie felt as if she were drowning. One step forward, three steps back. "But I was coming back when Dominico's goons intercepted me."

"Because you were in trouble." Tom smirked. "Have there been any further phone calls?"

Annie shook her head. "No, but—"

"My point exactly." Tom smiled, the expression lacking any humor. "Dominico is dead. Your part in this little farce is over. And there's no further threat to your son."

"As long as Kim Sun is out there, there's a threat. Surely you can see that?" She shot a look at Nash and Avery, hoping for support. "The man is looking for payback. He said so himself."

"I see nothing of the sort. If Kim Sun was involved, I'll concede that he should be brought to justice, but that doesn't change the facts as they stand. Which means that you also have to pay for your crimes."

"I didn't kill Dominico, and I'll be damned if I'm going to let you use me as a scapegoat." She shot a pleading look in Avery's direction.

"What's really going on here, Tom?" Avery asked. "Nash and Annie are right. You're just a little too zealous about bringing her to justice. The facts may not all be in place. But I, for one, think we've got something more complicated than just an ex-CIA agent taking out a diplomat to save her son. I can understand why she'd run. But if nothing else, I can't see her taking her son along while she offs a man."

"She had no problem putting him in the middle of a gunfight on the side of the highway."

"That wasn't my fault. Maybe I could have handled it better. But I was fighting for Adam's life," Annie responded, wondering if she'd every really known this man at all. "That's what all of this has been about. Fighting to free my son. And you of all people know how much he means to me. What I gave up for him." The minute the words were out she wished them back. It would be so easy for Nash to put it all together. But he wasn't paying attention, his concentration centered instead on Tom.

"I don't know anything about you anymore," Tom said, his tone dismissive.

"Well, I know that she saved two of my operatives." Avery frowned. "That's got to mean something."

"Yeah, that she played you. I saw the reports. Nash's gun jammed. And the only other fingerprints on the gun were Annie's. Are you saying those were transferred as well?"

"No." Annie shook her head, her eyes on Nash. "I did handle the gun. I unpacked the gear. But I didn't do anything to it. Even if I'd wanted to, there wasn't time. And besides, my son was in grave danger. Why would I want to thwart the effort to rescue him?"

"I have no idea what was in your mind. I'm just repeating the facts."

"And avoiding my questions," Avery said, pulling out his BlackBerry and punching in a number.

"Who are you calling?" Tom asked.

"Paul Jackson," Avery responded, lifting the phone to his ear.

"No, wait," Tom said, his voice losing all semblance of bluster.

Annie frowned as Avery disconnected the call. "Who's Paul Jackson?"

"A good friend of Avery's," Nash said, the corner of his lip twitching upward. "And an even closer friend of the president's. He's currently acting as the executive branch's liaison to the CIA. And interestingly enough, he also happens to be married to the head of Homeland Security, Mary Alice Branch, Tom's boss."

Avery shot a pointed look at Tom. "This isn't a bluff."

"You don't have anything to tell them." Tom's try for defiance was undercut by a flicker of fear in his eyes.

"Actually I do, because the order for the hit on Kim Jin didn't come from above, did it, Tom? The order came from you."

Annie sucked in a breath, waiting for something from Tom.

"What on earth would make you think that?" His voice was a little too casual, the note of surprise forced. Annie glanced over at Nash, but his attention was focused on Tom. His frown indicated that he, too, recognized that something was off.

"I did a little research on you, Walker," Avery responded. "Seems your career wasn't exactly cruising along in the fast lane. You'd been passed over for two promotions. Had requested a transfer and even that had been denied. Your ability to handle delicate operations was, shall we say, less than perfect. Your decisions consistently put your operatives in danger. In fact, you'd just been reprimanded again when the order to rescue Kim Jin came through.

"Now of course this is just supposition, but I'm guessing you decided you needed to get Langley's attention, to pull off something big. So you invented the story about Jin's allegiance to the insurgents."

"That's insane," Tom said, his eyes flashing with anger.

"I don't think so." Avery shook his head. "Look, Tom—this can go one of two ways. I've already reported everything we suspect to Jackson. Including Annie's version of what happened in Saida." He paused, his steely gaze impaling Tom's. "One way or the other there's going to be an investigation about what really happened in Lebanon. And the truth is going to come out."

"It's just Annie's word against mine. And Nash's."

"You can count me out," Nash said, his frown fierce now. "In case you've forgotten, I don't remember anything that happened."

"So," Avery continued, leaning forward, his tone deceptively calm, "the way I figure it, you can either come clean and I'll tell Paul you cooperated fully. Or you can keep lying, and when the truth finally comes out it'll be that much worse for you. It's up to you."

For a moment the two men faced off, Avery's dark eyes giving nothing away, Tom's fingers clenched as he considered his options. Then Tom sat down. "What do you want to know?"

"I want to know if you fabricated the information about Jin working with terrorists."

"Actually," Tom said, his face still mottled with anger, "it could have been true. There was some intel suggesting that the kid was in fact associated with Red Sword."

"In Malaysia?" Nash asked, his voice sharp. "What the hell does that have to do with Lebanon?"

"I believed the story that his academic journey was actually cover for his being in the area to train with the Lebanese resistance movement. And that his so-called kidnapping was, in fact, his attempt to cover his ass when his father suspected something was amiss."

"And you had evidence to back this up?" Avery queried.

Tom hesitated.

"I take it that's a no."

After a moment's bluster, Tom sighed. "I didn't have enough evidence to make my case, but I knew I was right. And I knew that taking action was the best thing for the country."

"The best action for you, you mean." Nash's tone was harsh as he stared at Tom, his eyes filled with incredulity. "You thought that if you pulled off the assassination— proved that Jin was a traitor—you'd get a promotion."

"I acted as a patriot." Tom shoulders were ramrod straight as his gaze dueled with Nash's. "Jin's death was for the greater good."

"But you weren't certain he was guilty." Annie's stomach clenched as she grappled with the enormity of what Tom had done. "Which means that it's possible that I shot an innocent man."

"Oh, please," Tom said, his voice harsh with contempt, "you're an assassin. What the hell difference did it make if they were guilty or innocent?"

"It mattered to me," she said, sinking onto a chair.

"The kid was guilty," Tom said. "And if things hadn't gone so terribly wrong I'd have been able to prove it. I'd have been a hero. But once everything went public, it was too late."

"So you covered it up," Nash said. "Pretended the secondary order never existed."

"That's why you wanted me out of the game," Annie said, her incredulity turning to rage. "So there'd be no chance of my telling what really happened."

"It worked for eight years." He shrugged.

"And thanks to your supposed heroics in rescuing me," Nash said, "it accomplished your real mission. You landed that promotion. A top job with Homeland Security."

Annie struggled to breathe. "So I sacrificed my job—my *life*—all of it, just so that you could get a promotion? Tom, we almost died in there. Hell, we lost Drew and Jake. And all of it because of a hunch?"

"You'd have been in the same situation no matter whether the mission was to rescue Jin or kill him. None of that was my fault. And I did rescue Nash. Just not as completely as I led people to believe."

"So Annie's version of the operation is the truth," Nash said, his voice shaking with anger. "She pulled me out of the building."

"Yes. But I was there to get you both out. If I hadn't come for you, you'd both be dead."

"If you hadn't changed the rules of the game," Avery said, "maybe none of this would have happened."

"So my cover was never blown?" Annie asked, realizing for the first time just how much had been lost that day.

"No." Tom shook his head.

"And Nash—you let him believe that I deserted him. That I left him to die?"

"It was better for all of us," Tom said. "I needed to keep

my part in the secondary mission buried. The best way to do that was for you to disappear. Look, I did what was best for everyone under the circumstances. The country had one less threat. Annie got her out. I covered my ass. And Nash was allowed to move on. It was win-win for everyone."

Avery's phone rang, the sound harsh in the emotionally strained atmosphere. "It's Paul Jackson," Avery said, checking caller ID. "I'd better take it." He walked out the door into the hallway, leaving the three of them alone.

"Why didn't you tell me the truth?" Annie asked, her nails digging into her palms as she struggled to maintain control.

"It would have defeated the purpose. And besides, you were always a little too high-minded. I couldn't be sure you wouldn't decide it was better to come clean."

"But we trusted you with our lives. And you threw that trust right back in our faces."

"And lied about everything," Nash said, shaking his head. "You son of a bitch."

"I'm pragmatic." He shrugged. "And if you're honest, so are both of you. So spare me the sanctimonious bullshit. Hell, I did you both a favor. Gave you just exactly what you wanted. Annie got her freedom. And you got A-Tac."

"And people died. Innocent people. And my son..." her voice caught in her throat as she thought of Adam. "My son almost died, too. If Kim is behind all of this, then it's on your head, Tom. Yours."

"You pulled the trigger, Annie."

"You son of a bitch!" Annie lunged forward, Nash catching her by the shoulders, holding her back.

"He's not worth it, Annie." She sucked in a breath and

nodded, tears threatening as she ran the gamut from rage to despair.

"Is everything okay here?" Avery asked with a frown as he strode back into the room.

"She was trying to attack me," Tom said.

"With good cause," Nash snarled, his hands still on Annie's shoulders.

"I should press charges," Tom threatened on a hiss.

"I don't think that'll do you much good." Avery shook his head. "Paul found the original orders. There was no countermand. Tom was definitely acting on his own. And for the record, there was nothing tangible to link Jin to anyone at Red Sword."

"Doesn't mean it wasn't true," Tom said, his tone defiant.

"No. But it does mean that your actions were unconscionable. And that there'll be a full inquiry."

"So I did shoot an innocent man."

"In self-defense," Nash whispered. "None of this was your fault, Annie. You were just following orders."

"Speaking of which," Avery said, his tone devoid of emotion, "A-Tac's been given the green light to go after Kim. Langley agreed with our assessment of the situation and the president's signed off on the operation."

"What about me?" Annie asked, her voice strained.

"You'll be working with us. I convinced Langley that it's in all of our best interest to have you on the team for the duration of the mission."

"What the hell are they thinking?" Tom asked. "Just because there are extenuating circumstances surrounding the events in Saida, that doesn't clear Annie of wrongdoing when it comes to Dominico."

"True." Avery nodded with the hint of a smile. "But Hannah and Lara managed to prove that the fingerprints and blood found on the balcony of Annie's room belonged to one Kim Chin-Mae, Kim Sun's younger son. And Jason found some evidence of erosion on the fingerprints they found on the gun left behind by Dominico's killer. Apparently the pattern's consistent with prints that have been lifted and then transferred from one medium to another."

"So I've been cleared?" Annie said, the rush of hope threatening to swamp her.

"Not completely." Avery shook his head. "But I'd say we're well on the way. All we need to do now is produce Kim."

"And me?" Tom asked. "What happens to me now?"

"Fortunately, for us," Avery said, his eyes narrowed in disgust, "you're no longer a part of the mission. Mr. Jackson has some questions for you. And when he's finished, I suspect your bosses will want to have a go. There are two men waiting outside. They'll be escorting you to D.C. If I were you, Walker, I'd find a very good lawyer."

Tom glared at them both, and then with a self-important harrumph, he turned on his heel and strode out the door.

"So what happens to Tom?" Annie asked, still looking at the empty space where Tom had been standing.

"He could be prosecuted," Avery replied. "Treason isn't out of the question. Which is kind of ironic considering the circumstances."

"That's why he wanted Annie back in Washington so badly, isn't it?" Nash's jaw was still clenched in anger. "He wanted to keep us apart. Keep Annie away from you and the rest of A-Tac, in case we managed to figure it all out."

"Turns out he was right." Avery shrugged. "Anyway, I meant what I said. I think the CIA will handle it internally."

"Take him out, you mean?" Nash's voice was cold. "I can't say that he doesn't deserve it."

"He was our friend," Annie said, the words coming out of their own volition.

"He was never our friend." Nash shook his head. "He was playing us from the very beginning."

"You're right. But it still feels surreal. In the blink of an eye, everything's changed. Like we're on the other side of the mirror."

"Who knows," Avery said, "maybe it's the better side. No one's ever pretended the life we've chosen doesn't come with great risk."

"But I'm not part of that world anymore," Annie sighed. "Although maybe the real truth is that there's never a way out. It's always there. Waiting to get you."

"It's an inherent part of what we do." Avery shrugged. "Something we all accept even as we pretend that it doesn't exist."

"So where do we go from here?" She'd meant the query for both of them, but when she lifted her gaze to Nash's the words took on new meaning, the unanswered question sucking the oxygen from the room. She lifted her hand to touch his face, but he stepped away, shaking his head.

"I don't know, Annie. Right now, I don't know anything. I just need to think." He held her gaze a moment, and her heart twisted at the pain reflected in his eyes. Then without another word, he turned and walked away.

CHAPTER **22**

Nash walked up the steps to his house, his mind racing. In the space of two days everything had changed, his perception of the truth no longer trustworthy. Tom had manipulated everyone, using Annie to further his career, only to discard her when things had gone wrong.

And then there were Tom's lies...

Nash shook his head, trying to clear his mind, but it was useless. There was simply too much going on.

Thanks to a teenage arrest in Korea, Hannah and Lara had proven conclusively that the DNA in Annie's room was in fact a match to Kim Chin-Mae. Unfortunately, the guy was proving as elusive as his father. In the United States on a student visa, Chin-Mae had been the model student until about six months ago when the visa had been revoked and Kim's son had disappeared. Although he and his father were supposedly estranged, Chin-Mae's presence in Annie's hotel room seemed to refute the idea.

Bottom line, father and son were out there somewhere waiting for the fallout from their latest attack on Annie. Or maybe even planning something new.

He slipped the key in the lock, fumbling in his haste to get inside. To get to Annie. Finally, the lock yielded and he stepped into the entryway. The house was quiet and dark. For a moment he considered the possibility that she'd run again. But even as he had the thought, he rejected it. No matter what her feelings were for him, A-Tac was her best hope for protecting Adam.

The hallway was quiet, the soft chiming of a clock upstairs providing the only sound. He climbed the stairs, senses on alert. Avery had added extra layers of security, men patrolling the perimeters both in front and back of the house, but Kim had breached their security once before, and Nash wasn't about to take a chance.

The upstairs hallway was empty and dark, and he relaxed as he stopped in the doorway of Adam's room. The boy was sleeping, an afghan puddled at the foot of the bed, Adam sprawled across the sheets. He was clutching an old, tattered bear, a favorite toy, according to Annie. She'd brought it from Colorado. In part, she'd said, to help her keep hope alive. Hope that had been rewarded as now boy and bear slumbered peacefully.

As if aware of Nash's thoughts, Adam smiled in his sleep, his little arms tightening around the stuffed toy. Nash pulled up the sheet, tucking the boy in, surprised at the warmth he felt in the act. Although he shouldn't have been. After all, Adam was a part of Annie.

With a last lingering look, he headed back into the hallway, intent on finding Annie. There were things they needed to hash out. Questions only she could answer.

Moving with determination, he rounded the corner, almost colliding with Annie coming from the other direction.

Acting on instinct, he grabbed her arm to keep her from falling, the soft silk of her robe sending less-than-pious thoughts racing through his head.

"I thought I heard you, but then I wasn't sure," she whispered.

They stood for a moment, just looking at each other, then with a groan he bent his head to kiss her, his mouth taking possession of hers. He pulled her close, her body heat radiating through the robe, the sweet smell of soap and shampoo teasing his senses.

He knew that they needed to talk. But just for the moment he wanted to hold her. To feel her heart beating against his. Her lips fluttered under his kiss, and he felt the fire growing in intensity. A tiny moan escaped her lips. With ruthless precision, he used the opportunity to deepen the kiss. Their tongues met, thrusting and retreating, dueling for some unknown prize.

He felt himself harden as he pressed against the soft flesh of her thighs. Images of last night flowed into his brain. The rain, the chaise, her eyes closed in abandon as she cried out his name.

His breathing coming in rasps, he moved his mouth, trailing moist kisses down the side of her neck. She threw her head back, allowing him access, her eyes still closed. Pushing back the edge of the robe, he kissed the soft smooth skin of her shoulder as his hand found her breast.

He felt her nipple tighten as he rolled it lightly between thumb and forefinger, satisfied to hear her breathing become labored. Exchanging lips for hand, he circled the taut bud with the tip of his tongue, enjoying the contrast between her nipple and the silken skin of her breast. He could feel the fire building, threatening to consume him.

Lifting his head, he found her lips again, his tongue invading the hot, wet sanctity of her mouth. She pressed herself to him and he placed his hand on her bottom, pulling her even closer, nestling against the hot crevice between her thighs.

He tangled his other hand in her hair, feeling the fine strands wrap around his fingers, clinging with almost a life of their own. He circled her lips with his tongue, tasting toothpaste, and Annie. All he wanted to do was hold her—never let her go. His hand dipped lower, but she jerked away, struggling for breath. "No," she whispered. "We can't. Not here. Not like this."

For a moment he was stunned, her withdrawal almost physically painful. But then he nodded, remembering her son just down the hall. He reached for her hand, already moving toward his room and his bed.

"I can't," she said again, resisting him, her eyes pleading. "Not until we've talked things through. Please?"

He sighed and nodded, pushing away his need. No matter how badly he wanted her, she was right. Too much had happened in too short a time. There were still too many shadows between them.

"I'm sorry," he said. "I shouldn't have assumed..."

"After last night, you had every right. But I need you to listen to what I have to say first. Then if you still want me..." she trailed off, suddenly looking uncomfortable.

"If this is about Dominico—my not believing you— look, Annie, I'm sorry. I jumped to conclusions I shouldn't have. It seems I've been doing that a lot."

"It wasn't your fault. The evidence was pretty overwhelming." She shook her head, her eyes dark with remorse. "Anyway, it's not about that, at least not directly. There's something I need to tell you."

He nodded, something in her voice setting off his internal alarm. Whatever she had to say, he had the feeling it was going to change everything. Except that considering the events of the past forty-eight hours, he couldn't see how that was possible.

"Come to my room," she said, her tone calmer. Stronger. "We can talk there."

He followed her down the hall, trying to collect his thoughts, to dampen the fire still burning inside him. It had always been like this between them. Fire and ice. One minute passion burning out of control and the next reality dousing the flames with cold-hearted abandon.

He followed her into her room, shutting the door behind them.

Annie twisted her hands nervously, sat on the end of the bed, and then jumped up again, walking over to the window. She stood with her back to him, her shoulders tense with trepidation.

"What is it?" he asked, his own stomach churning as he tried to guess what it was she wanted to say. "Just tell me."

"It's about Adam." She turned around, licking her lips in nervous anticipation. "I lied to you. His father isn't dead."

"What are you telling me? That Adam's father is still part of your life?"

"No." She shook her head, a tiny smile lifting the side of her mouth. "Well, sort of. Hell, I'm not handling this right at all." She frowned, clearly having trouble ordering her thoughts. "Do you remember when we were talking to Tom about Adam—and I said that he knew how much Adam meant to me. What I'd given up for him."

Nash nodded, his brain turning as he tried to figure out what she was trying to tell him.

"Well," Annie said, twisting her fingers together, "I was talking about my career. Nash, the reason I agreed so easily with Tom's suggestion that I go underground was because of Adam. I was already pregnant when we went to Saida."

He sucked in a breath, her words grinding home, his mind kicking into gear, the truth presenting itself front and center. It had been there all along. He just hadn't allowed himself to see it. He lifted his gaze to hers, the words coming out on a whisper. "Adam's mine."

She nodded, still chewing on her lip. Then she sucked in a deep breath, hands still linked together for fortification. "Yes. Adam is your son. I found out I was pregnant right before we were assigned the mission in Lebanon."

His mind went numb as he tried to grasp the meaning of her words.

He was a father.

Adam's father.

Annie's baby had been his. There was no other man.

His head spinning, he sank onto the bed, bracing himself with his hands. "So when Tom tried to railroad you, you gave in to protect our son."

"Yes. When Tom told me my cover was blown, it seemed the perfect opportunity to make my escape."

"And you never thought of telling me?" Somewhere beneath his confusion, he could feel anger stirring. He had a son, and she'd kept it from him for almost eight fucking years.

"Of course I did," she said, moving to sit in the chair

opposite the bed. "I tried to tell you that night in Vienna, before we left for Lebanon. But all you could talk about was A-Tac and your new position and how—"

"There was no room in our lives for commitment," he finished for her, his own words echoing in his ears. "Or for family."

"You were adamant about our relationship only being a product of the moment—the kind of life we led." She nodded. "I guess I'd always thought we were a team, in every sense of that word. But when you told me you were leaving, I couldn't tell you I was pregnant. I've always hated women who try to trap a man."

"And you thought if you told me, I'd react just like your father," he said, guilt diluting his anger.

"Yeah," she said, ducking her head to avoid his gaze. "The thought crossed my mind."

"So you kept quiet."

"Yes. Although I didn't think it was going to be forever. I thought eventually I'd find a way to tell you. I always believed you had the right to know. But then everything went to hell in Saida."

"Oh, my God," he said, horror replacing all other emotion. "When you went back into the building—to try to find me—you were . . . Oh, my God."

"It was the hardest choice I've ever had to make. But I couldn't let you die. I just couldn't." Her tears fell in earnest now. "And you have to know that if I had to do it again, I'd make the same choice."

"But you both could have died."

"And I could have lost you."

Silence held for a moment as Nash tried to sort through his cascading emotions.

"Did he know?" he asked, finally, clenching his fists against the emotions rocking through him. "About Adam. Did Tom know?"

"Yes, I told him. I needed his help."

"And he sent you into Saida anyway. You should never have been there."

"I didn't have a choice. I had to find a way out, and Tom promised to help me if I finished this last mission."

"I just can't believe you went to him instead of me."

"You told me I was clinging to something that never really existed. That our relationship was born of necessity and loneliness, not of anything lasting. What the hell did you expect me to do?"

"I was a real bastard," he whispered, his heart twisting at the pain reflected in her eyes.

"No." She shook her head. "You were honest. I was the one living in a fantasy world, believing that there was some way we could build a normal life together. But that didn't change the facts. I was carrying your baby. A child I found I wanted very badly. So when Tom offered me the chance to get out, I took it."

"So that's it? You never looked back?"

"I told you I came to see you, right after the explosion. I begged Tom to let me come, to see for myself that you were okay. At first he refused, saying it was too dangerous for both of us—especially you—but finally he gave in. And I was prepared to tell you then. I thought maybe it would help. Only you were completely out of it. You never even knew I was there. And then Tom insisted I had to make the break, for your sake as well as for mine and the baby's."

She leaned forward, resting her head on her hands.

"I don't know, maybe I let go too easily. But you'd been more than clear about what you wanted. So I just let Tom take over. He made all the necessary arrangements. And a few weeks later I had a new life"—her voice caught on a sob—"without you. But the baby was safe and that's what mattered the most."

"I see," he said, still trying to make sense of the nonsensical.

"I did try one other time," she said, looking up to meet his gaze, her eyes filled with tears. "I had a weak moment. I needed you, and I wanted you to know your son. So I called Tom. It was the first time I'd talked to him since the night he put me on a plane to Colorado. In the beginning, he sent me progress reports on your recovery, but once it was clear that you were going to be all right, the letters stopped. Anyway, I told him I wanted to see you. That I needed to tell you the truth. He didn't think it was a good idea, but I insisted, and finally he agreed to talk to you.

"I waited for three days to hear back. Hoping. Praying. Feeling stupid and vulnerable at the same time. But when the call finally came, it wasn't from you. It was Tom. He told me you'd refused to see me. That you'd gone on with your life and I should get on with mine." Tears dripped down her face as she angrily wiped them away. "I never tried again. In fact I never talked with anyone from the Company again. Tom included."

"He never talked to me, Annie." Nash's anger shifted toward Tom as he thought about what it must have cost Annie to reach out. And how much it had clearly hurt her to believe she was being rejected. "I never got the call."

"So many lies," she said, a tremor of pain in her voice.

"He has your eyes," Nash said, not sure where the thought had come from, but unable to stop himself.

"But he's so like you. I see it in him every day. Sometimes it feels like living with a ghost."

"So why did you decide to tell me now?" He sounded harsher than he'd meant to, but there was a part of him that still felt betrayed. Even knowing he'd probably brought it on himself with his callous comments on that night so long ago.

"I think I've wanted to tell you for a while, but I was afraid of what you'd say. What you'd do. Then we made love and I was so full of hope…"

"And I betrayed you again. Believing that you were involved in all of this somehow."

"It was hard to hear you say that. And also you'd made it so clear that you still didn't want anyone in your life, that the job was all that mattered to you. I was afraid you'd reject him. Then Adam got so upset when we ran away. He was certain that he was letting you down. And I realized that I wasn't being fair to either of you. I just had to have a little of the faith that you told me I should have. So I decided to come back, but in the meantime everything went to hell. And so here I am—telling you now. Adam is your son."

"And that's the only reason you're telling me?" He searched her face, not certain what it was exactly that he was looking for, only knowing that it was important. "Because you thought I had a right to know?"

She paused, looking down at her hands, then taking a deep breath, she looked up again, her gaze steady. "Yes. No matter what happened between us, you deserve the truth."

"Except that if Kim hadn't kidnapped your son, and if A-Tac hadn't been called in to run you to ground, you'd have let me go on in blissful ignorance." He knew he wasn't being completely fair. Tom had lied to her as well as to him. But she hadn't said anything about her feelings—about whether she wanted him back in her life. And somehow that mattered more than he could possibly have imagined. "I looked for you, you know. After I got better, I tried to find you."

"Tom and his people were really thorough."

"I don't think I really realized how much I hurt you the night we fought. But even after that—knowing how upset you were—I guess I thought we were still a team, at least professionally. So when I woke up in that hospital and Tom told me you were gone, I couldn't believe it. No matter how angry you were, I found it impossible to buy into the idea that you'd just leave me there to die."

"But Tom was very persuasive."

"Yes." Nash nodded, remembering how Tom had talked him down with just the right amount of remorse and support. "He was."

"But I didn't leave you. At least not in that building. And maybe not at all if things hadn't played out the way they did."

"You mean if Tom hadn't manipulated our lives?"

"Something like that." She nodded, her face reflecting his anguish. Years gone that they could never get back. "Look, I know this is partly Tom's fault, but I was the one who made the decision to keep the secret. So I understand if you're angry with me."

"Frankly, I'm not sure what I feel. Anger, sure. And betrayal. But I can also see why you made the decisions you made. It's my fault, too. If only I'd listened that night in Vienna, maybe all of this would have played out differently."

"You can 'what if' yourself to death, Nash. Believe me, I know."

He nodded, wishing there were a way to skip past this part. The hurt. The anger. But it was all there, building inside him, threatening to swamp him like a river cresting after a storm. Instead, he decided to focus on something else. "So tell me this. If you hadn't wound up here with me, would you have ever told Adam the truth?"

"Yes. When he was old enough to hear the whole story. Up until now, I thought I was protecting him. A little boy isn't capable of understanding why his mommy is in hiding. It's better that he believe his world is the real one, not a charade his mother's Company made up to protect her."

"And if something had happened to you?" he asked, frowning at the thought of Adam being left on his own.

"I made arrangements with an attorney. I figured with client confidentiality, I'd be okay as long as I didn't tell him too much. So I told him an abbreviated version of the story, and set it up so that on the event of my death, if Adam was old enough, he'd be told the truth about his father—about you. And if not, then the attorney was directed to find you and explain the situation."

"And when all hell broke loose, and Adam was kidnapped? You didn't think of coming to me then?"

"I thought I could handle it on my own."

"Some things never change."

"Look, I did the best I could given the circumstances. You can't imagine what it was like to find Adam gone, and to know in my heart that it was my fault, my past that put my son in danger." She pushed off the bed, her eyes flashing with anger. "You may think I'm horrible for keeping my secret, but I'm a good mother. And I love my son." She rummaged through her duffel, throwing things next to him on the bed as she searched. "Here," she said finally, producing an envelope. "I carry this with me, always. Just in case. It's a notarized letter, identifying you as Adam's father. You have to believe I never meant for this to be a secret. It just played out that way."

She tossed the envelope on the bed and walked over to the window, arms crossed, shoulders rigid.

He reached for it, but froze as his eyes fell on the rest of the stuff she'd discarded on the bed. Teetering on top of the pile of T-shirts and sundries was a black lacquer box. He reached out to touch it, some part of his mind expecting it to disappear.

"You kept this?" he asked as he cradled the little box, memories surfacing. Krakow. The market. One of the happiest days he'd ever spent.

She turned, her face softening when she saw the puzzle box, tears slipping down her face. Without a word, she reached over to take it from his hands. Then, moving her fingers in practiced motions, she released the catch and the lid sprang open.

Inside were the petals of a rose.

His rose. The one he'd given her so many years ago.

He reached out to touch the faded bloom, then lifted his eyes to hers. "Why?" he whispered. "Why did you keep it all these years?"

"Because I still love you."

CHAPTER 23

The minute the words slipped out Annie wanted to take them back. He'd caught her off guard, her heart speaking before her brain had the chance to censor the thought. "Oh, God, Nash, I didn't mean to..." she started, then stopped. "I'm sorry. I've dumped so much on you and now I..."

"Hey," he said, closing the distance between them, wiping her tears away with his thumbs. "You know I care about you, too."

She nodded, not trusting herself to speak. It wasn't exactly a declaration of love, but surely it counted for something.

"Annie, I know this is hard for you. But you've got to understand that it's a lot for me to deal with, too. You've just told me I have a son."

"I don't expect anything from you, Nash. I just wanted you to know, so that you could make your own choices about the kind of relationship you want with Adam."

"That sounds more simple than it is. God, everything is so fucked up."

"I know. And it's all my fault."

"No, not entirely," he said. "I sure as hell didn't make it easy for you to tell me. And after everything I said in Vienna, I can see how you thought it would just be easier to go."

"Maybe we should have just had a little more faith in each other."

"Maybe so. But we can't change the past. So it seems like a waste of time to sit here blaming each other. We were both at fault. We were young and arrogant."

"And so certain we were right," she said, tears welling again.

"See what I mean," he sighed. "This isn't doing us any good."

"So what do we do?" she asked, her voice catching in her throat. "Where do we go from here?"

"I honestly don't know, Annie." He shook his head, smoothing the hair from her face. "But I promise you, we'll figure it out together."

"I'm afraid," she whispered, her hammering heart testament to the fact.

"Not of me," he said. "Never of me."

"No." She shook her head, her gaze locked with his. "Never of you."

He slanted his mouth over hers, taking possession of her lips, the intensity of the kiss a physical embodiment of everything they'd lost—and everything they'd found. Framing her face with his hands, he pulled her closer, his mouth giving and taking, promising everything and asking for nothing.

She closed her eyes and reveled in the fact that he was here—with her. And that at least for this moment, they were together. He deepened the kiss, their tongues tangling together, their bodies moving to a rhythm belonging to only the two of them.

She pressed even closer, needing to feel his heart beating against hers. Wanting to feel the heat of his body. To erase the pain of the past eight years. To rediscover the magic she'd only ever shared with him. Before, when they'd come together in the rain, it had been out of a need so fierce there'd been no stopping it. But now, in this moment, there was something more. Something more than desire. Something soul deep—binding them together.

Reverently, he pushed the silk robe off her shoulders, and it slid down her body, pooling at her feet. Cupping his hands beneath her breasts, he traced the line of her nipples with his thumbs, his skin rasping against hers, slivers of heat arcing through her.

Then slowly he kissed her eyes, her nose, her neck. His warm tongue caressing the hollow of her throat and then moving to suck gently on each earlobe. Each stroke, each caress, a mark of possession, the heat from his lips sending shivers of need coursing through her.

She reached for the hem of his T-shirt, pulling it over his head and tossing it to the floor. She kissed his chest, circling each nipple with the tip of her tongue, reveling in the feel of him—the taste of him. She trailed kisses along his shoulders, her fingers tracing the scars that covered his torso. Some remembered, some not.

So many years gone.

His eyes locked on hers, he stepped out of his jeans, leaving nothing between them but skin and heat. She gasped as he pulled her to him, fitting her body against his, the hard heat of his penis nestled into the juncture of her thighs. Then she slid down, her hands caressing him as she kissed the line of hair stretching down over the taut muscles of his abdomen.

Then she enveloped his heat with her mouth, sucking gently as she moved her hands slowly up and down. His fingers twined tightly in her hair as she loved him. Sliding up and down, her tongue tasting and teasing. She felt a surge of pleasure as he responded to her ministrations. Growing harder—hotter.

Impatient now, he pulled her up again, his mouth closing over hers, the intensity of his kiss raising the bar, moving their loving to the next level. Swinging her into his arms, lips still locked together, he carried her to the bed and laid her on the cool cotton sheets, their soft comfort the perfect foil for his heat and hardness.

Straddling her body, he cupped her breasts, then bent his head as his mouth closed over her breast. He bit lightly, his fingers moving rhythmically across the skin on her hips and stomach. She closed her eyes as the pressure increased, the sucking stronger, more insistent. His hand found her other nipple, massaging and pulling, the combined sensations sending her bucking against him.

With a crooked smile, he slid lower, his mouth making a hot trail as it moved downward, kissing, licking, stroking until she thought she might cry out with sheer joy. Lower and lower he moved, lightly flicking his tongue. Teasing the soft skin of her inner thighs, his hands cupped now beneath her bottom, lifting her upward, opening her to him. And then he blew softly, the gentle kiss almost more than she could bear.

Her hands closed around the rungs of the headboard as he lifted her higher still, his tongue plunging inside her, driving deep and pressing hard against her secret spot. In and out. Her breathing coming in gasps now, she pushed against him, fighting for her release. And then his mouth closed around her throbbing core, his lips and tongue moving faster and faster until she couldn't think. Couldn't breathe.

There was nothing but the incredible sensation of his mouth moving against her. Sucking her, harder and harder, each wave of sensation carrying her higher and higher until she thought surely she'd die. And then with one final pull, she felt herself splintering into a million shards of color and light.

He shifted to cradle her spasming body as she came. She pressed closer, needing to feel his body hot against hers, as she continued to spiral out of control. Then, summoning her strength, she rolled to straddle him, her hair hanging like a curtain on either side of his face. She bent and kissed him, then lifted and in one smooth stroke impaled herself, the feeling of him deep inside her almost sending her over the edge again.

They stayed for a moment, bodies joined, gazes locked, and then she bent to kiss him, gyrating slowly as she did so, feeling him harden against her heat. She teased him for a moment, and then, her passion fully aroused, she began to move. Sliding up and down, her slick heat building the sensual friction until it was almost too sweet to bear. Then with a growl, he flipped her underneath him, his big body covering hers. Possessive and loving, embodying everything she needed—everything she wanted.

As he began to move again, his mouth found hers,

his lips and tongue caressing her as she tightened herself around him, stroking and squeezing.

He started to move in earnest, and she lifted her hips to meet his, the two of them establishing a rhythm as familiar to her as breathing. Still kissing, they moved together, in and out, in and out, each thrust taking him deeper—taking them higher, the years melting away as they moved together—until there was no past. No future. Only now.

The two of them. Together. Their union a covenant. There were no more secrets. Only each other, and the glorious feeling of their bodies as they moved as one.

Faster and faster they moved, the world spinning out of control, until the only thing left was the feel of his body inside hers and the sound of their hearts beating as one.

Then slowly Annie drifted back to earth, safe for the moment in the warmth of Nash's arms. There were no easy answers. She knew that much. And she knew, too, that tonight wasn't a panacea for their problems, but at least the shadows of the past were finally gone, which meant that there was hope.

And for now, that would simply have to be enough.

Nash moved slowly through the layers of sleep, his mind trying to hold on to the dream. He'd had it so many times, it had become a familiar companion. One that gave him great joy, only to leave him devastated once he realized it was nothing more than a figment of his imagination.

He opened his eyes to the dark night, his heart quickening as he felt her body there, warm against him. This wasn't a dream. It was real. And like all reality, it came with a price.

One they'd both paid in full. But there was still so much between them. So many questions. So many things left unresolved. His mind rebelled at the thought. Annie always said he made things more complicated than they really were. Maybe she was right. Maybe now was the time for simple things.

Loving each other. Loving their son.

He thought of Adam—with Annie's eyes and smile.

His son. The words echoed in his brain, and he tried to sort through the resulting emotions. On the one hand, he was delighted, the feeling akin to receiving an unexpected gift. On the other hand, he was terrified that he wasn't up to the task, that he'd somehow let them down. And then, in between somewhere, there was anger. Anger for all that he'd missed, for all that he'd thrown away.

Downstairs the clock chimed three, and his skin prickled, something alerting his senses. Beside him Annie stirred, then sat up, clearly roused by whatever he'd heard.

"What is it?" she whispered as he reached for his gun.

"Not sure. Probably nothing, but better to make sure. There's another gun in the bedside table. You go check on Adam and I'll check downstairs."

She nodded and slid the drawer out, her movements calculated and almost noiseless. Moving in tandem, they worked their way to the bedroom door, Annie covering him as he stepped out into the hallway. Everything was quiet.

"Be careful," she whispered as she headed toward Adam's room.

Moving on silent feet, Nash worked his way down the stairs, careful to avoid the creaking fifth step. Below him something or someone moved. Maybe in the kitchen. He moved quietly through the foyer, back to the wall, and with a silent count of three swung out into the kitchen, gun drawn.

A shadow shifted near the back door, and he took aim.

"Holy shit, Nash," Tyler's voice broke through the dark. "It's just me."

"What the hell are you doing in my kitchen in the middle of the night?" he asked, lowering the gun and reaching over to turn on the light.

"Your damned cell phone was off again. And I didn't want to wake everyone in the house."

"So you decided on breaking and entering?"

"No. I just got the key from one of the security detail." She held up the key as proof. "Avery called me when he couldn't get you. I should have known you'd be on red alert."

"Nash?" Annie said, appearing in the doorway wearing nothing but his shirt.

"Everything's fine. It was Tyler. Is Adam okay?"

"Yeah, he's still asleep. So what's the deal?" She laid her gun down on the counter and pulled up onto a barstool, the shirt sliding up her thighs in the process. Nash swallowed, and Tyler smothered a smile, then sobered.

"Hannah's found Kim. Or at least she thinks she has. Avery wants to mobilize as quickly as possible. They're waiting to brief you now."

"What about Adam?" Annie asked.

"That's another reason why I came in person. If it's

all right with you, I'll take care of the squirt until you get back."

Annie looked to Nash for confirmation, and he felt a rush of surprising emotion. Gratitude, fear, and an intense urge to protect.

"I swear I'll guard him with my life."

"Of course you will," Annie said, her smile warm. "We know that."

Nash glanced at Tyler to see if she'd noticed Annie's choice of pronoun, torn between wanting his friend to know, and wanting to keep his private life just that.

"Nash," Annie said, laying her hand on his arm. "We need to talk to Adam. He needs to know what's happening. And I think he deserves to know the whole truth before we go."

His body went cold, the idea of telling Adam sending every neuron in his body into overdrive. On the one hand he wanted his son to know, but, on the other, the idea terrified him more than facing an entire battalion of enemy combatants.

"It'll be fine," Annie said, as always reading his mind.

"I'll hang out here, until you guys are ready," Tyler said, pointedly ignoring the undercurrent. If she'd guessed the truth, she was keeping it to herself. "Maybe get some coffee going. The guys outside said that everything's quiet, but you need to get moving. Avery's expecting you ASAP."

"Right." Nash nodded. "We'll move quickly."

He and Annie walked into the foyer and started up the stairs. About halfway up, she stopped him.

"Nash," she said, her voice rough with emotion,

"before we tell Adam, I need to know that you want him. That no matter what happens with the two of us, you'll be there for him. You'll be his father. I know it's a lot to ask, but I can't do it any other way."

He'd expected to be torn but he wasn't. In that instant, he knew that he wanted his son in his life. More than he could have ever thought possible.

"I want him, Annie," Nash said. "And for the record, I want you, too."

"All right, then—" Annie's smile reached out to him, like a living breathing thing, the warmth settling deep inside him, in a place he'd forgotten existed—until now. "Let's go tell our son."

They walked to the top of the stairs, and Nash waited while Annie pulled on some sweats, and then together, they walked into Adam's room.

"What's going on?" Adam asked, his hair tousled from sleep, his eyes still groggy. "Is it morning?"

"No, buddy," Nash said. "It's the middle of the night. And your mom and I hated to wake you but we have something we need to tell you."

"And it couldn't wait until morning?" he asked, tilting his head in a perplexed way that reminded him of Annie.

"No, baby," Annie said, sitting on the side of the bed, motioning for Nash to do the same.

"Is this about the bad guys?" Adam asked, his little face clouding. "Are they here?"

Nash shook his head. "No way. You're safe here. But your mom and I are going to have to leave."

"What about me?" Adam asked, his voice trembling.

"Tyler's here," Annie said. "And I bet she'll play computer games with you if you ask her to."

"Now?" he asked, his expression changing to incredulous. "In the middle of the night?"

"Yup," Nash said. "It'll be like a special tournament."

"So when you get back," Adam asked, "are we going to stay here with Nash?" The last sentence landed somewhere between a question and a statement, his little face filled with both hope and trepidation as he waited for her answer.

Nash shot a look at Annie, not sure where exactly they stood. They hadn't had the chance to fully discuss their relationship or the future. Everything was still too new. Too fragile.

"Would you like that?" Annie asked, her voice deep with emotion.

"Totally," Adam said. "Nash is cool." He looked from his mother to Nash and then back again. "I'm glad you're friends again."

"Me, too," Annie said, reaching out to squeeze Adam's hand. "But it isn't permanent. Just until all this is over and we can sort things out."

Nash's heart constricted at the thought of either of them leaving. But Annie was right, there was no point in making promises that might not be kept. It was enough for now that she knew he wanted them in his life and that she wanted Adam to know the truth.

"Well, I think we should stay."

"Well," Nash said, his eyes shooting up to meet hers, looking for some kind of guidance, "I'd like for you to stay, too, so that we can get to know each other better. But first your mom and I need to take care of the guy with the games."

"Is that where you're going?" Adam asked, raising his chin to counter the quaver in his voice. "To stop him?"

"Yeah." Annie nodded. "And before we go, Nash and I wanted to tell you something." Annie met Nash's gaze, his own trepidation reflected in her eyes.

"What is it?" Adam asked, his brows drawing together in a puzzled frown.

"You know how you thought your father was dead?" Nash said, his tone matching Adam's solemnity. "Well, it turns out it might not be true."

"Really?" Adam asked, his eyes widening as he turned to Annie for confirmation.

"It's true, baby," she said, smiling even as tears shimmered against her lashes. "Your dad is alive. He just didn't know he was your dad."

"How could he not know?"

"It's really long and complicated. But the important thing is that he loves you." Annie lifted her gaze to meet Nash's. "And he wants to be a part of your life. That is, if you're interested."

"Of course I'm interested," Adam harrumphed. "Everybody wants a father."

"Even if it's me?" Nash asked, feeling as if he were walking barefoot across a minefield.

"You?" Adam asked, his eyes, if possible, growing even wider.

"Me," Nash said, heart in his throat.

"For real? Wow. I mean, you really are a hero, just like Mom said. I always figured she was making it up."

"So you're not disappointed?" Nash asked, holding his breath, surprised at how much he cared about the answer.

"It's really true?" Adam asked, his face a mixture of excitement and worry. "He's really my dad?"

Annie nodded with a soft smile.

"This is so cool," he said, eyes shining. "Now I've got someone to do stuff with."

"You've always had your mom," Nash said.

"It's not the same," he said, with the simplicity only a child can achieve. "She doesn't like to do guy stuff. Now you can teach me all kinds of things, like football and fishing."

"I'm not so good at fishing," Nash said, shaking his head. He'd always been too short on patience.

"All dads are good at fishing," Adam pronounced. "But if you want, I can show you how."

"Sounds like a plan," Nash agreed, his voice hoarse with emotion.

"So now we're a real family, right?" Adam asked.

"Yeah, something like that," Annie said, chewing on her lower lip. "There's still a lot to work out."

"Why don't we just take it one day at a time," Nash suggested.

"Okay." Adam shrugged, clearly at peace with the idea. "So when do you gotta leave?" he asked, his face tightening with worry.

"Pretty quickly. If we're going to catch Wii guy we have to act fast, but we'll be back before you know it. And in the meantime, why don't you hang on to this." He slipped off his watch and gave it to Adam.

"Wow," Adam whispered, staring down at the watch with reverence. "It's even better than the old one."

"And I promise you," Nash said, covering his son's hand with his, "I'll take really good care of your mother until we get back."

"Of course you will." Adam nodded solemnly, his

little fingers curling around his father's. "Cuz you're a hero."

"So what have we got?" Nash asked as he and Annie strode into the war room. The entire team was assembled, except for Tyler, whom they'd left deep in battle against Adam's dragon.

"Glad you could make it," Avery said, nodding at two empty chairs on the far side of the table. "I was just telling everyone that this is going to be a difficult operation."

"Tyler said you'd found Kim," Annie said, taking a seat next to Lara. "So where is he?"

"In Cyprus," Hannah answered. "Or more accurately on an island just off the west coast. It's a spit of land known as the Devil's Horn." She hit a button and a map of Cyprus popped up on the overhead screen. "Technically, it's considered a part of the main island, but when the tide is high, it's completely cut off with the only access by boat, similar to St. Michael's Mount in Cornwall." She hit the button again and the screen was filled with the photo of a small, rocky island.

"Why Cyprus?" Drake asked. "Seems a little far from home."

"Devil's Horn is owned by Anthony Zechar," Avery said.

"The arms dealer?" Nash asked, trying to connect the dots between Kim and Zechar.

"Exactly." Hannah nodded. "Although there's never been enough evidence to take him out, we believe Zechar's network is responsible for distributing munitions to some of the most powerful terrorist networks in the world. Including several groups in Asia."

"Red Sword," Annie said, leaning forward to study the man's face. "That's the group that Tom said Kim Jin affiliated with. Of course, one has to consider the source."

"Right. And while we can't definitely prove that connection, we do know that Red Sword has been involved for years in the plot for reunification of Korea under communist rule. And since we know that Kim Sun's reputed reunification efforts have brought him into that sphere, it's not that great a leap to assume that Kim knows Zechar."

"And Zechar offered him sanctuary?"

"It looks that way. And it makes sense from a strategic standpoint." Hannah switched the picture again, this new one showing a close-up of the island. No more than a couple of miles in diameter, it looked as if the landmass had simply been pushed straight up from the sea, sheer rocky cliffs marking the island's boundaries, and on top, just visible below the line of the trees, the white gleam of a compound.

"Jesus." Emmett whistled. "Not exactly a visitor-friendly place."

"It was originally a temple," Drake said, his advanced knowledge of ancient artifacts coming into play, "used at different times by both the ancient Greeks and the Ottoman Empire. Then, sometime during the fifteenth century, it was abandoned until the Second World War, when it fell into the hands of the Nazis."

"The building supposedly sits on a maze of tunnels," Hannah continued, switching to a closer view of the island, "some of them reputedly leading to the main-land. But as far as I can find, the only documentation to support that fact comes from ancient Greece. There's a rudimentary map," she said, hitting the computer button, and the map appeared above them, "but it dates back to the early fifth century."

"Tunnels are tunnels," Lara said. "It's possible they're still the same."

"Possible, but not probable." Drake shook his head. "Much of the compound was destroyed when the Allies attacked the island. It sat empty for years."

"I'm surprised you archaeologists weren't all over it," Jason said.

"Cyprus was at war much of that time. And when things finally did settle down, the country, in desperate need of funding, sold it."

"Since then," Avery continued, "Devil's Horn has had a string of private owners, most of them with reason to hide. Zechar bought the place about fifteen years ago, restoring the original buildings as well as some of the fortifications."

"Bottom line, this isn't going to be an easy in and out," Emmett said. "So how do we do it?"

"We climb," Avery said, switching to another slide, this one showing the stark face of a cliff springing directly from the Mediterranean.

"That's a hell of a rise." Nash frowned.

"Two hundred and ten feet at its highest," Hannah said, "about a hundred and sixty at its lowest."

"Definitely not for the faint of heart," Annie observed.

Avery reached over Hannah and clicked for another picture, this one a topographical rendition of the island. "I'm thinking we go up here," he said, pointing to a fairly smooth cliff face about 180 feet high. "There's a small beach to land and the cliff fronts the back of Zechar's compound."

"No." Annie shook her head, squinting a little as she stared at the map. "It's better to the right. That curve indicates a fissure." She stood up and walked to the screen, pointing to a small indentation on the drawing. "Do we have a photo of this part of the cliff?"

Hannah checked coordinates and then produced a split screen of the map and a photo of the cliff.

"Look," Annie said as she studied both drawing and photo, "there's a rock crevice here." She pointed to a darker area of the cliff. "Almost a chimney. It'll provide both cover and an easier ascent. Have you got the vertical figures for this section?"

"Looks like the chute tops out at about one-sixty."

"And is there beach access?" Nash asked.

"Yes." Avery nodded after consulting a sheaf of papers. "Not as wide as the other location, but it's there. You're sure this is better, Annie?"

"Absolutely. This is your best bet. It'll be quicker and more contained. And considering proximity to the original site, it'll still feed onto the backside of the compound."

"You sound like you know what you're talking about," Lara said, her curiosity evident.

"I live in Colorado, which means spending a hell of a lot of time in the mountains." She shrugged. "I needed a way to make a living and climbing is a huge sport with a high demand for guides. So for what it's worth, I'm AMGA accredited."

"AMGA?" Jason asked.

"American Mountain Guides Association," Nash supplied. "And she's being modest. Annie's been climbing for years. I remember several times in particular when she managed to climb in and out of things no one else believed possible. Hell, she's even been on K2."

"Yeah, well, I didn't make it to the summit." She shook her head. "And that was a hell of a long time ago. But I do know my way around a rope."

"Good, because you're on the team," Avery said, waving away her protest. "Normally, Emmett serves as our climbing expert. But since he took a bullet to the leg during a recent operation, I'm thinking it's better if he sits this one out."

"And you're okay with this, Emmett?" Annie asked as she searched the other man's face. "You were pretty damn certain I'd killed Dominico yesterday morning."

"I was wrong," he said, his gaze steady. "And Avery's right, I'm not up to that kind of climb. I'd just slow everyone down. It's got to be you. You're the only one with the expertise to get them safely to the top."

"Besides—Drake grinned—"you can't tell me you don't want to be there when we find Kim."

"The idea has a certain appeal," she admitted. "All right, then. I guess that means I'm in."

"Just like old times," Nash said, his gaze locking with hers.

"Two against nature." She smiled, using the phrase Tom had tagged them with almost twenty years ago.

"Or in this case, two against Kim Sun," Nash replied. "The bastard will never know what hit him."

CHAPTER **24**

The cliff stretched up out of sight, clouds cloaking the top as the surf crashed on the beach. Offshore, Annie could just make out the shape of the boat as Emmett maneuvered farther out to sea. He'd stay put until they'd safely reached the rendezvous spot, ready to call in backup should it be needed.

Already about 120 feet up the cliff, Annie carefully placed a camming device, and then, stretching out with her right hand, she felt for a handhold and carefully worked her way up along the crevice.

Just below she could see Avery. He shot her a thumbs-up as he braced himself against a rock and pulled upward, following her path. Drake came next, along with the haul bag containing their gear and weapons. And finally, bringing up the rear, she could just make out Nash's head.

Pressing her back into the side of the crevice, she adjusted the cam, making sure the carabiner was secure, and then waited for Avery to reach her previous position, tightening the rope to maintain tension. He in turn tightened the slack as Drake moved upward, and finally Drake did the same for Nash. At Avery's signal, Annie again began to move upward.

So far the climb had been routine, but they had only just reached the most difficult part. The chimney she had chosen was wider than expected, especially at the top, which meant that the final forty feet would be extremely slow going.

Because of the clouds, the moonlight was dim, a boon for keeping them concealed, but a definite detriment when it came to the climb. Every move she made was determined by touch. The crevice narrowed, and she was able to move upward using her feet, hands, and back. It sped up progress, but meant that there were fewer cams for protection.

Traveling in silence added an element of danger, and also gave the night an eerie feel, the hiss of the wind against the rocks swirling around them almost like a living thing. She stopped for a moment to adjust the rope's tension, waited for visual confirmation that everyone was all right, and then began her ascent once more.

She tried to keep her mind clear, but there were so many thoughts rushing through her brain. Adam. Nash. Their future as a family. It had been her dream for so long. And now here it was within her grasp, and yet, he hadn't told her he loved her. He'd shown her as much, maybe, but it wasn't the same. And then there was the question of A-Tac.

For so long she'd believed that distancing herself from her past had been the way to keep Adam safe. To give him a shot at a normal life. But instead, she'd set him up for Kim. And her little boy had been through more in his short lifetime than most people ever go through.

She shuddered as she thought about what could have happened.

But it hadn't. Adam was safe. And with a little luck, they were about to put an end to Kim Sun's threat once and for all.

She closed her eyes for a moment, pushing away her thoughts. She needed to stay focused. Reaching upward, she felt for a handhold, surprised when her fingers met something soft and warm. Instinctively, she jerked her hand away as a gull came careening out of the chimney, screaming in protest.

The resulting melee left her hanging by only her right hand and foot. She swung her body inward, reaching with her left hand for the rock face and the now-abandoned crevice. Connecting with a scraping thunk, her fingers closed on the tiny ledge, but the rock broke free, sending a hail of scree sliding down behind her.

She fought the urge to scream a warning, instead concentrating on securing herself as the rope tightened with a sickening jerk. Below her, Avery spun out away from the cliff, his body weight threatening to pull her with him.

Holding her breath, she braced herself, fighting to hold the rope steady as he swung out and then back, desperately scrambling for a second handhold before gravity had the chance to win the day.

Her shoulders tightened with the effort to hold on to the rope, and she pressed into the rock, bracing herself with her feet. Then, just when she was certain she couldn't hold on any longer, the rope went slack as Avery regained his footing.

She leaned against the mountain, gulping in air.

"Annie," Avery's voice crackled in her ear, "we've got a problem. The rope's splitting. I can see it. About four feet up. It's holding, but there's no way it'll take my weight again."

"Everybody just sit tight," she said, already climbing down to where Avery was clinging to the rock. Working quickly, she removed the damaged portion of the rope and spliced the remaining ends together. Then, after setting an additional cam, she moved back into position.

"Everybody okay?" Nash asked, his voice sounding tinny in her ear.

"Well, it's raining rocks down here," Drake said, as usual using humor to deflect the intensity of the situation. "But no bodies, so I guess that means we're good to go."

Annie smiled, despite herself. "I'm here. And in one piece. Rope should be secure."

"Avery?"

"Not to worry. I'm fine. Just went for a little ride," he said, his breathing contradicting his casual tone. "View is damn fine. But I think if it's all the same to you, I'd rather get off this rock."

"Copy that," Nash said. "Annie, we still good to go?"

"Yeah," she said, already beginning to climb. "Let's get it done."

The crevice fortunately proved to be less of a problem than she'd anticipated, or maybe after their close call it just seemed that way. They made good time, stopping only once when Drake needed to resecure the haul bag.

Nearing the top, Annie moved more cautiously. According to intel, there were three pairs of guards, two working the perimeter and one stationed at a gatehouse on the north of the island. She checked her watch, the luminous dial showing sixteen after. The guards should be about fourteen minutes out.

"Fourteen minutes," she whispered into her headset, reaching upward to pull herself onto a ledge about four feet below the top. She anchored the rope for the last time as Avery pulled himself up beside her, a long scrape down the side of his face serving as a reminder of their near miss.

"You sure you're all right?" she asked, wincing in commiseration.

"I'm fine. It's just a scrape. Damn bird's fault. Guess I must have severed the rope when I swung across the rocks."

She nodded as Drake climbed onto the ledge, pulling the haul bag behind him.

"Get up there and see if you can spot the guards," Avery said, checking his watch. "They ought to be visible in five."

Drake grabbed a pair of night vision goggles from the bag. He popped up for a quick look, just as Nash pulled himself onto the ledge.

"Good," she breathed in relief, "everyone's safe."

"So far." Nash shrugged, a half smile lifting the corner of his mouth.

"They're right on time," Drake whispered, dropping back down beside them. "ETA two minutes, coming from ten o'clock."

"Should we take them out?" Annie asked, pulling her gun from the pack.

Avery shook his head. "Only if absolutely necessary. We'll take them later, after you and Drake get inside. Better to have them reporting in for as long as possible."

Annie nodded, seconds passing slowly, until laughter in the distance indicated the men were finally approaching. Avery motioned them all back against the wall, as Drake pulled the bag deeper into the shadow.

The sounds grew closer until the men, speaking Turkish, stopped just above them. Frowning, Nash looked upward, muscles tensing for attack, but Avery shook his head and Annie held her breath as the smell of cigarettes wafted over the edge of the cliff.

Sons of bitches were taking a break.

She pressed back against the cliff, her hand tightening around her gun, finger lightly pressed against the trigger. A cigarette sailed over the edge, the end glowing as it spiraled downward, landing just to their left.

Rocks skittered across each other as something in the darkness moved. Crouching now, ready to spring, the team held steady as the men above grew silent, their flashlight beam sweeping back and forth across the face of the cliff, until it settled on the source of the noise, a mountain goat, clearly startled by the incoming tobacco.

The flashlight flickered off as the men walked away, talking again, their voices receding as they headed out, clearly satisfied that everything was as it should be. Two minutes later the area above was totally quiet, and Annie drew a deep breath in relief.

The goat bleated and Drake let out a soft laugh. "At least they didn't decide to take a piss."

Annie smiled, the tension of the last few moments easing as she holstered her gun and then carefully pulled herself up and over the cliff's edge. Nash and Avery followed suit, with Nash reaching down for the bag as Drake boosted it up. Then he slid it back into the shadow of a rock, while Avery offered a hand to help Drake.

The company fully assembled, Drake and Avery began to check the equipment, while Annie walked to the edge of the cliff to make sure their climbing ropes weren't visible from above.

The moon had broken through the clouds, bathing the rocky terrain in silvery light that fell off the edge of the cliff, cascading down into the water below. In any other circumstances she would have considered it breathtaking, but her overriding thought at the moment was that it robbed them of cover. Fortunately, due to the angle of the cliff and overhang, the ropes were hidden from sight.

"You okay?" Nash asked, the proximity of his voice startling her.

"I was until you scared the shit out of me," she gasped.

"Sorry." He smiled, his hand on her arm to steady her. "Occupational hazard. Everything look good?"

"Actually, no," Annie said, handing him the frayed section of rope she'd cut free after Avery's near miss. "This rope wasn't cut by a rock. Look at the ends. They're clean."

"You're sure?"

"Nash, I've been climbing a long time. Ropes never break. Which means one of three things can happen. They can sever after pulling across a sharp object—rock or ice. They can be chemically damaged. Or they can be cut by a knife. In the first two cases, the ends are frayed. In the last, it's a clean break."

"So you think it was deliberate."

"Looks that way." She frowned. "I checked the ropes

before we left Sunderland. Everything was fine." She waited while the weight of her words sank in. "I did a cursory check on the boat, but it was dark. I could have missed something."

"So somewhere between Sunderland and here, someone tampered with the rope. You mention this to anyone else?"

"No." She shook her head.

"Good. Let's leave it that way for now. And why don't you let me hang on to the rope. We'll want to be sure it gets safely back to Sunderland."

She handed him the piece of rope. "Should we be worried about the mission?"

"Not as far as the team is concerned," he said. "If the rope had severed completely, Drake and Avery would probably both be dead. Me, too. Wouldn't make sense for them to sabotage themselves."

"What about Emmett?" she asked.

"No way. He's risked his life for me on more than one occasion. If there was sabotage it had to come from somewhere else, which means we're probably insulated for the moment."

"Yeah, well, I say we still need to keep our eyes open."

"Roger that." They turned to walk back to where Avery and Drake were crouched by the equipment.

"All right, people," Avery said, "this is it. From here on we'll be separating into two teams. We'll be able to communicate through the coms. But we need to keep chatter to a minimum. If everything goes as planned we'll meet at the rendezvous in an hour. Helicopter's scheduled to pick us up at oh-four-hundred. There'll only be one chance, so I don't want anyone playing cowboy." He shot a look in Drake's direction, but the other man just grinned. "Everyone clear?"

They nodded and Annie stuffed some extra ammo into the bag she'd slung over her shoulder and headed back to the cliff for a last look. The plan was for Drake and Annie to make their way inside and grab Kim, while Nash and Avery worked to neutralize the perimeter guards. Once Kim was secured, they'd all make their way to the rendezvous, hopefully without serious resistance.

On its face, the plan seemed simple, but Annie knew better. In any operation, there were always unknowns, things that couldn't have been predicted and that, once they happened, completely changed the game. The seagull and the goat had been minor examples. The severed rope potentially a monumental one.

"Hey," Nash said softly, coming up behind her. "You ready?"

She nodded, arms crossed. "It all looks so peaceful out there, like nothing bad could ever happen."

"You having second thoughts?" he asked, his hand warm against her arm. "No one would blame you. I mean, you have a son to think about."

"So do you," she said, turning to face him. "And if we don't stop Kim, he'll never be safe. So, no, I haven't changed my mind."

"You're fearless, you know that?"

"Or foolish. Either way, this is all about Adam."

He frowned. "I guess I was kind of hoping this was about something more."

She shivered at the thought, but knew she couldn't go there. Not now. She had to stay focused. "I think we should concentrate on getting Kim, then when we're sure there'll be a future we can talk about it."

"All right. If that's the way you want it." She wasn't sure if she was relieved or disappointed. "But there's still something I want to tell you," he said, lowering his voice so that only she could hear. He shifted uncomfortably. "Whether you're ready to hear it or not. I mean, what if…"

"We're going to be fine." She shook her head.

"I know. But I still need to say it."

Her stomach knotted as she looked up into his eyes, a million different possibilities running through her head.

"I should have said something before," he said, looking decidedly uncomfortable. "It's just that I'm not exactly into baring my soul."

"I wasn't aware you even had one," she teased, trying to deflect the butterflies in her stomach.

"I'm serious." He framed her face with his hands, seeming oblivious to the fact that Drake and Avery were only a couple of feet away. "I wanted you to know that I still love you, too. I don't think I ever stopped, even when I believed you'd betrayed me. I should have told you eight years ago. But since I can't roll back time, for what it's worth, I'm telling you now."

She nodded, words completely deserting her, her heart in her throat.

"I love you, Annie." He bent his head and kissed her—hard. And then with a nod at Avery, the two of them were off, disappearing into the shadows of the night.

"That boy's got it bad," Drake quipped as he shifted his gun from one shoulder to the other. "What do you say we do our part, and keep you alive."

"Works for me." She smiled as they headed toward the white stucco building. "What about you—you got some-one waiting back at Sunderland?"

"Not a chance." He shook his head. "I don't do relation-ships."

"Now where have I heard that before?" She frowned over at him.

"Look," he said, "what you and Nash have is great, but that doesn't mean it's for everyone. Some people are just meant to be on their own."

"But don't you ever think about having a family?" she asked.

"I've got one." He smiled, his gaze meeting hers. "Half of it is right here on this island." He held up a hand, and they dropped down behind a stand of olive trees, the leaves whispering above them in the breeze.

"Two hostiles at three o'clock," he whispered, lifting his field glasses for a closer look.

"That'll be the house guard." Hannah's intel had iden-tified two men walking the walls of the building as well as the perimeter guards. "They should hold position for another few minutes and then separate."

They watched as the men lit cigarettes, talked briefly, and then, as if on cue, turned and headed out in opposite directions. In just a few seconds, they'd both rounded their respective corners and disappeared from sight.

"So we've got like ten minutes before they're back again," Drake said, glancing down at his watch. "Let's hope Hannah's right and there really is a door back here."

The entire building, though fortified, was a jum-bled mess from centuries of remodeling, outbuildings incorporated into what had originally been the temple to form a labyrinth of rooms, courtyards, and passageways. The entrance was carefully guarded, but the back was subject only to foot patrol, which meant that it provided the best chance for access.

Hannah had managed to obtain an old blueprint dating back to the sixties. It wasn't exactly up to date, but then neither was the monstrosity sitting atop Devil's Horn. According to the plans, there was an old gate in the back wall. Originally intended for livestock, it led directly into a goat barn that, according to the blueprint, had long ago been incorporated into the main house.

"You ready?" he asked.

She nodded, and the two of them moved across the open field, keeping to a crouch, the moon fortunately obscured by a bank of clouds. Shadows moved with the wind in the trees, and Annie tightened her fingers around her gun, keeping her eyes moving.

They stopped behind a pile of rocks about fifteen feet from the peeling stucco that marked the goat barn. As promised, the rusty iron of a gate showed black against the white wall.

"Go, Hannah," Drake murmured as he started out from behind the rocks.

Annie held out her hand to stop him, something or someone separating from the shadows at the edge of the gate. Drake pulled back behind the rocks with a soft curse. A man stood leaning against the wall, an assault rifle slung across his shoulder.

"That's not one of the original guards," Annie whispered. "He's too short." The man, although muscular, topped out at maybe five foot seven. "You think he's here to guard the gate? Or just sneaking a break of some kind?"

"I don't think it matters." Drake frowned. "Either way, he's standing between us and the prize."

"So how do you want to handle it?"

"We need a distraction. Got any ideas?"

"Yeah," she said, digging in her bag for a knife. "Give me a bullet, and I need a piece of paper."

Drake shot her a look that questioned her sanity, but he pulled a bullet out of his handgun and handed it to her. Using the knife blade, she levered off the end cap and took the folded paper he'd pulled from his wallet.

"Overdue electric bill?" she queried as she opened the paper, keeping one eye on the man by the gate.

"What can I say?" he said, shrugging. "I suck at paperwork."

Annie carefully poured the gunpowder from the bullet into the center fold.

"I get it." Drake grinned. "Greek fire."

"In its most rudimentary form." She nodded, adding some pebbles for ballast and then folding the bill until it was about the size of a small cigar. "Hopefully it'll have enough zip to grab our man's attention without the need for him to phone home."

"I like the way you think," he whispered.

She smiled, then sobered. "All right, then, I'll give you a few minutes to move closer to our boy there, and then I'll set this off. Once he turns to investigate, you neutralize him. And then, hopefully we'll be home free."

Drake moved out, circling to the guard's right, using trees and rocks for cover. When he was in place, Annie shouldered her pack, and after laying the improvised explosive on top of a boulder, she lit the end and ran backward to a stand of olive trees.

A popping noise, like wood on a fire, broke the still night, followed by a bright flash of light. The whole thing lasted no more than three seconds, but it was enough to capture the guard's attention. Drake moved swiftly up behind him, pulled him into a headlock, and with a simple twist, ended the threat once and for all.

Annie closed the distance between them and helped him drag the man out of sight. "Did you get his radio?" she asked as they moved back into the shadows of the wall.

"Couldn't find one. Based on the sheepskin and the smell, I'm thinking he's not part of the regular guard. Maybe a local. No way to know. But at least no one will be expecting him to call in."

The gate, as expected, was locked. But they'd come prepared, and it only took Drake a few seconds to cut through the metal. Careful to keep it from squeaking, they moved inside, waiting a moment for their eyes to get used to the gloom.

"Definitely a barn," Annie said, wrinkling her nose. "Anybody in residence?"

Drake cautiously pulled out a penlight and flipped it on, the beam cutting a path across the dusty straw-covered floor. Crates and boxes were stacked haphazardly against one wall and a feed bin full of grain took up half the adjacent wall. Opposite the bin was a row of stalls, the shining eyes of a couple of curious goats checking out the newcomers.

"Maybe our guy was the shepherd," Drake said, moving farther into the room. "He certainly smelled the part."

"Right," Annie said, moving slowly in a circle as she checked out the room. "A shepherd carrying an automatic weapon."

"These times, they are a changin'," Drake quipped, frowning as he dropped to his knees beside the feed bin. "Check this out. Looks like Hannah's tales of secret passages weren't just smoke and mirrors."

A small grated doorway had been cut into the wall, the panel rusted shut with age, but in the light from Drake's flashlight, Annie could see rudimentary stone steps curving downward into the dark.

"Probably just a cellar. Carving tunnels in this rock would be a pretty daunting task."

"So were the pyramids, but they still got built. Where there's a will there's a way. But you're right, those steps aren't going to take us any closer to Kim. To do that, we've got to go through there." He highlighted a wooden door with his flashlight.

Signaling her to cover him, he moved forward, turned off the penlight, and began to inch the door open. As soon as he was certain it was clear, he moved into the hallway, leading with his gun. Annie followed, the two of them turning full circle back to back as they cased the area for signs of danger.

The hallway was empty.

"According to Hannah's map," Annie whispered, "there's a couple of main rooms on the left."

Drake nodded. "I'll take the lead. You watch our backs." The hallway stretched to the left and right, dead-ending on the right about fifteen feet away. The only door was the one leading to the barn, and a little window cut high in the wall streamed with moonlight, indicating the right path led exactly nowhere.

They moved off to the left, and Annie counted the doors as they moved, stopping when they reached the fifth one.

"This should be it," Drake whispered, his back flat to the wall. "You ready?"

Annie nodded as she moved into place on the opposite side of the door.

Drake reached out and pushed the door handle down, the door swinging inward as they moved through the opening into the room, weapons at the ready.

For a second there was silence, the room shrouded in darkness, then the lights flashed on as shots rang out. Blinking at the sudden onslaught of light, Annie dove for the floor, hitting on a roll. Drake had managed to take out one man, but two more had rushed to fill the void, pinning him to the wall. Annie lifted her gun, finger on the trigger.

"Unless you want your friend to die, I suggest you lose the weapon," a voice called from behind her. She dropped the Beretta and slowly turned around.

"Welcome to the Devil's Horn, Ms. Gallagher," Kim Sun said, his icy smile every bit as lethal as the Walther in his hand. "We've been expecting you."

CHAPTER 25

S on of a bitch," Nash said, coming to a full stop
behind a group of sun-bleached rocks, Avery dropping down beside him.

"Looks like we've got trouble." Avery frowned. "That
sound like Kim?"

"I can't be sure." He shook his head. "But it's definitely Annie. And they're definitely in trouble."

"Could you hear Drake?"

"No. And now there's nothing at all." His stomach
churning, he clenched his fists as he imagined the worst.

"They're fine, Nash. Annie and Drake can hold their
own. And Kim needs them alive. At least until he figures
out who else is on the island."

"Which means we need to move. Now."

"Agreed."

"So how do we do it?" Nash said, determination setting in as he steeled himself against all other emotion.

"I don't know for sure, but I've got an idea. Can you

raise Emmett on the handset? It's got a secure channel as well. Oh-six-eight."

Nash adjusted his earpiece. "Emmett, you there?" Static. "Emmett?" Nothing but white noise. "Damn it."

"Shift over a little. The rocks might be blocking transmission."

He moved slightly to the left into the open, Avery covering his position. "Emmett, do you read me?"

"Roger that," Emmett responded, his voice choppy with static. "That you, Nash?"

"Affirmative. We've got a code yellow. I repeat, code yellow. Second team is down." He released the button.

"I copy."

"Look, Emmett, we need to move quickly," Avery said. "Can you patch us through to Sunderland?"

"On it," Emmett replied, the sound of him moving equipment accompanying his voice.

"What do you have in mind?" Nash asked.

"The only way we can help Drake and Annie is to get inside. But any attempt to use obvious entrance points will be anticipated. So I figure we'll shoot for something a little less expected."

"Hannah's tunnels. But we don't even know that they really exist."

"Well, you better pray that they do," Avery said. "Emmett, you got Hannah yet?"

"She's on the line."

"I'm here, Avery. Emmett filled me in," Hannah said, her voice steady, but full of concern. "I'm guessing you want me to walk you through the tunnels."

"Always said you had a quick mind." Avery chuckled, and despite the gravity of the situation, Nash smiled.

"Where are you?" Hannah asked, cutting right down to business.

"We're at the east end of the island about ten yards from the main guard station."

"All right, you want to move south about twenty yards. You should see a pile of rubble. Maybe a column or something? In my rendition it's still a building. But a small one."

"Got it," Nash said, already on the move. "It looks to be in use. An outbuilding of some kind. Maybe storage."

He and Avery made their way over to the building, careful to keep low and out of sight of the front guards.

"How many outside the compound?" Hannah asked.

"Six, possibly eight. We had visual contact with the two foot patrols but missed the opportunity to get up close and personal with the men on the gate. We saw two before we had to move. But there could have been more."

"And inside?"

"No idea," Avery said. "Can you use satellite to get us an approximate count?"

"Consider it done," she said, "but it'll take a few minutes to pull things together. Gotta hitch a ride on the right satellite."

"I can help with that," Emmett responded. "Avery, do you want me to try to join you?"

"Not enough time." Avery shook his head, even though Emmett couldn't see him. "I don't think they'll keep them alive long."

Nash swallowed back a wave of fear and used his silenced gun to shoot off the lock on the outbuilding's door. Inside, they waited a moment for their eyes to adjust and then looked around. "It's a generator room. Looks fairly new. I don't see any kind of access to a cellar or tunnels."

"How big is the room?" Hannah asked.

"Maybe ten feet square."

"Look behind it. Is there anything more? Ruins maybe?"

Avery moved to a second door in the back of the room, cracking the door open. "Looks like we're right up against a cliff. There's maybe three feet of clearance and then an outcropping of rocks."

"Wait a minute," Nash said, peering into the darkness. "There's something at the foot of the rocks. A shrine maybe?" They moved out the door into the little yard, circling slowly to make sure they weren't being watched.

"We're clear," Avery said, relaxing his stance. "It is a shrine. Or at least I think so. There's a small arched gate and a slab of stone."

"Can you get in the gate?" Hannah asked.

"There's no lock, but it's rusted shut," Nash said as he pulled on the structure. Picking up a large rock, he wrapped it in a handkerchief and slammed it into the latch a couple of times. The gate groaned and then sagged open.

They waited for a moment to be sure that no one had heard and then moved into the little alcove. "There's some carving on the rock, but it's not legible. Years of wind and rain."

"Can you move it?" Hannah sounded excited, and her enthusiasm carried over the air.

Avery shifted to the far side of the stone as Nash bent to get a solid grip.

"On three," Avery said. "One, two...three."

Together they lifted, surprised to find the stone much lighter than anticipated. And behind it yawned a dank, dark opening.

"It's here," Nash said as he stepped into the abyss.

"What the hell happened?" Drake rolled to his feet, rubbing his head. "Last thing I remember, we were surrounded by Kim's thugs."

"Said thugs clubbed you over the head. You weren't in the most cooperative of moods. How you feeling?" Annie asked.

"Head hurts like hell, but I'll manage," he said, searching the room for a way out.

"It's no good, I've already been over it. There's no way out."

"Any idea where we are?"

"No. We're still on the first floor, but I lost track of exactly where. I tried to keep up but there were too many turns, and it wasn't exactly a leisurely stroll."

"Fuck."

"That sums the situation up nicely. But I think I managed to contact Nash and Avery before they took our gear. At least I hope I did. It all happened really fast. Kim was talking and I was trying to use the conversation to give Nash a hint to our whereabouts. But then Kim noticed the headset. One of his men grabbed the earpiece and smashed it. So I've no idea if Nash will be able to decipher what I said."

"Did Kim know there was someone on the other end?"

"I told him there was just you and me. But I don't think he bought it. And he didn't seem inclined to chat.

After he found the communications equipment, he had his men drag us in here."

"How long?"

"Fifteen minutes, maybe twenty. They took my watch."

"At least they didn't tie us up. Evens the odds a little."

"Except that they're carrying guns."

"Hey, it ain't over till it's over."

"I hope to hell you're right. Our lives are riding on it." She crossed her arms, trying not to think about Adam. The best thing she could do right now was keep her focus. "So you got a plan?"

"Not yet, but I'm working on it. I think we can assume that Avery will come after us. But until then, we're on our own." He lifted the leg of his pants and reached down inside his boot to produce a small handgun complete with silencer. "Always bring a spare."

"You are a man of many surprises, Mr. Flynn."

"What can I say, I like to be prepared. Think you can make like a grieving girlfriend?"

"Somehow, I'm not buying you as Boy Scout," she said as he slumped down in the corner, playing dead. "But you're right, you're not looking very good." She gave him a nod and knocked on the door. "*Help*. Please. Something is wrong with my friend."

The door opened a crack and the guard looked in, his eyes suspicious. Annie knelt next to Drake. "I don't think he's breathing."

The guard stepped into the room as Drake came to life, getting off a shot before the man even realized what had happened. He fell forward, his eyes wide with surprise, Annie grabbing him under the arms to break his fall.

"Come on," Drake said. "We don't have much time. His buddies are bound to get curious when he doesn't check in."

Annie grabbed the man's rifle and they headed out the door. They hadn't made it more than about twenty feet when a cadre of men rounded a corner behind them shouting in Turkish and firing their guns. Annie ducked and pivoted, managing to get off a successful shot, then fired again.

"You really are a sharpshooter," Drake said as they rounded the corner, the others still in pursuit.

"Yeah, but there's no way I can get them all. We're still seriously outgunned, and you're not going to do us much good with that." She nodded down at the little handgun.

"Well, then I suggest we get a move on," he said, already sprinting away from the shooters. "That, and pray for the cavalry."

Nash worked to open the padlock on the grating in front of him. They'd already maneuvered around three blocked passages, so this latest encumbrance was only a minor annoyance by comparison.

"You got satellite, yet?" Avery barked into his earphone. Hannah had been trying for the past half hour or so with no luck. But at least they had light. The first half of the tunnel had been completely dark, their penlights not making much of a dent, but after they'd cleared the second rockslide the passage had smoothed out, opening off onto various storage rooms, a string of bare light bulbs stretching along the ceiling. Someone was clearly using this part of the tunnel as a cellar of sorts.

"Still working on it. But according to the blueprint

you should be coming out into the east wing of the building. Which according to my intel is unoccupied."

"Grate's open," Nash announced as they pushed
through it, the sheet-shrouded room confirming Hannah's
assessment. "Now what? This place is too big to wander
around blind."

"Well, you don't have to," Hannah said, her tone
relieved. "I've got satellite. Infrared showing your area
clear. But I've got warm bodies all over the west side of
the building."

"Any way to find Annie and Drake?"

"Not specifically, but two of the hot spots are moving pretty damn quick. If it's them they've got people on
their tail."

"All right then," Avery said. "Let's go."

They moved out of the room together, Nash taking the
left, Avery the right.

"Clear," Avery called.

"You need to go straight about ten feet and then take
your first left," Hannah said, her voice sounding tinny as
they moved farther into the old fortress.

They continued up the hallway until they reached an
intersection. "Left," Avery confirmed as they moved forward into the adjacent hall.

"Correct," Hannah said. "Now go about twenty-five
more feet and take a right. You're still clear of company."

"And Annie?" Nash said, unable to keep from asking.

"They're still moving, but the guys on their tail are
closing."

Avery and Nash swung around into the right-hand
hallway. "We're clear," Avery said. "Now what?"

"Okay, it's going to start getting dicey. I've got hot

spots coming up in the hallway. No way to know who, but I'm betting they're not friendlies. In about ten feet the hallway curves sharply and just around the bend you'll see a doorway. You've got people inside. I'm seeing what looks to be two people. With another one in the hallway maybe five feet farther along."

"Stationary or moving?"

"All stationary, but the guy in the hall was on the move just a few moments ago."

"What about Drake and Annie?" Avery asked.

"If I'm right, they're coming up on the same room. Different hallway. Looks like there's another doorway. Hostiles are still in pursuit." Hannah paused for a moment, the silence telling. "Look, guys, I hate to say it, but the shortest route to Annie and Drake is through the room."

"We've got a bit of a problem with that," Avery said. "If we round the corner we're going to have to deal with the man in the hall. I've no doubt we can take him, but not without alerting the people in the room to our presence. Which means our chances inside just got minimal. Any other options?"

"Maybe," she said. "Hang on a minute." Nash could hear Hannah shuffling paper on the other end. "Okay, I've got it. If you backtrack about eight feet, you'll see a door to your right. Once inside you should see a door in the far wall. According to the blueprints, it leads into the main room."

"All right," Avery said, motioning Nash back the way they'd come. "We're on the move."

The door was a small one and it protested with a squeak when they opened it. Nash pivoted into the hallway checking to see if anyone had heard. But everything was quiet. "The man in the hall still stationary?" he asked Hannah.

"He is. Nothing's moving. At least on your side."

"Annie and Drake are still headed the same way?" Avery asked as they slid inside the room and closed the door.

"Yes." Hannah concurred.

The room was small, and like the others they'd encountered, covered with drop cloths. There was only a smattering of furniture. And no second door.

CHAPTER 26

They still back there?" Annie asked as they dodged around a corner, the guys on their tail firing randomly as they closed the distance. They'd managed to take out another two, but there were still at least four in pursuit and Annie had no doubt that there were others heading their way.

"Yeah," Drake said. "And they're getting closer."

"So maybe we should find a way to narrow the odds a bit. I don't like the idea of a shoot-out in the hallway, too much ricochet. But maybe if we draw them inside somewhere."

"All right, pick a room." He nodded at the doors lining the hallway.

Back to the wall, she reached out to open a door, then swung into the room. It was empty, but too small for a face-off. "No good," she said. "We need something bigger. Better angles."

Drake nodded and they moved across the hall to try

another door. The second room was smaller than the first.
A closet or anteroom of some kind.

"What's that door?" Annie asked, nodding across at a
second door in the far wall.

"Only way to find out is to open it," he said.

"You go"—she motioned—"I'll cover the hallway."
She turned to face the door, lifting the rifle.

Drake started for the door, but before he could pull
it open, shots rang out, Annie firing as a man crossed
into the doorway. He clutched his chest and fell but was
immediately replaced with two more men, both also with
rifles at the ready.

Annie dropped her gun, hands raised, blocking Drake,
who managed to slip the pistol back into his boot.

"You, there." The guard motioned to Drake as another
man joined his comrades. Annie smiled. From six to
three. At least she'd managed to thin their numbers a bit.
"Get up."

Drake stood slowly, hands at chest height.

"In there." The man motioned to the door, his English
accented but passable. "Move." He shoved her forward
with the barrel of his gun. It took every ounce of strength
she possessed to keep from spinning around and kicking
him in the teeth. It was a delicious thought, and had he
been alone she'd have given it a shot. But there were two
other men, which meant the move would be suicide.

Drake shrugged slightly, the gesture indicating that
he'd had the same thought. With a sigh of regret, she
followed him through the door into what appeared to be
a library. Huge mahogany bookcases were interspersed
with gilded frames containing works by the masters.
Annie recognized a Titian and a Rembrandt.

"I should have killed you when I first found you here." Kim Sun sat in an ornate wing chair, a glass of cognac on the table beside him. Across from him, ensconced in a leather chair, Annie recognized the man who'd attacked her in her room, Kim's son—Chin-Mae.

"Why didn't you then?" she asked as two of the guards took up position in the doorway, the third keeping his gun on Drake.

"I have other plans. A slow, lingering death. Nothing is too good for the woman who killed my son."

"I almost got two of them," she said, anger getting the better of her.

"But you didn't," Chin-Mae said, his jaw tightening as he closed his fingers on the arm of his chair. "In fact, if I remember it correctly, it was you who almost lost your life."

"Yeah, but close doesn't count," Drake said.

"Enough." Kim raised a hand. "You are here. And so we have won."

"How do you figure that?"

"Your son grows up alone. And you will pay for my son's death with your life. I find that a fitting ending."

"Better that the kid was dead," Chin-Mae said, eyes narrowed as he looked at his father. "You should have killed him when you had the chance."

"I did what was necessary," Kim Sun said, his attention still centered on Annie. "I just hadn't anticipated her making it so difficult."

"He's just a child," Annie said, anger strengthening her resolve. There had to be a way. She just had to find it. And to do that, she had to keep Kim talking. "And you were going to blow him away."

"The bomb was not my idea." Kim frowned over at his son. "And he was well cared for. I told him you would come to get him. And I was right. Anyway, what's done is done. The child lives. And I, unlike you, Ms. Gallagher, have no innocent blood on my hands."

"Jin was far from innocent," she said, praying that it was the truth. "Did you know he was in Lebanon to train with the insurgents? That he was working against everything diplomacy stands for?"

"He was a child. And like most children he played with fire."

"You knew?" She fought against her surprise.

"Not at the time. No. I truly believed my son was kidnapped. But later, when I began to uncover what really happened, the truth of his youthful idealism came out."

"Idealism? His actions were treasonous. Against my country and yours."

"We have no allegiance to your country," Chin-Mae said, his voice colored with contempt. "Nor to the imperialistic regime that resulted from your invasion of my country."

"Looks like the apple didn't fall far from the tree. You and Jin are both traitors." Drake coughed beside her and from the corner of her eye she saw him tip his head toward the far wall. It was covered with two large tapestries, and unless she missed her guess, they were moving. First the left. Then the right. Then the left again. The movement was so slight she would have thought she'd imagined it, except for the fact that for a moment, she'd also seen the flash of a face.

Nash.

The cavalry had arrived.

"You have no idea what you're talking about," Chin-Mae

was saying, his face red with anger. "Our cause is a just one."

"Perhaps." Kim nodded. "But that doesn't mean that I approve of using violence to obtain one's goals."

"What do you call kidnapping my son? Yanking him out of bed in the middle of the night? Threatening to kill him if I didn't comply?" Annie protested, taking a step backward toward Drake as she forced herself to stay focused on Kim. She needed to keep his attention away from the tapestry.

As far as she could tell Kim wasn't armed. That left the three guards, each of whom had rifles, and Chin-Mae, who, although not brandishing a weapon, was still a bit of a wild card. The odds weren't perfect, but they also weren't as bad as they could be.

"I call it necessary," Kim was saying, "but we have talked enough. The time for action is at hand."

"No shit," Annie said as she swung backward with her elbow, catching Drake's guard in the gut. Taking the opening, Drake grabbed the rifle as Nash and Avery burst from behind the tapestry, guns blazing.

Two more guards ran into the room, and all hell broke loose as bullets went flying. Annie scrambled across the floor, intent on reaching Kim, who was trying to make it to the far door and the safety of the hallway beyond.

"Annie," Nash yelled as she moved past him. "Catch." He lobbed a handgun and she jumped in the air to catch it, then hit the floor again, running now, as Kim came within inches of his goal. "Move and you're dead," she said, leveling the gun at his head. The room had grown quiet, and she grabbed his arm, moving him in front of her as she turned to face the room.

More guards had arrived, but Drake and Avery were holding them back. Nash was bending over one of the dead guards, blood dripping from his hand.

"You okay?" she called.

"Fine," he said, wincing as he used his teeth to tie the dead man's handkerchief around his forearm. "It's just a scratch. Where's Chin-Mae?"

"I don't know." She shook her head, her gaze sweeping the room. "I don't see him."

"My son has escaped," Kim said, his tone gloating.

"Yeah, well, can't say the same for you," she said as she moved Kim farther into the room, her gun still at his temple. "Tell them to drop their guns and fall back or I'll drop you right here where you stand. And you of all people should know that I mean what I say."

Kim stood ramrod straight, his muscles bunched in protest. But he nodded and the soldiers complied, Avery and Drake picking up their discarded weapons as Nash kept his gun trained on the guards.

"Lock them in the anteroom," Avery ordered, Nash moving to carry out his instructions. "And if anyone tries anything, your boss is dead."

"They don't work for me," Kim said, shaking his head.

"Then I guess you'd better hope they're loyal." Drake shrugged, moving to take over with Kim. "And in the meantime, I'd say you've got a lot to answer for."

"In many religions an eye for an eye is not considered a crime."

"Yeah, well, we believe in the separation of church and state," Avery said as they moved out into the far hallway.

"I assume you've got an escape route in mind?" Annie asked as Nash rejoined them, and they moved backward, guns trained on the anteroom and hallway.

"Got it covered," he said with a smile.

"And your arm? It's really all right?"

"I'm fine. I swear. How about you? All in one piece?"

"Yeah, I'm good. Just ready to get the hell out of here."

"Your wish is my command," Avery said as they moved into a room filled with furniture covered with drop cloths. In the far wall an arch-shaped hole gaped black against the flocked wallpaper. "Our door to freedom."

"So how we going to handle this?" Nash asked, his gun trained on the door behind them.

"You and Annie take Kim. Hannah can walk you back through the tunnels. Drake and I will fix things here so that no one can follow us. We'll be right behind you. I've got com-links for both of you," Avery said, pulling the haul bag out from behind a sheet-swathed bureau.

Annie caught the earpiece Avery lobbed at her and fixed it into place. "Hannah, you there?"

"Glad to have you back in the fold, Annie," Hannah said.

"What, you're not happy to hear from me?" Drake asked, adjusting his earpiece, as he stepped through the opening.

"You know I love you, big guy, but there's no time to tell you how much. You guys need to get a move on. Looks like the forces are gathering. Emmett's on his way with reinforcements, but they're not in place yet."

"No worries, Hannah. We're outta here," Avery assured her. "Nash, you next," he nodded at the opening, "with Kim. And then Annie."

Nash prodded Kim with the barrel of his gun, the older man bending to step through the arch to Drake, waiting on the other side. Annie followed Nash through, blinking in the dim light.

"Okay," Avery said, pulling a timer and wiring from the bag, "you two head on out with Kim. Drake and I are going to leave a little gift for anyone who follows. We'll be right behind you."

Annie moved out behind Nash, keeping her gun at the ready. The tunnel was carved straight from the rock, water dripping along the sides and from the ceiling. It smelled of mildew and limestone. "How far does it go?" she asked.

"The whole island is riddled with tunnels," Hannah said, her voice crackling in Annie's ear. "You're in one of the main branches. It leads down to the bottom of the island and the main gate. Although I doubt there was a gate when the tunnels were built."

"There are miles of them," Kim said, unaware of Hannah's input. "But Zechar told me they are dangerous."

"I'll second that." Nash nodded. "We had to get past a couple of cave-ins just to get this far. The light ends about two-thirds of the way down. From there on, I'll warn you it's dark and pretty dismal. But I've got a flashlight."

"Sounds comforting. Anyway, I'm not afraid of the dark."

"Maybe you should be," Kim said, his expression unreadable in the dim light.

"Listen, Kim," Nash growled, tightening his hold on the little man, "if anyone should be afraid, it's you. You almost killed my son."

"Your son?" The old man nodded. "That explains

much. Would that I had shown you the same loss that you showed me."

Annie clenched her fists, anger rising as she thought about her son. If things has gone as Kim had planned, he'd be dead. She shook her head, clearing her mind, focusing her energy instead on staying alert. If they didn't make it out of here, there was no chance at all of bringing Chin-Mae to justice. And at least in the meantime, they had his father.

The three of them walked in silence for the next twenty yards or so, passing a crumbling passageway off to the left and then another angling off to the right. Annie tightened her grip on her gun, intuition sounding a warning. Behind her, rocks shifted as somebody moved along the passage. She spun around as Nash stepped forward, holding Kim in front of him as a shield.

"Whoever's out there," Nash called, "I've got Kim Sun and I'll kill him if you don't show yourself."

A guard stepped into the light, followed by Chin-Mae, both of them holding weapons.

"Drop your guns," Annie said. "Or your father is dead."

"So be it," Chin-Mae said. "My father is a weak man. An embarrassment to our cause." And then before she had time to realize his intent, he fired his gun, the bullet ripping into his father, who gasped and then slumped forward.

Annie tried to move as a second flash came from Chin-Mae's gun, but before she could react, Nash shoved Kim Sun's body in front of her. Annie heard the bullet tear into Kim's dead flesh, while above her, Chin-Mae was aiming again, this time for Nash, who was shooting at the guard.

"No," she screamed, buoyed by adrenaline and anger as she popped up from behind Kim and fired.

Chin-Mae's eyes widened as he looked down at the bloom of blood spouting on his chest. He tried to lift the gun, but it fell from lifeless fingers as the man dropped to his knees. "Our secrets die with us," he gasped as he fell forward onto his father.

"God willing," she said, stumbling to her feet, swinging her gun around on the guard. The man was dead, eyes open as he stared upward into the dim wash of light. Exhaling, Annie lowered her gun.

"Nash?" she called, her voice shaking as she spun around. He groaned, slumped against the far wall. She covered the distance in seconds, dropping down beside him. "Are you hurt?" Blood covered the front of his shirt, seeping onto the ground beneath him. "Oh, God," she whispered, ripping off her jacket to make a bandage. Something. Anything to stop the blood. "Can you hear me? Baby, can you hear me?"

His eyes were closed, but he moaned again and she pressed harder against the wound. "Don't you dare leave me," she whispered. "Damn it, Nash, not now. Not after everything we've been through. I need you. I love you."

"You guys all right?" Drake called as he and Avery ran into the tunnel. "We heard gunfire."

"It's Nash," Annie said, her voice strangled with her tears. "He's hurt. Bad, I think. Chin-Mae shot him. I tried to stop him." She stared up at Avery, tears filling her eyes. "But I was too late."

"It's going to be all right, Annie," Avery said, dropping down beside her. "His pulse is still strong."

"But there's so much blood."

"You know as well as I do that some of the most superficial wounds are bleeders," Avery said, reaching up to take the pressure bandage Drake was offering.

"But this isn't one of those," she whispered.

"No." He shook his head, replacing her makeshift bandage. "It's not. Hannah? You there?"

"Yeah, I'm hearing every word. What can I do?"

"You need to get Emmett. We need evac now. What's their ETA?"

"He's here. At the mouth of the tunnel. I'll apprise him of the situation. All the hostiles have been apprehended."

"All right then." Avery nodded at Drake. "Let's get Nash out of here."

Annie ran beside them, holding Drake's flashlight, sending up desperate prayers. *Not now. Not now. Please, God, not now.*

It seemed forever, but she knew it was only minutes, and they had him out of the tunnel, Emmett there, surrounded by men from the main island. Men here to help. Drake and Avery laid him on a stretcher, and together they all ran to the waiting helicopter, Annie still fervently praying for a miracle.

And then they were there, the big chopper's blades swooping through the air as it waited, the undergrowth bending to the ground in its wake. Ducking down, she stayed with the stretcher and Nash. And then waited while they pulled him on board, a medic ready with an IV.

"I'm coming with you," she said, already halfway on board. She settled in beside him and reached for his hand. "I'm here, Nash. I'm right here."

His eyes slowly opened, the corners of his mouth lifting in a half smile. "Never thought you'd be anywhere else." His hand tightened on hers, and she looked across at the medic.

"Is he going to be all right?"

"His vitals are good." The man nodded. "And the bullet doesn't appear to have hit any major organs. I'd say Mr. Brennon is a lucky man."

She sucked in a breath, wondering how long she'd been holding it. "You hear that, Nash? You're going to be all right."

"That's not what he said, angel," Nash whispered, grimacing as the medic gave him a shot for pain. "He said I was a lucky man. And he's right. I've got you and I've got Adam. So I can promise you, I'm not going anywhere."

She nodded as the helicopter lurched into the air, Devil's Horn growing smaller and smaller as they moved up into the sky.

The mission was over.

But life—with Nash—had only just begun.

EPILOGUE

"Mom, can I have some more ice cream? Dad said to ask you." Adam skidded to a stop in front of her, chocolate ice cream smeared across his face.

"Don't you think maybe you've had enough for one day?" Annie asked, shooting a glance over at Nash, who was in the middle of an animated discussion with Jason and Avery.

Nash's wound had proved to be less frightening than it had first appeared. He'd lost a lot of blood, but the medic had been right. No vital organs had been hit. And now, except for a rather angry scar, he was fully recovered.

Nash claimed he owed it all to Annie. Her shot throwing off Chin-Mae. But Annie wasn't so sure. Maybe it had been her prayers. Or maybe it just hadn't been his time. Either way they'd been given a second chance and she was determined not to waste it.

"You can never have enough ice cream," Adam was saying, looking longingly over at the ice cream maker.

They were all gathered in Avery's backyard. It was an all-American picnic. Burgers, hot dogs, chips and guacamole. Beer and margaritas for the adults. Cola and ice cream—lots of ice cream—for Adam.

"Just don't make yourself sick," she cautioned as he ran off to refill his bowl.

Drake dropped down into the chair next to hers. "He seems happy."

It had been two months since the kidnapping, and all things considered Adam was doing all right. There were still nightmares. And he hated being parted from either of them. But Lara said that eventually it would all pass, fading into memory. Annie prayed that her new friend was right.

"He's doing okay," she said. "And I think a lot of that has to do with Nash. The two of them are inseparable." She watched as Adam grabbed his now-overflowing bowl of ice cream and ran over to his father. Nash hoisted Adam into his lap and opened his mouth for a bite, then grinned over at Annie.

"I think you sell yourself short, Annie," Drake said, his tone turning serious. "You raised a great kid. And you've made it easy for Nash to find his way with Adam. The three of you belong together."

She looked down at the ring on her finger. "I still can't get used to the idea. I've been on my own so long. And I never would have believed Nash and I'd have a second chance like this. It's like a fairytale, and I don't believe in that kind of stuff."

"Me either." Drake shook his head. "But watching you and Nash, well, a guy could change his mind."

"Careful, Drake," Tyler said as she handed him a beer,

"a little more talk like that and I'll think you've turned into a romantic."

"Not a chance," he said, pushing out of his chair. "Hey, Adam, you want to play catch?"

Adam jumped off his father's lap and grabbed his glove, running out into the yard after Drake.

"I think he's a lot more of a softie than he lets on," Tyler said. "But don't tell him I said so." She smiled and wandered over to where Hannah and Emmett were trying to convince Lara to get into the pool.

Annie closed her eyes, letting the noise of the party drift around her. Her life had changed so much. And yet not at all. She'd left Nash to try to find a normal life, but it was only in finding him again that she'd accomplished her goal. And in doing so, she'd come full circle.

Avery and his higher-ups had worked to make sure her name was cleared of any wrongdoing. DNA evidence found on a cigarette butt at the scene had ultimately tied Dominico's shooter to Chin-Mae. But in an effort at diplomacy, the Kims' real part in the conspiracy had been covered up by Langley, the assassination of Dominico attributed to a radical student gone off the deep end.

The jammed gun and the severed rope were still a mystery. The idea that someone in their own organization was working against them was a bitter pill to swallow. But Annie and Nash had learned the hard way that trust could be misplaced. So they'd been working with Avery to find the source. To figure out who would want to sabotage A-Tac. Every puzzle had a solution, and eventually, Annie knew, they'd figure it out.

And in the meantime, the world ticked on, the balance upheld—for now.

"Penny for your thoughts," Nash said, bending down to kiss her neck. She shivered with delight and wondered if it would ever get old having him there with her all the time.

"I was just thinking how happy I am."

"I'm glad to hear it," he said, pulling her up into his arms. "I do aim to please, Mrs. Brennon."

"And you'll get no complaints from me, sir." She smiled up at him.

"Any chance you're going to put Avery out of his misery?" he asked, shooting a knowing look in his friend's direction. Avery had been after her to join the team. He insisted they needed a sharpshooter.

"Not quite yet. You know I'd do anything for Avery. Which means helping out any time he needs me."

"On a mission?"

"You talking about something in particular?"

"I might be." He grinned. "But unless you're part of the team I'm afraid the information's classified. Let's just say there's a certain insurgent involved."

"You're playing dirty. But I don't want to commit full-time. I'm still enjoying being your wife and Adam's mother. Is that so bad?"

"No." He shook his head, his eyes full of love. "I think it's fabulous—for Adam and me. But I know you. And I think maybe it's time you think about getting back in the game. You're good. And the world's full of people like Kim."

"You know, his son was a piece of work, but I'm not sure Kim Sun was really all that bad."

"Are you kidding?" Nash asked, his eyebrows raised in surprise. "He kidnapped our son."

"Yes, but I don't believe he really wanted to kill him. Just me. And that I can understand." She looked out as Adam jumped for a ball, grinning as the ball hit his mitt. "At the end of the day, we'd do anything for our kids."

"Maybe. But it doesn't change the fact that what he did was wrong."

"No. It doesn't. But it does make you stop and remember that there are two sides to every story." She looked up into his eyes, seeing the whole world.

"I love you, Annie Brennon," he whispered. "With all my heart."

And standing there, in the warm New York sun, content in her husband's arms, Annie realized that she'd been wrong—there was such a thing as happily ever after. And she'd found it. Here. Now. At Sunderland. With Adam and Nash.

Drake Flynn knows
how to survive behind
enemy lines. But he's about
to meet one adversary he
can't subdue…or resist.

Please turn this page
for a preview of

DANGEROUS DESIRES

Available in mass market in
July 2010.

CHAPTER 1

San Mateo Prison, Serrania Del Baudo, Colombia

Madeline Reynard squinted in the bright light. After three days of total darkness, the dappled sunlight hurt her eyes. She flinched as the guard shoved her forward, losing her balance and careening forward into the exercise yard.

"I've got you," Andrés said, his voice raspy, his English heavily accented as he steadied her. "I've been worried."

"They put me in solitary," Madeline whispered.

Andrés shook his head in disgust. "Are you all right?"

"I'm fine." Madeline nodded. "It's getting easier." This was the third time she'd been relegated to the dank, windowless cell in the bowels of the prison. "I just try to think of somewhere else and let my mind carry me away. It doesn't always work, but it helps to keep me calm. And besides, it's not as if I haven't had practice." She'd spent a good portion of her childhood locked in a closet only slightly smaller than the solitary cell. Her father had clearly believed the adage "out of sight, out of mind." But the experience had not been without value. If Madeline could survive living with Frank Reynard, she could survive anything. Even San Mateo.

A place for political prisoners, the prison lacked creature comforts. In actual point of fact, it lacked most everything. Which meant that days loomed long, the only bright spot the minutes spent here, under the canopy of trees.

"It's best if you find a way to separate yourself from the reality here," Andrés agreed. He nodded toward the people scattered about the yard. It was nearly empty, this hour relegated to women and the infirm, Andrés falling into the latter category.

She'd met him on her second day in the yard. At first, his matted hair and filthy clothes had been off-putting. In all honesty, he was the kind of person she'd have ignored had she passed him on the street back home. But she wasn't in Louisiana anymore. And after almost a week in this hellhole, she'd been desperate for human contact. Granted, theirs was an odd friendship. But there was no way she could have survived life here without him.

Her Spanish was limited to schoolgirl verbs and useless nouns, although that didn't matter when she was alone in her cell, or being leered at by the guards. It didn't take a vocabulary to interpret their catcalls.

Madeline closed her eyes, shutting out the small, barren exercise yard, its occupants wretched in their filth.

With hope almost nonexistent, she'd stopped counting the days, settling instead into a life lived moment to moment. At first she'd demanded contact with U.S. authorities. But her pleas had fallen on deaf ears, the only valuable commodity here cold hard cash. Which was unfortunate when one considered that she had none.

"Are you sure they didn't hurt you?" her friend asked, his voice colored with worry.

"I told you I'm fine," she reiterated as they walked slowly across the yard, her muscles protesting the movement even as her mind rejoiced in her newfound freedom. "I'm just a little stiff, that's all."

"You need to keep moving," he said, his hand strong against her back. "It's important to stay strong."

"I know you're right, but sometimes when I think about spending the rest of my life here, it doesn't seem worth it."

"You won't be here forever," he said, his tone soothing. "Someone will come for you."

Madeline laughed, the sound harsh. "Believe me, that's not going to happen. No one cares where I am. And even if they did, they wouldn't know where to begin looking. I didn't tell anyone I was coming to Colombia."

"Someone must have known." Andrés frowned.

"No." She shook her head. "There's only me. But at least I have you." They never talked about why they were here. As if there were some unspoken rule.

"Yes, but I'm a marked man," Andrés sighed. "My days are numbered."

Madeline dipped her head, tears filling her eyes, the idea of losing her only friend beyond comprehension. She'd heard the shots fired late at night. Men and women executed without benefit of due process. She was a long way from home, and her only ally was about to be taken from her.

"The only reason I was allowed out here with you was that I was so sick. But I'm better now, and that means

I will be returned to my original cell. I overheard the guards," he said. "I'm being moved back. Which means this is my last time in the yard with you."

"No." She shook her head, panic mixing with dread. "Maybe you can pretend to be sick again. Something. Anything that might keep you here—with me. I can't manage without you."

"Of course you can," Andrés said. "You're much stronger than you know."

"Señor Barras?" a guard called from the doorway, his machine gun held at the ready. *"Ven conmigo ahora."*

Madeline turned to the guard, then back to Andrés, heart pounding. "What does he want? I don't understand what he's saying."

"He wants me to come with him." Andrés shrugged. "I guess it's time."

"No. You can't go. I can't bear the thought of dealing with all of this on my own." She waved at the yard, and the guards.

"But you will." His smile was gentle, his teeth white against the dark growth of his beard. "Because you're a survivor."

Madeline frowned. "Clearly, you have more faith in me than I have in myself."

The guard moved impatiently, his lips curled in a sneer. *"Apurate!"*

"Uno momento," Andrés said, holding up a hand. "Here, I have something for you." He reached into his pocket and produced a grimy card. "Take this. It may be of help to you."

She took the card, the battered face of the Queen of Hearts staring up at her. "I don't understand."

"If you can get this to the American embassy, they'll help you. No questions asked."

"But it's just a playing card." She shook her head. "How can it possibly help me?"

"Trust me," Andrés said, reaching over to close her fingers around the card. "And keep it safe."

Madeline's gaze locked on her friend's. "Why not use it yourself?"

"Because it is too late for me. I have accepted my fate. And it gives me pleasure to think that perhaps I can be of some service to you. No matter what you have done, you don't belong here."

"Neither do you," she whispered, her voice fierce now. "Keep the card."

"It is yours, my friend. I give it freely. Now I must go." She hesitated, but he shook his head, waving a hand toward the guard. "Use the card to find your way home, Madeline. And then forget this place ever existed."

"I can't do that," she said. The playing card might be nothing more than the foolish imaginings of a feeble mind, but she had no doubt that he believed what he was telling her. And so even if it was without power, it remained a gift of the heart. "I'll never forget any of this. Because if I did, that would mean forgetting you."

Tears slid down her face, the first she'd shed since landing at San Mateo. She slid the card into her pocket and watched as her friend walked away. She wasn't the type to get sentimental. Andrés was right. She was a survivor. But something about the older man had touched her heart. Reached a place she'd thought long dead.

And now they were taking him away.

*   *   *

Sunderland College, New York—three years later

The air smelled like fall even though Indian summer was still holding court, the temperatures higher than normal for late September. Drake Flynn made his way across campus, smiling at students and fellow professors as he walked, his mind still centered on his last class.

"Professor Flynn," a breathless coed called. "Have you got a moment?"

He stopped, dutifully pulling his mind away from pre-Columbian artifacts. "What can I do for you, Stacey?"

"I had a question about the degradation of ancient ruins. You were taking about how much had been lost to deforestation and greed. And I was just wondering why it mattered so much. I mean, isn't it better to have progress? People working. Food on the table. At the end, isn't it really a tradeoff? 'What was' versus 'what is'?"

"There certainly is an argument to be made for the modern world over the ancient one," Drake said, watching as Nash Brennon emerged from the social sciences building. "But I'm not sure that stripping the land of everything it harbors—trees, animals, artifacts—is truly a step forward. There's got to be some kind of balance, a way for us to use our past to make a better future. And if we destroy everything that's old we lose a valuable tool in understanding not just where we've been but where we're going. Look, Stacey, since you seem to be so interested, maybe you should consider the topic for your paper."

"Thanks, Dr. Flynn. I'll think about it. And you're right." The girl licked her lips and flicked her hair provocatively, and Drake bit back a smile. "Not everything old is bad. I mean, look at you."

"Right. I'm positively decrepit." He nodded, laughing as she walked away.

"Fraternizing with the coeds?" Nash asked as he came to a stop beside Drake. The two of them worked together not just as professors, but as elite members of A-Tac. The American Tactical Intelligence Command was an off-the-books arm of the CIA. Operating out of Sunderland College, it was cloaked under the guise of the Aaron Thomas Academic Center, one of the country's foremost think tanks.

Members of the unit were adept at both academics and espionage, their unique abilities setting the stage for some of the CIA's most dangerous missions. Nash was the team's second in command and the chair of the history department. An expert in covert operations, he was the go-to guy when something needed to be accomplished under the radar.

"Are you kidding me?" Drake said, shaking his head. "She's like nineteen."

"If that." Nash grinned. "You on your way to Avery?" Avery Solomon was their boss. A hard-nosed ex-military man, Avery inspired fierce loyalty among team members. He'd successfully ridden out four political administrations and maintained contacts at the highest levels of government, including the Oval Office. There wasn't a man alive Drake respected more.

"Yeah," Drake said, patting the beeper on his belt. "He paged. I'm guessing we've been given new orders. Any idea what they might be?"

"Not a clue." Nash shook his head as they walked into

the center to a bank of elevators at the back of the lobby. Nash inserted a key into an elevator marked "professors only" and the doors slid open. They stepped inside, and Drake inserted a second key as Nash pushed a button behind the Otis Elevator sign.

The doors closed as the elevator started downward to the A-Tac complex hidden beneath the campus.

"Any luck convincing Annie to join the team?" Drake asked. Nash had recently married a former CIA operative, and although Avery had done everything possible to convince her to come on board, she was still holding out.

"Not yet. But I think maybe she's weakening. Avery asked her the other day for about the millionth time if she'd be interested in being reactivated. Usually she just says no. But this time she told him she'd think about it."

"Sounds like progress. I predict she won't hold out much longer. Truth is she's as much of an adrenaline junkie as the rest of us. She's got to be itching to get back into the saddle."

"Well, there's Adam to think about." Adam was their son and they'd nearly lost him to a kidnapper. "I know he's safe here, but I worry about both of us being gone."

"So you split your time." Drake shrugged. "It's doable."

"Hey, I'm not the one saying no." He held up his hands in defense as the elevator doors slid open. They walked into what appeared to be a reception area, and Nash slapped his hand on a bust of Aaron Thomas—the center's namesake. Then, palm identification completed, a panel in the far wall slid open, and Drake followed Nash into the A-Tac complex.

"Wondering where you guys had gotten to," Hannah

Marshall said as the panel slid shut again. Hannah was the team's intel expert. She looked more like one of her students than an expert in both political theory and ferreting out information. Her spiky hair was streaked with purple today, the glasses perched on the end of her nose a contrasting green. "Everybody's waiting for you in the war room."

"So what's the mission?" Nash asked.

"Extraction. Seems pretty straightforward." Hannah shrugged. "Avery will want to tell you himself though."

The three of them walked into the war room. The oversized space was the heart of A-Tac. With computer banks flanking the walls and LCD screens above and behind the oblong conference table, the room was stocked with state-of-the-art equipment.

"All right then," Avery said as everyone sat down at the table. "Now that we're all here, why don't we get started. As I'm sure Hannah's told you, we've been charged with an extraction." He pressed a button in front of him and the screen filled with the picture of a woman.

"Her name is Madeline Reynard."

"French?" Tyler asked. Tyler was the team's ordnance expert. Drake doubted there was a bomb in existence that she couldn't put together or tear apart. She was also the chair of Sunderland's English department, the dichotomy a testament to her diversity.

"No. American," Hannah said, looking up from her computer. "Louisiana originally. A town called Cypress Bluff. But for the last three years she's been living in Colombia with Jorge di Silva."

"The drug racketeer." Jason nodded, clearly recognizing the name. Jason handled the unit's IT needs, as well as computer forensics. A whiz with everything electronic, he was an invaluable asset to both the college and the team.

"Actually, di Silva's gone a step beyond that," Hannah said. "They've even coined a new term—narcoterrorist. Not only is he producing and dealing cocaine, he's using the proceeds to obtain and sell weapons to the highest bidders. No questions asked."

"Hell of a guy." Drake frowned. "So how does Madeline Reynard fit into all of this?"

"She's his mistress," Avery said. "He plucked her out of a Colombian prison three years ago. Place called San Mateo."

"I've heard of it." Nash nodded. "Some kind of fortress in the Chaco region. I thought it was reserved for political prisoners."

"And foreigners," Hannah said. "We've got no physical record of her arrest or conviction, so no idea why she landed there."

Drake nodded, studying the woman in the picture onscreen. She was tiny, her long, dark hair curling wildly around her face. Her features were sharp, her chin a little long, her nose aquiline. But even so, she was still a looker. Full lips and a body that begged a man to touch her. Tottering on heels that should be declared illegal, she stood on a corner, arm held up as she tried to hail a taxi.

"Not exactly the shy and retiring type," Tyler observed as she, too, examined the photograph. "When was this taken?"

"About six months ago," Avery said, shifting to the side so that he could see the photo as well. "In Bogotá. That's di Silva behind her." The man in the picture had his back turned, his attention on someone out of the frame.

"Here's a better one of him," Hannah said. The chiseled flat-nosed face that filled the screen was almost identical to the ones that decorated the burial mounds and ancient monuments of the pre-Columbian ruins scattered along the Cauca River, generations of genealogy pooled into one man. Drake shook his head, pushing away his anthropological thoughts in favor of more practical details.

"Is the woman in Bogotá now?"

"No." Hannah shook her head. "But until recently she was living there, and it's where she first made contact with our people. Through the embassy. But shortly thereafter, her contact was killed and Madeline was removed to di Silva's compound in the mountains."

"I take it our man's death is being linked to di Silva?" Nash asked.

"There's no hard evidence. Guy was gunned down at his apartment. But if you play connect the dots I'd say di Silva or one of his henchmen is a likely candidate."

"Any chance the woman set him up?" Jason asked as Hannah put Madeline Reynard's picture back up on the screen.

"Higher-ups seem to think she was legit," Avery said. "Di Silva is known to have a temper. And he's always been overly protective of his possessions."

Hannah switched the photograph again, the new one depicting a sprawling stucco home. "This is di Silva's hacienda. *Casa de Orquídea.* The area's known for its orchids. Anyway, the house is part of a compound located about twenty miles due west of Cali. It's officially listed as a coffee plantation. But as we know, there are other, more lucrative crops that grow well in that part of the Andes."

"Like the coca plant," Drake inserted.

"Exactly." Hannah nodded.

"And that's where Madeline is?" Tyler asked with a frown. "Not going to be an easy in and out."

"That whole area is pretty inhospitable," Nash agreed. "I'm assuming he's got guards."

"Full-meal deal." Hannah nodded, switching to a map of the area. "Surveillance, perimeter rotation, and at least four men on duty in the house. He's also got eyes on all approaching roads."

"We can helicopter in," Drake said. "Then hike through the jungle and enter from the back."

"Makes sense," Nash agreed. "But we'll need to disable the cameras somehow."

"I should be able to do that from here. With Jason's help."

"Not a problem." Jason nodded.

"Maybe more so than you think," Avery said. "I'm going to need you on site as part of the team. With Emmett still in Russia, you're going to have to coordinate communications and retrieval."

Emmett Walsh served as the unit's communications guru. He also headed the college's economics department. He and Lara Prescott, an expert in biochemical weapons, were currently in Minsk helping their Russian counterparts neutralize a recently discovered stockpile of chemical weapons.

"Shouldn't be a problem." Jason shrugged. "Hannah can handle it from here, and if there's a problem, I can just advise from the field."

"So why is Langley so interested in this woman?" Drake asked, tipping his chair back to lean against the wall. "I mean, this is a hell of an extraction. And it's not like them to make this kind of effort for someone who isn't somehow connected to the government. Is there something you aren't telling us?"

"As far as I know the woman's a civilian," Avery said. "The rest is all need to know. And basically we're not on the short list. But the basics are that she's agreed to flip on di Silva in return for her freedom."

"Word on the street is that he plays a little rough," Hannah said. "Maybe she's had enough."

"Or maybe she's looking for a payoff." Drake scowled as Hannah switched back to the photograph of Madeline Reynard. "I know women like her. She's not the wave-the-flag-while-turning-on-her-meal-ticket type."

"Doesn't matter what she wants. Washington's buying. And our job is to deliver her safely to Langley."

Drake shook his head. "This extraction doesn't seem like much more than a glorified babysitting gig."

"Well"—Avery smiled—"there's a little bit more to it than that. Di Silva has been suspected of dealing arms for quite some time now. But we haven't been able to establish tangible proof. There have been all kinds of rumors. Everything from a warehouse in Bogotá to a terrorist hideout in the mountains of Chaco."

"But nothing has ever been substantiated," Hannah added.

"Until now." Avery's expression turned grim. "According to the original source, Madeline Reynard knows the location of the weapons cache. And it's somewhere in the vicinity of di Silva's compound. So if she's telling the truth—"

"Then we'll be able to nail di Silva," Nash said.

"Exactly." Avery nodded.

"And if she's lying?" Drake asked.

"Then"—Avery shrugged—"we leave her to di Silva."

THE DISH

Where authors give you the inside scoop!

♥ ♥ ♥ ♥ ♥ ♥ ♥ ♥ ♥ ♥ ♥ ♥ ♥ ♥ ♥ ♥ ♥ ♥

From the desk of Dee Davis

Dear Reader,

The American Tactical Intelligence Command (A-Tac) is an off-the-books black ops division of the CIA. Hiring only the best and the brightest, A-Tac is made up of academicians with a talent for espionage. Working under the cover of one of the United States' most renowned think tanks as a part of Sunderland College, A-Tac uses its collegiate status to keep its activities "eyes only."

I suppose my love of academia is in part responsible for the creation of A-Tac. I graduated from Hendrix College in Arkansas. A small liberal arts school, the campus is dotted with ivy-shrouded buildings and tree-covered grounds. So although I moved my fictional Sunderland to upstate New York, it's still very much Hendrix that I see as I write. And like Nash Brennon (the hero of DARK DECEPTIONS), my degree is in political science. Although, unlike Nash, I have never worked for the CIA or taught in the social sciences.

But I have been in love. And I know how easy it is to let things get in the way. To let fear and distrust rule the day. To let a twist of fate stack the cards against finding happily-ever-after. Thankfully my situation was never quite so dire, but I can understand how Annie Gallagher feels when her path crosses Nash Brennon's again. Eight years ago, he betrayed her in the most basic of ways, and now they find themselves on opposite sides of a dangerous game. Annie with a desperate mission to rescue someone she loves, and Nash charged with stopping her—no matter the cost.

To get some insight into my world as a writer—particularly as the writer of DARK DECEPTIONS—check out the following songs:

"When I'm Gone"—3 Doors Down
"Into the Night"—Santana (featuring Chad Kroeger)
"Fields of Gold"—Sting

And as always, check out www.deedavis.com for more inside info about my writing and my books.

Happy Reading!

Dee Davis

♥ ♥ ♥ ♥ ♥ ♥ ♥ ♥ ♥ ♥ ♥ ♥ ♥ ♥ ♥ ♥ ♥

From the desk of Jennifer Haymore

Dear Reader,

When Katherine Fisk, the heroine of A TOUCH OF SCANDAL (on sale now), entered my office for the first time to ask me to write her story, I realized right away that she wasn't like one of my normal heroines. She was obviously of the lower orders, dressed in plain brown wool and twisting her hands nervously in her lap. Still, there was something about her dancing brown eyes that intrigued me, and I asked her why she had come.

"I'm in love," she said simply.

I laughed. "Well, that *is* what I write about. But tell me about this man you love."

"Well—" She swallowed hard. "He's a duke."

"Hmm." I studied the calluses on her hands, evidence of a life of hard work. "That makes it . . . difficult."

"I know," she sighed. "But there's more—much more."

"All right," I said. "Tell me."

I was already feeling doubtful, and I hesitated to encourage her. Don't get me wrong. I mean, I love Cinderella stories—but this girl really didn't look like a match for a duke. Plus, she didn't look like she could pay me what my last client had (my last client was a duchess, and she was loaded).

"Well . . . I think he wants to kill my brother."

I tapped my pen against my desk. A servant girl besotted with a duke intent on killing her beloved brother? Impossible, but also . . . "Intriguing," I said, "but you're making this difficult, you know."

"I know." She clasped those calloused fingers tightly together. "There's still more. There's the matter of the duke's wife . . ."

Well, that was that. I rose, intending to politely show her out. "I'm so sorry, Miss . . . Fisk, was it?"

She nodded.

"Miss Fisk, I'm sorry. If the man is already married, there's nothing I can do for you—"

"Oh, he isn't married!" Her brow furrowed. "Well, I don't think he's married . . . But he has a wife." Her frown deepened. "At least . . . he had a wife, but . . ."

I lowered myself back into my chair. "Okay. You're

going to have to start from the beginning. Tell me everything. Don't skip any detail."

She nodded, took a breath, and began. "When I first saw him, he was naked . . ."

And that was how it began. With a servant and a naked, married (or not!) duke seeking retribution from her brother. By the time Miss Fisk finished telling me her story, I was so hooked, I had to put pen to paper and write the entire, wild tale, and, believe it or not, I offered to do it pro bono. I'm usually pretty mercenary about these things, you see, but I figured if I pulled it off, at the end Miss Fisk would be more than capable of paying me, and quite handsomely, too.

I truly hope you enjoy reading Katherine Fisk's story as much as I enjoyed writing it! Please come visit me at my website, www.jenniferhaymore.com, where you can share your thoughts about my books, learn some strange and fascinating historical facts, and read more about the characters from A TOUCH OF SCANDAL.

Sincerely,

Jennifer Haymore

♥ ♥ ♥ ♥ ♥ ♥ ♥ ♥ ♥ ♥ ♥ ♥ ♥

From the desk of Rita Herron

Dear Reader,

I've always loved small towns. They feel homey and friendly. Everyone knows everyone else, trades recipes, and watches over one another's children. A small town is a safe place to raise a family.

But have you ever noticed that there seems to be one news story after another about the man or woman next door in those small towns who turned out to be a serial killer? Then there's the soccer mom who killed her husband. Or the man who slaughtered his family.

I've always been fascinated by this idea and it occurred to me one day, what if I took it one step further? What if brutal killers are living among trusting people in small towns . . . and they're not the scariest and most dangerous hidden element? What if there are demons, too? An entire world of them who live underground and mingle with the normal citizens.

And nobody in town knows about those demons . . . except, of course, for the local sheriff, Dante Valtrez . . . who is one of them!

There, I had my setup. But that wasn't enough. I needed to get into the heart of my hero and heroine.

Having a degree in Early Childhood Education, I've always been intrigued by the effects of parenting and society on young children. Our parents teach us to be nice, to follow the rules, to respect others and not to be naughty. But what if my hero wasn't taught that behavior as a child? What if he was taught to be naughty, to be evil? What if Dante Valtrez was raised by demons?

But even if Dante was a demon, I wanted him to be a hero. Like his brothers Vincent in INSATIABLE DESIRE and Quinton in DARK HUNGER, he has both good and bad in him (don't we all?), so he struggles with his own evil side throughout his entire life.

But how to showcase this struggle between good and evil? And then it occurred to me—what if he had to choose between killing a little girl to earn the acceptance of his fellow demons and doing what he knew was right and being forced out of the only community he ever knew? I chose to have Dante put to the ultimate test at age thirteen because that's the beginning of adolescence, a confusing time when a boy changes from a child to a man. This is a pivotal moment for Dante, because he's so torn at the sight of the little girl and her happy family, something he secretly craves, that he can't kill her. He fails the demon test because his humanity surfaces.

From that point on, Dante can't go back. But he doesn't fit into the mortal world either or think he deserves love. Still, he becomes determined to protect innocents from the monsters who raised him.

But Dante has suffered a painful childhood and has been tortured, He does deserve love, and the romantic in me had to find the perfect woman to give him that love. And who else could possibly save Dante but the one he was supposed to kill? The little girl he saved as a child who becomes the woman who wants to destroy all evil through her work?

Romance, suspense, murder, demons, family issues, secrets—this story is chock-full of them all. I hope you'll enjoy the surprise twist at the end and the final installment in the Demonborn series, FORBIDDEN PASSION—out now!

Rita Herron